The Orphanage Girls

Mary Wood was born in Maidstone, Kent, and brought up in Claybrooke, Leicestershire. Born one of fifteen children to a middle-class mother and an East End barrow boy, Mary's family were poor but rich in love. This encouraged her to develop a natural empathy with the less fortunate and a fascination with social history. In 1989 Mary was inspired to pen her first novel and she is now a full-time novelist.

Mary welcomes interaction with readers and invites you to subscribe to her website where you can contact her, receive regular newsletters and follow links to meet her on Facebook and Twitter: www.authormarywood.com

BY MARY WOOD

The Breckton series

To Catch a Dream
An Unbreakable Bond
Tomorrow Brings Sorrow
Time Passes Time

The Generation War saga

All I Have to Give
In Their Mother's Footsteps

The Girls Who Went to War series

The Forgotten Daughter
The Abandoned Daughter
The Wronged Daughter
The Brave Daughters

The Jam Factory series

The Jam Factory Girls
Secrets of the Jam Factory Girls
The Jam Factory Girls Fight Back

The Orphanage Girls series

The Orphanage Girls

Stand-alone novels

Proud of You
Brighter Days Ahead
The Street Orphans

The Orphanage Girls

Mary Wood

PAN BOOKS

First published 2022 by Pan Books
an imprint of Pan Macmillan
The Smithson, 6 Briset Street, London EC1M 5NR
EU representative: Macmillan Publishers Ireland Ltd, 1st Floor,
The Liffey Trust Centre, 117–126 Sheriff Street Upper,
Dublin 1, D01 YC43
Associated companies throughout the world
www.panmacmillan.com

ISBN 978-1-5290-3343-4

1 3 5 7 9 8 6 4 2

A CIP catalogue record for this book is available from the British Library.

Typeset by Palimpsest Book Production Ltd, Falkirk, Stirlingshire
Printed and bound by CPI Group (UK) Ltd, Croydon, CR0 4YY

Visit **www.panmacmillan.com** to read more about all our books
and to buy them. You will also find features, author interviews and
news of any author events, and you can sign up for e-newsletters
so that you're always first to hear about our new releases.

For my brothers: Charles RIP, Frank RIP, Eddie RIP, Matthew, Bernadine, Christopher RIP, Dominic RIP and Damian RIP. Love you all.

Chapter One

1910

Shivers trembled twelve-year-old Ruth's body at the sound of footsteps approaching the dormitory.

As the door opened, light splashed over her bed seeming to carry with it the voice of the man all the girls hated and feared. 'Shut yer noise up, girl. I ain't hurt yer.'

This compounded the misery that had clothed Ruth since the girl had been taken away earlier.

Her mind had screamed memories she didn't want to think about. Memories of herself being 'the chosen one'.

There had been no peace for her in the relief of not being taken tonight as she'd lain awake praying for the girl whilst trying hard not to think about what was happening to her.

But now, the heart-wrenching sobs she could hear denied her attempts to continue to shut it all out as vivid images of Belton, the night warden of Carlton Orphanage in Bethnal Green, came to her. His smarmy face, blackened teeth and how his sour breath mingled with the stench of stale tobacco, strong body odour and unwashed hair. But worse than this was thinking about the feel of his hands touching her and hearing his heavy sighs.

A tear seeped out of her eye and as always, she wished she had a mum to love her and take care of her.

1

Left on the doorstep of a priest's house when a newborn, Ruth imagined her mum had been poor and lonely to have done such a thing, as that way she could excuse her and love her. Loving a mum – even one she didn't know – gave her comfort.

Not daring to move, Ruth clung to the one sheet that covered her and watched the light become a thinner strip and then disappear as the door closed behind Belton.

The darkness left little specks dancing in her eyes. She blinked, trying to adjust, wanting to go to the girl to tell her she had a mate, but a harsh voice stopped her in her tracks.

'Shurrup, can't yer? How can anyone sleep while you're making that racket?'

Gwen the grump! It was easy for Gwen to say such a thing. Pimply, snotty-nosed, with hair that hung like greasy string and a huge nose that dominated her face, *she* didn't know what it was like to be chosen.

Another – kinder – voice called out, 'Leave her alone, Gwen . . . But hey, luv, crying won't do yer no good. Yer have to learn to accept it, snuggle down in yer bed when it's over and get some sleep. That's what I do.'

Ruth wondered if Doris really did this and wished that she could. Most nights she lay awake, waiting for the door to open, wondering if the heavy footsteps would stop at her bed and feeling relief if they didn't but at the same time, sorry for the chosen girl.

With the dormitory quietening and Ruth's eyes more used to the dark, she slipped out of bed to go to the girl to offer comfort. The lino-clad floor iced her feet as she crept along the row of beds.

When she reached the sobbing girl she found her screwed

up into a ball. Touching her made her jump. 'It's all right, mate. I want to help yer.'

With light from the corridor trickling through the small window above the bed, Ruth could see how distraught the girl was. Her heart went out to her. 'I can get in with you if yer like, luv. Me friend does that when Belton brings me back and it helps to comfort me. What's yer name, you're new ain't yer?'

'Amy. Yes, I came yesterday.'

'Hotch up.' As she said this Ruth lifted the sheet and put one foot in the bed.

'No, stop . . . I – I don't want you to get in.'

The feel of the warm damp sheet gave Ruth the reason for Amy's refusal. But with the realization came visions of being hit with a wet sheet, and then wrapped in it and made to stand on her bed till supper time. She had to do something to protect Amy. 'Shush, don't say anything out loud about this. Yer can come to my bed for a while, but first we have to sort the bed out.'

As Amy got out, Ruth gathered the sheets in a ball and dropped them onto the floor before whispering, 'Go around the other side and help me turn the mattress over.'

With this done, she took Amy's hand and led her back to her bed. From what she could see, Amy wasn't as tall as herself. 'Get yourself in, then when all quietens down, we'll deal with the sheets.'

As they snuggled up together giving each other warmth, Ruth told Amy her name, but then wasn't sure if it fell on deaf ears as Amy's deep breathing, interrupted by the jerking of rebound sobs, told her that she was already asleep. Ruth held her close.

Not daring to sleep herself, she waited until she thought

3

all the girls in the dormitory had settled before getting out of bed and tiptoeing along to Amy's bed, stopping at Grumpy Gwen's to listen a moment. She wanted to be extra sure she didn't disturb her as Gwen was known to snitch on anyone just to put herself in a good light.

With the reassurance Gwen's snores gave her, Ruth ran, scooped up the wet sheets, and was out of the door with them, in a flash.

Fear gripped her as she looked this way and that along the dimly lit, draft-filled corridor, but all was quiet. Now, all she had to do was to get safely past Belton's office.

A strip of light across the floor ahead made her heart sink even further – his door was ajar! Ruth slowed her pace, then wanted to take flight back to her bed as a distressed voice made her jump. 'No, I ain't doing that.'

It was one of the lads. The orphanage housed girls and boys but kept them separate most of the time.

Ruth couldn't bear to hear any more, but couldn't block her ears.

Mr Belton's, 'Why yer like boys is beyond me, Alf,' made her feel sick.

'Shurrup, it's easy for you. The girls don't fight back.'

The second voice belonged to Gedberg, the night manager. Ruth waited.

The door opened wider, and the boy came dashing out, his tear-filled voice screaming, 'Leave me alone . . . Come near me and I'll kick yer in the knackers.'

Ruth fled in the opposite direction then stood around the corner of the passageway. *Don't let them have seen me, please!*

Her tummy ached with suddenly wanting to pee. She clenched her legs together.

When she peeped around the corner, she saw both Belton and Gedberg chasing the boy.

Her sigh held relief for herself, mixed with pity for the boy. But with nothing she could do to help him, she tried to put out of her mind what might happen when they caught him and ran like the wind to the laundry.

Closing the door, she switched on the light. It was then that she saw the blood on Amy's sheet. Her temper rose, as she realized Belton had truly hurt Amy. But she couldn't think about that now, she had to hurry.

Dumping the sheets into the huge cloth-bag of dirty laundry, she grabbed clean ones off the shelf and was back out in the corridor, running as if her life depended on it.

Once inside the door of the dormitory, the sounds of sleeping girls – rows and rows of them – helped to calm her.

No one stirred as she felt the mattress to make sure it was dry on its upside, dumped the sheets on it and ran to the water closet to relieve herself. Once there, the fear that had zinged through Ruth brought tears as the wretchedness of their situation filled her with despair.

But as she began the chore of making the bed, she told herself that at least she'd saved Amy having to go through with more than she already had, and this cheered her.

Tired now, she wearily woke Amy. 'Come on, mate. Yer bed's made for yer . . . Only you won't wet it again, will yer?'

'No, I ain't a bed wetter, it were . . .'

Her sob tore at Ruth. 'Shush, luv, it's all right. Don't cry. I know . . . Did he hurt you badly?'

'Yes . . . He . . . he—'

'Look, I'll get in with yer a mo, eh? Then you can talk, but yer have to keep your voice down, there's them as would tell of us, then we'd both be for it.'

5

Once under the sheets, Ruth asked, 'When did you come in here? I ain't seen much of yer.'

'It was yesterday evening . . . That man was with Matron when I was brought in.'

'Have yer just lost yer family, then?'

'No, I was found at the gates of a convent when I wasn't many hours old.'

Ruth gasped. 'Something like that happened to me.'

'I don't know how a mum can give a baby away, do you?'

'No. But I think of my mum as not being able to help herself. I'm going to find her when I leave here.'

'Is that soon?'

'When I'm thirteen on the twenty-first of August. That's if they don't keep me on working in the kitchen or the laundry. Miss Flynn, the housekeeper, is always saying I'm good at both and they kept Hettie on. You'll meet Hettie, she's Mr Belton's favourite, but it don't seem to bother her. She says she makes the best of it and gets favours because of it. But I couldn't do that, I'd rather they sent me into the workhouse than that.'

'I was in the workhouse for a time. The nuns wanted rid of me when I grew up a bit. They said I was a pest and caused trouble, but I didn't. Other kids blamed me for everything, so when I wasn't well, they took me to the infirmary and didn't come back for me.'

As she listened, Ruth's heart felt heavy with pity for Amy. 'Was it bad in there?'

'No, the women were good to us kids, and the warden was kindly. She said I didn't belong there as I didn't have parents, so she got me a place here. I wished she hadn't now.'

'How old are yer, Amy?'

'Eleven, only I ain't sure when me birthday is.'

The sound of someone stirring made Ruth shush Amy. Once it became quiet again, she told her, 'I'll look out for yer, don't worry. I know all there is to know about here. Anyway, as soon as whoever that is settles, I'll have to get back to me bed.'

Amy gave a soft moan when she moved away. Ruth guessed she was sore. 'Don't go to the matron with how you're hurting, Amy, and don't tell no one nothing. You'll only get a beating for telling lies.'

'But it ain't a lie.'

'I know. Just don't, that's all.'

Back in her own bed, Ruth sought the place where Amy had lain as it was still warm, and it was nice to think of her being there.

The clanging of the bell woke Ruth with a start the next morning. Every part of her ached from lack of sleep. Dreams of Mr Belton had disturbed her, making the rest of the night a torturous nightmare, but she dared not dwell on this and so jumped out of bed as fast as everyone else did as the morning routine had to be followed.

She soon had her bed made and her nightdress folded under her pillow before donning her grey surge frock and topping it with a wraparound pinny. She didn't own a comb so she gathered her long black hair, shoved it into a net and covered it with her mob cap.

The hive of activity around her showed that everyone was doing the same, but for Amy. 'Amy . . . Amy, get up, mate!'

Amy gave a muffled moan.

'Please, Amy, you'll get a whipping with Matron's cane. She's a tartar.'

'I can't.'

Torn between carrying on with the regimented morning routine – she'd still to go to the lav and then swill her face with the rest of them in the washbasins at the other end of the dormitory – or helping Amy, Ruth sighed. She glanced both ways. Queues of wriggling girls at the closet end and chattering ones at the washbasins told her she had at least five minutes before it would be her turn at either. She just had to help Amy and pray that Matron didn't appear before she was stood in line.

Feeling how hot and sweaty Amy was deepened Ruth's concern, but despite this she knew that she had to get her to try to dress, as Matron didn't tolerate anyone being unwell. 'Amy, come on, mate. Please.'

Too late, the door of the dormitory swung open with a vicious slamming against the wall. Ruth froze.

'What are you doing? Why isn't this girl out of her bed!'

'She's unwell, Matron Hecton.'

'Unwell?'

Matron often repeated what you said, as if to say, 'How dare you!'

Ruth trembled – she knew the consequences of Matron's temper and could hear it rising in her tone as she barked at Amy, 'Get out of bed at once, girl!'

Amy tried to put her legs out of the bed but flopped back down again. Ruth jumped forward to help, but a stinging slap sent her reeling. Matron's face came within inches of hers. 'Get in line for your wash, little miss interferer!'

Ruth scurried away, holding her smarting face, unsure whether to head for the lav or the washbasins. The closet won as her fear had made the need of it an urgency. But then she wished she'd gone the other way as she came up behind a smirking Gwen. 'Serves yer right. Yer've always got yer nose in where yer shouldn't have, Ruth Faith.'

Ruth seethed with anger. The need to lash out overwhelmed her. Her fist cracked into Gwen's nose. Blood spurted everywhere. Gwen's screams brought Matron flying up the dormitory.

It seemed to Ruth as if doomsday was on her. She couldn't react or make a move to defend herself as a violent jerk of her head gave her excruciating pain. It felt to her as though every strand of her hair was being pulled from its roots. She tried to keep to her feet to release some of the pressure but lost her balance as Matron dragged her along the wooden floor.

One voice protested. Ellen. Her lovely mate, Ellen. 'Let her go! That's cruel!'

'Shut up, big mouth, I'll deal with you later. I'll show you cruel!'

This pained Ruth. Ellen was a bright light in her life, as was Hettie. Both made some of the drudgery bearable.

The youngest in the dormitory at ten years old, Ellen was also the prettiest, with how her dark hair fell in soft curls and her large brown eyes dominated her oval face. She'd latched onto Ruth from the moment a heavily veiled woman had brought her into the orphanage a year ago.

Whilst trying to comfort the weeping Ellen at the time, Ruth had learned that the woman was Ellen's stepmother who had treated her cruelly and had constantly reminded her that she wasn't her daughter and seemed to begrudge every minute of her being in her house. 'She always calls me me dad's bastard. But— but me dad loves me.' Ellen had told her.

It seemed to Ruth that the love Ellen had for her dad had kept her going through all of his wife's mistreatment of her, as she'd described him as being loving and kind. Poor Ellen still missed him every day. Often, she would stand by the railings looking up the street, sure he would come and fetch her home.

Seeing the wretchedness of this, it occurred to Ruth that it was better to be like herself and not remember anything of your parents.

When they reached the isolation cell in the basement, Ruth knew an easing of the dreadful pain as Matron let go of her hair and shoved her inside. Though the feeling of relief didn't last long as the truth of her predicament dawned on her and compounded as Matron, a burly woman with hairs coming out of her chin, raised her bushy eyebrows and glared out of her beady eyes. 'You . . . you, *Pig*, will stay here till you learn you cannot mess with me. Understand? You're nothing but a stinking tyke!'

The last bit of this was muffled as Matron pulled the heavy creaking door and slammed it shut behind her.

With no air coming into the near-dark room, the putrid stench surrounding Ruth brought the bile to her throat, its sting choking her as she lay in a huddle on the cold stone floor.

Chapter Two

Ruth didn't know how long she'd been in the room but gradually she'd become accustomed to the dark and could now see quite well with the aid of the light coming through a high, gridded window.

Cold had seeped into her bones and her stomach ached.

Somehow she managed to stand on legs that didn't feel as though they would hold her and grope her way over to the corner. Here, she found the source of the stench – the bucket. Almost overflowing, it had formed a crusty-looking layer over the top of the fetid urine. Her crouching over it and adding to it, sent the contents leaking over the top. Ruth retched again as she steadied herself by holding onto the stone wall.

Despair filled her. This cell was Matron's punishment room. Ruth was sure the governors – all good churchgoers – knew nothing about it, or of Belton's treatment of the girls and Gedberg's of the boys.

The vicar of the church where all the governors greeted them on a Sunday was kindly. He had a smiley face and a little word for each. He visited their classrooms and told them wondrous stories about Jesus and his mother, Mary. Ruth loved Mary. When she prayed it was always to the sweet little lady with her lovely smile and blue cloak.

Always she felt warm and protected as she talked to her. She tried it now. 'Holy Mary, help me.'

As if her prayers were to be answered, the door opened.

'Blimey, Ruth girl, what yer been up to, eh?'

'Hettie! Oh, Hettie.'

'Crying don't help nothing, come on, get a hold of your gumption, luv. Look, I've brought yer some broth and some water, only I've gotta make meself scarce as I sneaked it down and I've to get the key back on the hook before anyone notices it missing.'

'Ta, Hettie. I – I'll try.'

'It's the only way, luv. Look, drink the water quick and I'll take the mug back with me, but when you've done with the broth, you can hide the dish under that sacking. I'll try and get down later and get it.'

Ruth drank the water in one and felt better for it. 'Hettie, do yer know how Amy is?'

'That new nipper?'

'Yes, she's ill, I was trying to help her. It was that Gwen who got me in this trouble.'

'Oh, her! Anyway, I know the new kid ain't well as I had to take her some broth too. That's how I got enough for you out of the kitchen, I was to feed her and knew she wouldn't be able to eat all that I'd put in the bowl. As it turned out, she couldn't eat hardly any, so you've got plenty.'

'What's wrong with her? Is she going to be all right?'

'I'm not sure, she ain't good, she's got a fever. I'm sorry, mate, but I don't give much for her chances. Weren't she chosen last night?'

Ruth's world rocked. For some reason, Amy was so important to her and she hated to think of her in the infirmary.

12

Her own memories of being in what was no more than a sick room really, with about five beds in it and not much more, weren't good.

Presided over by Matron as everything was, it was a place of little care.

'Yes, and Belton hurt her. She wet the bed and there was some blood on her sheet.'

'Poor cow. Sounds like he didn't stop at touching her. When he did that to me the first time it hurt like mad because I fought him. Did he do it to you, Ruth, luv?'

'No, I – I don't know . . . he touches me in places . . . and he makes me . . . well, do things to him.'

Hettie sat down on the bench next to Ruth and took her hand. 'Look, if ever he does, don't fight. It's the best way. Cook looks out for me, and she told me that when she had it done to her as a girl it didn't hurt when she just let it happen.'

'Cook?'

'Yes. But I'll tell yer about it some other time. Anyway, at least Belton's careful not to put yer in the pudding club.'

Ruth shuddered. She didn't know what 'it' was nor why Hettie thought Belton not making you have a baby made any of it any better.

For one moment she wanted to leap at Hettie and stop her laugh, which made her more than ample bosom for a fourteen-year-old bounce up and down. But she'd never hurt Hettie.

Dark haired like herself, Hettie's beauty was in her smile as it lit up her eyes. They had the same dark-coloured eyes, but whereas Ruth's were set in a heart-shaped face, Hettie had a rounded, dimply face.

Ruth hoped that her own slender body didn't end up as

buxom as Hettie's but worried that it might, as already her bosom seemed to be growing bigger every day. She wanted to stay as Ellen described her when she said she saw her as beautiful and elegant, like she imagined a princess to be. At the time Ruth had laughed at this but had secretly loved it. It made her feel worthy and confident.

'Well, come on, girl, give me that mug. And eat that broth, like I told yer to. It'll put hairs on your chest.' Hettie laughed as she closed the door.

Ruth wanted to call her back as it felt as though someone had turned a light off. Not the shutting out of the extra light from the corridor, but with Hettie leaving her.

The broth was like a salve to Ruth's empty stomach, but she couldn't savour it, she had to eat quickly in case someone came. She'd never want to get lovely Hettie into trouble and couldn't believe she'd ever felt like going for her.

But the comfort given by the hot food didn't last long as Amy's plight played on Ruth's mind.

Pacing up and down, she prayed to the Holy Mary that Amy would get well until, exhausted, she flopped down onto the bed.

What began as small, stinging tears soon wracked her whole body with achingly deep gulps of pain.

The door opening woke her and the wonderful vision of Hettie cheered her until Hettie's urgent tone ground a fear deep into her heart.

'Gimme the bowl, luv, quick, I heard that bleedin' Matron saying she was coming down here . . . Oh, Ruth, luv, she . . . she said she were going to get her cane first. I'm sorry, mate.'

The trembling Ruth had experienced before was nothing

14

like she knew now. Even her teeth clattered together as she saw the tears streaming down Hettie's face.

Hettie quickly wiped them away with her sleeve. 'Be brave, luv. Yer'll be all right. Us cockneys can take it, can't we, eh?'

'I don't know . . . I don't even know if I am a cockney. I only know I was left at a priest's house somewhere in Southwark.' Ruth didn't know why she was saying this when she really wanted to scream and scream for someone to save her.

'Well then, that's in the sound of the Bow Bells, so yer a cockney like me, and we don't give in. We're strong and have the spirit of a horse. So, grit yer teeth, take yer punishment and you'll soon be out of here, won't yer?'

Ruth tried to latch onto this courage but failed. Inside she dreaded what was to come and could already feel the lashes of the long cane cutting her skin.

'I've got to go, mate. Think of me when it happens. I'll be rooting for yer.'

As the door closed, Ruth heard Hettie's loud sobbing and knew she'd stood a moment outside. Her love for Hettie made her call out, 'I'll be all right, mate,' but she knew in her heart she wouldn't be.

When it opened again a few minutes later, Ruth cowered in the corner. Matron loomed like a monster, her cane held high. 'Start a ruckus in me dormitory, would you? Well, you'll pay, lady. You'll pay to within an inch of your life.'

Matron stepped closer with every word. Ruth held her head and tried to do as Hettie had said as she dug her teeth into her bottom lip. But when the cane came down and tore into her shoulder, she screamed out in agony. This seemed to increase the savagery of the whipping, as Matron went

15

into a frenzy, making an ugly 'ugh' sound with each lash as if putting all her effort into it.

Ruth's agony increased with the slicing of the cane as it ripped the straps off her pinny, shredded her bodice, then cut deep into her bare flesh.

Unable to take any more, she sank into the blackness that offered her peace and freedom from the agony.

Her smarting wounds woke her. Her whole body seemed to be drowning in sweat. Her throat rasped with pain when she tried to swallow, and her head ached.

Unsure of where she was, she looked around, wanting to call for help, but then saw she was in the infirmary and knew it would be useless to try to get anyone to come to her. She lay back on the rock-hard pillow and wept.

'Ruth?'

A croaky voice trickled into her mind. Ruth opened her eyes. She tried to say Amy's name, but nothing would come out. With a great effort she raised her hand.

'Oh, Ruth. I'm dying. Don't let me.'

A streak of terror shot through Ruth, giving her strength. Her own voice croaked and hurt her throat as she called out, 'No, Amy, fight back. Don't die. I won't let yer die, mate. We can beat them by getting well.'

'Beat who? Just you try, young tyke and see where it gets you. More of the same, if yer ain't careful.'

Ruth's fear couldn't get any deeper than it was already. The evil Matron could do no more to her than she'd already done. But Ruth wouldn't let her win. She'd survive and one day she would have her revenge.

She hadn't known Matron was in the room, but now heard her steps receding and knew some relief. But the rallying thoughts she'd had increased her determination. She lay back. Hearing, but not able to do anything about Amy's sobs, she prayed to her beautiful Holy Mary.

When she next woke, a man stood looking down on her. Matron stood next to him. His voice was kindly, 'Tell me, who did this wicked thing to you, my dear?'

Matron coughed, drawing Ruth's attention to her. Her look defied Ruth to dare mention who.

Ruth remained silent. The man turned to Matron. 'Surely, you know how this happened, Matron, these children are in your care.'

'I don't, Doctor. And if I find out . . . But then, these kids are always fighting amongst themselves. They bully this one in particular as she gets on all of their nerves, so I'd say a few had a hand in it. Not that you'd ever get her, or any of them, to tell you who were involved.' Matron's head bobbed on her neck.

'Well, maybe you need to see they are more closely supervised. Now, you have a problem on your hands. For apart from her appalling injuries, this young lady and the one called Amy look likely to have diphtheria.'

Matron's 'No' came out following a deep gasp.

'I'm afraid so. I will need to carry out tests, but I'm almost certain. This could now run rife through the home and take the lives of many of these poor souls. They need careful nursing and keeping in isolation. Everything used for them must be either destroyed or sterilized by boiling.'

'But I haven't got the staff to cope with that. Can't they be taken into the charity hospital?'

'No, it's best to keep them where they are. Besides, they have an outbreak in most of the charity hospitals and work-house infirmaries.'

'Well then, that explains it. That one,' Matron nodded to where Amy's voice had come from, 'came from one of those just recently. No doubt, she's the reason we've got it here, then.'

'Well, whatever the reason, you have to put measures into place. I will try to get hold of some antitoxin. I have a supplier who may have some.'

Ruth's terror increased, and yet she couldn't completely take it in. *He said I might die! What is being dead like? I don't want to die, and I don't want Amy to.*

As soon as the door closed on Matron and the doctor, she called out in as loud a voice as her sore throat would allow, 'Amy, are yer all right, luv?'

A similar croak came back. 'Yes, but I feel so ill.'

'Hold on, luv, don't die.'

A little sob came from Amy. Ruth didn't know what to do, she couldn't raise her head, or hardly move her aching limbs. She closed her eyes.

A voice that seemed to be coming from a long way off woke her. 'Ruth, Ruth, open your eyes.'

Ruth tried to respond to it, but her eyes felt weighted down and wouldn't open, and her head hurt so much.

'If she doesn't wake, we may lose her. She needs to respond. Has she spoken at all, Matron?'

'Not that I know of.'

'Look at the state of her. What's going on? She's lain here for three days now. Have you bothered to bathe her and change her soiled gown?'

'I told you, I haven't got the staff, and I can't do it all myself.'

'What about the other one? You're very lucky it was confined to these two only . . . Let me take a look at her.'

18

Ruth drifted off again, liking the oblivion. Not wanting to wake up until a different voice pleaded with her. 'Ruth, wake up. Please wake up.'

Amy? 'Amy, are you all right, Amy?'

But it seemed Amy hadn't heard her as she carried on calling her name. Then a different voice, that of the doctor came to her, 'I think she's trying to speak. Amy, will you try again, but don't tire yourself as you're far from well yourself yet.'

Amy's cry of 'Ruth, Ruth' encouraged Ruth to make a massive effort, and she opened her crusted eyes.

'Ahh, some response, good . . . Now then, my dear, you're doing well and responding to treatment, but I need you to fight this too . . . Matron, prepare a bath at once. Get someone . . . anyone, to come along and bathe these two poor souls. I shall report this to the board.'

'Huh, you won't get anywhere, I told them myself, that if I put someone on cleaning and doing for them, the whole home could become infected. They agreed I should keep these in isolation and do what I can – well, as you can see, that isn't much. But at least I kept it confined.'

The doctor sighed. 'Well, I think it's safe now to let someone come and clean them up and change their beds. I'll give them one more dose of the antitoxin, and then they both should make a full recovery. I'll come back tomorrow, and I want to see a different state of affairs.'

Ruth closed her eyes again but found herself being shaken. 'Ruth, please, keep your eyes open. Get better, Ruth, don't leave me.'

Not able to answer Amy, Ruth tried to nod her head, but the pain was too much too bear. Though she knew with a sense of relief that Amy had beaten the disease enough to get out of bed.

'Doctor said yer injuries are a lot to do with how badly yer hurt, Ruth. That pig! Did she beat you?'

Ruth nodded. 'St-stinging.'

'Oh, Ruth. That's because the doctor put iodine on, but he has to or you'll get infected.'

Ruth heard the door go and stiffened. She knew Matron wouldn't be in a good mood after the way the doctor had spoken to her and that could mean consequences for her and Amy. But then a familiar voice had her wanting to smile. 'It stinks in here. Bleedin' hell, ain't yer washed for a fortnight?'

Hettie! Lovely Hettie.

'Right, let's get the bleedin' bath ready. You can go first, Amy, as yer don't look so bad. How's Ruth?'

'She's badly, but the doc said none of us are infectious now.'

'I know, I wanted to come before, but the old cow wouldn't let me. Let me help yer to wash. I've brought a clean night-gown for yer both and I'll go and get some sheets.'

Ruth heard Hettie approaching her bed. She opened her eyes.

'Oh, Ruth, luv . . . look, let me help yer into a chair and start to get them things off you, eh?'

Ruth nodded, but then screamed out in pain as Hettie tried to move her.

'Nearly there, mate, scream as much as yer like, I can take it. But I've got to get yer cleaned up. Yer'll never get better in that stinking pit.'

Ruth gritted her teeth and allowed Hettie to bathe her. Tears streamed down her face, but she didn't murmur.

'Yer made of strong stuff, Ruth, luv. You can get through this. Only a few more months and you'll get to go to a placement.'

Through chattering teeth and wanting to distract herself, Ruth asked, 'What they like, Hettie?'

'Well, I ain't ever been out of here and the workhouse, but I get to go to the market sometimes and once I met a girl who works in a big house as a scullery maid. She don't do too bad. She says she'd look out for something going for me, but I don't know if I can leave Cook. Anyway, this girl told me the work's hard and the hours are long, but she gets fed well and has mates there who're more like a family and on days when the owners of the house have a celebration, they're allowed a glass or two and to sing songs.'

To Ruth, this sounded like heaven.

'She gave me hope, because she told me that she ran away from the workhouse and just went knocking on kitchen doors. She fell lucky on her sixth day, mind she near starved in that time. And she is no more than a dogsbody as she has no references but she seemed happy.'

The idea began to take root in Ruth. She could run away. She could do as this girl had done . . . *I will, I'll do it. One day, I'll take me chance and run away.*

With this thought giving her hope, Ruth felt the life coming back into her. These last days she hadn't cared if she lived or died, but now, she wanted to live.

Chapter Three

The metal landing of the stairs that led to the playground had been warmed by the June sunshine, making it a welcome place for Ruth, Ellen and Amy to sit on this lovely summer's day.

They dangled their legs through the railings, watching the other kids. Some sat on the steps huddled together with their mates, others ran around, screaming with joy and happiness as if they hadn't a care in the world.

Didn't they feel trapped in this awful place – abandoned? Unloved and unwanted? What was it that made them different? Why was it that they seemed invisible to Matron and Belton and could carry on their lives as if everything was normal?

Not so for the ones on the steps. They were like her, Amy and Ellen. Their pain and misery visible in their eyes. Ruth knew their need to hold hands as she was doing with Amy and Ellen.

But then despite it all she was glad that she hadn't died, and even more so that Amy hadn't. But she knew they'd been lucky – herself in particular.

Six weeks had passed since that awful day and now her cuts were scabbed over and more comfortable and she was getting stronger every day.

She looked from Amy to Ellen. 'Yer know, all the while I were ill, it was me need to get me own back that kept me going. A feeling I had that no matter what, they weren't going to win – that and, well . . . I wouldn't have got through any of it without you two and Hettie.'

Amy snuggled in closer, her mousy hair covering her freckled face as she looked down at the ground. She did this a lot, as if she felt that looking up would give her the reality of her world. She didn't speak much either, but wherever Ruth went, Amy was by her side or not many paces behind, as was Ellen. The three of them were becoming inseparable.

Ellen squeezed her hand a little tighter. 'You would. You're stronger than you think. Me dad always said that of me. He said, "Your calmness is your strength, Ellen. You don't rebel, when anyone else in your position would and that saves you a lot." Funny, but he said it saved him too. I suppose he meant that me accepting things made for a peaceful life. But to me, you're the strong one as yer fight back.'

'I suppose. Did yer dad ever tell you where you came from, Ellen – I mean to them, not that birds and bees stuff.'

They all giggled at this.

'No. I didn't ever ask them. It all seemed normal as I can't remember anything but being with them and anyway, me dad is me real dad, I know that. As I told yer, me mum always called me his – his bastard. I looked that word up once. She used to take me to the library, and they had a big dictionary. It means "born out of wedlock".'

Ruth knew this and had wondered if she was a bastard child too.

'That's why I think me dad really loved me – mind, he did tell me so when we were on our own. I asked him once, why me mum didn't love me and he just said it was

23

complicated. But once I knew what the word meant, I thought she couldn't be me real mum – not the one who gave birth to me. But it all became too much so I didn't think about it a lot. Anyway, I have you and Amy now, and that makes up for a lot.'

Ruth knew this feeling; if you didn't think about things, they couldn't hurt you, and to have someone you felt close to and who you knew loved you meant the world.

Sometimes she felt guilty at her plan to run away, for as much as she needed them, Ellen and Amy needed her. But she couldn't let that alter her resolve and she decided now was the time to tell them about it. 'I'm going to run away.'

'What?!'

Both looked stricken as they said this in unison. Ellen recovered first, though still looked devastated as she asked, 'When?'

'I don't know yet. The time has got to be right. But it will be during the summer in case I don't get set on somewhere and have to sleep rough.'

'I'm coming with yer.'

'No, Amy, you stay with Ellen and look out for each other, and try to keep yerselves out of trouble. I'll come for yer when I'm set up. But before that, I'll sneak up to the railings to see yer whenever I can, so look out for me.'

Ellen had tears in her eyes as she asked, 'How will yer do it, Ruth?'

Ruth hesitated. She had a plan, but she couldn't tell them about it. She'd decided she'd be like Hettie, she'd gain favours from Belton. She'd get Hettie to tell him she was willing to let him do anything with her.

This thought tightened her throat. She swallowed hard. She'd asked a lot of questions of Hettie and learned how she played games with Belton. All of it repulsed and frightened her, but she saw Hettie as so brave to do it, and knew it was the only way for herself to stand a chance of getting out of here. She could do it . . . Anything if it meant she'd be free!

Ellen brought her back from these thoughts. 'Have yer got a plan, Ruth?'

'No, but I'll find a way. If yer look for stuff, yer find it. And I watch all the comings and goings, so, one day, I'll get me chance.'

'You really mean that you'll come for us?'

'I do, Amy. Look after each other and one day we'll all be together again.'

It was later that day, while she was helping Hettie to load the huge dinner trolley ready to take into the dining hall that Ruth plucked up the courage to tell her of her plan.

Hettie looked horrified. 'What? No, Ruth. No, not that, luv . . . Don't ask that of me. Besides, yer'll never make it. Out there, where would yer go?'

'That girl yer told me about did and if she can, then I can.'

Hettie was quiet for a moment. 'You really mean it, don't yer, mate?'

'I do and I need yer help, Hettie.'

'But not that way. Not by using Belton. No! Yer don't know what it's like, Ruth.'

For the first time, Ruth wondered what happened to Hettie and doubted if what she'd always thought was the truth. Did Hettie do what she did, willingly? Cunningly even, to make her life better?

But whatever it was like, Ruth had no other plan and this made her determined to endure it to help her cause. She went to plead with Hettie but instead tears tumbled down her cheeks, making her feel weak. The tears were of despair, of the kind she didn't seem able to control since her illness.

'Aw, don't cry, luv. Come here.'

Hettie's hug as she rocked her backwards and forwards helped.

'There'll be a way, luv, but not that way. But promise me, if you do go, yer'll keep in touch. And don't starve. I'll make arrangements with yer to meet me at the kitchen bins when I empty the slop bucket and if I can't get anything fresh for you then yer can have something out of the bucket, as believe me, yer'll be bleedin' grateful for it.'

'Ta, Hettie. And ta for hugging me, luv. I love to be hugged.'

'It still feels strange as the first time was when yer were in the isolation, but nice. We should do it more. Me arms have ached to hold someone and have someone hold me in a loving way.'

Ruth looked both ways and seeing no one had come to find her, she hugged Hettie again. 'I luv yer, Hettie.'

'Ha! Yer a dafty, but I bleedin' luv you too, girl.'

They both laughed at this.

'Hettie, you will look out for Ellen and Amy if I go, won't yer?'

'I will, luv, as they'll be lost without you. Tell them, I'll always be here for them.'

'Ta, luv.'

'Now, let's get the dinner dished up, or we'll have Matron on our heels.'

Ruth's chance came sooner than she thought. She lay asleep a few nights later, dreaming that she was walking the streets of London, when was she catapulted awake by someone shaking her.

'Shush!'

From the shadowy form she could tell it was Hettie.

'Grab yer clothes and come to the kitchen.'

With this Hettie turned and almost ran out of the dormitory.

Ruth didn't know how she made it to the dimly lit kitchen, as every step of the way was fraught with danger of being caught.

Each door she passed gave her signs that someone was awake. A cough, or the sound of someone having a pee. But the worst sounds of all came from Belton's office as a boy screamed, and she heard Gedberg shout, 'Hold the bleeder still, Belton, will you?'

Her heart went out to the boy and urged her to burst through the door, but her head told her that wouldn't do any good, so she prayed to her lovely Holy Mary for him and for herself.

Her prayers got her to the kitchen.

When she opened the door it was to find Hettie pacing up and down.

'Are yer all right, Hettie? What have you planned for me, mate?'

'No, I ain't all right, and I didn't plan anything, it just became something I've got to do . . . Oh, Ruth. You will take care, won't yer?'

'I will. But why, what's happened?'

'Look, mate, just remember that I wouldn't do this if I weren't trying to save you. Yer see that bleedin' Belton's got his eye on yer.'

'You mean . . . ?'

'Yes. You couldn't make it up. Here you were asking me to arrange it and then a few days later, he's telling me he wants a fresh girl to be his regular and asking me to work

27

on you – tell you the benefits, make yer want the same. Ha, he told me to tell yer how good it was, but it ain't, Ruth. He hurts yer and he enjoys doing so. It makes you feel dirty . . . Anyway, he said he'd noticed how you were developing, and he liked how beautiful you were. I said I wouldn't do it, so he thumped me in me back. Took me wind away. I doubled over and that's when he kicked me, so I agreed, knowing I would help you to escape instead.'

Ruth had been dressing as she listened. Terror clutched at her and she wanted to say she couldn't do it. She couldn't go out in the dark by herself, but what she was hearing spurred her on. But what of Hettie?

'Come with me, Hettie. He'll know what you've done, mate. He'll hurt you again and again. I can't bear that.'

'No. I can't. Don't worry about me, I'll get me revenge. I serve his meal at night when he comes on duty. He's not going to be very well for a good while. By the time he can think straight, he'll have forgotten this and want to get back to normal. But if me plan don't work, then I'll run away too. Now, stop worrying about me. Here, I've put some grub up for yer, luv.'

Ruth took the cloth bundle.

'Make for the market square, cross the Old Ford Road and just keep going. You'll see a few stands and things as some leave them up all the time and yer'll get some shelter under them. But hide out of sight if yer see anyone coming towards yer, as there's some rogues about at night. In the morning start looking for a placement, though sometimes, someone from the countryside will come to the market looking for workers. Yer'll know if this is likely as yer'll see a queue of down-and-outs, hoping to be took on. Wait in the queue, you might get lucky.'

Ruth nodded. She wanted to run back to her warm bed, but the thought of Belton spurred her on. She'd been shocked since knowing that Hettie didn't really like going with him and that he hurt her. In the past Hettie had always spoken as if it was a good thing to be the favourite. But then, that was Hettie. She wouldn't want Ruth worrying over her, or worse, trying to protect her. Hettie knew she was known for flying off the handle to stand up for what was right. Though after what happened when she last lost her temper, she'd think twice now.

'Give me another hug, love, and make sure yer come to this back door regularly to get food and to let me know how yer are.'

Ruth didn't want to come out of the hug. It seemed to her it would be the last bit of comfort she'd ever have. 'Tell Ellen and Amy that I'll come to the railings when it's safe to do so, but if I can't, they're not to forget me as one day, I'll come for them. And you, Hettie. We'll all be together one day, won't we?'

'We will, luv, we will. Good luck. Be strong and remember, you're a cockney, and cockneys have spirit and courage. And the majority out there'll help yer, so don't be afraid to ask, eh?'

Shivering from the cold of the damp night air, Ruth pulled the shawl Hettie had given her around her shoulders, trying to get the feel of the safety of Hettie's arms as much as to shield herself.

The smog that was a permanent part of London thickened in places making it hard to see where she was going, but eventually, she made out the shapes of some wooden stalls ahead. She quickened her pace, but then stopped dead as another shape became clearer and she realized there was a huddle of shadowy figures perched against one of the stalls.

Dodging into a doorway, she peeped out. None of them moved.

Hoping they were asleep she took her wooden-soled shoes off and crept in her stockinged feet towards them, hardly daring to breathe.

When she reached the first stall, she could see it had a skirt of canvas around it. Crouching down, Ruth crept under this but was assailed by the stench of rotting vegetables. Taking deep breaths, she crawled closer to the crates that were giving off the awful smell, seeing them as a back rest in this cramped space.

Voices woke her. Cheery voices calling out to one another. ''Ere, Bett, you going to make a killing today then, luv?'

'Ha, I've to shift this bleedin' lot first . . . Ger out of it, yer drunken layabouts.'

'Come on Bett, give us a break.'

'Give yerselves one, get down the docks, go on, yer'll most likely be given a day's work. Not that any of you bleeders know what one of them is.'

'Give us a sup of tea first, Bett.'

'Cheeky buggers. Yer can 'ave a mug between yer once I've brewed it. Let me get me brazier going.'

Not daring to move, Ruth could see a woman's feet shuffling backwards and forwards and hear sounds that told of the stall she was under having goods put on it.

'The cart's turned into the street, Ruby, luv, looks like yer delivery's here, do yer need a hand with yer crates?'

'Ta, Bett. Me back's giving me some gip today.'

Ruth held her breath as the canvas was lifted.

'Bleedin' hell, what we got 'ere? Blimey, it's a waif and stray! Come out, girl, no one's going to bite yer.'

As Ruth crawled out, she looked into two weathered, wizened, but kindly faces.

'What the devil?'

'Leave it out, Ruby, mate, the girl's frightened out of her wits . . . Now then, young miss, where did you come from?'

'I ran away, and I don't want to go back.'

The one called Ruby put her hands on her hips. 'We'll be the judge of where yer go, girl. How old are yer, and where did yer run from?'

A few of the men and boys who'd been sleeping rough had gathered round. One piped up, 'I bet she come from that kids' home, I've 'eard some tales of that place. Young Robbie here ran away from there, didn't yer, son?'

'I did, and I ain't never going back. Did Belton get at yer, girl?'

Ruth looked from one to the other and nodded her head. 'Me name's Ruth and I'm tw— thirteen, and I'm going to look for work.'

'Not before yer 'ave a hot cuppa tea and a crust of toasted bread and dripping you ain't, Ruth girl. Get yerself by me brazier and warm yer bones.'

'Here, Bett, it's one thing these men and boys sleeping rough, but we can't let a girl do it. We should take her back.'

Ruth felt the terror of this. She broke away and ran for all she was worth not stopping to look back. A hand grabbed her. 'Hold yer horses, Ruth, no one's going to send yer back. And if they try, they'll have to get by me first.'

Gasping for breath, Ruth slowed down.

'Ruby ain't a bad ole girl, she'll come round, she always takes the high ground. And Bett'll always look out for anyone, she's the salt of the earth is Bett. She didn't mean any of that she said to us just before you appeared, it's all part of our regular banter. Come and have a dripping butty and a hot drink, eh? None them blokes I'm with'll harm you. They're a good bunch, just down on their luck like me and you.'

Feeling better, Ruth let the young man she'd heard called Robbie guide her. 'Ta, Robbie, I were scared for a mo.'

'I know how yer felt, you don't have to tell me. I was . . . well, I had problems in that bleedin' home. Did Belton have a go at yer?'

She nodded, feeling her cheeks redden.

'Well, I ain't saying you're safe now, but you are from the lot I'm with, they won't touch yer, I promise, they're a decent lot. Come on.'

When they got back to the group, Bett handed her a mug of tea. 'Well, yer've got cockney spirit, girl, I'll give yer that. Now, get this down yer, and take no notice of Ruby.'

'Well, I only thought I was doing right, Bett.' Ruby shrugged then turned to Robbie. 'Anyroad, Robbie, mate, if yer want a day's work today, you've got it. Finish unloading me cart for me, son, as me back's breaking. Then yer can help me to load me barrow and take it around the streets for me. Jack ain't coming in today, he's got a gammy leg.'

'Ta, Ruby. Ta very much. Yer won't be sorry, I'll work hard.'

'You'd better. And mind yer Ps and Qs in them posh streets, none of yer bleedin' swearing.'

A roar of laughter went up at this. And as each of them introduced themselves to her, Ruth had a warm feeling of being amongst friends.

'I'm Reg. I was injured in the Boar War. Fought for my country and now on the scrap heap, trying to get by. Good to meet you, Ruth.'

Reg, a gangly-looking man who Ruth imagined might be in his thirties, smiled, showing a mouthful of even but decaying teeth. His posh voice didn't go with his situation and she felt most sorry for him.

'And I'm Mick. Mick the Irish. Known for the blarney. What is it you're for having in your cloth?'

'Food, and yer can all share it if yer like.'

'I'll be for tanking you, as it is that I am fair hungry this morning.'

Mick looked older than Reg. Ruth loved the way he expressed himself and his lovely blue eyes that held kindness.

Then there was Ted the Flute, another older man, named, they told her, because he played the flute on the street corners and earned a few coppers to buy them a jug of ale now and then.

Ruth liked them all and wished she could help them. They presented a motley crew with their ragged trousers tied with string at the ankles and old coats also tied with string around their waists. Each wore a flat cap and were grubby and had a look of being half-starved. But all had a cheery word.

When she opened the cloth she found sandwiches made with thick slices of ham. They were gone in no time. Biting into the one she had, she found it delicious with just a light taste of mustard. She thought of Hettie and had the feeling that she was hugging her again.

A voice cut into this thought. 'You can come with me if yer like, Ruth. It'll be a good chance to knock on kitchen doors or to ask them as they come out to buy off the barrow if they have any jobs going.'

'Ta, Robbie, I will.'

'Robbie, stop yer flirting and come 'ere.'

Robbie blushed. 'What is it, Ruby? I've got the cart ready, I'm just having a bite to eat.'

'It ain't all about pushing a cart. You need to be more presentable to the folk who might consider buying from yer. They won't want to buy from the dirty-looking tyke that you look like. 'Ere, take this farthing and get yerself over to the slipper baths and 'ave a wash. Then yer can put Jack's overall on, it should fit yer and it's been washed and ironed.'

It was Ruth's turn to feel embarrassed but feeling as desperate as she was, she had no choice but to ask, 'Is there a lav in the slipper baths, Ruby?'

'No, yer go behind that bush, like the rest of them. Though I should 'old yer nose as it's been used as a lav by a good few.'

'Ruby, girl, I don't know what's got yer goat this morning, but can't you find a civil word for the girl, eh? She's one of us, anyone can tell that. Come on, Ruth, I'll take yer to the cafe. I rent a storeroom around the back of it and they've got a lav.'

'Ta, Bett.'

'Morning, Joe. 'Ow are yer today?' Bett cheerfully greeted the man behind the counter of the cafe but didn't get the same kind of response.

'Where shall I start? I ache all over.'

'Well start by pulling a jug of ale for the lads. They're going to the docks to try their luck. Put it in a bottle and it'll keep them going for the morning. Add it to me tab, ta.'

Whatever Joe said to this, Ruth had no idea as it was growled out, but she felt lifted by Bett's cheery giggle as she followed her around to the back of the building.

'That door, there, luv, it ain't all that clean though. Folk should be given a peg to put on their nose, but it's all right, and if you've to do yer business then yer can read the bits of the newspaper on the hook while yer do and then use it afterwards.' Bett laughed as if she'd told a joke that was really funny. But Ruth didn't mind this crudeness as it made her giggle and helped to cover the awkwardness she felt.

When she came out, Bett was waiting for her. 'There's a job going here with Grumpy Joe, but I'd worry about yer. I know the bloke you were talking about – Belton. He comes down 'ere for his ale before he goes 'ome to have his kip.'

Fear zinged through Ruth.

'Don't worry, luv, if yer ain't on the road with Robbie by then, we'll hide yer.'

'But Ruby might tell him!'

'No, don't you worry about Ruby. She's a good sort. She's feeling her bones this morning, but when it comes to it, she won't give yer away.'

Ruth didn't feel so sure. She hadn't taken to Ruby and didn't trust her and was glad to find when they got back to Bett's brazier with the spuds from Bett's storeroom that the men had all gone to seek work and Robbie was ready to set off.

Robbie looked different. The brown-cloth work coat hung on him and his grubby face had turned into a shiny clean one. She could see he had freckles across the bridge of his nose. His sandy hair shone, though was still damp on top where it was a lot thicker. Ruth loved how it curled up where it touched his collar. In Robbie she felt she'd met a kindred spirit and knew they were going to be friends.

'I'm heading for Victoria Park area. There's a few big houses around there. It's about a fifteen-minute walk, are yer up to that?'

35

'I am, I can walk you off yer legs, mate.'

They both giggled.

'I can remember seeing yer about in the orphanage. You're younger than me, about two years I'd say. I remember that one or two of the lads thought yer pretty.'

Ruth blushed. 'Well, I can't remember seeing you, so pull the other one, it's got bells on it.'

This set them off giggling again, and Ruth knew this was the happiest she'd ever felt in her life. She breathed deeply, ignoring the wafts of horse dung and the smell of the smoke belching out of the factory chimneys. Her freedom was in every breath. She thought about the home and imagined Matron's face when she found her gone. And Ellen and Amy, how distressed they'd be at not having said goodbye. And Hettie. 'Please, Holy Mary, don't let Hettie suffer for this, and look after Ellen and Amy for me.'

'What did yer say? It sounded like a prayer. Are yer a churchgoer, then?'

Ruth felt silly, she hadn't meant to say her prayer aloud. 'No. Well, I am really I suppose. Anyway, yer should know, we all had to be. But I saw a picture of the Roman Catholic Mary and I liked it. I had a feeling she'd help me if I prayed to her and she has done up to now.'

'What did yer pray for then?'

'For me mates, Hettie, who helped me to run away, and Ellen and Amy, who are younger than me but I were close to.'

'I know Hettie. She works in the kitchen, don't she? She's a good sort, but how she puts up with what Belton puts her through I don't know.'

Ruth felt the pity of this, as she'd been so naive thinking poor Hettie was all right with what was happening. At this moment she felt like running back and begging Hettie to leave.

They'd been walking in silence for a while now and as they neared the park, Ruth was amazed at this glimpse of the outside world. How people had these lovely houses just to themselves and their families. It set her off thinking about her own mum and wondering if she was still alive and if she ever thought about her, and if she knew who her dad was, and what he was like, and what it would be like to live with your very own family. She sighed heavily. Maybe when she got a placement, it would feel like she had a family too, with all the staff. She hoped so. With all her heart, she hoped so.

Chapter Four

As soon as they entered Victoria Street, Robbie made enough noise to waken the dead, but he wasn't the only one as the hawkers in the street numbered at least six, shouting out their wares.

'Oranges, two a penny. Cherry ripens a penny a pint. Come and get them before they go.'

It seemed women in grey frocks, white aprons and white mob caps came out of every side entrance to every house, all clambering to get the best bargains for their master and mistress. Some bartering, others taking the price and running with their purchases. Robbie had a queue, and they all nattered away to each other, increasing the level of noise.

Robbie nudged her a few times, 'Go on, ask. Ask them all. Shyness never got anyone anywhere.' Then suddenly without warning, he shouted, 'Here, any of yer looking to set on a maid?'

'Yer not trading in maids are yer, mate?'

'I am as it happens. Ruth here is looking for work. She's in good fettle. Ripe for training and willing to learn. She'll put a twelve-hour shift in without complaint.'

Ruth felt like kicking Robbie. Her face burned bright red.

'Have yer references, girl?'

Ruth went to shake her head, but Robbie spoke before she could. 'She has. And the best going, from honest traders in Bethnal Market. Bett the spud lady, Ruby, whose fruit and veg you've all bought for years, and war veteran, Captain Reginald Higginbottom. All can speak for her honesty and her willingness.'

'I'm the housekeeper for number eighteen, girl. I'm looking for a scullery maid. Can you start straight away?'

Ruth, amazed at this, bobbed a curtsy, and said she could.

'What experience did yer have with Captain Higginbottom?'

'Maud, are you mad? You can't take a waif and stray into service. She'll be trouble, I can tell. And I bet she don't know the first thing about how a big house is run.'

'Not mad, desperate. I can't seem to keep a scullery maid. They go off to better things, or end up having babbies . . . So, girl. What have yer to say for yerself?'

'I can light fires and clean, and wash and iron, missus.' Ruth had never felt so grateful for the drudgery of the home as all of these tasks had been taught to the girls and carried out by them on a regular basis. She really was skilled in them all and couldn't believe the work she hated was now going to be her saviour.

'Well! That's good enough for me. Work today and we'll see. If you do all right, you can come back tomorrow with your belongings and your references, and if they're in order, you'll be moving in.'

Ruth bent her knee again.

'Come along, girl, don't stand there bobbing up and down. There's work to do.'

As Ruth followed the thin little woman with a pointed face, she listened as she was told, 'I'm Mrs Casson. You will address me as that, or Housekeeper, at all times. Now, Cook

39

will tell you what will be expected of you, so, presuming you come up to scratch and are kept on, you will be paid twelve pounds a year, be given food and board, and half a day off every month.'

Ruth was astonished. A pound a month all to herself! That was a massive sum to her. All of a sudden she didn't care what she had to do, she'd do it cheerfully and she'd use her afternoon off to go and see Hettie, Amy and Ellen. But would they worry about her till then? She didn't want them to and thought she would ask Robbie to get a message to Hettie.

The door they went through led into a kind of pantry, with shelves stacked with gleaming copper cooking pots.

'This is one of your jobs; keep this lot as you see them now. Through that door is the coal house. In the winter, you'll be up before us all and you'll need to clean out and light all the fires in the house. There's a basket of kindling, under that shelf there, you've to keep it topped up from the woodman who calls every fortnight and you're to collect all the newspapers around the house every evening to make them into firelighters. Is that something you know how to do?'

'Yes, Mrs Casson.'

'Good. Through here is the main kitchen, this is Cook. You will do her bidding as and when she bids you to do anything for her. Understand?'

Before she could say yes, the fattest woman she'd ever seen, with a red face that looked as though it would explode from the heat, asked, 'Who you got 'ere, now, Casson?'

'This is . . . what's yer name, girl?'

'Ruth Faith, miss.'

Ruth didn't know if this was her real name, but it was her given one from the priest who'd found her and baptized her, which made her a Catholic, but she'd never talked much about that as the home was run by the Church of England. Though she did wonder if this was the reason that she loved the Holy Mary. She'd heard that all Catholics loved Mary.

'She's a waif, I'd say.' Cook gave a heavy sigh. 'Sometimes, Casson, I think you lose yer marbles.'

Mrs Casson harrumphed.

'Right, apart from the fires, the pantry and anything Cook wants you to do, you have to do anything the upstairs maid needs you to do. Is all that clear?'

'Yes, Mrs Casson.'

'Good. You can start by working with Cook.'

When Mrs Casson left the kitchen, Cook scowled. 'If yer ain't any bleedin' good you're out that door, understand? Now, get them pots scrubbed, and bring in some coal for me stove, then I need them spuds peeling, and be quick about it all.'

The blackened pans resisted all Ruth's efforts.

'Don't yer know anything, girl? Look, right before your eyes, a wire brush – hanging there. Get It down and use it!'

Ruth couldn't think why she hadn't spotted the brush, but now she had it the task became easier but for Cook bellowing every few minutes for her to quicken her pace as she was losing the heat from her oven and needed it topping up.

After a few minutes, the banging of the rolling pin on the wooden table made Ruth jump. Shivering with nerves she stood straight.

'Leave that and get the coal!'

'But I've nearly done, I've only half of the bottom of this pan to do.'

Cook's growl turned menacing, she lifted her rolling pin and struck Ruth a painful blow across her shoulder.

Drawing in a gasping painful breath at the sting of her still tender skin, Ruth scuttled to the coalhouse. But back at the stove with her heavy load, she looked at the five doors with beaming brass handles and hadn't a clue which one contained the fire and which the delicious smelling bread.

Another blow brought a cry from her as it caught her. 'I – I'm . . . sorry, I ain't never seen a stove like this.'

Cook's shove made Ruth almost lose her balance, then she opened one of the doors that revealed what looked like a raving furnace. How it couldn't be heating the oven, Ruth couldn't think.

Her shoulder stung with pain as she lifted the heavy bucket to throw the coal in, losing some on the floor and causing a cloud of dust. The blow this time sent her to her knees, sobbing with agony.

'You imbecile! What do yer think them tongs are for, eh? Decoration!'

Cook's foot dug into Ruth's hip. Ruth could take no more. Her screams hurt her own ears as she got up and went for Cook but they were no match for Cook's hollers. The door to the kitchen burst open and the housekeeper stood there, astonishment making her poker face look hideous. 'What the blazes!'

Ruth crumbled, sobbing huge racking sobs that vent all her anger, disappointment and humiliation, and hurt her throat. 'She . . . she beat me with . . . her rolling pin.'

'Get up, girl, get yer shawl and get out of 'ere!'

With her back and shoulder smarting, Ruth stood outside the house not sure what to do next, until she looked across the road. Victoria Park looked lovely – a green oasis. It drew her to it.

Broken and exhausted, she flopped onto a wooden bench, empty of tears now, and feeling desolate and lonely.

Leaning back hurt, so she sat forward and held her trembling hands clasped in her lap, at a loss as to what to do. Into her despair came a small voice making her jump, 'Why are you crying?'

Lifting her head, Ruth looked into a face like none she'd ever seen. Big black eyes looked back at her. 'Can I make you better?'

The little boy's skin was as black as the coal she'd just been handling. 'Are yer from Africa?'

'No, I live across the road.'

Ruth didn't know what to say. The boy who she thought might be about five years old was beautiful, his eyes were almost liquid, his lips perfectly bow-shaped, and his hair curled so tightly it looked like soft wool.

'Are you sad? You can play with me if you like. I've got a yo-yo.'

He fished the brightly coloured yo-yo out of his pocket. 'Here, you can have it. What's your name?'

'Ta.' Ruth held the warm, metal yo-yo. 'Me name's Ruth. I came to work in the house across the road but Cook beat me and I lost me temper.'

'I'm Horacio. My momma often gets beaten. She's a maid in that house over there. My father is the butler. He's treated well.'

Ruth couldn't take this all in – the boy didn't seem as though he belonged to parents who worked as servants. She felt compelled to ask, 'How come yer speak posh?'

'I'm educated with the family's youngest child, but her nanny doesn't like me. She calls me names. She's over there with Elizabeth. Elizabeth's four years old and nice and I'm five. Nanny brings me to the park with Elizabeth, but she doesn't like me to be around them and makes me go off to play. But I don't mind. Are you ten?'

Ruth liked him very much. She felt like picking him up and putting him on her knee. She'd never seen a Black person before, only in books, and he was the most beautiful person she'd ever seen. 'I'm almost . . . I'm thirteen.'

Horacio wanted to know where she lived, and why she was sad, and where her mother and father were. He fascinated Ruth and seemed fascinated by her.

Wanting to keep him with her longer, she asked, 'Can yer keep the yo-yo going? I can do thirty – well, I did once.'

Yo-yos were just about the only toy she'd ever played with and she was quite skilful. She showed him a few of her moves, twisting it round and bouncing it up and down. Horacio clapped his hands, his face a joy. 'Teach me, please teach me.'

The next ten minutes were full of giggles and Ruth began to feel more carefree than she'd ever known, until a shrill voice stopped their fun. 'You, boy, come here, we've got to go.'

Horacio's face fell. 'Will you meet me in the park tomorrow? We come here every day at this time.'

'Horacio!'

The nanny came marching over, her hand raised. Horacio dodged behind the bench.

'Don't yer dare hit him! He ain't done anything wrong.'

'And who might you be to tell me what to do? A common maid? How dare you even speak to me until I have spoken to you, let alone challenge me!'

'She's my friend, and her name's Ruth, and she's not a maid as Cook beat her and she had to leave.'

'Oh?'

Ruth felt like dirt under the foot of this stick-like, cold-fish of a girl. Everything about her was straight – her hair, her nose, her back, which she held so stiff and upright that she had no option but to look down her nose.

'Well, if you don't come at once, Horacio, you'll be beaten too, and you don't like that, do you?'

'No! Nanny's not to beat Horacio!' This tearful plea came from the pretty little girl standing back a little. 'If you do, Nanny, I'll tell Mama.'

Nanny's face coloured. Through gritted teeth, she commanded Horacio, 'Get here, now!'

Horacio came out from behind the bench. He sidled onto it next to Ruth, his trembling hand found hers. 'I'm staying with my friend.'

Nanny swivelled on one foot, and marched away, roughly grabbing the hand of the little girl as she went. 'You'll be sorry for this, miss.'

When her stiff back disappeared out of the gate, Ruth put her arm around Horacio. His little head rested on her chest.

'Can I stay with you forever?'

'No, I ain't got a home, or anywhere to take you. You've to go home. I'll see yer across the road.'

'I will, but not yet. I don't want to leave you.'

Ruth held him closer. She couldn't understand the feeling she had for this little boy; it was akin to love. A feeling she thought that girls might have for a little brother.

A sudden shout catapulted her out of the dreamlike world she'd gone into, 'What are you doing? Let my son go at once!'

Ruth straightened. Fear zinged through her as Horacio jumped down.

'She's my friend, Poppa. Nanny was going to beat me.'

The man Horacio called Poppa was magnificent. He wore a red jacket with a stand-up collar and a row of gold-braided

45

loops around shinning brass buttons that stretched from his neck to his hips. A lace cravat sprouted from the collar and his white breeches fitted snugly to his legs. With all of this, and his hair hidden under a white turban, he looked like a king.

'I was only giving him comfort, mister.'

'You have no right . . . Horacio, come here at once!'

Ruth didn't know what made her blurt out, 'I need a job, mister,' but the words were said before she could stop them.

His huge black eyes stared out at her. 'I don't hire and fire. Go around to the kitchen and ask there.'

His voice had softened, giving Ruth courage. 'You shouldn't let that nanny beat your son, nor anyone beat your wife!'

The man looked astonished. He took a moment to answer. 'You don't know the way of the world. It is our lot. I can't do anything about it. If I tried, I would lose my job. Why do you think I allow it? I'm a slave, not a man of means.'

'I'm sorry, I didn't realize. You look like a king.'

The man smiled. His face shone with beauty. 'My ancestors were royalty – chiefs, in my own country. We were brought low when the British came and took us for slaves. My great-grandfather was brought to England, but many were taken to America.'

Ruth had learned about slaves at school and had cried at their plight. Tears brimmed in her eyes now.

'How old are you, child?'

'I'm not a child, I – I'm thirteen!'

'Well, you have a lot to learn about my world, but if you really want to enter it, then do as I say and try your luck at the kitchen door. I'll tell the housekeeper to expect you.'

Ruth rose. Her sore, stiff muscles made the movement painful.

46

'Are you hurt?'

'I – I'm all right.'

'Well, follow me.'

'Can I hold Ruth's hand, Poppa?'

'No, son, you mustn't be seen to hold the hand of a white girl, especially one who may become a maid in the house. You'll earn another beating.'

As Horacio took his father's hand, he looked back at Ruth. His bottom lip quivered.

'We can be secret friends, Horacio. No one will know. I'll pray to the Holy Mary to help me to get a job and to stop anyone beating you and your mama.'

Horacio did a little skip and a jump. 'Is that all right, Poppa? Please say it is.'

'Just be very careful. But yes, I think Ruth will be a nice friend for you.' He turned to look at her. 'When we get to the gate, Ruth, wait and watch. The house hasn't a side entrance, so when you see which one I go into, count how many it is from the corner, then go along and make your way around the back. Give it a few minutes, enough time for me to talk to Mrs Randell, the housekeeper. She's all right – a bit of a tartar at times, but a good sort.'

When she saw them disappear, Ruth felt the weariness of all she'd been through. She leaned heavily on the gate – afraid, hungry, and worried that she'd never get back to Robbie, Bett and the menfolk. She thought of Ellen, Amy and Hettie, and for a moment wished she was back with them. But then Belton's ugly, clouded eyes came to her, and his deep grunts as he carried out his vile acts, and she knew she would never, ever go back, and only wished she could get the others out too.

Chapter Five

Around the back of the houses, Ruth counted five along till she came to the gate to the yard of the one she needed. The latch gave with a click, but the gate didn't open. Ruth stared at it, not sure what to do as she didn't think anyone would hear her if she knocked on it, even though happy sounding voices came from what she assumed was the kitchen.

Just as she thought this, a loud bellow of a laugh reached her and made her giggle. Full of hope she shouted, 'Is there anyone there?'

The sound of footsteps set her heart racing and stomach fluttering with nerves.

'What do yer want, we don't allow no pedlars 'ere.'

The woman staring at her was small with beady eyes.

'I want a job if there's any going.'

'Yer'd better come in and I'll see if the housekeeper can see yer.'

The outer scullery and kitchen were the same as the house she'd just left.

As they walked in, a kind sounding voice asked, 'What we got 'ere then, Aggie?'

'A waif looking for work, Cook.'

Cook could have been a twin of the last cook. A big woman with many chins and wiry hair escaping her mob cap, the only difference seemed to be that this one had a pleasant expression and didn't growl.

'Well, you look a poor soul, luv.'

The kindness of this undid Ruth. Tears rolled down her face.

'Well, bless you, yer in a desperate state, ain't yer? Well, I should think we could spare yer a cuppa, even if you ain't set on . . . Where's that Ebony? Always missing when yer want her. She's a bleedin' nuisance.'

This sudden change of tone shocked Ruth. What Horacio had told her about his mother came to her and had her wondering if Cook was talking about her.

'Go and find the lazy cow, Aggie, she can get us all a cup of tea.'

Aggie laughed. 'That's if she can remember how to make it!'

The door opened just as Aggie reached it and a thin, frightened-looking Black woman came through. She had Horacio's eyes, but her skin wasn't as dark, and her hair bushed out around her small face as opposed to his tight curls.

A vicious shove of the door almost knocked Ebony off her feet. Ruth gasped, then felt sickened as Aggie gave Cook a satisfied smile and Cook laughed out loud.

'You should watch yerself when yer come through a door, someone might be standing behind it.' Cook smirked as she turned to Aggie, 'I think she should knock before she enters any room in future, don't you, Aggie?'

'Yes, it's only polite, ain't it? Especially when yer a slave girl.'

They both laughed at this.

Ebony stood still, her fear visible, her eyes shining with tears. Ruth's temper rose and she wanted to go for the pair of them but Cook had her rolling pin in one hand drumming it onto her other, her look defying Ebony to protest. This put a fear into Ruth that if she interfered, she too would get a beating. She knew she couldn't stand another one.

Cook's face looked ugly as she growled at Ebony, 'Get us all a cuppa, girl. And you'd better make it properly this time.'

Ebony scurried over to the stove, giving Cook a wide berth. Cook's smirk at Aggie increased Ruth's anger, but though she wasn't very worldly-wise her young mind deduced that she should be careful of any woman who had power over her. She was coming to know that there was no fighting back, she had to accept it.

'Right, we'll 'ave the stewed dishwater that she's bound to serve up, then we'll see if the housekeeper's free. Yer might just get lucky . . . what did yer say yer name were?'

Ruth couldn't remember saying, but as she answered she was plied with further questions: Where did she come from? Had she done this work before? Did she have references as the housekeeper was a stickler for references.

The lies tumbled from her, 'Me mum's just died. I've to get out of our house, she's been ill for a long time and I've been looking after her.'

'What about yer dad?'

'He – he died when I was little.'

'Oh dear, you poor thing, yer've had it rough. But yer'll get nowhere without references, someone as can speak up for yer.'

Ruth smiled at Ebony as she took the mug of tea from her, Ebony jerked her head round to look at Cook, but Cook hadn't seen the smile. When Ebony looked back at her, she gave the most beautiful smile that changed her face. All the haggard lines disappeared, and her eyes came to life.

Cook's stern voice asking 'Well?' made Ruth jump.

'I have a reference I can bring from Captain Reginald Higginbottom.'

'Blimey, who's he when he's not at 'ome?'

'A – a friend. He's known me a long time.' Knowing this wasn't enough, Ruth added on more fibs. Where they came from she didn't know, but she had always been told she had too much imagination for her own good. 'Me mum worked for him before she was ill.'

'Well, couldn't he 'elp you more than just write yer a reference, girl?'

Ruth felt cornered for a moment, but then spurted out, 'He did. He paid for doctors for me mum, and he didn't let her have a pauper's funeral. But he only has a small household, and he has all the staff he needs. He did say he'd be able to speak for me though, to help me get a place.'

At last Cook seemed satisfied. Ruth lifted her eyes heavenwards, but this time she didn't speak her prayer aloud. *I'm sorry for me lies, Holy Mary.*

'Right, Aggie, you go along and see if Housekeeper'll see her.'

Ruth crossed her fingers. Not that she wanted to work here, but she had to do something, and this kind of work provided a bed and board and seemed to her to be her only choice.

'You, girl!' Cook addressed Ebony again. 'You scum. You can brush up the flour I've dropped, and be quick about it.'

For all the world, Ruth wanted to protest at this way of speaking to Ebony, but she bit her tongue.

It seemed that all Ebony's movements were done in a scurrying way, as if driven by fear. She did this movement now as she went over to the cupboard in the corner and brought out a brush and pan. As Ruth watched her, she had an urge to hug her and make her world better. But just as she thought this, Cook gave Ebony a vicious kick as she bent to sweep up the debris and Ruth, without stopping to think, blurted out, 'That were cruel!'

'What!'

Cook's face looked menacing. Ruth's stomach churned.

'You a Black lover, then, eh? 'Cos you'll 'ave no place here if yer are.'

Ruth didn't know what to say. She couldn't bear to see anyone suffering as Ebony was, but the sight of Cook, red in the face as if she'd burst with anger, had frozen her.

'Let me tell you, girl, you should think on. Here's you walking the streets, begging for a job and a bed, and this scum 'ave all of that. And I'll tell yer something else: me own son works here, and he's nothing but a lackey' – she pointed at Ebony – 'when he could 'ave been promoted to being the butler. But, oh no. Them upstairs want a status symbol. A handsome Black man they can dress in all the finery and show off to their friends. They educate his kid and give jobs to his family and all on a plate. While our own scrimp and scratch for a living, with many on the streets because they can't get work . . . And you pity her! Save yer pity for yerself and watch out for the likes of her and her kin. Keep them down in the gutter where they belong.'

Ruth couldn't answer. She hated the way Cook looked at things. As she understood it, it wasn't that way at all and she couldn't imagine how it was for the Africans who were kidnapped and taken to a foreign land where everyone looked on them as slaves. She wanted to ask how she would feel if it happened to her, but the door opening and Aggie appearing saying she would be seen by the housekeeper, saved the moment.

Sighing with the relief of being taken out of the situation, Ruth gladly followed Aggie.

The housekeeper was surprisingly friendly and nice. Not at all what Ruth had expected. She couldn't imagine that this homely woman knew what was happening to one of her staff.

'So . . . Ruth, isn't it? A waif off the streets and sent here by Abdi Nana, our butler, who tells me you asked for a job when he went to get his son. Well, I'm all for a trier, but I cannot just take you without someone to speak for you – a priest, or vicar, maybe?'

Ruth gave her story.

'Well, that sounds all in order, though I know most households in this area. Where does this captain have his house?'

'I – I can't remember the name of the street. I can go there though.'

'Hmmm, well, never mind. I'm sure that being an army officer he can have his credentials verified. Now, have you had any experience?'

'No, but I can do most things – make a bed nicely, clean and scrub and polish and light fires and wash clothes and bedding.'

'Well, well, an all-rounder.' The housekeeper laughed, but Ruth didn't feel that she was making fun of her. She liked this woman and felt she could trust her. Without thinking she blurted out, 'Did yer know Ebony is being bullied?'

'I beg your pardon?'

Ruth's insides shrivelled up. She wanted to bite her own tongue off to stop it running away with itself.

'What Cook does in her own domain, is Cook's business.

It may not be the way of us all, but it's not to be frowned on, or talked about, do you understand?'

Ruth nodded.

'Never answer my questions with a gesture. Speak your answer out loud and in an honest manner, girl.'

'I understand, miss. I'm sorry.'

The housekeeper was quiet for a moment. When she spoke, her voice was back to the kindly tone she'd started the interview with. 'Well, I understand too. Some ways of a large household can come as a shock, but most are there for a reason – the smooth running of the home and the comfort and wellbeing of the family we serve.'

'Yes, miss.'

The housekeeper looked at her in a quizzical way. 'Why do you call me miss? Have you been in some kind of institute?'

Holy Mary, help me.

'Well, no matter, but you address me as Mrs Randell, and refer to me as the housekeeper.'

'Yes, Mrs Randell.'

'And on that subject, Cook is always Cook and the butler is Mr Abdi. Abdi tells me that Nana isn't his surname but means "king". It's all very fascinating. His actual surname is unpronounceable, and so we settle for Mr Abdi. Do you understand all of that?'

'Yes, Mrs Randell.'

'Good. I feel you may be the person I am looking for, Ruth, and I'm willing to give you a try. The job will entail several duties. You'll be responsible for cleaning and lighting fires. You will work alongside Ebony and you both will be under the supervision of Aggie, the upstairs maid. Part of your job will be to clean the living areas, stairs and banisters but you must not go further than the top of the stairs. The landing, bedrooms, nursery and school room are the domain of the chambermaids, the nanny and the tutor, and their cleanliness is overseen by Aggie. You will sleep in the attic rooms which you will access from the back stairs and share a room with Ebony. Have you any objection to that?'

'No, I'd like that.'

Ruth couldn't think why Ebony didn't sleep with her husband and was beginning to wonder at his character.

'Those above you in station are everyone except Ebony, who is below you and must do everything you ask of her. The chambermaids are of the same rank. You will be allowed one bath a week and will make your own bed and keep your room clean and tidy. You will have a half-hour break for breakfast, an hour break for your evening meal – all meals are taken in the kitchen – and a half-hour break in the afternoon for exercise. One day off every month is allocated to you and your pay will be fourteen pounds a year paid quarterly.'

This thrilled Ruth. She'd have been happy with the twelve offered at the last house, but the extra two would be heaven.

'Have you any money at the moment, Ruth? As you're required to buy your own uniform.'

Ruth's excitement died. 'No, Mrs Randell.'

'Oh dear, that's a problem. Can you ask anyone for help?'

Ruth didn't know who, but she said, 'Yes.'

'Very well, report in two days' time at six a.m., ready for work wearing a grey surge frock, white pinny and mob cap. Bring your case of personal things with you . . . Goodbye, Ruth, you are dismissed.'

The suddenness of this felt strange, but Ruth gladly took her leave.

*

Outside the office Abdi came towards her. 'Well?'

'I got the job, but I don't know if I can take it. I've to buy clothes. I don't know where from and I don't have any money.' Then she remembered she was speaking to the butler, not the kindly man she'd met in the park . . . 'I mean, I'm sorry, Mr Abdi. Ta, I did get the job.'

Abdi smiled. 'When do you start?'

'The day after tomorrow, but it's hopeless, Mr Abdi.'

'Well, that's the day you start to call me Mr Abdi, so you haven't done anything wrong. But we need to solve your problem. I want to help. I think my son needs you around, Ruth.'

'And I'll look out for Ebony too. I've already seen her being bullied.'

Abdi sighed. 'You can't do anything about it, Ruth, and you mustn't try, but it's nice to know you'll be a friend to her.'

Abdi looked both ways. Seeing the coast was clear, he took a coin out of his pocket. 'Take that. Go to number three Little Collingwood Street, Bethnal. My aunt lives there, and she is a dressmaker. She knows our uniform and will have rolls of the cloth. Tell her I sent you and she's to kit you out. She'll have you a frock and two pinnies made in time. Give her this shilling and tell her we are all right. Don't be telling her any more. Now, off you go.'

'Ta, Mr Abdi.'

'Don't be late.'

With this, he walked away, his stance giving her the same feeling she'd had in the park, that she was in the presence of royalty. But then, Mrs Randell had said his surname meant 'king' so to her, he was.

Walking back along the road in the same direction that

Robbie had brought her, Ruth pondered on what it must be like in Africa, and how exciting to meet someone from there, though she didn't think Abdi, Ebony and Horacio had ever been there as Abdi had said his great-grandfather was brought over as a slave.

'Penny for 'em.'

'Robbie! Where did you come from, eh?'

'I sold everything and waited a while, but if you hadn't come now, I couldn't have waited any longer as Ruby'd skin me alive. She don't trust no one with her money.'

'Did yer make plenty?'

'I did. And I put a farthing on stuff when I could, so we can have a bun on the way home, I'm starving. Only don't tell Ruby. Anyway, how'd you go on?'

Ruth told him all that had happened in the few hours since he'd left her.

'That's good news. Though I'm sorry yer went through that at the first place. But the second don't sound much better with how they treat that woman, and the kid getting bullied by the nanny. It ain't right. No one's a slave these days.'

'It was awful, Robbie, and they're so nice.' She told him about the shilling.

'I'll take yer there after I've dropped the money and barrow off. It can be a bit rough up that end.'

'But what about me reference? I've to take it back with me.'

'That ain't a problem. Reg is an educated man. The drink brought him low, but he really was a captain, and can write a good letter for yer. He sometimes earns a copper or two writing letters for folk, but he won't charge you, you're one of us. Ahh, here we are, Bloomsberry's Bakery. I'll get us an iced bun each. Then I'll still have enough to get some pie and mash for us later as Ruby should give me something for the job I've done.'

Robbie disappeared into the shop. Ruth didn't think what he'd done was right, but then, she supposed when you were homeless you had to be up to all sorts of tricks to survive and she wasn't going to refuse the bun, her grinding stomach wouldn't let her, even though she was sure Holy Mary would be shaking her head. Hunger didn't care about sinning, so Holy Mary would just have to cluck her tongue and get on with it.

This thought made her giggle.

Chapter Six

The bun was delicious.

'Ha, you'd better wipe the end of yer nose or yer'll give the game away. Ain't yer never ate an iced bun before then? You've to tackle it from the bottom up till it gets thinner and you can take a clean bite, like mine, look, none of me icing has gone yet, which means I've that treat to come.'

Ruth felt silly, but she didn't care, she'd never tasted anything like the icing, and now she could lick it off her lips and would try to save the bit on her nose to eat too.

'With a tongue like that you should get a job at the post office licking stamps.'

This tickled Ruth. She guffawed, sending a shower of crumbs towards Robbie. The pair of them went into a fit of laughter, and suddenly Ruth knew a feeling that lifted her higher than she'd ever felt in her life. It was mixed with a feeling of not being alone, as she had Robbie, and the best feeling in the world, one of being free. She danced ahead, throwing her hands in the air . . . 'I'm free . . . free!'

'You daft sod.'

But though Robbie said this, he soon lost the grown-up air he had and skipped alongside her, twirling on his toes and posing his arms. The moment was a joyous one for Ruth and, she thought, for Robbie too, as his mucky face glowed with the biggest grin.

'Yer a great dancer, Robbie.'

He stopped abruptly. 'I weren't dancing. That were just skipping. Dancing's for girls.'

'It's not. Boys can dance.'

Robbie kicked a stone. 'I'd like to dance. Only don't tell anyone or they'll call me a sissy.'

'I won't, but when we're on our own we can dance, can't we?'

Robbie didn't answer.

Ruby had been pleased with what Robbie had done and had given him twopence. He was over the moon. 'Ruth, mate. Pie and mash are definitely on the menu later, for sure.' He became serious then. 'Ruth, yer can share me blanket tonight if yer like, only it gets cold in the early hours and yer'll freeze to death without something on yer.'

Ruth didn't think this would be right – not to share with a boy, but she didn't say anything as she knew Robbie was just looking out for her.

When they neared Little Collingwood Street, the cobbled roads became narrower. A strong smell of sewage and rotting waste carried on the breeze.

'I told yer, it's a bit rough around here . . . Right, this one's Collingwood. Number three, yer say?'

Ruth nodded, afraid that if she spoke, she would retch. How could folk live in such conditions?

But she forgot this, and the feeling of wanting to be sick, when a lovely, rounded lady, who looked so like Abdi but with a darker, more weathered skin, opened the door to them. She wore a swathe of material of many colours wrapped around her body and over her shoulders and shiny bangles around her neck and arms. A tall head-wrap, matching her dress, sat proudly on her head. Her face beamed with the brightest smile, though when she saw them both, she frowned. 'Who've we got here, then? Who's come to see Rebekah, and why?'

'I'm Ruth and this is Robbie. Mr Abdi sent me.'

'Abdi? Well, come along inside, girl. How is me Abdi, eh? My, he's got a good position, I'm proud of him.'

'He's very well. He sent me to get a uniform made. He sent this shilling for yer . . . It's to pay for a frock and two pinnies for me. Only I need them by Tuesday.'

'That's not a problem, Rebekah does have your size just by looking at you, girl. Come in, come in.'

Ruth looked back at Robbie.

'And you, young man. You'll all find a welcome in Rebekah's house.'

'Ta, missus.'

Inside the house, everything was draped with material. Scarlet wool cloth covered the sofa. Blue curtains didn't just hang, but swathed, across the windows and doors. Brightly coloured patterned cushions looked like they'd been thrown into place, not placed neatly, and yet the effect was beautiful – like Ruth imagined a palace to be.

'So, you all tell Rebekah your names and where it is you live. I ain't never seen you around these parts before.'

'I'm Ruth and this is Robbie. We ain't got a home.' Feeling she could tell Rebekah anything, Ruth blurted out, 'We ran away from the orph—' Robbie's shove stopped her in her tracks, but Rebekah showed that she knew what Ruth meant to say.

'You mean that place for children not far from the market?'

Ruth nodded, afraid now that she'd betrayed them.

61

'I heard tell that place was a good place and the kids were taken care of. Why did you run away, girl?'

Robbie answered. 'It ain't a good place. Bad things happen there. Come on, Ruth, I've gotta go. Yer shouldn't have told on us.'

'Now, you hold on young man. Rebekah ain't about to send you back to no bad place, nor tell anyone in authority about you. Sit yourselves down and let me get a good look at you. I can tell if I can trust someone by their eyes.'

Ruth sat gingerly next to Robbie. It upset her to have angered him.

'You, young man, need a good wash for a start, then you'll look like the honest fella you really are, though Rebekah knows you've done wrong, she knows it was to survive and even the Good Lord will forgive that.'

'I had a wash this morning, but I've done a good day's work with veg and fruit and the veg was muddy.'

'I can see the dirt is only skin deep, boy. Now, you Ruth, look like a good girl, but you ain't no one's fool. And your tongue gets you into trouble as you defend right from wrong. Rebekah likes what she sees in the pair of you. And I tell yer what she's gonna do for you. Rebekah is a Christian and cannot see two of God's children sleeping on the streets and going hungry. I have two beds upstairs and they're yours for as long as you need them. And you'll all get yourselves settled if you take me offer. Because, with a home and an address to call your own, you'll stand a chance of a job, or getting an education. Now, what do you say to me offer?'

Ruth's mouth dropped open. Never had anyone shown her this kindness, and yet, it struck her to ask, 'What about Ebony and Horacio? They aren't happy. Ain't it right that they should live here with yer?'

'Rebekah knows your thoughts, Ruth girl, as I have the same ones. But Ebony, even though she's bullied, and knows Horacio is, sacrifices a home here with me to be sure her boy gets a good education, and to at least be in the same house as her man. And that's the way of an African woman. As it is for us to help them in need, because us Africans, we know the ways of suffering, girl. We've suffered more than most.'

'If me and Ruth stay here, where would I find work? There ain't any work around.'

'Boy, there's always work for a white boy. You done work today, and where me niece and nephew live, there's work there for you.'

'If I had a barrow of me own there would be, but I was selling for a mate.'

'And did you do good?'

'He made over what the market trader wanted and . . .' A dig in the ribs from Robbie shut Ruth up once more.

'That's the way you have to do it sometimes, boy, you did good. My Abdi did get me over here, and he did buy me me first rolls of cloth. From then on, I've made me money with me sewing. I make garments for some rich folk and one day, Rebekah Ababia, she going to have her own shop. So, now, you're obviously good at selling. Well, that'll come in good and handy. You'll need to get your own barrow. And then buy vegetables from the market gardens and make your own profit.'

Robbie seemed to come alive as he said, 'I know where there's a barrow been dumped. I could do it up and if I got a few jobs on the docks, I could save enough to get me first lot of veg.'

'Now you're thinking right, boy. And I could make you curries to knock your socks off, with any veg you didn't sell, no matter if it is rotting. Mind, Ebony's the cook in the family. Her curries are sweet to the palate. I defy anyone not to like them.'

Robbie grinned. 'Would yer really give me a bed, Rebekah?'

'It's yours. Go up and get it made, boy. You'll have to take the one in the rafters, it's a shake-me-down. It's cold in the winter, but you're young. You'll find blankets and a quilt in the chest of drawers on the landing. Ole Rebekah ain't going to do that for you.'

Robbie got up, but then hesitated. 'What about Ruth, she ain't got a bed for tonight, tomorrow, or Monday.'

'You're welcome to the only bedroom, Ruth. Up you go and get the bed made. It's aired as the sun keeps it so in the summer, it does shine through the little window straight onto the bed. Wakes you up nice and early. Ole Rebekah sleeps down here, as when I'm on me own, I like to hear what's going on in the street. We get the odd bad person down here who would rob anyone.'

'Ta, Rebekah. We won't be any trouble, will we Ruth?'

Ruth couldn't speak for the tightness of her throat. When she nodded her tears spilled over.

'What yer crying for, Ruth?'

'You men don't understand us women, we cry at good things as well as bad. Ruth's tears tell me she's overcome. Well, Rebekah's pleased to see that, Ruth girl. That home has toughened you up, but you still have a good soft centre. Now, away with you, but mind, boy, your next job will be to get the tin bath in and fill it. You're not sleeping in me bed in that state.'

Robbie grinned. He had a lovely grin that could melt the hardest heart. His blue eyes twinkled. He was taller than Ruth and was strong. He'd told her that some of the crates they had to haul about on the dockside had given him muscles.

A happy feeling entered Ruth to think that he was going to be all right now. She'd dreaded going on Tuesday and leaving him to sleep on the streets.

As they went upstairs, Robbie said, 'Let's do this bed making thing together, as I ain't never made a shake-me-down.'

'I don't even know what one is!'

As soon as they opened the door to her room, Robbie sprang towards the bed and jumped on it. Its springs groaned in protest. 'A real bed, Ruth! I ain't seen one of these in a couple of years.'

She giggled as he jumped up and down on it and then threw the pillow at her. 'Stop it, you'll break it, and that's no way to pay Rebekah back.'

Robbie sat on the edge. 'What do yer reckon to it all, eh? There ain't many as would offer a roof to the likes of me.'

'I know. I've been wondering. I haven't known much kindness from a grown up. But being an African, I think Rebekah has been through a lot of bad times and knows what it's like and that makes yer want to help others. I always like to if I can.'

'I suppose. Anyway, I like her. She's a straight talker, we cockneys like that.'

'We do. Are you cockney born and bred?'

'I don't know. It's the only place I've ever known.'

'Didn't you ask where you came from? I did.' She told him what she knew of her beginnings.

'Boys don't ask things like that, they just get on with it. Let's get this bed done, eh?'

Ruth detected a sob in Robbie's voice, but she didn't say anything as she knew that was another thing that boys got on with – life – and they didn't cry easily, either.

The shake-me-down had them giggling. It was no more than a tick mattress of straw that you could shake to distribute the filling how you wanted it, or just fold away.

Robbie played the same trick of jumping onto it but this time, he couldn't bounce and ended up on the floor leaving Ruth helpless with laughter and desperate for a pee. 'I'll be back.'

She rushed downstairs, 'Where's the lav, Rebekah? I need to go.'

'Through the scullery, girl, go on, second door in the yard, the first is the coal house.'

If Ruth thought she'd seen it all in this house, she was amazed at the lav. Pink brick walls were hung with lovely cross-stitch pictures, and there was a pink and black rag rug on the floor. The newspaper was cut into precise squares and stuck through with a knitting pin which had been somehow implanted in a round piece of pink-painted wood. Rebekah, to Ruth's mind, was an island of colour in a drab street.

When she went back into the house, Rebekah called her. 'Let me see now. Step up onto this stool, girl.'

In her hand she had a skirt, with three pinned seams which she held against Ruth. 'Perfect. It's going to be a very good fit. You're going to be the belle of the kitchen, Ruth girl.'

Ruth giggled. She felt like hugging Rebekah. And impetuously she did when she got down off the stool.

Rebekah held her to her. She smelled of cleanliness and love. 'You'll be all right, girl, and if you're not, Rebekah's always here to come to.'

It wasn't easy for Ruth to understand what was happening. Did the world really have such lovely people who could give you their love after only just meeting you? But then, hadn't Bett done that? She'd fed her and been kindly to her. And what about Robbie? He'd given her friendship, and Abdi, and little Horacio. A warm feeling crept over her that wasn't just because of the hug, as suddenly she knew the world wasn't all bad and that she would be all right.

As she stroked Ruth's hair, Rebekah hummed an unknown tune. 'You know, girl, I had a daughter once. I lost her to the fever. She were your age. She was . . . so beautiful.'

Rebekah's body heaved. Ruth felt sad, but didn't know what to say, so she just tightened her hold around Rebekah's waist and stayed quiet.

The door opening and Robbie saying, 'What's up? Has something happened?' changed the mood as Rebekah laughed.

'No, just an old woman and her memories. Anyway, boy, you can run an errand while I get on with fitting Ruth for this frock . . . Now, where did Rebekah put her purse?'

'I've got a couple of coppers, I can get what yer want, Rebekah.'

'No, you keep that for a rainy day, boy. Rebekah does all right, but when you get yourself a regular job, then you can pay board and lodging. Ah, here it is. Get yourself to the corner shop and get me a penneth of spuds. I've a nice stew I can heat up for us, but it won't go around without adding something to it. I have rice meself, but you won't be used to that, and it's hard come by.'

'I can get you some from the docks. It comes in by the sackful, and the odd sack gets a hole in it, accidentally on purpose. Joel, who runs a cafe, buys it.'

'I know Joel. His food's good. I like his authentic African food, not his attempt to please the white folk with his pie and mash muck.'

'Well, I ain't living with yer if yer don't like pie and mash!'

Rebekah laughed out loud. 'You and me are going to get

on just fine, boy. And I ain't saying I don't like it. I just don't like Joel's, and nor does anyone else, but he don't learn. He thinks as he's in London he has to make London food, but all the Londoners buy his African dishes!'

Robbie grinned as he went out of the door.

'I like that young man. He makes me laugh. I think ole Rebekah's going to remember this day when you two came into her life.'

'Ta for taking him in, Rebekah. He ain't had much of a life. He's been sleeping rough since he ran away from the home.'

'Well, it ain't all from the goodness of me heart, girl. Ole Rebekah gets lonely and a little feared too. There's a lot as don't like us Black people and they ain't above showing it. I'll feel better with someone in the house.'

'Are your neighbours a trouble to yer?'

'Not me immediate ones. They're always polite. But some up the street give me hell at times and others don't seem to want to talk much to me, though they ain't unkindly and I try to be good to them. Sometimes, me door gets kicked during the night, or something is smeared on me windows. They do it to the West Indian family up the street too. They look on us as scum, but we're not.' Rebekah told of how her grandfather had been captured. 'He was a prize for the British, you see, being one of the chiefs. With him gone, there was a huge hole left in the tribe.' Rebekah sighed then took a deep breath. 'Anyways, Grandfather became well-loved here. This was his house. He rose to be able to buy it. And he left a little money. Abdi's mother, my sister, she come over to find Grandfather when she was a girl. Then she did go and find a man to marry and had Abdi. When she died, she left enough for Abdi to get me over here for a better life. But the house, it did pass on to me as the next granddaughter.' She shook her head. 'But this life ain't been better. Rebekah do miss her country. The colour, the music – especially the music.'

With this, Rebekah began to sing and then her body moved and her arms went up in the air. Suddenly, she didn't seem old as she began a kind of hopping dance and made a rhythm with her feet. She picked up a scarlet cloth that had been draped over the settee and twirled it around in the air, making it coil and spiral. Ruth began to want to dance too. She copied Rebekah's movements. Excitement gripped her as they stamped faster and faster, and Rebekah, sweating now, began to make a noise like a yodel. Her eyes closed. Ruth felt caught up in whatever was happening.

Suddenly, Rebekah stopped. Her body seemed to fold as she found the nearest chair and slumped down. Tears rolled down her face.

Ruth went to her and held her shoulders. 'Don't cry, Rebekah. Robbie'll take care of you.'

'Ole Rebekah's being silly. For one moment there, I was back with me tribe. I could hear them laughing, see them dancing and smell the cooking pots outside their mud huts.'

'Me friend at the home, Hettie, she says you can be wherever you want to be in your dreams. And we can dance like just now whenever I'm here . . . And maybe, one day, we'll both sail to Africa on a big ship.'

'Aw, that's a nice thought. You've a kind head on your shoulders, Ruth girl. Ole Rebekah's going to thank the Lord for the day Abdi sent you to me.'

When Rebekah looked up with her bloodshot eyes and smiled, Ruth knew that she loved her as if she'd known her all her life. She smiled back. 'If I can, I'll bring Horacio to see you, one day.'

'Rebekah is lucky like that as I do see him and Ebony at church on a Sunday. Them as own them big houses have to let their maids come to church, but you know, it pains me to see the sadness in Ebony. She wants to be a good wife to her man, but she can't be. It ain't right . . . but wait a minute, I just got an idea, honey child. You should come to church with her. I could see you more often than once a month, then.'

'That's a great idea, I will. I want to make friends with Ebony. We'll be sharing a room now.' As she chatted on with Rebekah, Ruth had the strange and lovely feeling that she'd come home.

Chapter Seven

Robbie took ages to return from the shop. Rebekah sat there fretting about whether he was coming back at all, but Ruth knew he would. When he finally did, he had her reference letter. He'd run all the way to the market to get it and to tell Bett what was happening. He was beaming when he came in as he'd spent his own money on buying Mick, Ted and Reg a bun each and given his blanket to Reg.

The first evening with Rebekah had cemented the bond between them, as the dancing happened again with Robbie joining in and Rebekah praising them both for the talent they showed.

Now it was Tuesday morning, and they were walking to work.

The morning seemed to shimmer with brightness as the early sun came up and the air resounded with the birds trying out their songs as they flew from tree to tree in Bethnal Green Gardens.

'Are yer nervous, Ruth?'

'A bit.'

'It's all right at Rebekah's, ain't it?'

'Yes, it's lovely. I feel like it's me proper home.'

Robbie kicked a stone. 'It won't feel so good without you there. You seem like you're family to Rebekah . . . I mean, you ain't the same colour, but . . .'

'I know what yer mean. She does feel like family to me. I didn't want to leave today, but I've to earn a living.'

'Well, there's plenty of industry around. I hadn't ever thought to try me luck in that quarter, but now I'm settled I'm going to try a few today.'

'I thought you were going to do a barrow up.'

'I was, but when I told them all the other night, Ruby had a blue fit going at me saying I'd be in competition, and anyway, I checked and the cart was gone.'

'She's a funny one. So, which factories will yer try, then?'

'There's the furniture-makers. I fancy that. It seems an interesting job.'

'I hope so, Robbie, and I'll keep me fingers crossed that yer get set on.'

'So how yer going to haul coal buckets with yer fingers crossed, then?'

They both laughed, but stopped when a window of one of the houses they were passing in Pitsford Street, opened. 'Get out of here with yer bleedin' noise!'

Ruth felt her arm being grabbed and her body dragged just before she heard a splash.

'Yer dirty old hag!'

As Robbie shouted this, Ruth saw that it was the contents of a piddle pot that had just missed her.

'Run, Ruth. The door's opened.'

Ruth ran faster than she'd ever run in her life and didn't stop till Robbie, who was ahead of her, did. They were by the railings of Victoria Park by then.

Panting for breath she clung onto the iron bars to steady

her shaking body and jelly-like legs, made weak from fear, running and uncontrollable giggling.

As Robbie wiped his eyes, he sobered her as he told her, 'At this rate yer going to be late on yer first day. Come on, let's get yer there.'

When they reached the turn into the back alley behind the houses he asked, 'What time will yer have the break they said yer could have?'

'I don't know. I think she said afternoon.'

'Well, I'll be in the park. I'll wait for yer.'

Ruth felt suddenly shy. She nodded her head.

'See yer, then, good luck.'

As she walked away her heart lay heavy in her chest. She had an urge to run with Robbie again, and not to stop until they got to Rebekah's, but she walked steadily towards the back gate.

'Ahh, yer here, then? Good girl, ten minutes early. That's the way to go on.'

'Yes, Cook.'

'Don't look so glum, it ain't that bad here. You should be glad of a job, young miss.'

Ruth didn't know what to say to this.

'Right, yer to make a start, Ebony's to show yer the ropes, but mind yer make sure she knows you're the boss! She'd get away with murder if yer let her.'

'Where is she, do I go to her?'

'No, she's to come to you. Ring that bell. The third one along. That's the front withdrawing room, she should be in there and the bell'll bring her running.'

Though she didn't like the idea of summoning Ebony in this way, Ruth did so, as she thought it too soon to raise objections. Ebony seemed to come through the door before Ruth had let go of the cord. She bobbed her knee at Ruth. Ruth, shocked at this, felt a giggle bubbling up, but swallowed it down and followed Ebony when she beckoned her.

The hall they went through seemed like a vast place, even though it wasn't that wide. It was the height of the ceiling that gave the impression. The staircase to her right curved round and round and as she looked up, she could see it visited many floors. Pictures adorned the walls each side of her and up the walls of the stairs, and a soft, blue carpet softened their tread.

'In here, I'm just cleaning and laying the fire, miss.'

'You don't have to call me miss, I'm Ruth. Pleased to meet you, Ebony.' Ebony stared out of large, black eyes. 'It's all right, honest. I'm no different to you. I'm a maid, ain't I? Anyway, it don't seem right. You're a woman and I'm only twe— thirteen.'

'But you're white. I can't call you by your name.'

'Why not? What's the colour of our skin got to do with anything? Anyway, if it means trouble for yer, yer can just call me Ruth when we're alone, no one will know.'

Ebony looked afraid.

'I ain't trying to trap yer, I promise. I'm living with yer Aunt Rebekah – at least, that's where me home is when I'm not here. She says to give yer her love.'

At this, Ebony's eyes opened even wider.

'How did you come to be with Rebekah, girl?'

As she helped Ebony to clear the ashes from the grate, she told her how it was she was now living with Rebekah. 'Not that I can go there until me day off, but I hope they let me stay the night. She says to tell yer, she's looking forward to seeing you and Horacio at church . . . She invited me to go, and I'd love to, if yer don't mind?'

Ebony looked at her. Still she had a mistrust about her.

Ruth didn't know what to do to change this. She sighed and wished she was older and more worldly-wise as she feared getting everything wrong and not having Ebony as a friend.

As if Ruth hadn't spoken about church, Ebony said, 'Right, Ruth, do you know how to lay the fire?'

'I do. We had to do this at the . . . I – I mean, well, I've done this work before.'

'There's something about you, girl, that I'm not sure of. Where did yer come from? How come you knock on the gate looking for work?'

Ruth decided the truth was the best, and thought maybe Ebony might warm to her if she knew her circumstances.

Ebony listened without comment. But when she'd finished, she said, 'You and me, girl, we are in the same boat as I see it. We'll work well together and look out for each other.'

'Ta, Ebony. I do want to be your friend.'

'We'll see. Friends when you're grown up is something that grows, it ain't like the friends you've been used to. Falling in and out, having your tantrums, ganging up on someone because it suits you – you'll find out that adults make friends in a different way. It all has to be built on trust, not just whether it suits you to be friends.'

'You can trust me, Ebony.'

'Well, girl, I will, till proven otherwise. I've been hurt real bad and it takes a lot for me to accept someone.'

Ruth could understand this – she'd felt the same at times. But she'd been wrong to think she could help Ebony. Ebony didn't need that, she just needed a friend she could trust. Ruth made up her mind she would do her best, but she knew in this moment that she had so much to learn about this new world she'd entered.

It was when they were polishing the banister that Ruth caught a glimpse of her first member of the family. Ebony was just telling her that the family were called Peterson and were very wealthy. 'They own property all over the country and let to industries. They do have two sons, Abraham, he's seventeen, Andrew, fourteen, and a daughter Lucinda, twelve. Abraham is at home till he's eighteen and goes to big college, but the other two ain't home often as they go to boarding school. Then there's little Elizabeth, Mr and Mrs Peterson done have her a lot later.'

'I've seen Elizabeth.'

'I know, Abdi told me. I did mean to thank you for looking out for Horacio, but be careful, sometimes a kindness to him or to me can get you into trouble, girl. Anyway, if we see any of the family, we have to get out of sight as quietly and quickly as we can. We mustn't be seen to see anything that happens, though I know a lot about the goings on that the other servants don't know, because my Abdi tells me.'

As Ebony finished saying this, a young man, who Ruth guessed was the son Ebony had said was at home, appeared at the top of the stairs. Ebony turned quietly and went down. Ruth went to do the same, but her nerves got the better of her and in her haste, she stumbled and fell.

Strong arms caught her. 'Are you hurt?'

Ruth kept her head down. 'No, ta . . . I – I'm sorry . . . I'll go now.'

'Don't be sorry, it was an accident. I know you were trying to disappear.' Then in a whisper, he said, 'Not that I think you should, so if it's only me about, don't hurry so that you hurt yourself.'

She looked up at him. He had the loveliest grin. The fringe of his dark hair fell forward and almost covered his deep blue eyes. Ruth went to brush it back, but just stopped herself as she heard Ebony's desperate whisper of her name.

'Let me help you steady yourself . . . There, no harm done.'

As soon as she had hold of the rail, Ruth flitted down the stairs. When she reached the bottom, the young man said, 'What's your name?'

Ruth shivered with fear, knowing this was too familiar. She looked back. He was still grinning. 'A name won't hurt, will it? Mine's Abraham, known by my friends as Abe.'

'Ruth, sir.'

'Ha, two biblical characters of courage.'

Ebony beckoned her away. Not feeling as afraid now but excited about the encounter, Ruth took her time, holding Abe's look as she went to where Ebony hid. They stood just under the stairs until Abe disappeared into a room on the left. Ruth was sure she heard him giggle as he did so. Was he making fun of her, or did their paths crossing make him feel happy? Something she didn't understand told her that he was happy to have met her. She knew that she was to meet him, and knew too that she would never forget Abe.

Over the next few hours Ebony became friendlier. They giggled a lot together and especially as they made a pact that they would be careful to let it seem that Ruth was in a higher position, but mostly they would just work together as friends.

Mid-afternoon Ebony said they needed to go to the kitchen as it was her job to make a pot of tea to serve to the rest of the staff along with a plate of cakes.

'I'll help yer, Ebony.'

'No, you mustn't, Ruth girl. You'll be getting yourself

into trouble. Don't worry about it, I'm used to the treatment they give me and I just close meself down so that I can't feel the pain I used to at their jibes. I'm a strong person. Stronger than you think.'

Ruth found it was hard to hold her tongue as Aggie deliberately spilled her hot tea on Ebony, and Cook spat out hers making it spray all over her. Then, they were all allowed a cake but for Ebony, so Ruth craftily put half of hers in her pinny pocket, even though she was hungry and could have eaten it all.

When she went outside to the lav, Ruth sat a moment and allowed her tears of sorrow and frustration to rain down her face. *How can people be so cruel?*

Not able to understand this and feeling sad that it should happen, she now knew she couldn't change the world so would do what Ebony wanted her to and keep quiet.

And she would be a good friend, sharing what she had, as she knew Ebony would share with her. Thinking this, she felt glad that she'd saved that piece of cake.

As Ebony ate the cake, Ruth told her, 'They shouldn't be allowed to treat you how they do, Ebony.'

'I told yer, girl, I can cope with it, so don't you be worrying.'

Ruth had no time to carry on this conversation as Aggie summoned her and told her to go for her break. As she went through the kitchen Cook warned, 'Only go to the park, Ruth, and for no more than ten minutes. You can have longer when you've proved yourself.'

'How will I know when ten minutes has gone by?'

'You'll have to guess, won't yer? Just don't be long.'

Not stopping to get her shawl, Ruth ran outside. Not that she needed it as the day was beautiful.

As soon as she reached the end of the road, Robbie appeared. 'Hey! Where did you come from?'

'I've been waiting. I had some good luck, Ruth, and I wanted to share it. I can start at Woodstock's Cabinet Makers on Monday. I'll learn the trade next to skilled men.'

'That's great, Robbie. I'm pleased for yer.'

'I won't be paid much, but if I work hard and learn some skills, yer never know where it'll take me.'

'Ooh, yer might even have yer own place one day making furniture for big houses.'

Robbie laughed. 'Ha, and pigs may turn orange, but yer know, it ain't a bad idea. I loved the smell of the place and the sound of the saws and how the men were covered in sawdust . . . Only thing is, I don't know when we'll see each other, Ruth.'

'We'll find a way. I don't know how the land lies yet, but I'm planning on going to church with Rebekah, so you could come too. It seems we're allowed the time off to go to church.'

'I ain't much for all that stuff. I mean, how can a God who's supposed to love children let such things happen to them as happened to me and you?'

'I don't know. I ain't never understood it all. I have the Holy Mary and pray to her, and talk to her, and that does me. And I have known her to help me many a time. You should try talking to her yerself.'

'I thought you said she belonged to the Roman Candles?'

'I didn't, I don't know what a Roman Candle is?'

'It's what yer call them Catholics.'

'Oh. Well, I did say they love her. But then, I'm one of them, I think, as me mum left me with a priest not a vicar.'

'It don't count if yer not practising.'

Ruth couldn't see the logic of this, but she didn't say anything.

They'd reached the park, but before they did, they heard music.

'It's the brass band, I love them! Come on, Ruth, let's go and see. The bandstand's this way.'

To Ruth, the sound was magical. 'It makes me feel like dancing, Robbie.'

'Me too . . . I mean, well, swaying anyway.'

'I don't see why it's sissy for a boy to dance. Girls and boys dance together all the time, I've seen pictures of it.'

'That's them posh lot, not the likes of me.'

But even as he said this Ruth saw his body sway in time to the music. She didn't know what the tune was, but it seemed to bring something alive inside her. Lifting her skirt, she began to move in time to the beat, and then to twirl. 'It's wonderful, Robbie. Come on.'

'No! Don't be so daft. Everyone's looking at yer. You'll get into trouble if anyone from the house sees yer.'

This stopped Ruth in her tracks. 'Oh no, I forgot the time. I'd better go, Robbie, it must be ten minutes since I left.'

'No, yer all right, but it will be by the time we get back there, I'll walk with yer.'

When they got to the bottom of the road, Robbie caught hold of her hand. 'I'm going to miss yer, Ruth. Maybe I will come to that church, but only so as we can be together.'

'All right then. See yer there. And tell Rebekah that I'm all right, won't yer? Oh, and tell her Ebony is as well, and that me and her are going to be friends and'll both come along to church.'

'I will. Ta-ra.'

Robbie looked so forlorn that Ruth wanted to grab him and hug him, but she knew he'd shove her away. She didn't understand boys. What was the harm in dancing when you felt like it? Since her escape, she'd wanted to dance often with the sheer joy of being free. And why wouldn't you hug your friend?

Thinking of friends, she turned back to call after Robbie, 'Another thing, Robbie. Are you scared of going back near to the orphanage, mate?'

'No, why?'

'Would yer go to the back of the kitchen and try to speak to Hettie for me, eh?'

'Course I will. Be good to see her, and that lot can't do anything to me, I'm going on sixteen.'

'Ta, can yer tell her to let Amy and Ellen know too, and give me love to them all.'

'I don't know about that last bit, it's a bit soppy, but it'll be good to see Hettie. Why don't yer write a letter and give it to me on Sunday?'

'If I can get paper and pen, I will. See yer Sunday.'

With this, Ruth ran to the gate of the house hoping she wasn't late back after her first break.

Relief flooded her when all Cook said when she returned was that she was to help 'that slowcoach to peel the potatoes'.

Ebony struggled with the knife she had as it didn't seem sharp enough whilst the one Cook had given to Ruth sliced through the peel easily. Ruth nudged Ebony and winked at her as she handed her her knife. 'Give me that. I'll take the eyes out and you peel.'

Cook nodded approvingly. 'That's the way. Remember, you tell 'er what to do at all times, don't let 'er get ahead of 'erself. Give them an inch and they take a mile, that lot.'

Ruth wanted to giggle, not at Cook's words but at managing to hoodwink her.

Ebony and Ruth exchanged a knowing smile, making Ruth feel that she was starting to gain Ebony's trust.

Dinner in the kitchen was at times funny – as Abdi and his assistant, Fred Ruman, who Cook said would be called a footman in a larger household, had them all laughing with their tales – and sometimes awkward, as Aggie wasn't friendly at all. Ruth learned that she doubled up as a lady's maid when Mrs Peterson needed any assistance, and this seemed to give her airs and graces. She was a sourpuss and never missed a chance to have a go at Ebony. This visibly upset Abdi, to the point that he asked her to mind her manners.

Ruth found that hers and Ebony's positions were unusual to what would be expected of them in a larger household as they did the work of a scullery maid and laundry maid, as well as downstairs maid – downstairs to the upper part of the house, occupied by the family, that was, as Cook pointed out when she had a moan about the amount of work that she was expected to do. 'Most households have housemaids as well as scullery and laundry maids.'

'Well at least Ebony now has Ruth to assist her in these tasks, so that should make your job a little easier, Cook, as you have two of them to call on. And it isn't as if this is a large establishment.'

As Abdi said this, Ruth caught the glance he gave to Ebony. To her it was full of love, and it made her feel sad that they couldn't live as other husbands and wives did.

She hadn't seen Horacio. The day had been so busy learning new things and trying to take in the layout of the house that she hadn't thought to ask after him.

It was when they finally retired after washing up and cleaning the kitchen that Horacio appeared.

Ruth had found it was all her legs could do to carry her up the three flights of back stairs that led to the top floor where the household staff had bedrooms. Hers and Ebony's was at the end of the landing and very small, with just enough room between the beds to manoeuvre if you turned sideways. At the bottom of her bed was a cupboard with no doors, containing a rail and a shelf.

'You ain't got much by way of clothes, girl. 'Ow you going to manage?'

'I need to wash the gusset of me knickers out at night, Ebony, and hope they dry, but I have two uniforms and Rebekah said she'd have some more clothes ready for me to pick up at church.'

'That's good. And I can help. We're not far off the same size.'

Ebony rummaged through some of her clothes on the shelf. 'Here you are, girl, pantaloons to do you proud. Real silk they are.'

Ruth giggled as she took them.

'And have you a nightdress? I have a spare one, here, take it. You can't go trotting to the lav in your all-together!'

They both giggled now, and Ruth felt she truly had made a friend in Ebony.

Getting back from the bathroom just as Horacio came dashing into the bedroom renewed Ruth's energy. His voice filled her with joy.

'Momma, I got away. No one saw me, not even Poppa.' He ran straight into Ebony's arms. She held him tightly to her, rocking him backwards and forwards. 'My boy, me darling son.'

Horacio caught sight of Ruth. 'Ruth! Ruth! You're here!'

Ruth laughed out loud. 'Yes I am.'

Horacio was a bundle of joy as he threw himself at her, knocking her off her feet so they both landed on the bed.

'Horacio, my boy, be careful, you'll hurt Ruth. I told you she was coming today, didn't I? Now come and tell Momma what you've been doing today. You learned some good things, boy?'

'I did, Momma. I learned to divide into quarters, and then fifths. It was good fun and I helped Elizabeth to do her counting. But she's hopeless, she only gets to six.'

'No, she's not, son, it takes some a bit longer to grasp things, that's all. Never say anything bad about anyone who isn't as quick as you are, or for any other reason, as that makes you no better than them as beat Momma.'

'Sorry, Momma.'

'Now, say goodnight to Ruth, then give me a cuddle and get yourself back to your room before you're missed.'

'Can I stop off at Poppa's bedroom?'

'If there's no one about, you can. Night, my darling boy.'

Ruth felt tearful as she watched them cuddle, but that passed as Horacio came to her and gave her a huge hug. 'Will you be in the park tomorrow?'

'I'll try. I'll look out for you.'

It didn't take long for Ruth to fall asleep. The small bed was comfortable, and the winceyette nightgown Ebony had lent her snuggled around her making her feel cosy and safe. But though she slept well, the strange noises of the house did wake her a couple of times, especially when the bedroom door opened again.

For a moment her heart was in her mouth, but then she heard a whispered, 'Ebony, my darling, are you awake?' This told her it was Abdi. She smiled as she closed her eyes again just as Ebony crept out through the door with Abdi.

They did have time together, then. This thought made Ruth happy, but she vowed, no one would ever know from her lips.

Chapter Eight

By Sunday, Ruth was beginning to think that life wasn't going to be so bad. She and Ebony had fallen into a way that helped them both to cope with their situation. They made fun of Aggie and Cook without them knowing it. They giggled a lot together and they had fun times with Horacio when he came to their room in the evenings. Now, with the housekeeper having given them permission to go to church as long as they had their work done before going, they were getting ready – Ruth in borrows from Ebony: a cerise pink blouse that was over-fussy with its frills and much too bright a colour for her age, but which Ebony said looked lovely on her, and a long brightly coloured skirt that picked out the cerise in splashes between blue and yellow flowers on a white background. Both garments were far too old for her years, but she felt so grateful not to have to wear her uniform.

'Now, girl, you must cover your head. It ain't right for a woman to go into church with her head bare.'

What Ebony presented her with, Ruth did not want to wear – a bright pink hat with a large bow on it. 'Oh no, Ebony, I couldn't wear that. I'll just borrow one of your scarves and tie that around my head when we go into church, eh?'

'They ain't scarves, girl, they're geles. I'll show you.'

Ruth watched, fascinated, as the head-wrap grew and grew in height as Ebony swathed the scarf around and around her head, making patterns as she went. The scarf she used matched her multicoloured wraparound frock of rainbow colours splashed over the silky material. When done, Ebony looked beautiful, but it wasn't anything Ruth dared to wear.

'Haven't you a smaller scarf I can borrow, please, Ebony?'

'I have something better . . . Now, where is it? Ah, it's under my bed in a box.'

Ruth dreaded what she might pull out, but then was pleasantly surprised by the lovely white bonnet with a stiff brim that stuck out like a sunshade, and long satin ribbons. 'Oh, it's lovely, ta, mate, I'll take great care of it.'

'You can put it on when you get to church if you like. Aggie might make fun of yer.'

Ruth felt she would anyway in her colourful outfit, and she did feel a fool. She only hoped that the clothes Rebekah had promised her weren't all influenced by their culture and she began to dread that they might be.

With little Horacio skipping along as he held their hands and the sun shining brightly, Ruth really enjoyed the walk to what was more a chapel than a church. As Ruth looked up at the shabby brick building, with its leaded windows and peeling paint on its thick, heavy door she asked, 'Is it Catholic or Church of England, Ebony?'

'It's a house of God, girl. A Christian community place that belongs to the Black community of Bethnal Green. Our preacher is ordained by the Church of England. He gives conventional services in Saint James the Less church, but also gives a service here that is for the African community.

But all are welcome, and many white people come as they enjoy our service more.'

They arrived early so stood outside waiting for Rebekah. The sight of the many African people arriving was like a kaleidoscope of colour and jolliness as laughter filled the air and people called greetings to one another. Ebony and Horacio received many cuddles and besides the gaiety of it all, Ruth could feel the love they all had for each other.

Ebony transformed. Her downtrodden look disappeared, and she became a glowing, beautiful picture of happiness. Horacio jumped up and down with excitement and Ruth began to feel she was attending a carnival rather than going to church as the joy Ebony's friends showed was infectious and filled her whole body with a feeling of warmth and love.

She heard Rebekah before she saw her. 'Ebony, child. Oh, Ebony, you look wonderful.' This was followed by a profusion of colour as the two women embraced and the multicolours of Rebekah's kaba – as Ebony had told her the beautiful cloth she'd wrapped around her to make a frock was called – mingled with Ebony's.

But another voice caught her attention. 'Ruth!'

Robbie! He'd come! She'd doubted he would but there he was pushing his way through the crowd to her side and looking so handsome in a brown suit and polished brown shoes.

'Look at you! Did Rebekah make that for you? Yer look really smart, mate.'

'She did, she's a tailor as well as a seamstress. I've never seen such talent . . . Ruth, d'yer really want to go in, or shall we go for a walk . . . I mean, well, I'd rather.'

'I would too, but no, Ebony and Rebekah'll be hurt if we don't. Let's give it a try, eh?'

Horacio came up then. 'Is this your boyfriend, Ruth?'

Ruth coloured. 'No, he's Robbie and he's just a friend.'

'Good, because I want to be your boyfriend.'

Robbie laughed, but at the look Ruth gave him he quickly covered it up by saying, 'So, yer must be Horacio, Ruth told me about you, mate. She said how handsome yer were. Yer a proper bobby-dazzler.'

'What is a bobby-dazzler?'

'It's a little smasher.'

Horacio grinned and looked up at Ruth. 'I like being a bobby-dazzler . . . Does that make you want to be my girlfriend, Ruth?'

'I am already. Not like a courting girlfriend, but I'm a girl and you're me friend.'

Horacio looked satisfied with this but placed himself firmly between her and Robbie as they filed into the building and found a place on the bench where Rebekah and Ebony already sat waiting for them.

Ebony gave Robbie a lovely smile as she greeted him while they all settled down.

The service was a revelation to Ruth. The congregation interacted with the preacher the whole way through. If he said something, in his lovely sing-song voice, they chanted a reply, of 'Amen to that', or a collective 'Alleluia', or 'Praise be'.

The atmosphere seeped into Ruth and made her feel that she truly was praising God. She glanced at Robbie a couple of times and saw him looking uncomfortable and as if he'd make a dash for the door at any moment. But then the singing began. This wasn't the usual flat voices dominated by one loud screeching voice, but a jubilant singing and dancing along and clapping to the rhythm. It seemed to sweep you along with it till Ruth found she was doing just the same as everyone else and feeling a strange mixture of embarrassment and joy.

After a while, Robbie began to join in, his movements those of a natural dancer, his face alight with . . . freedom, yes, that's what she'd call the look he had as he grinned at her, and that's what she felt too – free.

Outside, the atmosphere continued as groups stood around chatting and laughing. Ruth felt a deep love for everyone surrounding her and was glad she'd become part of their community as that's how they made her feel.

But suddenly a voice cut into all the love surrounding her and made her blood run cold. 'Ruth Faith! You bloody tyke!'

The hand that gripped her dug into the flesh of her arm. 'Got yer! Yer coming with me, you little bleeder!'

Ruth shrivelled as she looked up into Belton's ugly, fat face and felt the fear of his beady eyes boring into hers.

Ebony gasped, but Rebekah waded in with her handbag. 'Leave her alone. Let go of her. She's free now, she ain't yours to take. She be thirteen and has a job. Get away from her.'

'She ain't thirteen and she's in me charge. She's coming back with me, and if any of yer try to stop me, I'll call the coppers to yer. She's a charge of the Carlton Orphanage and I'm a warden there.'

Ruth couldn't speak. Her world crashed around her. Horacio's voice full of anguish came to her as he kicked Belton's shins. 'Leave Ruth alone, you! You can't take my Ruth.'

Belton pulled her to face him, his hand on her chin, his face close to hers. His foul breath wafting over her, he whispered, 'A Black lover are yer, eh? Well, I'll show yer different, you'll not like any Black when I've had yer.' His spittle sprayed her face. She could do nothing, as it was as if she'd been turned into stone.

But suddenly, Belton crumbled as a vicious kick from Robbie sank into his groin leaving him doubled over and foaming at the mouth. His cries were like that of an injured animal as tears flowed down his bulging face.

A cheer went up. Robbie grabbed her. 'Come on Ruth, run!'

But the preacher's authoritative voice stopped them in their tracks. 'No. Don't do that. This is something that needs sorting out.' The crowd hushed. 'Ruth, are you a charge of the Carlton Orphanage?'

Ruth nodded.

'I take it you ran away?'

'She works with me, Reverend Jafari. She's a maid in Mister Peterson's house. She be thirteen.'

'Well. I know the trustees of the home, they are all church members, I will speak to them. Are you really thirteen, Ruth?'

'I – in August, Reverend.'

'And did you run away?'

'Yes, Reverend . . . but I had to . . . He . . .'

She stared down at the recovering Belton as he growled, 'Shut yer mouth!' He gasped in a deep breath. 'They're all liars, Reverend. They say anything – wicked lies, to get what they want.'

Belton's voice changed then and became pleading and sickly. 'We do all we can for them. But some of them, like this one, are sinful. They play up to the male wardens to try to get favours, and when that doesn't work, they run away. Mostly they become prostitutes. But if we can protect them until they are of an age where we can place them in work, they go on to live good lives.'

91

'He's lying, Reverend. I know. The manager . . . well, he does things to the boys and . . .'

Robbie reddened as he looked from one to the other horror-struck face.

Belton looked at him for the first time. 'Robbie Hayden! I remember you. You ran away after stealing from the manager's office . . . Stole two quid, he did, Reverend, then vanished in the night.' He looked at Robbie. 'No one takes the word of a thief, and when the cops come they'll arrest yer and you'll be behind bars for a long time with the evidence we have . . . And now, Hayden, I'll add assault to yer charges, as I've all these witnesses as to how yer assaulted me.'

With Robbie looking terrified, Ruth came out of the stupor that the shock of Belton's appearance had put her in. 'He's lying, not Robbie. It's true what they do to us. I – I couldn't take any more. I had to get out. Don't make me go back. Please don't.'

'Reverend, I can take care of her. I'd love her like me own and teach her to sew and become a tailor, too. She's only two months off leaving that place.'

The preacher seemed to hesitate, but then gave Ruth hope. 'If the board who preside over the orphanage agree, then I think that's a good solution. Would it suit you, Ruth?'

'Yes, Reverend and I'd work hard and never give Rebekah any trouble.'

'If you speak for her, Reverend, it might be the Petersons keep her on. She be a good worker.'

'Well, all that's to come, and to think about, Ebony.' The preacher turned to Belton. 'Mr . . . ?'

'Belton, Reverend.'

'Well, Mr Belton, what do you say to what these good ladies propose?'

'It ain't down to me. And anyway, none of it can happen without the proper people saying it can. She has to come back into the charge of the home. It's where she legally belongs.'

'Yes, yes, I know, but in the meantime, I can get things into place for her, as one of my upstanding parishioners is willing to take her.'

'Begging yer pardon, Reverend, but they never to me knowledge put a white girl in the home of a Black family, besides, yer parishioners don't know her. She's a liar, and a girl who's out for herself only. She'd get anyone into trouble to save her own skin, she's not liked by the other children as she's always trying to get them into trouble.'

Ruth was aghast, she couldn't believe what she was hearing, she looked around to get some help from Robbie, but then saw he was gone. For a moment her heart sank, leaving her with a deep sense of despair, but then it came to her that Robbie was safe and a feeling of rejoicing at this knowledge soared through her. Robbie had taken his chance and disappeared and she was glad.

She hoped he went far away where no one could ever find him, but then a deep sadness filled her and spilled her tears, for she couldn't bear to think of never seeing him again.

As Belton recovered and was helped to his feet, he looked mockingly at her.

'Ha, that's another of her tricks – turning the taps on. Well, it don't wash with us back at the home anymore. Look, whatever happens, the legal position is that she belongs in the home until she's thirteen and can be found employment, so I'm taking her back there.'

'No, please don't let him, please . . .'

'I can't do anything about it, Ruth. I'm sorry. I don't believe all this man says, but I have to go down the legal route.'

Belton turned and hailed a cab from those tethered on the other side of the road.

The sound of the horse's hooves clip-clopping on the cobbles seemed to be like a bell tolling her doom. Ruth looked around her. Her eyes fell on Rebekah's distraught face. 'Help me, Rebekah, please!'

Rebekah sobbed. Her sobs were joined by a wail from Horacio. Ruth looked over at him, his beautiful face screwed up with grief and fear. She didn't want that. She took a deep breath, 'It's all right, Horacio. I'll be free in two months. I'll come and see yer then, I promise.'

'I don't want you to go, Ruth.'

Ruth looked heavenward. *Help me, Holy Mary.* Then, knowing she was amongst believers she said out loud, 'The Holy Mary will ask baby Jesus to help me, Horacio. Don't worry.'

'Ha, another of her tricks. She makes out she's a believer in the powers of the mother of God, always spouting about it when the kids at the home are good Anglicans. I'm a God-fearing man meself, Reverend, having just come from the service at Saint James the Less. I've never met you before but know you're one of the clerics who serve that church and that yer know the Reverend Arthur. Well, he can speak for me as a proper Christian. While this one plays at it for her own purpose, she leans towards the Roman Catholic faith. Our manager calls her sanctimonious.'

Ruth had no idea what this word meant but didn't think it a good thing to say about her. The Reverend's look held something different when he glanced at her – a kind of distaste. 'And now I find you in my church, which looks very much like you may well be trying to hoodwink my parishioners when I, and them, were willing to believe in you and give you the benefit of the doubt . . . I think you should take her back, Mr Belton, and deal with her as you think fit . . . Rebekah, Ebony, come with me. I believe you need counselling after this encounter.'

Both ladies looked from her to their preacher. Ruth's heart sank as they went to turn away.

'No! It ain't true. It ain't. Rebekah, Ebony, please believe me . . . Help me, help, please.'

Horacio broke away from Ebony and ran to Ruth. His little arms hugged her waist. 'I won't let them take you, Ruth. Let go of her, you beast. Momma, help me. Momma!'

Ebony dashed over and took hold of Horacio. Her whisper gave Ruth hope, 'Hold on, girl. We believe you, me and Rebekah. We'll help yer.'

'Get away, nigger!'

The crowd gasped. The preacher turned on his heels, his face angry, 'What did you call Ebony?'

'I – I'm sorry, Reverend. I – I didn't mean it. I thought it was a term of affection. I – I have an African mate, and he calls me Honky. I didn't think.'

'I don't think that was said in the same manner you describe. You insulted Ebony, sir.'

'I beg yer pardon, Ebony. It was a slip of the tongue, no more. I'll be on me way with me charge now. Good day, Reverend.' He doffed his cap at Ebony and said, 'Madam,' before turning back to Ruth. 'Now, you, get in there. Yer going back to where yer belong. And don't think that Robbie's got away with what he's done, as this time we'll get the cops on to him.'

Ruth had never known the depth of misery she felt at this moment as the wheels rumbled over the cobbles, shaking her body as if emphasizing the tumbling of her world. Her unhappiness was compounded by the fear that zinged through her when Belton stroked her hand before she snatched it away. 'Don't be like that, Ruth. It'll be nice having yer back, girl. I've plans for you.'

His eyes held a look she'd seen many times and loathed. His voice had a deep note to it.

In a sudden fit of temper, she lashed out and dug her nails into his fleshy cheek. With the action she knew the satisfaction of the skin giving and blood seeping out of the wheals she'd made.

A slap sent her reeling back in the seat. 'You bleedin' bitch!'

Pulling his handkerchief out of his pocket, Belton dabbed at his cheek. When he saw the red stains on it, he seemed to turn into a baby as he wailed, 'You made me bleed! You bleedin' bitch, yer made me bleed.' But then his tone changed. 'You'll pay for this. When I'm on duty tonight you hadn't better sleep. You'd better watch for me coming, as I will.'

Tears streamed down Ruth's face. Her situation seemed hopeless. No one could save her from her fate. The only thing she had to cling onto were Ebony's words.

Please, Holy Mary, please, please. But at this prayer, begging for Rebekah and Ebony to truly be able to help her, the grown-up feelings she had had over the last weeks left her and she wailed like a baby.

'Shut your bleedin' mouth, girl!'

But Ruth couldn't obey. 'Help me-ee-ee. Someone help me!'

The cab came to a halt.

'Shurrup, will yer.'

Belton shook her roughly but stopped when a face appeared above the half door. 'Here, what's going on, mate, eh? What's the matter with her? I ain't liking this. I pick yer up amongst a crowd of Blacks, and this young girl ain't for going with yer, and now this. Something ain't right.'

'He's going to do stuff to me, don't let him.'

'What stuff? What's she talking about, mate? I'd thank you to get out of me cab, both of yer. Pay yer dues and get on yer way. I'm having no part of this.'

'Take no notice, driver. She ran away from the children's home and I'm taking her back. She's not safe out here on the streets. She thinks I'm going to punish her . . . well, I won't, but the matron will, and she deserves it.'

'I see . . . Well, quieten her down. I ain't driving around London with that going on.'

As he moved away, Ruth took her chance. Her hand shot through the opening, found the handle on the outside, and clicked the door open. In a flash, she jumped down to Belton's cries of 'Stop her! Stop her, man!'

Fear gave Ruth wings. Her mind screamed against the possibility of Belton catching her as she dashed into a side street, not stopping to see where she was headed, but praying she'd get away.

Chapter Nine

Despairing of what to do and where to go, Ruth gasped for breath as the streets became a maze. Painful collisions with others sent her stumbling. The sound of her name and 'Stop her!' spurred her on until, unable to run anymore, she leaned heavily on the wall of a house.

The bricks chaffed through the thinness of her damp blouse as she turned to look back. Terror gripped her as she saw a running figure turn into the street. Spinning round to run in the opposite direction, she screamed out 'No! No!' as a feeling of being trapped engulfed her – there was nowhere to run. She was in a cul-de-sac!

Panic, and the need to find a way out swivelled her head one way and the other as she desperately sought refuge somewhere, but the cobbled street only gave her rows of terraced houses looking like identical boxes. No people . . . No one to help her.

Frantic, Ruth banged on the door of the house she stood next to. When it opened an old lady leaning on a stick looked at her with distrust.

'Help me, please . . . please help me. There's a man after me.' A painful jab had her bending double and almost losing her balance.

'Git away from me door, I don't want the likes of you bothering me.'

Ruth jumped back to avoid a vicious swipe with the stick but lost her footing as she stepped off the edge of the pavement.

'Go on, git out of it!'

As she tried to scramble backwards to get out of range of the stick a hand grabbed her and pulled her upright. Panting for breath, the police officer spoke in a kindly way, 'Now then, miss. I'm not going to hurt yer. I'm PC Veners. I understand you've run away from the orphanage?'

'Damn prossie. Keep away from me door.'

'That's enough, Enid. She's no prossie. She's just a runaway kid who turned to you for help. But she picked the wrong one there, didn't she, eh?'

'Bugger off.' With this, Enid slammed the door. The policeman chuckled, then sighed as he said, 'Don't mind her. Now, I hear you've only a few weeks left to be in the home, so why don't yer go back quietly and wait till yer reach yer birthday, eh?'

The gentleness of his voice broke Ruth. Tears streamed down her face. 'If I told yer why, you wouldn't believe me. No one ever believes us.'

'Oh, I see. Well, Mr Belton said yer'd come up with some story about mistreatment by him. He's mortified by the lies you're telling. It's wicked to slander such a good man. I've known him all me life and I've never known him hurt a fly. And as for what you're accusing him of, well, the poor bloke broke down as he told me. What are you thinking of? To bring a man like that, who's devoted his life to the care of those such as yourself, into disrepute by saying such things is criminal! Never mind being allowed back to the home, which he is willing to do for you, to my mind you should be prosecuted for malicious lies against him and assaulting him. Now, come on.'

Defeated, Ruth went without protest.

Belton stood at the corner of the next street, his face red and sweaty. 'Yer caught her! Thank God. I'm worried sick about her, Jack. She's a handful, I'll tell yer. I only hope she settles down again for the few weeks she has left with us.'

'Well, if yer have trouble along the lines of her spreading malicious lies, you let me know, mate. I've given her a warning as to what can happen.'

'I think the Blacks had something to do with it, she was with them when I found her and it accounts for why she's dressed like she is. They need a visit from you as there was another absconder of ours with them.'

Ruth held her breath, but Belton didn't repeat his accusation of Robbie.

'They're all right. They've got kind hearts and would just be taking care of them. Yer should be grateful to them, at least she's been fed and clothed. A lot worse could have happened to her. But I'll look out for the lad.'

'Don't bother with him, Jack, he's been gone a long time and too old to return now. I'm just saying, seems funny they were both with the Blacks.'

Ruth wished she could tell Robbie that he needn't be afraid. She hoped he'd go back to Rebekah's but didn't think he would.

Back at the home the familiar smells of boiled cabbage and musty corridors assailed her, deepening her misery.

Belton didn't heed her sobs now but dragged her relentlessly towards Matron's office. As they passed the open door of the kitchen, she heard an anguished, 'Ruth, oh Ruth, mate.'

But Belton gave her no time to call back to Hettie as, holding her arm in a painful grip, he kicked open Matron's door and shoved Ruth inside the office.

'A present for yer, Matron.'

Matron stood. Her movements a slow walk around her desk. Her look grinding fear into Ruth as memories of the stinging caning came to her.

'So, you return . . . Well, aren't we miss fancy pants?' Every word came out slowly and felt like a threat, but then, Ruth jumped as her tone changed and she snapped, 'What on earth is this ridiculous outfit you're wearing, girl?'

Ruth kept her head down as every part of her trembled. She was at a loss as to what to do. Matron sometimes wanted answers but often didn't. But Ruth knew whichever you chose to do, Matron would get angrier and angrier as she asked if the cat had got your tongue, or yelled at you to stop talking.

'Well? Answer me, girl. Where did you get these clothes?'

'Fr-from a friend. A lady who took me in.'

Belton sneered, 'She got them from a Black woman, Mabel!'

'A . . . Black woman? You've been mixing with the Blacks!'

The clout around Ruth's ear stung. She cowered away.

'Get her out of my sight! Take her downstairs, we'll let her cool off for a few days. Then get yourself home, Belton, you'll be in no fit state to do the night shift at this rate.'

When they came out of the office, Ruth saw the other children lining up to go into the dining hall. Her own stomach rumbled.

'Ruth, Ruth!'

The tears stinging Ruth's eyes spilled over once more as she looked towards the voice and saw Ellen's lovely face. She

101

stood with Amy. Amy lifted her head, her expression one of happiness until she saw how Belton yanked on Ruth's arm. Both now looked afraid.

Ruth wanted to run to them, to have them hug her and for everything to be all right. But Belton shouted at them to get back in line and to shut their mouths. They did as he bid.

The room Ruth hated loomed like an evil black hole that would swallow her. She wanted to scream at Belton not to leave her there, but her dry mouth wouldn't let her do more than utter a pitiful moan.

'Right. I think you're in here for the long haul, girl, so you'd better make yerself comfortable. The stench is probably yer own piss from last time, as no one's been in here since.' He laughed as he said, 'It's reserved for wicked little tykes like you.' His tone zinged a new terror into Ruth as this last was said in a husky voice.

Ruth moved away from the nearness of him, but he followed her till she reached the bed then gave her a shove. Losing her balance, she fell forward, saving herself by putting her hands out.

Belton's hands dug into her thighs. She could feel his body close behind her. He pulled her further into him and thrust himself at her.

'No!'

'No? Well, I say yes!'

His hands grasped her thighs.

'No . . . please.'

She tried desperately to struggle out of his grip. But he pushed harder at her and she landed face down on the bed.

Holding her down with one hand, he fumbled with her skirt, her petticoat, and finally she felt him pull at her pantaloons.

Then his weight came on her, squeezing the breath from her. She felt him fumbling with his trousers.

'Please, don't . . . p-l-ea-se!'

Tears, salty, and mingled with her snot, ran into her mouth as she felt him touching her and then shoving at her again, only this time a ripping pain and the feeling of being stretched made her grasp the sheet and cry out.

Begging made no difference. Trying to kick her legs was useless. His groans and grunts disgusted her as they wafted stale tobacco over her. His spittle sprayed her.

'Ha! At last!'

His grunting repulsed Ruth, she felt her anger boiling inside her. With it came a strength that helped her to twist her elbow back in a strong jerking movement that caught him in the eye.

As he had in the cab, he wailed like a child. Ruth, incensed now and sensing his weakness, twisted herself. This released her from him.

Filled with courage, she kicked out at him. He staggered backwards. Ruth lunged and, as if she was an animal that would tear him to pieces, flailed him with her fists, clawed at him with her nails and then as he went to his knees, pulled his hair to jerk his head back and spat into his face.

'You little bitch!'

It seemed he'd turned into a raging giant as he stood up, but Ruth was no longer intimidated by him and, as she'd seen Robbie do, she lifted her foot and viciously kicked him in the groin.

He sank back down. His hands clutched between his legs. His face turned purple as he gasped for breath.

'What's going on here? What have you done, girl?'

Ruth tried to get out of the way, but the ugly grimace on

Matron's face held her as if suspended in time as the cane she wielded sliced across her back.

The painful breath Ruth drew in on a croaking sound rendered her weak as a sharp sting compelled the air to stay in her lungs. She swayed, found the bed, and flopped down on it.

Blow after vicious blow rained down on her.

Vomit rose into her throat almost choking her. No begging came from her. No screaming. No prayers.

'Stop, Mabel! For Christ's sake, stop, you'll kill her!'

At last, the onslaught stopped.

In a voice Ruth didn't recognize, Matron said, 'Get yourself dressed, Bert . . . Oh, Bert . . . why, why?'

'I – I can't help meself, Mabel. I'm sorry.'

'You have those who will let you . . . and, well, you know how much I want . . . Anyway, let me help you up. Let's get you to my office and I'll look after you. Oh, why do you do it?'

'I told yer, I can't help it, Mabel, it's a sickness in me. Like the one you have in you. You enjoy beating them, don't yer? You relish the chance. Well, I think you've gone too far this time. We both have. Yer'd better see to the girl, or there could be dire consequences.'

'Huh! We've dealt with those consequences before.'

'Please, Mabel. I – I don't want to do that again.'

Ruth heard a sniffle. She opened the eye that wasn't pressed into the bed and saw a Matron she didn't know, gently soothing Belton, her voice coaxing. 'Come on, lean on me. That's it, you'll be all right. I'm always here for you. Forget her, we'd be better off without her, she's nothing but trouble.'

As the door closed behind them, Ruth sank into the pain-free blackness and accepted the peace it gave her.

*

'Ruth, Ruth.'

Hettie's voice seemed to be coming through a long tunnel. Ruth wanted to go towards her but didn't know how. She hadn't the strength.

Something cold slapped on her cheek. She opened her eyes with a start.

'Ruth, sit up, me luv.'

With Hettie's help, Ruth somehow sat up. Hettie's arms came around her making her wince in pain.

'Belton told me Matron had caned you again, luv.'

The gentle stroking of her hair gave Ruth no comfort. None of the warmth and love that she knew Hettie had for her seeped into her. It was as if all the feeling part of her had shut down.

'You'll be all right, Ruth. I'll look after you. I've to take you to the sick bay and tend to your wounds. Oh, mate . . . I – I'm sorry.'

Hettie's body shook with sobs, but all Ruth could do was reach out her hand to her. They stayed like that for a moment until Hettie took a deep breath. 'Try to stand, luv.'

Ruth tried, but her body began to tremble in a violent way that clicked her teeth together and took the last ounce of strength she had.

'All right, luv, don't worry, I'll fetch Belton to—'

The sound that came from her own mouth was alien to Ruth and was akin to a growl. It was prompted by fear, disgust, and a hatred that had an intensity she'd never felt before.

'Oh, Ruth, Ruth, I can't help yer down here, luv, and I can't carry you . . . wait a minute, Cook might be able to. She lifts massive bags of spuds.' A little giggle came from Hettie. 'Not that I'm saying you weigh as heavy as that, luv.'

Ruth couldn't even smile at this but closed her eyes against it. Nothing in this world was funny and light-hearted anymore and never would be again.

'Ruth, Ruth, I'm sorry, mate. Ruth! I shouldn't have made a joke. It's me nerves . . . I . . .'

Ruth heard no more. Her world was fading again, and she allowed it to. In the blackness there was a refuge.

When she next woke, Hettie looked down on her through a film of netting.

'Oh, Ruth, mate, fight, please fight . . . Please don't die.'

A strange feeling came over her as Hettie said this. She imagined herself floating and yet she could see herself in the bed beneath her. The bed was draped with curtains and the space around it filled with steam.

It seemed she had a choice – go back towards Hettie's call of, 'Come back . . . Don't leave me', or to float away, to where she didn't know, but it felt like a good place and she wanted to go there.

A sudden scream shocked her. She looked down again. Ellen and Amy were there with Hettie. Both were sobbing and shouting, 'No! No!'

Ruth couldn't bear their agony, she needed to go to them, to make everything right for them. With this thought, she felt a tug. She opened her eyes.

'Ruth! Ruth! Oh, Ruth, you're alive!'

Confused, Ruth tried to answer them, but then Hettie put her arms around them and steered them away. When she came back to the bedside, Hettie took her hand. 'You're going to be all right, luv. You've got pneumonia but you've passed the crisis point now . . . Oh, Ruth. Thank God, I thought I'd lost yer then, mate.'

*

It shocked Ruth to learn that she'd been ill for so long, that the awful thing that had happened to her had been over two weeks ago. Now she was sat up in bed trying to eat some broth, but she felt so weak.

From not knowing anything that was going on, thoughts began to crowd her. Tears welled in her eyes. 'He . . . he did that thing, Hettie.'

'I know, love. But you gave him what for. He's been out of action since, so no girl has had to suffer his filth. Amy's recovering. But Ellen, well, you can never tell with Ellen.'

'We've got to stop him, Hettie. You . . . you shouldn't let him.'

'I ain't as brave as you, Ruth. I just feel as though it's something yer have to get through.'

Hettie was talking as if it was a ritual. A shudder of disgust trembled through Ruth. 'No, Hettie, it ain't. It ain't right. And nor is what Matron does.'

Mentioning Matron brought the strange conversation back to her. 'They're in it together, Hettie. Belton and Matron, Bert and Mabel.'

'What're yer talking about, who's in what together and who's Bert and Mabel . . . Are yer feeling all right, love?'

'Belton and Matron. That's their names, Hettie.' She told Hettie what had happened.

Hettie was quiet for a moment. When she looked up, her eyes were full of tears, 'I – I went to Matron when . . . when it first happened to me. She laughed and then gave me a clout and locked me in *that* room for lying. Even though I was in the same state as you were in.'

'But . . . but you said yer let it happen.'

'I do now, but I didn't, I just got defeated and things got better when I played along with it.'

Hettie sat down on the bed. She stared ahead. 'But at first, he . . . he did the same to me as he has to you . . . he forced himself on me.'

'Oh, Hettie. No one believes us.'

Ruth reached for Hettie's hand. It was as if they were lost – uncared for, nothing more than bits of meat that Belton and Matron could do as they pleased with. 'But why? Why? Why won't anyone listen and believe us, Hettie?'

'Because Matron's all sweetness and light to them at the church and holier than thou when she's around them. She's some sort of weird pervert, Ruth. She hates kids. And takes pleasure from seeing them suffer. But, mind, I didn't know there was something between her and Belton. It's as if they cover for each other so they can both have the pleasure they want, her beating kids and him . . . well, you know.'

'But what about Gedberg?'

'He probably takes advantage of his knowledge of them. He's a pervert too, only his pleasure is boys. Oh, Ruth. It's all so hopeless . . . Hotch up, luv, I want . . . need to get on the bed with yer.'

As Hettie lay beside her, Ruth felt in despair. She rested her head on Hettie's shoulder.

After a moment, Ruth felt better that she had said what was on her mind. Hettie had talked as if what Belton did to her was bad, and yet she'd always said to just let it happen. Is that what she'd have to do herself? The thought repulsed her; her mind screamed out against it. 'Hettie, I could never do what you do. How could yer let him? How?'

Hettie sighed. 'I can't do anything about it, so I shut meself off. I just let it happen and get it over with. That way, I can cope with me rotten life . . . I only said you should do the same as I don't think yer have a choice. I mean, they'll win in the end, but how many beatings can you take before they do?'

'Until I die . . . But Hettie, you don't have to take it. There's a world out there. I've seen it. It's where people live a normal, decent life. It's where I met Robbie, Hettie, and he helped me and then . . .' she told Hettie what had happened to her and how happy she'd been. 'You should leave, Hettie. You're old enough to. Just go! Get yerself a living-in position. Get away from here.'

'I can't, Ruth. Here and other institutions are all I've ever known and I ain't as brave as you are, mate. I may seem it, but even when I've to go to the market, I feel sick. I hate the crowds, the noise, the feeling that I'm alone out there. I have to stay here.'

This was a different Hettie. A girl Ruth didn't know. She'd always thought of Hettie as strong, and worldly-wise. Not someone afraid, who let anyone do anything to her so that she didn't have any upset. Pity for the girl she'd always looked up to came into Ruth. She turned her body and put her arms around Hettie. The gentle hug felt good.

When Ruth rolled back to lie straight again, she asked, 'When me time comes to leave here, will yer come with me? I can help yer, Hettie. I've done it once and there's people out there that'll give yer love and take care of yer, lovely people like Rebekah, and Bett.'

Hettie didn't answer.

'Hettie?'

'I'll see.' She got up off the bed. 'You need to rest now, luv. And you didn't finish the broth. Close yer eyes now, and then I'll fetch yer something to eat later. You have to eat, Ruth. Yer can't do anything if you're weak from hunger.'

As Ruth closed her eyes, she felt more alone than she'd

ever felt. To her, finding out how fragile Hettie really was made it seem as if one of the rocks of her life had crumbled.

But then, she knew a strength come to her that made her truly grow up, for there was nothing she didn't know about the grown-up world now. But mostly, she knew it wasn't all she'd thought it to be, and she'd to be strong if she was to truly make a better life for herself, Hettie, Amy and Ellen.

Chapter Ten

Ruth's dreams gave her pain and caused her to toss and turn in her sleep as she relived over and over what she'd been through. They came at her in swirls that made her feel dirty at times, and at others, made her the conqueror of her despair and gave her courage.

She cried tears of frustration. When she woke with a start, she sat up expecting to see the tormentor looming over her, but there was nothing but blackness. She was alone, truly alone. She screamed out against it.

The clicking of the door and light flooding the room woke her fully. And though her mouth was open, she knew she hadn't really screamed.

'Ruth? It's me, Hettie.'

'Oh, Hettie.'

'Are yer all right, Ruth, mate?'

'Yes, I had a bad dream. What time is it, Hettie?'

'It's three in the morning. I didn't wake you for something to eat as you went into a deep sleep. But I've checked on you and though you were restless, I thought it better that I left you.'

'I'm hungry, Hettie.'

'Good. I brought porridge with me, just in case. I left it on the table outside the door. I've brought it up a few times, so it's been reheated, but I like it like that. I'll fetch it in for yer.'

Ruth felt the strength coming back into her with every spoonful of the delicious porridge. 'I want to get up today, Hettie, and get outside.'

'That's a good idea, luv. I can walk yer around the playground, only once yer start to get about, I'll have to go back to me duties in the kitchen full time. Poor Cook's weighted down with the work. Not that she's minded as she keeps saying that you, and you getting better, are the most important things.'

'Will yer thank her for all the nice broth she's made me, Hettie?'

'I will, luv. That'll please her, she gets very little praise.'

'Hettie . . . I ain't standing for Belton coming near me again, you know.'

'I do, mate, and I don't think he will, not after yer put him out of action for such a long time.'

'Me, and Robbie. I only did what I did because I'd seen Robbie do it earlier that day.'

'Well, two blows down there is more than anyone could take. By the way, Cook said yesterday that Robbie came to the back door asking after yer. He said to tell yer that Rebekah sent her love and said not to worry, as the preacher is doing his best to get yer back with her.'

This news really lifted Ruth, she felt her old energy coming back and wanted to get out of bed there and then and run out of this ward, out of the building and not stop running till she got to Rebekah's, but she knew she had to wait. Doing so would be easier knowing that Rebekah was keeping to her promise and that Robbie was with Rebekah and was all right.

'If Robbie comes again, will yer tell him that he's truly free, that Belton didn't press charges with that copper, but told him to just let it drop as Robbie was over the age to be in the care of the home.'

'What's all that about, then?'

Between mouthfuls, Ruth told her about the policeman.

'That rotten Belton. No wonder he ain't afraid. He's got coppers for friends and made himself look like a holy man, going to church. It all makes me feel sick.'

'If Rebekah don't come for me soon, will yer run away with me, Hettie?'

Hettie hesitated. 'We'll see. Now, lie back down, as I need to get back to me bed. I'm exhausted.'

'Ta for all yer've done, Hettie, yer've saved me life.'

Hettie bent over and kissed her cheek. 'I'd give me own life for you, Ruth.'

The intensity of how Hettie said this felt strange and a little embarrassing, though Ruth had no idea why it should.

'And me for you, Hettie.'

When Hettie got to the door, she turned and blew a kiss. Ruth lay down. Her mind went to the two girls who everyone called 'queer' because they held hands everywhere they went, and they'd been seen kissing like a man and woman would. Did Hettie feel like that towards her?

No. Hettie's just glad I'm getting better, and I wouldn't be but for how she has looked after me. I'm being silly.

But the thought wouldn't leave her.

The noise of the playground frightened Ruth for a moment as she walked around on unsteady legs. It seemed to her that everyone was screaming. She reached out for Ellen's and Amy's hands as they were walking beside her. Hettie hadn't been able to take her out after all as Cook had burned her arm and needed Hettie's help.

'Shall we go and sit on the veranda, Ruth? You don't look like yer can walk much further, and I'm scared someone's going to knock into yer and really hurt you.'

'Yes ta, Ellen, mate. I think that's best.' This came out breathlessly. Ruth was finding it hard to fully fill her lungs with air and wanted nothing more than to sit down.

Climbing the steps was what she thought climbing a mountain might feel like and she was glad when they reached the top and perched as they had done before with their legs dangling through the railings.

As Amy sought her hand again, Ruth thought how much older than these two she felt.

'Yer won't go again, will yer, Ruth?'

'I have to, Amy, mate. But I promise yer, I will come back for yer and take care of yer.'

'What was it like?'

She knew this question would come. Amy was like herself before her break out, and she knew nothing of the outside world. But it left Ruth feeling torn. Would it upset her to know how wonderful it was? And would it conjure up painful memories for Ellen?

Trying to avoid answering, she turned to Ellen. 'No luck with your dad coming then, luv?'

'No, but I know one day he will.'

With this, Ellen's head turned towards the railings. Ruth's heart went out to her.

'Well, there ain't anybody to come for me, as I haven't got anyone.'

'Never forget that you've got a mum, Amy. She may have left yer but maybe she couldn't help herself. Anyway, yer'll always have me. I promise. I'll come to the railings and bring you stuff and chat with you till the day comes when I can get you out of here.'

'Tell us what happened to yer, Ruth. I'm dying to know.'

With this from Ellen, and Amy saying, 'Yes, tell us. Was it really good?' Ruth decided to tell them almost every detail up to the minute she was brought back here.

'It sounds wonderful . . . Though I'm sorry that yer went through what yer did when they got yer back, that Matron's a pig.'

'Do all yer can not to upset her, Amy. Be good and do everything you're told. I can't bear to think of you being beaten. Nor you, Ellen, though I think you've been here long enough to know that, mate.'

Ellen nodded. But Amy asked, 'What, even go with Belton, and let him do his dirty stuff?'

Amy's eyes were wide open. Ruth found it difficult to look into them with the same honesty that Amy showed. How could she tell her 'yes' when her soul screamed 'no!'? And yet, she'd seen what she'd seen – Matron and Belton worked together. If Amy played Belton up, he would see to it that she got a beating.

Feeling like she was betraying Amy, she nodded her head. 'If yer don't, Matron will take the cane to yer, and I can't bear that. You wouldn't stand it, Amy, you're not tough.'

Amy's eyes filled with tears. 'I don't want to, Ruth. I'd rather have the beating, or run away. Take me with yer, Ruth, please.'

Ruth hugged Amy to her.

Ellen's head came onto Ruth's other shoulder. 'He . . . he touches me and I hate it, but he did that thing to Amy, Ruth.'

Ruth had guessed this, but having it confirmed made her want to scream. Suddenly, she felt like a child again, with no answers and needing an adult to help her – to help them all. A decent adult like Rebekah, Ebony, Bett, Ted, Mick or Reg. She had to escape again and get to them. They would help her; she was certain of it.

'Look, I want yer to be brave. I'm going to get out again. The folk I told yer about will help us. If I stay, we'll all go through it again and again with no one who can stop it. I have to do this. It's the only way. But promise me, Amy, that you won't do anything to upset Matron.'

Amy nodded.

'Nor you, Ellen.'

Ellen's eyes were trained on the railings now and her expression was as if she was praying fervently.

'Ellen?'

When she brought her eyes back to look at Ruth, she nodded. The action caused the tears that filled her eyes to tumble down her cheeks.

They went into a huddle again. As she held them, Ruth vowed she would find a way to get out and get help. She couldn't wait until the preacher had sorted it all out properly – she just couldn't.

Back in the ward, Ruth went over to the window. She'd never looked out of it before and was surprised to see that it looked out onto the street. Watching the horse-drawn carriages weaving in and out of the motor cars and the people, who looked to her like a rainbow of colour moving this way and that after the drab grey and white of those in the play-ground, gave her the feeling of life being so unfair. Outside these walls, everyone could do as they pleased, could wear what they liked, and if anyone did bad things to them, they could get help from the police. They were the folk who gave to charities. Whose money funded this home. If only they knew what it was that they were paying for.

With an even greater determination to escape, Ruth sat on the bed and tried to think how she could do it. Would Hettie help her again? It was her only chance.

Hettie looked tired when she came into the ward an hour later with Ruth's food. 'Have yer got a mo, Hettie, luv? I need yer help.'

Hettie looked at her. Ruth could see she knew what help she was going to ask for. Her look showed she was afraid of hearing it.

'I've got to get away, Hettie. I've to get help for Amy and Ellen. Belton has to be stopped and the only way is to get someone to believe us. There's folk out there who will.'

'No, Ruth, don't ask me. Please. Yer've only got a few weeks left. Yer know that Rebekah is doing something to get yer out sooner . . . I can't. I'm scared. I – I think they suspect I helped yer before. I couldn't take a beating. I've had enough, Ruth. I just want to live me life as it is and not get into trouble.'

'Please, Hettie.'

Hettie came over to her. 'Don't beg me. Yer know I love yer, mate, and would do anything for yer, but—'

'But yer were lying when yer said you'd give yer life for me.'

Hettie sat down on the bed. Ruth felt sorry to see the look of dejection on Hettie's face, she'd been a sturdy and dependable rock for so long.

'It's all right, mate. I – I didn't mean to upset yer. I'll find a way that won't involve you.'

'Please don't do it, Ruth. Just wait. It's the safest way. I'm scared for you.'

'Don't be. Once I'm away, like I told yer, I have folk who will help me. I still have a very badly injured back. I can show them. Show the police. They will have to believe me.'

'I've to dress yer wounds on yer back after you've had your meal. Is it really uncomfortable, luv?'

'It's smarting again. Did they get the doctor to me, Hettie? You know, when I was unconscious?'

'No . . . They daren't. Not after the last time. The doctor was suspicious then.'

'Hettie, don't that make yer want to help me? They were willing to let me die . . . Wait a minute . . . Oh God, Hettie . . . they have killed kids!'

'What? What are yer saying, mate?'

'I heard something. When Matron was beating me, Belton stopped her. He said there'd be consequences. And Matron said, they'd dealt with them before. But Belton was like a baby and said he didn't want to do that again. Oh, Hettie, that kid . . . what was her name? It was a couple of years ago. She was a defiant girl, always in trouble. I think she was your age. I remember Belton fetched her one night. He hadn't done anything to me back then. In the morning, she was gone, and we were told she'd been found a place . . . Oh, Hettie, do yer think they—'

'No! Don't be daft. Yer imagining things.' Hettie trembled. 'Hettie?'

'No, Ruth. I don't think that. Look, I remember waking up and Matron was in the room. She was getting stuff out of Hilary's drawer – her clothes and some bits she had. She used to steal paper and pens as she was writing a story, she said. Anyway, Matron didn't seem agitated or anything, she was calm. I think there was a placement, and they hadn't said. They don't because of upsetting those who have to stay. No one knows till they just come and get you, and that's that.'

'But in the middle of the night?'

'There's loads of trains that leave in the night. Especially if she was going somewhere like Scotland. Scotland's a long, long way away.'

Ruth didn't think this an explanation. Her heart had dropped. She felt sick. What if Matron beat Hilary to death? What if Belton had to help get rid of the body? 'I – I'm scared, Hettie. Please, please help me.'

Hettie put her arm around Ruth. Ruth leaned into her and rested her head on Hettie's shoulder. And though she didn't think she could cry any more tears, she sobbed out her fear and her pain.

'Look, mate, I've got to get back. Eat yer food, and I'll think about it, eh?'

'Ta, mate.' This was all Ruth could say. She'd done her begging, now with this new fear, she made her mind up that she would go with or without Hettie's help – climb out the window if she had to. The street was a long way down, but she'd once read about someone escaping through a window by tying sheets together. She looked around the ward. There were three other beds besides hers. All empty, but all made up with sheets and blankets.

Hope filled her. She could do it. She'd have to work at it after dark, but she could, and she would.

Lying awake for what seemed like hours, Ruth's heart thudded with fear as all possibilities visited her – what if the sheets came apart and she plunged to the ground? What if there wasn't enough of them to reach the ground? And there were other windows below hers. One of them was lit up. It must be either Belton's or Gedberg's office. *I might be seen and then they'd kill me and get rid of me and tell everyone I'd been found a placement!*

All this thinking was weakening her resolve. To her, Belton and Matron were murderers who'd taken on the guise of monsters in her mind, and this had filled her with terror.

The latch of the door clicking woke Ruth, though she was surprised to realize that she'd fallen asleep. She clutched the blanket that covered her and cowered beneath it as she watched the light in the room slowly grow to a flood. Then she saw who it was. 'Hettie! Oh, Hettie!'

'Yes, it's me. Are yer all right, mate? Yer sound desperate.'

Taking a deep breath and letting out a sigh of relief, Ruth told her. 'Yes, yer scared me, that's all.'

As Hettie crept into the room she looked back along the corridor as if she was afraid someone would see her. Once she'd closed the door behind her, she said, 'I'm going to do it, Ruth.'

She crossed the room on her tiptoes and plonked herself on the bed. 'I've planned something. I've some stuff ready and I've decided that I am going to help yer. And I'm coming with yer. But we'll have to go where they can't find us – well, you. They can't do anything about me. I'm not in their charge.'

Ruth sat up. 'Really? You'd go with me? Now?'

'Yes, but hurry. Belton's asleep. He always sleeps after . . . Anyway, if he wakes, we've had it.'

'Has he done that thing to yer again, Hettie?'

Hettie nodded. 'But never mind that, we've got to hurry. I've left everything in the kitchen for us.'

Ruth jumped off the bed. She wanted to pee but knew there was no time. 'I've only got me nightdress on, Hettie, have yer brought some clothes for me, mate?' As she asked this, Ruth wondered why it hadn't occurred to her before to worry about not having any clothes, but she hadn't been thinking right.

'Not here, they're ready though, we just have to get to the kitchen without being seen. I've got all we'll need. Let's just hurry and do it. Yer can put a shawl and shoes on and then when we're away from here we'll stop somewhere and sort yer out. It's a warm night, so you'll be all right. Come on, hurry.'

They stood in the kitchen, both trembling with fear. When they'd passed Belton's door, they'd heard him make a massive snoring sound and then smack his lips together. It seemed the snore had woken him as it was followed by the sound of the legs of his chair scraping along the floor. They'd both taken flight.

After a moment, Hettie reached for a shawl off the hook behind the kitchen door, 'Right, get those clothes on quickly and put this shawl around you. It's Cook's, so it's really big, and'll keep yer warm.'

'What time is it, Hettie?'

'I think it's around three. I saw Belton's clock when he fetched me and that was at two, he took a while, kept saying he didn't know if he could, but wanted to.'

Ruth shut her ears. She didn't want to know any details, or to hear anything that beast said, she just wanted to get away and try to get help to stop him ever doing that thing again.

Chapter Eleven

The chilled early morning air wrapped them in a damp smog that made them both cough. But high above them a small glimmer of a shimmering sunrise could just be seen through the bleakness.

'Let's head for the market square, Hettie. Bett, me friend that I told yer about, will help us. She'll be setting her stall up in a couple of hours.'

'Do yer think we'd be best to go further away, just in case?'

'But we'll be safe with Bett and Rebekah, besides, they didn't come looking for me last time, did they?'

'No. There was a big to-do and Belton got a strip torn off him by Matron as did the manager, but they didn't even tell the police. They're scared yer see. I heard a lot, and they argued about reporting you gone, but decided to leave it and not make a fuss. They don't want the coppers round asking the kids questions.'

'Well, it wouldn't make any difference, I've tried telling a copper, but he turned out to be a mate of Belton's.'

'It would if all the kids told at once, they'd have to believe them then. Or, at least, that's what Matron was afraid might happen. So, they just shrugged your disappearance off. But

I reckon, with how you're injured, they might not do that this time as they're scared as it is. And what if Belton sees you again?'

'He won't, me birthday's soon and I won't go anywhere until then, so there's nothing stopping us going to the square. And then on to Rebekah's later.'

'All right. But I still feel scared.'

'You've got this far, Hettie. It's going to be all right, I promise.'

Hettie had her arm through Ruth's and now squeezed it tightly. The action brought home to her how much she used to depend on Hettie, and now, she felt she had to be the stronger one – but then another thought hit her, and her heart dropped. Ellen and Amy wouldn't have either of them to take care of them now that Hettie had left too.

It was strange to her how much she cared about Amy and Ellen. She'd had longer to get to know Ellen and for their friendship to deepen, but Amy she'd only known for a short while. Both mattered so much to her.

Hettie cut into these thoughts. 'So, what was it like, working in a big house then, Ruth, luv?'

'It was hard, and there's the ones above yer that can be mean, but I was only there for a few days and it was a million times better than the orphanage. I felt I belonged and was an important part of something. I wish I could go back but I don't think they'd have me. Not after going out to church and never returning.'

After a while of walking in silence, Hettie asked, 'Can't we go to this Rebekah's now, we'd be safer then?'

'Later today we will, but we can't wake Rebekah up at this time. It'll be all right. And, Hettie, ta for this. For getting me out. Yer've given me another chance.'

'You were the one that gave me the courage, mate. I never thought I'd do anything like this and I feel frightened out me wits, even now, but I'm hanging onto you and hoping all will be all right.'

'Yer certainly doing that, you're like a ton weight on me arm!'

This made Hettie giggle and set Ruth off. 'Stop it, I need to pee!'

The giggling made it urgent that she did now. 'Hold on, and keep a look out, I'm going to nip into that garden there, the one with a hedge.'

As she squatted, a light came on in the house behind her. She froze. Hettie's scared voice didn't help. 'Ruth, hurry. Don't get caught!'

Dashing out of the gate, they ran down the road. When they stopped, they were laughing again, and it felt good. 'Oh, Hettie, I don't remember laughing much in the home, or at all ever, but I laughed a lot with Robbie and Ebony, and all the time with little Horacio – hey, I'll tell yer what, why don't you go for the job at the house? You would fit in so well, and I know yer'd be on Ebony's side. If they haven't replaced me, they will be looking for staff. And it was easy to get taken on. All I did was go to the back gate . . . Only if you do try for it, don't say yer know me.'

'Would they take me without a reference?'

'Well, I don't see why yer can't tell the truth. I couldn't because I'd left the orphanage before me time, but you're quite legal to leave. Tell the housekeeper how it was. Tell her that yer had to leave in a hurry as you were afraid of the attentions of the warden. She's all right. I think she'll take you on, but if not, well yer won't be destitute as I know Rebekah will give you lodgings for a bit till you get sorted.'

'So, why can't I say that I know you?'

'I'd worry that they might think yer'll do the same as I did.'

'Would it work to tell them that story, will they believe me?'

'Yes, because it's the truth. And yer could get a reference from Cook anyway, as you could go to the back door to ask her. I think she'd help yer. And another thing, make sure the housekeeper knows that you can cook as the cook they have is getting on in years and moans about the hours, and how she has no help. You might get kitchen work and one day take over the position!'

'Oh, Ruth, that'd be me dream. I love cooking. And in them houses they don't just cook slops, they cook real food – banquets, even.'

'I don't know about banquets, but I had food like I'd never had before and plenty of it. And some good banter around the table in the kitchen.'

The more she talked about it, the more Ruth felt sad that it had lasted for just a short time.

'Right then. I'll call there later. Oooh, it's like Christmas 'as come early.'

'I know. There is another life. And even being on the streets is better than that bloomin' place we left.'

When they got to the square, it was almost light. The dawn chorus had already begun filling the air with the loveliest of sounds of birds tweeting to each other, expressing their joy, practising their notes, and flapping their wings as if very pleased with themselves.

Ruth's heart lifted to see that Captain Reg was already awake. She ran to him and almost hugged him, she was so pleased to see him.

125

He looked at her for a moment. 'Well, well, it's . . . Ruth! Are you all right? We heard that man from the orphanage had taken you.'

She wanted to cry and scream that she wasn't all right, but she held it in. 'Yes, I'm all right, I got away again with me friend. 'Ave yer seen Robbie, then?'

'Yes, he came back here after it happened, but then a Black lady came looking for him, and they were both really pleased to see each other. Robbie didn't want to go with her, afraid the coppers might come for him, but she was having none of it and he went with her in the end. It was the lady who had offered you both a home.'

'She's called Rebekah. I sort of knew he was back with her as he came to the home with a message.'

'So, you got away again? Will you be safe?'

'I'm hoping Rebekah will have me back too, then I'll stay at hers and not go out at all until me birthday passes.'

'Oh, that'll make a difference, will it?'

'Yes. They can't make me go back after I'm thirteen. This is me mate, Hettie, she's over that age, but been working in the kitchens. She's escaped too.'

'Pleased to meet you, Hettie.'

'Hettie's going to try for the job that I lost.'

'Good idea, so you'll need a reference then?'

Hettie nodded.

'She has the cook at the home, but she can't have one off you as I've already used one.'

'I could still help. I have friends who do the same thing I do, only they will need paying and you'll have to have a story as to why you left their employ, Hettie.'

'I'll sort something out for her. They believed my story. Ta, Captain Reg.'

Captain Reg laughed, 'No one's called me that for a long time, girl.'

His laughter wafted stale alcohol fumes over Ruth. She shuddered as memories flooded her of Belton.

'It's not very warm, is it my dear? I might start up Bett's brazier for her, I often do in the wintertime, but usually by now in July, it's not needed. Must be a cold front.'

What a cold front was, Ruth didn't know, and didn't ask.

Hettie spoke up then, telling Reg, 'Ta for the offer of a reference, mister. But I can't pay yer.'

'Don't worry. I've got to do some work for one of the better off stall-holders. There's a lot of them who are self-made men and women and yet can't read and write. I write for them and sort their finances out – their bills and accounts and write letters to their banks. I'll charge my client a bit more and pay for the reference for you.'

Hettie beamed at him. 'Ta. That's kind of yer. I'll pay yer back one day in the future.'

'No need. Now, help me out by getting some kindling from around and about. I know where Bett stashes her coal, so I'll fetch that.'

As Reg cleared out the brazier, Ruth asked, 'Why are you up so early, Reg? When I stayed here it was a lot later and the others haven't stirred yet.'

'Well, I wasn't able to get a good quantity of my soothing liquid yesterday, Ruth, and that means sleeping with dreams, so I've kept awake most of the night. And now, besides a warm, I could really do with a cup of tea, but there's nothing to make it with so I will have to wait for Bett to arrive.'

'Well, that's something I can help yer with, mister. I've got a Billy can in me bag. I filled it with tea before we left. I'll get the kindling, and then we'll have some.'

127

This was music to Ruth's ears. 'Oh, Hettie, I'd love a cuppa, mate.'

'Well, there's plenty for the three of us. Only we hadn't better wake any of them over there up, as it won't go around more than us.'

'They won't wake. They'll be out until Bett gets here and then she makes sure they get up and out of her way, feeding them and then sending them off to the docks to look for work, not that they get much and usually end up begging on a street corner somewhere.'

Despite the captain saying this, once they'd fetched some bits of stick and the fire was going, they were like conspirators as they drank their tea and chatted in whispers.

'What else did yer bring, Hettie?'

'I've a pack of sandwiches, Ruth, and a pork pie I made over the last few days.'

'Pork pie! I never knew us to be served that!'

'No, that was for Matron, housekeeper, Belton and the night manager.'

The captain leaned forward. 'Well, if you would be so kind as to let me have a slice now, Hettie, I would be very grateful.'

'Of course, be glad to. I've a knife in me bag. I'll just lean on this wall, it's wrapped in paper, so it won't get dirty from the stones.'

As Hettie left them to do that, Reg made Ruth swivel around as he said, 'Well, would you look at that. You're early, Bett.'

'I couldn't sleep for worry over Ruth and now, here she is, so I'm very glad I came. Oh, Ruth, me darlin', you're all right and yer got away again, then?'

Seeing Bett had an effect on Ruth. All her strength of mind ebbed away, and tears flooded her face. She ran towards the homely woman.

Bett put down her many bags and put her arms out to her. 'Now, now, what's to do? Yer here now, ain't yer? And yer look all right, though a bit pasty.' Bett turned towards, Hettie. 'What's your name, luv?'

When Hettie answered, Bett patted Ruth's back, but didn't notice her wince. 'Well, then, Ruth, yer've Hettie to be a companion this time and to look out for yer.'

But Ruth couldn't be consoled, huge sobs wracked her body.

'What's wrong with her, Hettie? Did that bleedin' bloke . . . No! Me luv . . . No!'

Taking Ruth by the hand, Bett said, 'Come with me, and you, Hettie, luv. Me flat's just round the corner. I'll take yer there and sort yer both out.'

Bett's flat was the bottom half of a house. She had the use of the front door, and the flat above her used the back door, which led up the stairs.

The feeling that Ruth got as they entered was of cosiness. It was how she imagined a home would be, with two armchairs and a sofa around a fireplace, a log box next to the hearth, china ornaments on the mantlepiece and pictures on the wall. The colours were beige and green, but nothing stuck out more than anything else, it all just blended.

'Now, tell me, luv, what's been happening to yer?'

'He – the night warden, Belton, he did that thing to me,' Ruth blurted out all that had happened. Hettie helped her, giving the full picture of how ill she'd been. Bett's reactions went from horror to anger to trying to offer comfort.

'Oh, me little darlin'. I've got yer now. Come on, let me see.'

Bett gasped when Ruth showed her back to her. 'Them bleeders! Right, luv, yer all right now, yer with us and I know

129

Rebekah will take care of yer. Only yer might be left with consequences. When men do that to yer, it could result in having a baby. Have yer started yer monthlies yet?'

Ruth nodded.

'Nothing will happen, Bett. Belton makes sure as we don't have babies.'

'Oh my God! You as well, Hettie?'

'Yes.'

'I'll get them sorted, the bleedin' lot of them. I know just the man to do it.'

This put hope into Ruth. She looked up. 'Do yer, Bett? Can yer really have them stopped?'

'Yes, luv. The bloke I'm thinking of will make that Belton disappear off the face of the earth, but he'll make sure he suffers before he goes into oblivion. You leave it to me.'

'Ta, Bett.' Little Amy came to Ruth's mind. 'He has to be stopped, Bett, one of me mates is only ten and she's had it done to her, and it'll carry on happening if no one helps them.'

'Poor mite. Them little ones must be living in terror. It'll stop, I promise yer. But you've to thank me by getting yerself strong and making something of yer life. You can do it, Ruth. We'll all help yer, darlin'. Now, I've not a lot of time as I have me regulars, and I can't let them down. A lot come on their way to work, for me morning toast and butter. So, yer can help me to catch up, eh?'

'We will, Bett, but I think Ruth's back needs attention, I noticed it was weeping again, and yet it had scabbed over.'

'You should be a nurse, luv, what do yer do?'

'I'm a cook.'

'Well, well, you should handle me toast then, so that'll help me. Right. I've got some cream that might soothe your back and give it protection. One of the stall-holders sells it, she's a herbalist and her potions and creams work really well. This one always soothes any burns I get, which is the nearest I can match your wheals to, luv. I'll get it, then Hettie can put a good dollop of it on yer. Then, well, luv, yer needn't help me, but rest here for a bit, and then get yerself to Rebekah's as I know she'll give yer a home. But you let me know how yer are, won't yer?'

'I will, Bett. I'll get Robbie to call on yer as I'm not stepping out until after me birthday, I daren't.'

'Good idea, what about you, Hettie?'

Ruth told Bett what they had planned for Hettie.

'Good. That should work. Now, do you want something to eat?'

'No, ta, Bett. I'll just see to Ruth, then I'll come along and give yer a hand.'

'No, that's all right, luv, I've changed me mind. Reg'll sort things for me. Stay with Ruth.'

'Ta, Bett, we'd both be glad to take a bit of time just resting, wouldn't we, Ruth, mate?'

Ruth nodded. She had an urge to return the love Bett had shown to her, so rose and went to her. She put her arms around Bett and kissed her soft chubby cheek.

Bett gently patted her arm. 'You'll be all right, luv. You leave everything to me. And I'll tell the bloke who'll do the job to make sure each pain he gives to that lot is for one or the other of yer. And this Belton won't live to tell the tale, but he'll sure as hell know the reason why he's facing his maker. And good riddance to him.'

Ruth couldn't let herself think this was wrong as to her there was no other way – no one to turn to other than the likes of Bett and her way of dealing with things. All she would let herself think was that Belton would get his just desserts and never hurt anyone again like he hurt her and Hettie, and that he'd never hurt Ellen and Amy again either. They were all going to be all right and this meant the world to her.

Chapter Twelve

By the time they got to Rebekah's, the temperature had risen from the overnight chill, but spots of rain were falling and Ruth knew this would be welcome as it would settle the dust. The last week of July had been very hot.

Rebekah greeted her with open arms, giving Ruth the feeling of how difficult it was to understand how some people could give such love after only just meeting you, as Bett and Rebekah did, and yet others, who were supposed to give you love and care, treated you cruelly.

After answering Rebekah's many questions, as to if she was all right, and how she got away, and who was this with her, without going into the real truth of everything, Ruth asked, 'Is Robbie here?'

'No, he's gone to that wood place, he starts early, love. But he'll be a happy young man to find you here, luv.'

'Can I stay, Rebekah?'

'You can, Ruth girl, and welcome. But we'll have to take care. That man heard me name and the police could make the preacher tell them where I live. Robbie's living in fear of them coming for him.'

'He has no need to be scared.' She told Rebekah what Belton had said to the policeman about not bothering with

Robbie. 'And you don't have to worry about me, Rebekah, I'll stay in me bedroom all the time till . . . well, till me birthday.' She didn't say till Bett told her the coast was clear and the deed done. Something in her didn't want to hurt Rebekah with such details.

'And yer friend? Do you need a place, Hettie?'

Ruth answered, 'Just for a couple of nights. At least, we hope it's only that, don't we Hettie?'

Hettie seemed to have clammed up as she hadn't said a word other than 'hello'. Ruth knew this house had overwhelmed her. It was a lot to take in, but Ruth knew she would love Rebekah. To her mind, no one could do any other.

Hettie nodded but didn't offer an explanation, so Ruth told of their plans.

'Them's good ideas. And'll be a good thing for my Ebony. She was upset by it all and sorry to her heart to lose you, Ruth. Poor little Horacio was heartbroken.'

This hurt Ruth. She wanted to say she would go to the house and see him, but she knew that would be foolish. Instead, she would send him a little note with Hettie and then when it was safe for her to go out, she'd go to the park to see him and she would see him and Ebony at church. But Rebekah carried on talking. 'Well, you two have had a long day already and it only be early, yet. Take your bag to the bedroom and ole Rebekah'll put the kettle on and make you a pancake.'

'We don't need anything to eat, Rebekah, ta. We had sandwiches that Hettie had brought with her. We've been at Bett's since, just resting.'

'That Bett be a nice woman. A good friend.'

'She is.'

As she said this, Ruth knew a feeling of a miracle having happened the day she came across Robbie and met Bett and everyone she now thought of as her family. She went to thank the Holy Mary but stopped herself. For now, she didn't think herself fit to talk to her. Not with what she knew would happen to Belton and her being glad about it.

Once in the bedroom, Hettie plonked herself on the bed. 'Oh, Ruth. I didn't know such people existed. All I've ever known are wicked folk – except Cook. She's a good woman. But yer fell on yer feet when yer found all these folk.'

'I did. And I want to live with them forever and be like them. You can too, Hettie, only, well, yer will meet a few bad ones if yer do work at the house – bad in a different way as they hurt with their tongue. You have to take that in yer stride as they're above you. And like I said, you'll love Ebony and have a giggle with her and that'll keep yer going.'

Once again, Hettie didn't seem like the Hettie she'd always known, she had a look of fear on her face. 'Ruth, I know you said yer'll not go out of this house, but will yer just take me there? I ain't never been far out of the orphanage all me life and like I said, I used to get nervous when I left to go to the market.'

Ruth wished with all her heart that Hettie hadn't asked this, she wanted to say that no, she couldn't do it, but seeing the look on Hettie's face, she agreed. She couldn't see how Belton could find her in that area, he'd have no reason to be there.

But this thought didn't help her when they set out later that day, nor did Rebekah's pleading with her not to go and she wished with all her heart that Hettie didn't need her to.

They linked arms again as they walked. Ruth could feel Hettie's fear now, and in wanting to help her, she found strength herself. But to cover the nerves she still felt, she told Hettie the tale of the piddle pot being emptied out of the window and how it just missed her and Robbie. And this helped her further as at last, Hettie seemed to relax as they giggled together.

'I always liked Robbie. It's good to know he's safe.'

'It is. I can't wait to tell him that he doesn't have to worry, that he truly is safe.'

'If I get this job, will I see yer both, Ruth?'

'We'll make sure of it. I told yer, you'll be able to go over to the park in the afternoons, so when I can, I'll come there to yer. And you have the option of coming to church on Sunday.'

'I don't believe in all that.'

'I know, but yer don't have to. It'll just be a way of getting away from the house and seeing me and Robbie.'

'I won't have to pray and all that, will I?'

'You can sit out on the wall outside if yer like, till the service is done.'

'Well, that might suit me better.'

They chatted on until they reached Victoria Park. 'There, that's the house, Hettie, only you go up that street and take the first turn into where the backs of the houses are, and then you count four gates then call out at the fifth. It's a nice day now it's stopped raining, so Cook will have the kitchen door open and hear you. Just say yer looking for a job.'

Hettie trembled. 'Can we go into the park for a bit until I get me courage up?'

'Yes, if yer like. Only we'll need to go well away from the house as the nanny brings Horacio and Elizabeth over about this time, and if Horacio sees me it'll alert the nanny. Come on.'

They walked around the perimeter of the park until they came to a gate. Just inside, they saw a bench nestled under a tree. 'There, that'll be fine, you can't see the house from here.'

They sat holding hands.

'You'll be all right, Hettie. Just remember, don't mention me, or give any hint that yer've heard of Ebony or Horacio. I know it'll be difficult, but yer mustn't slip up. It has to look like you've come out of the blue. And then yer can tell Ebony when you can't be overheard.'

'I won't. And I've been thinking about me story and have an idea so that I won't slip up . . . Only, I'm not good at stuff like that as you are, Ruth. So, it's better that it's more above board.'

'What's yer thinking, Hettie?'

'Well, I could say that I've wanted to get away from the orphanage for a long time and that Cook knew. And then, when you were brought back you told me where you'd been, it gave me the idea of trying me luck as they'd be short of a member of staff again. Then I could say that Cook and the housekeeper will give me a reference, as I know they would.'

'But, Hettie, I told yer, it won't be a good thing to mention me.'

'I can't not, really, can I? Think about it, Ruth. If I tell them that I come from the same place, it's a bit too much of a coincidence.'

Ruth hadn't thought of this, but still didn't like it. 'But yer've walked out on Cook and left her with no help, and it would mean going back there . . . What if they forced you to tell them where I am?'

'Cook will be glad for me. She was always telling me to get away from there. She used to say that she'd cover for me while I went looking for a job, but I never had the nerve to do it. And Housekeeper were the same. They were different with me. I was considered one of them – one of the staff. And I can go around the back of the kitchen in the daytime when no one goes anywhere near there and see Cook. I know she'll be pleased for me and'll write me a good reference. She's all right, is Cook.'

'Did Cook know what was happening with Belton?'

'Yes. Everyone knew.'

'Well, in my eyes, she ain't all right. She should have done something about him.'

Hettie became defensive. 'What can she do, eh? What can anyone do? Anyone, that is, except your mate Bett. 'Cos that's what it'll take to stop him.'

'Cook could have gone to the coppers. They'd have believed her.'

'Against Matron and the night manager? They wouldn't have believed her, Ruth, and Cook would have lost her job. She's no different to us. She was a kid in that home, only it weren't where it is now, it was somewhere in Lambeth, it moved to Bethnal twenty-five years back when Cook was twelve years old. She's known no other life. She's never had the chance to meet a bloke and get married. They put her in the kitchen, like they did me, and that's where she stayed. Only she always wanted different for me. She treated me like she was me mum.' A tear plopped onto Hettie's cheek.

Ruth squeezed her hand, she was learning so much about Hettie that was different to her assumptions, and now about Cook too. 'Well, I think it a good idea, then, as like yer say, it'll mean you can't slip up, it'll be known that you know me and I'm the reason you took yer chance.'

Hettie nodded.

'So, are yer going over, then?'

'I'm scared.'

'So was I, Hettie, but I did it. Look, if yer don't want to we can go back and then yer can look for a different kind of work, eh?'

Hettie stood. 'No. I'm going to do it.'

With this, she marched off and all Ruth could do was call after her, 'Good luck, mate.'

The wait seemed endless till Hettie finally appeared again beaming all over her face. 'I got took on!'

Ruth jumped up, ran to her and straight into her arms. They held each other close in a hug that Ruth didn't want to come out of. 'Oh, Hettie, mate, I'm so glad. What did Housekeeper say?'

'She said she was very grateful to see me. She said with having you there for those few days she realized how valuable the extra help was, and she asked after you, telling me that they hadn't been able to get it out of Ebony what had happened, only that a man came along, and you disappeared. She was relieved you were back in the care of the home – I didn't put her right, but she did say that if, when you were truly old enough, you wanted to come back, you could. And she'd overlook the trickery you played of providing false references as she liked you and understood why you did it. I got the feeling that there's more to her, Ruth. Maybe she was in a home once, you never know.'

Ruth couldn't believe it, she thought with Hettie's story exposing the lies she'd told, about her family and her reference, that they would never want to see her again. 'If

I did go back, we'd be working together and that would be lovely, mate.'

'It would. Oh, Ruth, luv, it would.'

Rebekah was thrilled with their news.

'Though Rebekah ain't wanting you to go, Ruth, even if they do want you when the time comes as I've an idea to teach you me trade. Especially how to make hats. You see, Rebekah used to make quite a bit making hats, but I can't keep up with all the dressmaking as it is, so I thought, you could work on that side of things for me.'

'I'd love that! To learn a trade would be smashing. Ta, Rebekah.'

'I was thinking while you were gone that you could do it in your bedroom till the time comes that you can be free to go out and about. I'll get Robbie to get all me tools out. I have them in the attic room next to his bedroom.'

Ruth felt an excitement enter her at this, she didn't even know that hatmakers had special tools but the thought of being able to make lovely creations like the ones she'd seen ladies wearing as she walked along the streets, thrilled her. Even the thought of being in the upstairs bedroom for so long didn't worry her now.

She knew she'd feel safer up there and would be able to see anyone approaching the house from the window by the bed, then she could hide if it was a copper, or worse, Belton.

'I can't wait, Rebekah. Ta for all yer doing for me.' She flung her arms around Rebekah. Rebekah hugged her to her. 'It was a good day, girl, when you knocked on me door. Now then, did you say you start in the morning, Hettie?'

'I do.'

'Can yer help her with her uniform, Rebekah?'

140

'It's all right, Ruth. Housekeeper said that if I couldn't get a uniform in time, I could wear a wraparound pinny.'

'We'll get it done – at least, one frock. I'm on to it already. I looked this out while yer were gone in the hope you got the job. It's the rest of the material I used to make yours, Ruth. I've enough on this batch to make one frock at least.'

'That's all you'll need to start with, Hettie, as you change your pinny most of the time rather than yer frock. There should be two spare white pinnies there that were mine. The navy one for doing the dirty work is supplied.'

'Well, I'm ready to start drawing out the pattern, and your first task in your new career, Ruth, will be to help me with the sewing of it.'

Rebekah hummed as she cut the frock out. Her movements fascinated Ruth, she so wanted to be able to do the same. She could sew as they were all taught to and had been responsible for mending many of their clothes and darning their socks.

'This reminds me, Ruth, the things I brought to the church for you are still in the bag over there. I'd made yer a nice walking out frock and some undies, so while I do this, you can take them upstairs.'

Ruth loved the plain navy frock with a set of collars that Rebekah had made for her. There were three different lace collars that could be attached to it and each one had a matching set of cuffs too. The bodice fitted to the waist and had a row of pearl buttons from the collar to the waist. Dancing round the room with it on, she felt like a princess.

Hettie, always prone to the giggles, which Ruth had now

concluded covered up what she was really feeling, laughed her head off. 'We've landed on our feet, Ruth, we really have.'

By the time Robbie came home, the uniform frock and a white pinafore for Hettie had been made. Ruth had been fascinated by the action of Rebekah's treadle sewing machine and couldn't believe the speed that the material went through it. And she enjoyed sitting sewing the hem up while Hettie, who'd offered to make tea, had been busy in the kitchen.

Robbie was over the moon to see them. Though when he looked at her, he asked, 'What's made yer cry a lot today, Ruth, yer eyes are swollen.'

Just seeing him and the look of concern on his face, undid Ruth. She'd thought she was all right, but now she sank into a chair and the tears just flowed without her bidding them to.

'It was Belton, Robbie, he did . . . you know. And Matron beat her again. She's been really poorly since and gets emotional. But she's all right. And we're both sorted and it's nice to see yer, mate,' Hettie told him.

'It's nice to see you too, Hettie, but yer can't say Ruth's all right, I've never seen her cry like that. One of these days, I'll kill that Belton.'

Rebekah was by Ruth's side in a flash. 'What is it, girl?'

Ruth couldn't speak, she thought she'd been drained of tears, and had put the horror of what happened into a corner of her mind out of the way, but it was back with her.

Robbie crouched down in front of her. 'Yer all right now, Ruth. I'm glad you got away again.'

She nodded.

'I'll sort him out, I promise.'

'What is it, Robbie? Is it that man? Did he do something to Ruth? Oh no, not that, not that?'

Seeing Rebekah so upset had the effect of calming Ruth as she couldn't bear to see Rebekah so distraught. 'I'm all right. It was seeing Robbie that made me break down. I was so glad to see yer, Robbie. And . . . well, you don't have to worry about Belton, Bett's going to see to him.'

'Bett? Blimey, that'll be good and proper then, no one messes with Bett and her boys. They're notorious up west. I'd say that'll be the end of Belton for good, and good riddance.'

Ruth felt the tremor of Rebekah's hand as she gave her a hanky. Wiping her eyes, she looked up as she blew her nose. Rebekah's face showed her horror. 'Rebekah ain't never heard of anyone being killed before.'

This brought home to Ruth the enormity of what it really meant for Belton. But then it would be a good thing, wouldn't it? But suddenly, something she'd accepted and welcomed didn't feel right. Rebekah's reaction had given her this sure knowledge.

Robbie tried to reassure her. 'It's the only way with them, Rebekah, believe me, but still if they get rid of Belton that would leave Gedberg so no boy would be safe.'

'There's another bad man doing these bad things?'

Robbie hung his head.

'You mean . . .' Rebekah backed towards the sofa and sat down. Her huge dark eyes stared out at Robbie. 'We should go to the police. It be their job to stop this. It ain't right to . . . to have them . . . well, it just ain't right.'

'Nor is what they're doing, Rebekah, and no one'll listen to us. There's others at the home that know it's going on and do nothing, they'll deny it. And besides, if Ruth goes to the coppers, she'll be taken back there and left at the mercy of Belton.'

Ruth went cold inside. She felt torn, because she knew in her heart Rebekah was right, but also knew that to try to do the right thing was hopeless.

Hettie calmed things by changing the subject. 'Don't upset yerself, Rebekah. I made a nice pie with that chicken you had, and I boiled some spuds and made a thick gravy. It's all ready. Let's have our tea and forget all about it, eh?'

'Pie? I ain't never had chicken pie, Hettie. I was going to spice the chicken and make it with rice.'

'Oh, sorry. I'm not sure how to do that sort of cooking, but I'd love to learn.'

Seeming to forget all they'd been talking about, Rebekah rose. 'I'd be happy to teach you, girl. Next time you come here, we'll do some proper cooking. Now, let's get it before it spoils. You two lay the table while I help Hettie dish up this pie she's made.'

Robbie stood from where he'd been squatting. 'Are yer all right, now, Ruth?'

'Yes. It was horrible, Robbie. I don't ever want anyone to do that thing to me ever again.'

'What? Yer don't want to be married or to have kids?'

'Not if it means doing that, I don't.' An involuntary shudder shook her body.

'Well, you might change yer mind. Not all blokes are like Belton. Come on, we'd better try to forget it.'

He offered his hand to her. When she took it and stood, he didn't let go. 'I'll always look out for yer, Ruth. I won't let anyone hurt yer again.'

'Ta, Robbie . . . Robbie, do yer think Belton will be killed?'

'I don't know. He might just be taught a lesson he won't

forget. I'll talk to Bett. I'll tell her about Gedberg too. And I'll ask her to not have them killed, but just, well, sort of put out of action. Make it so they can't do them things to other kids ever again.'

'That'd be better than murder. I thought at first that I wanted Belton dead, but Rebekah's made me think again. It ain't right. You will tell Bett, won't yer?'

'Yes. And, Ruth, I'm sorry about what happened to yer. It sort of changes everything. I mean, in yourself and how you think. One day you are you, then that happens and you're never you again.'

'Was it bad what happened to you, Robbie?'

Robbie coloured, then too quickly said, 'No, I told yer, I got away, so they didn't have the chance.'

A wisdom older than her years came to Ruth. She guessed there was more to it than that. She didn't know what, nor could she imagine, but she knew that for boys, it was something they could never admit to.

Hettie, coming in from the kitchen carrying a large pie and looking triumphant, distracted them. 'There yer go. Rebekah says I'm a genius to produce this from the chicken she had for her and Robbie. But I have me tricks, and yer'll find plenty of vegetables in it, oh, and herbs. Rebekah has fresh herbs growing in a box on her windowsill, I've never seen the like and don't know what half of them are, but they smelled nice so I plonked them in.'

'It looks lovely, Hettie, luv.'

'And smells good. I'm starving, so half for me as the man of the house and the rest between you three.'

For some reason this really tickled Rebekah, she laughed as if it was the funniest thing ever, and then held the plate of steaming mashed potato in the air and did a dance. They all ended up giggling as they joined in. For Ruth, it was a tonic and gave her the knowledge that she would be all right. With these three by her side, she could recover. Already, they were the family she'd never had.

'Well, I ain't never tasted anything like this, girl. It's delicious. And that's a compliment as I'm not much for English food, I like a bit of spiciness and what the English eat is all bland, but this . . . Mmm mmm.'

'I love cooking. I like it that I'm good at it and I ain't good at much.'

'Everyone has a God-given talent, girl.' Rebekah turned to Robbie. 'You, boy, have the gift of dancing. You have a way of moving your body that's in tune with the rhythm.'

Robbie blushed. Ruth knew he was batting the attention away from him as he asked, 'And what about Ruth?'

'Ruth has a way of uniting folk. We all want to help her, and yet all get something from being with her. And she's strong. Strong enough to take all the knocks life deals out to her.'

It was Ruth's turn to blush; she hadn't thought that she had any of these gifts.

'And Rebekah's a mind to find other talents in you, Ruth, and hoping that you're good at me trade.'

'Ta, Rebekah. And you've got the talent of loving everyone, as well as having a talent for yer sewing, and you're kind. I don't know anyone who'd take in us three like you have.'

'God sent you to me, and when He calls, we do his bidding.'

Ruth smiled. She didn't know if God had a hand in it or not, but she would thank Him anyway just in case. Maybe Holy Mary asked Him to take care of them. This was a nice thought and made Ruth feel better to think her prayers were listened to.

Chapter Thirteen

Ruth's birthday fell on a Sunday but it had seemed like an age for the three weeks to pass. Now at last it was here.

A feeling of joy filled her on waking, making her want to skip around her bedroom – cluttered as it was with hat-making tools, felt material, and her first creation, which she would treasure forever.

Rebekah had two types of hat blocks – or hat shapers, as she sometimes called them. One, in three different sizes, was for making the crown for brimless hats or cloches, and it was one of these that Ruth's special hat had been fashioned on. 'Learn from the bottom up, girl, it's the only way,' Rebekah had said.

It had taken her a day of failures and a sore thumb from hitting it with the hammer while she tried to pin her shape to the block before she'd finally mastered making the plain cloche in grey felt. Now the one she'd made for herself looked lovely with the little net rosette Rebekah had made and that she had sewn to the side.

The other shape, again in two sizes, had a brim, and Ruth couldn't wait to learn how to make a hat on them as she was bursting with ideas.

The irons which had to be heated by candles, were sat on

a shelf above her head. Robbie had made and fixed the shelf up for her. And she was to use the irons. They had patterns on them for decorating the hats, then she had boxes of pins and nails and a pile of felt fabric in all colours and sizes. All of it excited her as she looked around.

Rebekah told her she was a natural for someone so young, but to Ruth, hat-making was a different world and offered her so much, so she could lose herself and forget the outside world.

Until today. Now, at last, turning thirteen years old, she no longer had to hide away. She was free! Truly free. No one could do anything to her. And today, after church, she was going with Hettie to see Bett, and then they were coming back here as Hettie had sent word that she'd make her a lovely cake as soon as they got back to Rebekah's.

It seemed Hettie had arranged it all with Rebekah on her visits to the church with Ebony.

And, oh, to see Ebony and Horacio as well as Hettie, Ruth knew, would make her birthday wonderful.

Throughout the past weeks she'd sent little notes with Rebekah to them all, and loved the ones Horacio had sent back telling her what he'd learned in his lessons and drawing her pictures, all of which were on her bedroom wall.

Running down to the lav, Ruth found she was the first up. Rebekah still lay snuggled up on a put-you-up bed in the corner of the living room.

Creeping past so as not to disturb her, Ruth moved the pan of water over onto the stove as she passed by. They'd all need some to have their wash before getting ready for church. She wished that Robbie was already up and finished his as it was awkward getting ready knowing he might suddenly come through her bedroom.

Over the weeks, she and Robbie had become like brother and sister. Though sometimes she thought Robbie would rather it was boyfriend and girlfriend as he hinted at how beautiful she was and often held her hand.

Rebekah told her that he was a growing young man and had feelings, but Ruth didn't want him to have feelings like that about her. She didn't want any boy to.

These thoughts made her blush when she came back in from the lav and Robbie stood just inside the kitchen. She covered up by giggling at the sight he made in his nightshirt.

'I heard you about, Ruth. I thought I'd come down and have me wash down here and leave yer in peace.'

'Ta, Robbie, mate.'

'And I got yer a present, Ruth. Happy birthday.'

'Oh, you shouldn't have. A present! A real present? I ain't never had one of them.'

'Can I give it to yer now as I'll feel daft in front of anyone.'

Ruth hesitated, feeling a bit silly and awkward herself but not knowing why. She nodded her head.

'Hold on then. I'll get it. I bought it off that stall near to Ruby's stand.'

Ruth knew the stall sold second-hand jewellery and felt a tickle of excitement in her tummy as she waited.

When he came back down, he asked, 'Is this yer real birthday on yer certificate, Ruth?'

'I don't know, I've never seen any certificate, but it's the day the priest found me. When's yours?'

'I don't know either, I put it as the day I ran away. I know I was twelve then. That was almost four years ago now on the tenth of March. So, next year, I'll be sixteen.'

'Oh, we'll have Christmas before then, so I'll get yer a present back for Christmas.'

'You don't have to get me nothing in return. Here you are.'

The gold-coloured box looked a bit worn, but that didn't matter to Ruth. She couldn't wait to open it. When the lid gave, she gasped. Shining back at her was the most beautiful brooch. Gold in colour, it had two delicate petals coming from a stem and a red stone set into the carving of a bud.

'Close your mouth then, yer look like a fish.'

His laughter as he said this brought Ruth back down to earth. 'It's lovely, Robbie. Ta, mate. I'll treasure it.'

The colour rose up over his face and his smile lit his eyes. 'I hoped you'd like it. Anyway, seeing as how it's yer birthday, I'll carry the jug of water up for yer then I'll try to get me own wash before Rebekah wakes.'

Rebekah didn't look like she'd ever wake out of the deep sleep she was in. She lay on her back now. Her lips flapped with every breath she took. This made them both giggle as they crept past her.

Once upstairs, Robbie filled the bowl on her washstand. 'There yer go.'

'Ta, Robbie, and ta ever so much for the brooch. I really will treasure it.'

'I know yer will. But I bet the best present of all will be getting out of this room. Yer've only had the evenings when we've sat on the doorstep to get any fresh air.'

'It will. I can't wait. And to see Hettie and Ebony, and oh, Horacio, will be the best of birthday presents. I can't believe Hettie's first day off has fallen on me birthday.'

Catching a look on Robbie's face she added, 'But none of that comes near to me brooch. Nothing can ever be better than that. And it'll last longer than any memory of a visit. I'll be able to pass it down to me grandkids.'

Robbie brightened. 'Oh, so you've changed yer mind on marrying then?'

Ruth picked up her pillow and threw it at him.

He ducked and grinned as he left. 'See yer in a mo.'

Once washed, Ruth dressed in the skirt and blouse Rebekah had made for her especially for this day. The colours weren't bright which was something that pleased her, as though she loved colour, she didn't want to stand out in a crowd – not that you could with the folk who went to the church as all the women wore wonderfully coloured wraparound frocks.

The skirt was a plum-colour, and the blouse had a frill that went from the collar to the bodice. This was edged with the same colour as the skirt. Ruth loved the image of herself as she did a twirl in front of the mirror.

The urge to skip took Ruth as at last she walked out of the house and breathed in deeply. Her shawl hung loosely around her shoulders and the hat, made with her own hand, sat on top of her head.

Robbie and Rebekah laughed at her as she did just that when they turned out of the end of the street. 'I'm free!'

'You won't be if you get run over by a horse and cart, you daft devil,' Robbie teased.

Though this wasn't really funny, Ruth laughed her head off at Robbie. 'Come on you two, hurry up, I can't wait to get there.'

'Rebekah's old bones won't take her any faster, girl. Slow down.'

When at last Hettie, Ebony and Horacio came into view, Ruth ran towards them with her arms up in the air. The hug they gave her brought tears to her eyes. But they spilled over when little Horacio's arms came around her waist and she went down on her haunches to hold him tightly to her.

'I've missed you, Ruth, though Hettie is lovely and I like her very much. She makes me laugh.'

'Oh, Horacio, I've missed yer too, mate. So much.'

'Do you know what the very best thing about today is, Ruth?'

Not sure, Ruth waited.

'I can stay. I can stay all day and overnight with you and Hettie and Aunty Rebekah.'

'Not if you don't come and give me a cuddle, you can't, boy. What's this, you not love your Aunty Rebekah as much now, eh?'

Horacio giggled as he ran towards Rebekah and went into her wobbly arms.

'Well, it will warm Aunty's heart to have you stay. I have another shake-me-down that I can put in with Robbie. That's if Robbie will have you.'

'I will. Hello, Horacio. My, yer grow taller every week.'

Horacio beamed as he politely shook hands with Robbie.

'Two men together, eh?'

'I'm not a man yet, Robbie. When I'm as big as you, I will be.'

They laughed at this, which made Horacio beam as he loved to make them happy.

The service was joyous and even more so when the reverend suddenly said, 'Let's praise the Lord for bringing our Ruth back to us.' And all replied, 'Praise the Lord.'

'And, on her birthday, too. So, as we end our service, let's sing "Happy Birthday", for never was there such a joyous song, and never more so than today.'

Ruth's colour rose as the attention focused on her. As they

sang, an inner glow of happiness filled her, and she knew that this truly was the happiest birthday she'd ever had.

'Now, Ruth. I have a surprise for you.' The reverend turned and picked up some papers. 'While you've been in hiding, I have been working away at making you the legal charge of Rebekah Ababia to work as her assistant milliner. You are now free of anything binding you to the orphanage.'

Ruth gasped. She looked from Hettie to Robbie to Ebony, then finally, to Rebekah, who stood and opened her arms.

The hug was a fusion of tears, thank yous and laughter to the background of clapping and voices chanting, 'Praise be to God.'

'Oh, Rebekah, ta. Ta from the bottom of me heart.'

'It's me birthday present to you, honey child.'

'It's the best ever. Well, the equal best and matches me brooch from Robbie.'

Hettie asked, 'What brooch is that, Ruth? You never said.'

Ruth dropped her shawl. The light caught the rose and highlighted its beauty. Hettie gasped. 'It's beautiful.'

Robbie beamed.

''Ave yer come into money, Robbie?'

Robbie laughed. 'No, Hettie. It's not real gold.'

'Well, it is to me, Robbie. I love it so much.'

Ruth could see that she couldn't have said anything better as Robbie looked as though she'd made his day.

Outside, clutching her papers, Ruth told Hettie and Robbie, 'I want to go to the home. I want to stand openly by the railings and see Ellen and Amy. That would be me fourth best present.'

'Oh? So, what was yer third then?'

'Seeing you, Hettie.'

The three of them giggled and as Hettie and Ruth went into

a hug, to Ruth's surprise, Robbie joined them. They just accepted him as it all seemed natural – they'd come through a lot, but Ruth felt that this was a new beginning for them. The beginning of the rest of their lives and no one could ever spoil it again.

They said their goodbyes and left a protesting Horacio with Rebekah.

'You can't come with us to where we're going, Horacio, but I promise we won't be long and then we'll have all afternoon and evening together.'

Horacio accepted this but it tugged at Ruth's heart to see his little face looking rejected.

Bett stood on her usual patch, calling out her wares, 'Hot spuds, soup to die for and tea like yer mother used to make!'

Some wisecracker shouted, 'Yer wouldn't want tea like me mum made, Bett, stewed and horrible! So, if yours is no better, I'll give it a miss, ta.'

A few people laughed, till Bett shouted, 'Any more of yer cheek, mate, and yer'll be drowning in me tea. I've got a good aim, yer know.'

This turned the laughter on the bloke who'd dared to make fun of her but before he could make amends, Bett caught sight of them. 'Oh, me darlin's, it's good to see yer.' Turning, she shouted, 'Oy, loud mouth, watch me stall for me, I'm taking five minutes.'

'Can yer trust him, Bett?'

Robbie answered Hettie, 'Course she can, Bert's been after getting Bett for his bride since her old man passed away. He wouldn't do anything to Bett, his banter is just to get her attention.'

Ruth felt sorry for the bloke, when she'd only just felt cross with him. 'He's good-looking, Bett.'

'Ha, and worth a bob or two, but no matter what he looks like, there ain't no one for me now me Fred's gone. Anyway, I'm really pleased to see yer all. Happy birthday, Ruth girl, I've got yer something; a little present.'

Ruth couldn't take all of this in. She'd never once had a present in her life and here she was being showered with them.

She watched eagerly as Bett dug deep into the pocket of her pinny.

'I hoped you'd come by, luv. Here yer go.'

Ruth stared at the Fry's chocolate bar. On the wrapper were five pictures of a little boy wearing a sailor suit, his expressions changing from desperate in the first picture of him to happily chomping on a piece of chocolate in the last. In the top left corner of the wrapper, she read, 'Chocolate makers to the King and Queen'. This made her feel like a princess. 'Oh, Bett . . . Bett!'

'Yer worth it, luv, and I've got news for yer.'

This dampened Ruth's spirits a little. She knew it would be about Belton and didn't want to hear the worst.

'Let's all nip to mine.'

As they walked, Robbie held Ruth's hand. Hettie got the other side of her and linked in. She winked at Ruth in a way that said she thought the news would be good.

Robbie was different, he just stared ahead. He knew how Ruth dreaded hearing the worst and had been trying to warn her that Bett's boy didn't stop at hurting people.

As soon as they entered Bett's front room, she said, 'Now then, me darlin's. It's done. Belton is out of action, and so is Gedberg. Both are in hospital. My men waited outside one morning in the week. They've been watching the place and there's a particular morning that both leave together. My main man got out of his van and greeted them so they could confirm they were who he was after, then he signalled his gang and bundled them both into the back of the van. No one saw it happen. Then, when they were dropped off again, they were in a bad way. They'll end up crippled for life, but no names were mentioned. They won't have an inkling that it was because of you, Ruth girl. I wanted them to know, but me men said it was better this way. They knew why they were being done over, but not which kids were responsible. Anyway, you can rest assured that neither will work again. And they had such dire warnings about what would happen to them if they even tried to put the police on anyone.'

Though she knew it was wrong, Ruth felt relief flood her. For no matter how bad and wrong it was, the kids who would come to the home for generations wouldn't be hurt how she, Hettie and Amy were, ever again.

'I see that's made yer smile, well, there's more. That matron was sent a note, that unless things improve, she'll be next. And she was told that they had insider information, so would know if the kids were badly treated or underfed. Now, Ruth girl, to my mind that's a good thing. What do you say, eh?'

'I think it's wonderful. I'm so glad. I know a lot of girls in there that it was happening to and I worried about them, but the two we told you about in particular. I'm so happy that they're safe now.'

'And it does me heart good to see yer smile, girl. How have yer been, then?'

Ruth told Bett about all she'd been doing and about her legal status. 'So, now I can go to see me mates at the home and make sure they have everything they need, and I'll let yer know if nothing's changed.'

'You do that, girl. No kid should suffer what you and Hettie and Robbie have . . . I'm only guessing, Robbie, luv.

I know it ain't easy for yer to talk about such things. So, now, what have yer planned for yer birthday, Ruth, me darlin'?'

'First I have to thank yer for me chocolate. I don't know what chocolate tastes like, but it looks delicious, and for everything, Bett.' Ruth put her arms out and Bett swamped her with her squishy body. Once more Ruth felt the love and warmth of this woman, who she knew had a hard side to her, but also had a heart of gold. 'Will yer come to tea, Bett? We're going to buy one of your spuds for our dinner and Rebekah is getting a lovely tea ready for us.'

'Ahh, you enjoy, but I can't today. I have two sons, yer know, and they visit on a Sunday and take me to the pub for a beer and pie and mash, it's the only chance I get to see them, but another time, mate, eh?'

'Yes, another time, Bett. And now that I'm free, I'll come to see yer regular.'

'That's lovely, girl. Well, I've to get back to me stall and close it up, but not before I serve you all.'

Outside, all three linked arms as they walked behind Bett, but they didn't speak for a while. Robbie broke the silence when he freed himself and punched the air. 'Yes! We beat them, girls . . . we beat them.'

For Ruth, it was a victory but it still didn't sit right with her. She had to keep reminding herself why it had to happen, and that it wouldn't have if anyone had believed them. She made her mind up to only think of how Ellen and Amy were safe now, as that mattered so much to her.

Chapter Fourteen

They juggled the hot spuds from one hand to the other as they walked and took tentative bites, frequently having to wipe their chins clean of the melted dripping that Bett laced the potatoes with, all savouring the taste of the lovely soft flesh and crispy, smoky, peel.

She and Hettie giggled when a bit dropped off Robbie's.

'Let's go into the park and eat them. I can't manage like you girls, you're like professional spud eaters.'

This made them laugh even more, though Ruth agreed it was a good idea, especially for Robbie as he wasn't coping well with eating and walking. She worried about missing Ellen and Amy. 'What time is it, Robbie?'

'It was only a quarter past twelve by Bett's clock, so can only be about half past now.'

'That's plenty of time, then. All right, let's, then Hettie can tell us all her news. We ain't had time to ask yer anything about how it's all going at the house, Hettie, luv.'

As they sat down, it was as if having the chance to tell them everything she'd been up to brought Hettie to life.

'It's great working at the house, I love it there. The work's a doddle to what I was used to, and me and Ebony have a giggle. And like yer said, Ruth, Horacio creeps in at night

158

and we have a lovely time with him. And every night, Abdi comes in silently and Ebony goes with him, but she don't know I know as I pretend to be asleep.'

'Ha, I saw that happen and did the same. I felt all happy about it.'

'Me too. It ain't right how they treat Ebony.'

'Huh huh, not another job for Bett's man is it?'

Hettie sounded alarmed as she said, 'No, Robbie, it ain't. Cook's all right really, she just has a thing about Blacks, I don't know why.'

'She's like two people . . .' Ruth found it hard to explain. 'To me, and it sounds like to Hettie, she's stern but kind. But I hated how she was with Ebony. It ain't nice to see. But Ebony copes. She turns most things into a giggle until it feels like she's the clever one, not Cook or the horrible Aggie.'

'That's what we do too, Ruth. But yer know, I think in time I can change things as Cook's very interested in me having worked in the kitchen and loves how I take an interest in what she's making. She started to talk about retiring, and said she'd speak to Housekeeper about it, so there might be a chance for me to take over from her sometime in the future. That'd be like a dream for me.'

'I'm so glad yer like it there, Hettie, and I love what I'm doing too. I haven't told yer yet.' Ruth told Hettie about her millinery work. 'I made this hat, and can make you one if yer like, a different one that I can design meself.'

'You made that! Oh, Ruth, it's smashing, mate. I'd love one . . . Just think, if yer make me a really posh one and House-keeper asks about it, or even better, if Aggie does, it might get to Mrs Peterson's ears and yer might get orders from her!'

'That would be lovely. Yer never know, I could end up with me own hat shop!'

'Blimey, yer getting ahead of yerself.'

Hettie spluttered at this from Robbie. Robbie looked mystified, 'What? What did I say?'

'Ahead, haha, she'll certainly do that. Yer should call yer shop that, Ruth. "Ahead of yerself".'

They all giggled, and Ruth felt that she couldn't be happier than she was at this moment. 'Right, let's share me chocolate. Have any of yer tasted it before?'

Both said they hadn't.

The squares of chocolate Ruth dished out, keeping some for later, kept them quiet for a while. Ruth wanted to savour every bit; she thought it blissful heaven when she bit into it and a delicious cream came out of the centre.

When she could talk, she said, 'Never mind about cooking spuds, veg and meat, Hettie, yer should learn to make chocolate, yer'd be rich in no time.'

When they reached the home, they all fell silent and Ruth had the feeling that the bottom of her lovely new world dropped a little and she feared that someone would come and drag her in through the gates. 'I hate this place. I wish we could get Ellen and Amy out.'

'Don't forget it'll be a better place now, Ruth, luv. They'll be all right. And if they ain't, they'll tell us. 'Cos we can do this every Sunday and check on them if yer want.'

'Ta, Robbie. I would like that. Yer'll love them, they ain't as old as me, but there's something about them, I just know I want to look after them and make sure nothing happens to them.'

'The bell should go soon. Then we'll know what it's like now since Belton and Gedberg were put out of action.'

Ruth didn't answer Hettie as her stomach had knotted with anticipation and yet a trickle of fear too.

She needn't have worried. When the kids started to come out of the door and onto the balcony, Ellen, always the one to look towards the railings hoping to see her dad there, spotted them straight away. Her squeal of delight carried over all the noise the kids were making as they spilled into the fresh air. Amy came through the door a second later and Ruth saw her face light up as she spotted what Ellen was squealing at.

The pair of them pushed their way down the steps before tearing across the playground. When they reached them, Amy, gasping for breath, blurted out, 'Belton's gone . . . He's gone, Ruth', then burst into tears.

Ruth wanted to hold her to her. 'It's all right, Amy, luv. I know . . .' Robbie nudged her and gave her a look that said to be careful what she said.

'I – I mean, I know how yer feel, even mentioning his name, Amy. Did he hurt yer after I left?'

Amy nodded.

'Well, if he's gone that's a good thing ain't it? He can never hurt yer again . . . I – I mean, he ain't coming back, is he?'

Ellen stepped forward and put her arm around Amy. 'No. Matron told us that he'd gone forever, both him and Gedberg and that there would be some changes made. She told us that if we were ever asked by anyone, we must say how good the changes are.'

'And are they?'

'They are, Ruth. Today we had meat pie for dinner, and it had loads of meat in it. And besides that, we had a bread and butter pudding. I'm bursting.'

Amy cheered as she put in, 'And we have a drink of milk in the morning and water and two biscuits in the afternoon. It's blooming smashing.'

Ruth couldn't help but laugh out loud, the news was so good.

'So, who looks after the place at night, Ellen?'

'A woman does, Hettie, and she's kindly. Matron said she's only here for a bit as she works at another home, but she says she'd like to stay as she lives nearer to this one. She looks after the boys and the girls, but she told us that her husband also works at the other home and she's hoping that they both get a job here.'

Amy jumped in with, 'She tells us stories and the other night, she started to bath us six at a time, and then six the next night, till we were all done. It was lovely.'

'Oh, that's really good to hear. Look, I've a square of chocolate here for each of you. Can yer manage it after yer banquet?'

'Chocolate! I ain't tasted chocolate since me dad . . .'

Ellen's eyes filled with tears.

'Well, yer've got a bit now, so shove it in yer cake holes, before the others see it.'

Hettie's voice sounded harsh, but Ruth knew she was just trying to stop Ellen dwelling on her dad.

'Are you all better now, Ruth? Yer look nice.'

'I am, Ellen, mate.'

'I've missed yer, Ruth, I wished you could get us out.'

'I can't yet, but I will one day, I promise you both, I will. But yer'll be all right now, and me and . . . Oh, this is Robbie, by the way. He's a friend and used to be here a few years ago. Well, he's been looking out for me and we'll come every Sunday together to see yer both. We can bring more chocolate sometimes, or anything yer want.'

'And I'll come with them on me days off.' Hettie puffed out her chest, 'I work at a big house, now.'

They wanted to know what that was like, and what Ruth

was doing. And before they knew it the whistle was blowing, and they had to go.

Ruth felt strangely sad as she watched them walk away. She wanted to call them back, but then felt better as Ellen turned and smiled and waved. 'See yer next Sunday, Ruth.'

Then Amy did the same and Ruth's heart warmed. She had the urge to shout after them that she loved them as that's how she felt at this moment, but she just waved and grinned at them.

'Have we got time to nip to the kitchen door for a mo, Ruth? I'd like to let Cook know I'm all right.'

'Yes, we've got time, tea's not till four, though I want to help Rebekah out a bit.'

'You're not doing a thing. You and Robbie can sit on the step or something. I'm the cook around here, I'll help her, and I'll see to making a cake.'

'Ta, Hettie, luv.'

At the kitchen gate, Hettie rattled the handle a few times. They could hear pots clanging together, but no voices. 'Cook!'

At Hettie's loud shout, the noise in the kitchen stopped.

'Oh, me Hettie, is that you?' As the gate opened, Cook, with suds clinging to her arms and looking hot and bothered, almost knocked Hettie over as she jumped at her and hugged her. 'Oh, Hettie, Hettie, yer all right, luv.'

'I am, Cook.'

'And you, Ruth. But oh, should yer be taking this chance?'

'It's all right, Cook.' Hettie told her about their changed circumstances.

'Well, that's bloomin' lovely news. Though God knows, I miss you, Hettie, luv.'

'And I miss you too, Cook. Have you anyone helping yer?'

'I've been given that Gwen to train, but she's driving me mad, mate. Never known such a Moaning Minnie. I feel like giving her a clout. But it's all changed here, I've so much to tell yer.'

'We know, we just saw Ellen and Amy. So, you have a lot more work to do, having to feed them more and make a pudding too.'

'I do, but they deserve it and all of yer should have been fed like this. The budget was there to buy the food in, but Matron . . . Oh well, that's another story. And all in the past as she's a changed woman. I always thought of her as a leopard but suddenly, she *has* changed her spots, and is all sweetness and light. I can't understand it, nor what's happened to Belton and Gedberg. I'm not sorry, though. I'm glad. And I'm glad yer all right, luv.'

'I am, Cook. I'll come and see yer on me days off, I promise . . . Oh, I want to ask yer. You don't know how to make chocolate do yer, Cook?'

'That's a funny question, but I do as it happens, well, chocolate icing anyway, but they'd never afford the cocoa for it here.'

'Well, I'd love to know. Can yer write it down for when I come again?'

'I will, and I'll look through me old books. I might find a recipe for solid chocolate . . . ooh, I could just eat some. I ain't had any since I were a girl, when the cook at the home where I was before we moved here used to make it at Christmas. I was put to work with her but gradually things changed . . . Anyway, as things look, I might be making it meself this Christmas.'

Ruth felt in her skirt pocket for the last piece of chocolate that she'd planned to keep until she was in bed tonight.

'Here you go, Cook, it's me birthday and a friend brought me some. I've one piece left for yer.'

'No, Ruth, I couldn't take yer last piece.'

But though she said this, Ruth didn't miss the longing in Cook's eyes as she gazed at the chocolate.

'Please, Cook, it'd make me birthday if you did as Hettie's told me how good yer were to her and this'll be me gift to thank you for that kindness.'

'Ahh, happy birthday, luv. But yer know, I'd have been good to you all if I dared. Ta, I'll enjoy that. I'll finish me pots then put me feet up for an hour and eat it really slowly.'

'We'll have to go now, Cook. I'll see yer in a month, eh?'

'Come here, Hettie, luv. Ooh, it's made me day seeing yer and knowing yer all right.'

As Hettie and Cook came out of the hug, Ruth told Cook, 'We're going to come every Sunday to see Amy and Ellen, so we'll pop round here and see if yer all right and if yer need anything. And if yer get that recipe, I can take it to Hettie as I'll be meeting her in the park some afternoons and seeing her at church on Sundays.'

'Ta, Ruth. You go to church then, Hettie?'

'I do. It's a way of getting a bit of time off and seeing Ruth and Robbie.'

Cook looked at Robbie. 'I know you, don't I?'

Robbie reminded her how she knew him.

'Aah, I remember, you were a weedy little chap with a lovely face – which yer still have – and I was glad when yer got away as you were put through a lot. Nice to see you're all right, and yer look like yer doing well, togged up in yer Sunday best.'

The emotions that showed on Robbie's face as the colour flooded his cheeks and he cast his eyes to the ground tore at Ruth's heart. She'd always known that Gedberg had tried something on him, but now she realized that Robbie had been through hell too. She reached for his hand and held it. 'We're all OK now, Cook. See yer next week.'

'I'll look forward to it. Be the highlight of me week that will.'

Ruth felt the pity of this; poor Cook stuck in that kitchen from morning till night, day in and day out. What kind of life was that? At this moment, she wished she was older as then she could make things better for everyone. You couldn't do that when you were still looked on as a kid.

She kept hold of Robbie's hand, but didn't ask any questions, she didn't need to. Her mind gave her the thought that it must be awful being a boy sometimes, as they could never talk about things like girls did, or cry over them, they always had to be brave. She knew she couldn't be like that and was glad she didn't have to be.

All this was forgotten when they reached home, and Horacio ran at her. Hugging him, Ruth filled with love for him as he looked up at her. 'Today is a very good day, Ruth. Aunty let me help her to make African-style meatballs for our lunch. I loved them. You see, I am African.'

'I know. Like your momma and poppa and Aunty Rebekah.'

'But here I have to be English.'

'You can be both. And yer can say "dinner" for yer midday meal when yer with us as we don't have lunch. We have breakfast, dinner, tea and supper as we're not posh.'

Horacio's expression was one of bewilderment; he looked so funny that Ruth burst out laughing.

'I shouldn't be teaching him stuff like that, if I was you, Ruth. That boy could slip up and get himself into trouble.'

'Oh, I didn't think, sorry, Rebekah . . . I'm only joking, Horacio, it is lunch, and me Hettie and Robbie had a lovely hot spud for ours.'

'Is that all, no meat and vegetables?'

'No, it was just a whole spud baked over hot coals, then cut open and a dollop of dripping put inside. One of these Sundays, if yer can come and stay again, I'll take yer for one.'

'I can come every Sunday, now you're here, as Aunty can manage me then. Before, she would have had to walk me back to the house, and that's too much for her.'

Rebekah chuckled. 'Ole Rebekah can do a lot more than yer think, boy. But I have yer visits to look forward to now, and that's all that matters. Well now, I suggest you, Ruth and Robbie go off to the park, so yer can have a good run around, while me and Hettie get busy for the special tea we're going to make.'

Tea was lovely. Little hard-boiled egg sandwiches, jam tarts, and then the best of all, a lovely sponge cake.

'Oh, Hettie, this is delicious, mate.'

'I loved making it for yer, Ruth. I've seen Cook make a few and watched how she beat the eggs and all the steps she took. I couldn't wait to have a go meself.'

Robbie made Hettie beam then, as with crumbs coming from his mouth, he told her it was the best thing he'd ever tasted.

After tea Robbie asked about Rebekah's life before she came to England, and they all sat enthralled as Rebekah told of growing up in West Africa.

She explained how, once a week, the women of the family washed their clothes and bedding in the water hole. 'Them were happy days, as we used to sing while we worked, and dance while the washing dried on the stones. And then we would plait each other's hair.'

Ruth was fascinated to hear the next bit.

'When I was widowed I took on the role of looking after all the women and helping them with their kids, making their clothes and dressing their hair. I was good so I progressed to being the hairdresser to the wife of one of the chiefs – my grandfather's cousin. Since I came here, it ain't all been as I thought it was going to be, as at times it has been lonely and ole Rebekah ain't no longer looked up to and sought after.'

'We look up to yer, don't we, Robbie? You've saved our lives, Rebekah.'

This brought a lovely smile to her face.

'Could you plait my hair?'

'I can, Ruth girl, and would love to. Let me go get me tin of beads and ribbons, you're going to look something special for your birthday, girl.'

Everyone watched fascinated as Rebekah plaited Ruth's hair into dozens of plaits and then intertwined them closely to her scalp, weaving tiny beads into the braids as she went. The effect was beautiful.

The sight of her set Rebekah off. She began singing and dancing. They all joined in, and to Ruth, it was the best and happiest birthday she'd ever had.

Chapter Fifteen

When Sunday dawned the following week, Ruth was filled with happiness and eager anticipation. Loving the service as she always did, today she was impatient for it to end.

At last it was over, they'd said their goodbyes, and now she and Robbie held Horacio's hands and skipped and jumped him along.

'I think he's tired now, Robbie, mate.'

Horacio had begun to drag on their hands.

'Come on, big fella, up on me shoulders and I'll give yer a lift.'

Horacio clapped his hands, 'I can see everything, like I'm a big man like my poppa!'

'Well, you're not eating your spud up there, I can tell yer.'

Robbie tickled him as he lifted him down, sending him into fits of giggles and taking away any protests he might make.

They'd reached the market and there was Bett as usual.

As Ruth came out of her hug, Bett said, 'So, this is Horacio. My, yer a smasher, boy.'

'What's a smasher?'

'We'll have two of yer spuds please, Bett. This little man is full of questions and'll keep yer hours. He's going to share mine to see if he likes it and can have one of his own another time.'

'I like a kid who asks questions, mate, shows their intelligence. My lads always asked questions and now they want for nothing. Built an empire they have.'

Ruth sensed Robbie's look, but daren't look back at him. She could guess what their 'Empire' was.

'So, how's things coming along with the pair of yer, eh? It wouldn't hurt yer to drop by more often yer know.'

'Sorry, Bett. I'm at work all week, and Ruth's busy with her hat-making.'

'I'm learning new skills every day from Rebekah, Bett, and loving it.'

'Well, that's good, luv. I should imagine that ole lady has a lot to teach anyone. Anyway, come and see me as often as yer can, I like to know how yer both are.'

Ruth kissed her cheek. 'We will, Bett, but we have to hurry now.'

After greeting Reg and having a chat with him and learning Mick the Irish and Ted the Flute were off begging, they crossed over to the park.

'Yer cut Bett a bit short, mate.'

'I know, Robbie, do yer think she was hurt? I didn't mean to hurt her but I worry about the time and Bett can talk for ages when she gets going, and I can't be late.'

Robbie didn't say anything to this but sat on the bench eating his spud. Ruth broke a piece off from hers and blew on it to cool it, but Horacio didn't like it. 'Ugh! It tastes of fat!'

'That's the best part. Here, try a bit that hasn't been touched by the dripping, then.'

This he loved and left Ruth feeling hungry as he devoured all the outside edge and the lovely crusty peel.

Riding on Robbie's shoulders again as they made their way to the home, Horacio was once more happy, singing about being on top of the world. 'A huge giant, I am.' But when the children began to come out of the home, Ruth could see the noise and the rush of bodies frightened him. He slid down willingly at her bidding and clung to her waist, seeming to be all right with her arm around him to reassure him as she scanned the crowds of children – there was no sign of Amy and Ellen. 'Where are they? Oh, Robbie, do yer think they're sick?'

'No, mate, don't worry, they'll be out in a minute, there's still loads coming out.'

This didn't stop Ruth's heart from sinking. Ellen and Amy knew she'd be there, they would have been the first out, if they could be. She just knew something had happened.

When the door to the building finally closed, and she knew the key would be turned to prevent any children sidling back inside, despair settled inside her.

Robbie touched her arm. 'Let's go around the back to see Cook and see what's happened, shall we? I can see you're thinking the worst, mate.'

Ruth was so worried; she couldn't even think what the worst thing that could have happened was.

Cook shook her head. 'They're gone, Ruth girl. Ellen's dad came for her. She was so happy. And Amy, poor little mite, well . . . I don't know if yer'll see her again. You might see Ellen, but Amy's gone to be part of the Canadian programme, quite a few of them have.'

Ruth couldn't speak. But Robbie asked, 'What's that?'

'I hadn't heard of it till it happened, but it's where they send kids to Canada to live with families, especially them families that need help with farming and such like.'

It seemed to Ruth that her world stopped as she listened to Cook. She couldn't imagine not ever seeing Amy and Ellen again, or not ever knowing how they were. 'Will Amy be gone yet? How do they get to Canada? Do they sail from London? I want to give her me address. And Ellen . . . gone. I didn't have a chance to say goodbye to either of them. How will they know how to get in touch with me?'

Cook shook her head again. 'Slow down, luv. I don't know none of the answers for yer. Were them girls special to yer? Didn't yer make other friends here?'

'No! Not ever like them. Yes, they were special, but I don't know why. I – I just . . .' She was at a loss as to how to explain her feelings for them and how empty she felt, as if a big part of her life had gone. And all her plans too. The dreams she'd dreamed at night when the house was still. She'd imagined her being able to look after them, and them all living happily together with no more fears ever again. Now it would never happen.

'Are you sad again, Ruth? I like it best when you're happy.'

'Yes, I am sad, luv. Me mates have gone away, and I didn't want them to.'

'I can be your mate.'

'Oh, you are, Horacio.' She snuggled him into her.

'So, who's this, then? Yer a handsome little fella, I know that much.'

'I'm Horacio, I'm Ruth's friend.'

'And mine, mate.'

'Yes, and Robbie's. Me and Robbie share a bedroom when I sleep over and he shows me how to play football in the park. One day he's going to take me to see the Hammers to see real football played because I really liked it.'

'Well, then, that's nice.'

172

'And Robbie's saving up to buy a real football, as we used a pig's bladder which Robbie blew up, but it burst.'

'Oh my, you've a good tale or two to tell, young man. I like talking to yer.'

Horacio smiled. 'And I like you. I like it now that I get away from the Petersons' house. But I like having Hettie there, she's funny.'

'My Hettie?'

Cook looked at Ruth. Ruth just wanted to scream and scream, not stand here listening to Cook and Horacio, but she nodded her head and explained Horacio's connection with the house.

'Yes, Momma's a maid, but she gets beaten. But not anymore, since Ruth came and then Hettie, as now she can get all the work done and be at the beck and call of Cook.'

'Oh, I see. That's how it is, is it? Well, I ain't that kind of cook.'

Ruth just wanted to go. She wanted this talking to be over. She wanted to run down every street in London to try to find Ellen and then go to the docks and watch every ship to see if it carried children to Canada.

As if sensing this, Robbie said, 'We'll go now, Cook. Hettie sent her love and asked us to ask yer if yer needed anything.'

'Give me love back to her, and no, I'm fine. Things are getting better here all the time. Oh, I nearly forgot. I found a recipe for making chocolate in *Mrs Beeton's Cookery Book*. It was left by the old cook and I've used it hundreds of times, but never looked at the sweet section. Will yer give it to Hettie for me?'

'We will.'

'And Ruth, let me give yer a hug, love.'

A hug was just what Ruth wanted and yet didn't as she

173

thought it might break her. But she didn't resist and was glad. Cook's fleshy arms held comfort for her.

'That chocolate yer gave me were such a treat. Ta again, luv. And yer will come back, won't yer? I looked forward so much to today.'

'I will. Ta, Cook.'

'Why don't yer call me Flo? No one calls me by me name now. Cook makes me feel like a thing, instead of a person.'

Robbie answered, 'That's a nice name, Flo.'

'Ta, Robbie . . . I don't suppose you'd like a hug, would yer? Young men are past having hugs, I'd think.'

'No. I'd love a hug.'

'Ahh, come here, duckie.'

Robbie looked so awkward in Flo's arms that Ruth felt herself smiling, when she'd thought she would never smile again.

Horacio stood waiting. Ruth hoped Flo would cuddle him too, which she did when she let go of a red-faced Robbie.

'Now, come here, buggerlugs. Yer not getting away without one of Flo's hugs.'

Horacio giggled as he put his arms around Flo's neck.

On the way home they didn't talk a lot and it was how Ruth wanted it to be. The feeling she had was how she imagined you would feel if someone you loved died. Because Ellen and Amy were like that to her now – gone forever.

'What's a buggerlugs, Ruth?'

Ruth shrugged. She had no idea; she hadn't ever heard the term. But Robbie said, 'It's what someone calls a child they really love. But yer need to keep it a secret word. Not even whisper it to yer momma because she may not understand, but yer can whisper it to Hettie, she'd have a laugh about it.'

'Ooh, I like secrets. And I can keep them too, Robbie, and I like Flo.'

'Funny that, ain't it, Ruth? Cook to us was always someone in the kitchen. She seemed a bit aloof, really. None of us but them 'as worked in the kitchen ever had any contact with her and yet, she's such a nice person. Kindly.'

Ruth agreed. Though a small part of her still wished Cook had found the courage to go to the police and try to stop what had happened.

When Robbie came in from work the next evening, he was shouting Ruth's name as soon as he came in the door.

Ruth put her head up to listen. She rubbed the ache in her neck from where she'd been bending over a hat block trying to work on Hettie's hat – a chocolate brown cloche but with a small brim that curled up on one side. This was a new skill she was learning but wasn't yet getting right.

Robbie's voice came nearer. She heard the latch to the bottom of the stairs, then, 'Ruth, Ruth, I've got some news for yer.'

Rushing to the top of the stairs to meet him, Ruth felt an excitement build in her. Just his voice gave her the feeling that this was good news.

'I called by to see the market gang . . . and Bett, of course. She sent her love. Ted was there and I asked him how things were at the dock and he said busy as there was a ship sailing on Wednesday to Montreal – that's in Canada!'

'Oh, Robbie. Really? What will happen, will everyone be on it by now?'

'No, when I worked there, it took a long time to board everyone, but once they boarded, then the ship left the dock that day, it didn't board them then stay in dock overnight.

Everything else is loaded on it – food, water, fuel . . . all sorts, and the crew work away at sorting everything out. That takes a few days and is what Ted's been doing.'

Hope gripped Ruth. Was there a chance she could see Amy?

'I'll go there, but how will I know what time it sails?'

'Ted said he was told it sails on Wednesday at two in the afternoon. From what I know, that means the passengers will start to board from about nine or ten in the morning.'

'So, where do you think they are keeping the kids till then?'

'I don't know, I can't think.'

'It must be some place where they can kit them out ready, but where?'

Robbie shrugged. 'I suppose it depends on how many kids are going.'

'I'll just have to go there on Wednesday and take me chances of seeing her.'

Wednesday seemed to take an age to come round, but when it did, Ruth was up bright and early. Robbie was going to walk her to the docks before he went to work.

'Now, you're sure yer'll be all right? Ole Rebekah will worry about you, honey child. There's some unsavoury characters hang around them docks.'

'I will, Rebekah. If I see anyone I'm frightened of, I'll run away as fast as I can.'

'You'll be all right, Ruth,' Robbie told her. 'I can stay with you till seven, and they might start boarding then so everyone'll be busy. I don't think anyone will bother about yer.'

'I'm not scared, Robbie.'

Though Ruth said this, she did have butterflies in her stomach.

On the dock Ruth felt as if she was in another world. The Thameside was a hive of activity. Crates were stacked everywhere, and it seemed hundreds of men worked at shifting them, and loading some, while others were marked with chalk.

'The marking tells the dockers what has to go where,' Robbie told her.

The ship looked enormous, making Ruth feel the size of an ant as she stood in awe, her neck bent as she tried to see the top of it.

Counting the many decks, she shielded her eyes against the brightness as the ship dazzled with what looked like a new coat of white paint. Smoke billowed from its two funnels.

'Mind yer back, you two, what yer doing here anyway, get yerselves away, it's bloody dangerous 'ere.'

'Where should we be to see a passenger off, mate?'

'Stand over there under that shelter. Opposite the gangplank, yer'll see from there. The passengers'll walk along between them barriers, but it won't be for about an hour.'

The protection of the shelter was welcome as the breeze coming off the Thames had a keen nip to it.

'I don't see how yer can fail to see her from here, Ruth. The pathway for the passengers isn't that wide, and they have to queue for a good while as each one is boarded – all their papers have to be checked and that causes delays. I've seen relatives chatting for ages to them they're seeing off. But I've to go now, will yer be all right?'

'I will, mate. I'll not move from here until the passengers start to arrive.'

'Good luck. I hope yer see Amy.'

It seemed like an age till the passengers began to file in to form a queue in the allocated space. Ruth couldn't believe her eyes when the first ones were two adults with a line of kids. She ran forward, calling Amy's name.

'I'm here, Ruth! Oh, Ruth, Ruth!'

They were in each other's arms. Their tears wet each other's hair and cheeks. 'Oh, Amy, luv. I can't believe you're going so far away.'

'I know. I'm excited, but scared too.'

'You don't mind going?'

'No, they said it's a wonderful opportunity for us to travel to Canada. To see a new world. I've got all new clothes.'

'And they've cut yer lovely hair!'

'I know, they said it will be better. I don't know why. I'm going to miss yer, Ruth.'

This spilled the tears again. 'I've written me address down. You can write and send letters from Canada. Robbie asked around at the place where he works and one of the men has a brother who emigrated there, and he gets letters from him, but they take a long time.'

'Ta, mate. I will write, and I'll let yer know where you can write back to . . . Will I ever see yer again, Ruth?'

This made them cry again.

'I'll never forget yer, Amy. When we're older, maybe things'll be different and then we can travel to see each other.' Trying to cheer Amy up, Ruth said, 'Look, I'll definitely come to see you, so hang on to that. I'm going to make me fortune making hats. And when I do, I'll buy a ticket to travel on this ship to Canada, and that's a promise.'

They clung to each other again.

A stern voice forced them apart. 'You there, what are you doing? Amy, who is this?'

'It's me friend, miss. She's come to say goodbye.'

'All right then, but hurry, we'll be moving forward shortly.'

178

'Amy, before yer go, do yer know where Ellen went?'

'I don't. But she was so happy, Ruth. We came out to the playground the next day after you visited and there he was – her dad! He told Ellen that he was making arrangements to fetch her out as his wife had died and he now lived on his own. When he'd gone, she said she didn't know where he was taking her as he didn't tell her. She said, she didn't know if she could, but she'd try to get back to see me like you did. But she went the next afternoon, and then the next day, they came to fetch me. I didn't have any idea that would happen, and I was scared at first, but they took us to this house, and everything was like a whirl, as they fitted us out with new clothes, and we had a lot of talks on what it was going to be like. We could be put with a family who has a farm and have to help out, it all sounded so exciting.'

Amy was smiling again and looking eager to go on her journey.

Ruth put her arms out to her. She swallowed hard, determined to smile as she said this last goodbye.

When they parted and the line of children began to worm its way forward, Ruth did smile and wave. But just as Amy was about to disappear, she shouted, 'I love you, Amy. Don't forget me.'

A voice came back, 'And I love you, Ruth. I won't, I promise.'

And then she was gone.

Ruth stood for a moment peering at the deck where she could see folk had gathered and were leaning over the railings, but no children appeared. Amy was gone.

With her face awash with tears. Ruth turned to go home. Nothing would be the same again. The dream she held had been shattered.

Chapter Sixteen

'Ruth girl, there ain't nothing gained by sitting moping. You can't change anything. What you gotta do is get on with making a life for yourself. And you're gonna do that through work. You have talent, girl. Rebekah did see that.'

Ruth stared out of the window. For the last hour she'd been watching the comings and goings of the street and wondering about the people going about their lives and none of them seeming to care about Rebekah.

Across the road two women gossiped, and kids played. She'd never seen any of these women even say hello to Rebekah, though they were always gawping out of their windows at the comings and goings of herself and Robbie.

'Ruth, honey child, you've got to get yourself out of this morose mood. Things are not looking good. We only have what Robbie can bring in as I ain't had any orders in a while and the little money I have is dwindling away.'

This shocked Ruth. Rebekah gave her a home, fed her and made clothes for her, and she hadn't contributed anything to help. 'I'm sorry, Rebekah. I just feel so sad. It seems there's nothing folk like us can do about anything.'

'There is. We can use the talents God did give us to make our way in life. I will teach you many skills, Ruth girl, so that you will be able to make good. Already you make a fine hat and work on one that is better. I can teach you dressmaking and look, I show you.'

Rebekah opened a cupboard under the stairs that was lined with shelves full of the materials she used. Twisting her body, she stretched her arm inside and pulled out a picture.

Ruth gasped. The picture was made of beads – a young, very beautiful African girl dressed in yellow. Her eyes looked alive and as if they were smiling, and yet the chiselled features of her face were set in a regal expression.

'Oh, Rebekah, it's beautiful. Did you make it?'

'I did. At home we did have the missionary nuns come and they encouraged our traditional arts. They sent them back to England and donations came to keep their mission going.'

'I'd love to hear about your life in Africa. Will you ever go back?'

'I don't know, girl. All Rebekah can do is work, and praise the Lord, and do His work. You are His work, Ruth girl. My mission is to set you up in life. He did send you to me.'

'I should get a job, Rebekah. I could go back to the house where Hettie works, they've already said they'll have me.'

'No. Rebekah needs you here, girl. If we work hard we can make a success. The hat like you made for yourself and the one you work on for Hettie, would be sought after as the winter comes. That's how we should start. We should make lots of them and then we could have a stall in the market. Rebekah has always wanted a stall.'

Ruth began to feel excited. She remembered telling Ellen and Amy that she would one day have a hat shop and be rich, and this could be the start of that.

'What you say, girl?'

'Can we make it happen? How do we get a stall, what do they cost?'

'We go to the council. They rent out the pitches. Rebekah did think about it a lot. Robbie could make us a stall. He's getting really good with making shelves for us with what he is learning at work, and he only been there a couple of months.'

Suddenly, it all seemed a reality. Ruth, smiling now, stood up. 'We're going to be rich, Rebekah. I'm going to start this minute. If I stick to making the plain cloches like mine, and you decorate them in different ways – bows, rosettes, ribbon bands around the brim – beads even! We could make enough in two weeks to start our stall!'

'Before that, girl. We only need six or so to start and we can carry on from there. You running the stall and making the hats, and I can knit scarves, gloves, mittens and muffs, to complement the colours. By winter we will have a full range of warm accessories to offer.'

They both giggled. Then Rebekah began her little dance and Ruth joined in as excitement set her stamping her feet and swaying her body to the same rhythm as Rebekah. As always, the joy of dancing seared hope through her as she raised her hands and allowed the feeling to soar high.

When Robbie came home, he looked at Ruth with concern. 'Did you see her?'

Ruth told him what happened, 'But we have news, Robbie. Me and Rebekah are going to be rich!'

Robbie grinned. 'Well, this is a turn up. Here was me thinking I was going to have to cheer yer up and yer full of the joys of spring!'

Ruth told him their plans.

'That's a great idea. I'll start asking for a few offcuts to make the frame, but we'll have to buy the slats to go across the top and for the four legs as there ain't never any offcuts that long or the thickness we'd need.'

Suddenly, with Robbie being just as enthusiastic it all seemed that it would truly happen.

Two weeks later, with fingers beginning to blister and bruised hands from where she'd missed the tiny tacks with the hammer as she'd moulded the felt to the shapes needed, Ruth had finished her tenth bonnet.

She'd worked from early morning till late at night and now, her bedroom seemed to be full to the brim of hats and all that went with them – boxes holding the hats that were finished, materials and the three completed cloches awaiting decoration, and in a corner, more cardboard bought from a papermill near to the docks and waiting to be made into boxes, a process which Robbie did for them.

Looking around at all she'd achieved, Ruth's eyes fell on her pride and joy that stood at a jaunty angle on the model head she'd fashioned it on – a hat for Hettie in chocolate brown with a small brim decorated with a black feather. It looked lovely and Ruth couldn't wait till Sunday when she would give it to Hettie.

The making of it had given her other ideas and had led to her working on a fashionable hat with a much wider brim. Excitement, as it took shape, zinged through Ruth as she knew this kind of hat could fetch a lot more money and maybe lead to them one day doing really well – maybe even owning a shop and not just a market stall.

But, they had to walk before they could run and the first steps were in place as today was the day they were applying for their pitch on the market. Rebekah had left the house an hour ago and Ruth had been glad of the distraction of working on the special hat as she was on tenterhooks, wishing she'd gone with her and hoping and praying they were successful.

As if on cue, the sound of Rebekah coming home had Ruth jumping up and running downstairs, eager to know the news.

One look at Rebekah's face told her it wasn't good.

In answer to her unspoken question, Rebekah shook her head. 'The council man did make every excuse in the book, but Rebekah knows he refused me application because I am a Black woman.'

'Oh no, Rebekah! Why should he? I don't understand!'

'White men in authority, they don't want to see the likes of me and my kind making good. It is twice as hard for us to do well.'

Anger rose up in Ruth. 'I'll go. And I'll tell him he has no right to refuse!'

'It won't do any good. When I argued, he said the vacant pitch I want is now twice what it was advertised for due to there being a lot of interest, but Rebekah knows that ain't right. But we have no argument, girl, and we can't afford such a rent. Even the going rate would have been hard to find as he tells me I would need to pay three months upfront.'

Ruth felt defeated for a moment, but then something occurred to her. 'How about if we don't have a stall?'

'What yer mean, girl? We gotta have something to sell our hats from.'

Robbie opening the door stopped Ruth from telling her idea. 'What's up? I ain't used to coming home to doom and gloom. Your faces look like someone's smacked you with a wet lettuce.'

184

Ruth couldn't laugh at Robbie's joke this time, even though his quips could always make her smile. She told him what had happened. 'But I have an idea, Robbie.'

'Well, what is it, Ruth girl?'

'How about we have a handcart, and not a stall. We could walk up and down then, and no one could stop us as we ain't taking a pitch. Could you make us one, Robbie?'

'I think I could. I'd have a good go, anyway.'

'No, it ain't possible. Me thinks that might upset folk as they are paying rent and they will see us make a profit from the crowd that attend the market and we ain't having to pay nothing. I think they would hound us out.'

'What about Bett? She might help.'

'That's a good idea, Robbie. We could ask her to rent a stall in her name and we pay.'

Rebekah sank down onto the sofa, almost losing herself in the many colours of her wraparound frock as they blended in with those swathing the sofa.

'Rebekah did think of that. I called on Bett and talked to her, but she says we need to cover any risk she'd take by giving her a cut. We ain't going to be making a big profit, as we were going to keep our prices low to get us a name. What with the rent and giving a cut to Bett, we ain't going to keep our head above water.'

'Bett said that? I can't believe it. Let me go and talk to her.'

'Ruth, you've got to remember, Bett has a hard core. She'd give you her heart if you needed it, but if you're going to be making money out of her she's a different person. I've seen her thump the man who brings her spuds because he put the price up more than she thought it should be. She's a businesswoman. She has her fingers in a lot of pies, and if you want anything to do with business, then you pay.'

185

'Oh, Robbie.' Ruth sat on the arm of the sofa. But never one to be defeated for long an idea occurred to her, 'We could give her free hats!'

Rebekah burst out laughing.

'What?'

'Rebekah did see a picture in her mind of Bett working at her brazier with hats piled high on her head!'

The picture made Ruth giggle, but Robbie put his head back and let out a real belly laugh.

Rebekah stood. 'She'll be champion over any African woman who likes to pile her head-tie high on her head.' With this, she went to her cupboard and brought out a swathe of royal blue silk. Her expert tucks and swirling of the material around her head had Ruth and Robbie watching in awe as it grew and grew in neat rows, sometimes tight sometimes twisted and curved. 'There, Rebekah now has the tallest head-wrap, but does still see Bett in her mind with ten hats on so it be taller.'

Her giggle set them off again and as always happened when Rebekah got into this mood, she danced. Robbie soon joined in and once again, Ruth was mesmerized by how his body seemed to be made of rubber. His movements were graceful, and yet, held an excitement. To her, he was like the poster she'd seen of a ballet production as the shape of his body mimicked that of the man holding the girl in a white frilly frock.

'You am a natural, boy – you too, Ruth – you both have the grace and the rhythm, even without music, but the music is in your bodies, in your blood. Rebekah's thinking you should go to lessons and become a dancer, Robbie!'

Robbie blushed but in a way that showed his pride. He covered this by saying, 'I'm hungry, what's for tea?'

'Rebekah did leave everything marinating, I only have to rapid cook in my special pan, and you'll be eating my special curry in no time.'

When Rebekah had disappeared into the kitchen, Robbie wiped his brow with the tail of his shirt front. 'I'll go along and see Bett later, see if I can do a deal with her. She might consider a low payment that you can afford at first and then more as you get on your feet. I'll point out to her that anything is more than she has now.'

'That's true as she'll have no extra cost.'

'It's the risk she's thinking of. If yer don't make enough to cover the rent, then she'll have to pay it as the contract will be in her name.'

Ruth hadn't thought of this and with hearing it a little understanding came to her.

The curry was the most delicious yet. They both loved Rebekah's African cooking. It was spicy but not hot. Laced with fruit, it had so many flavours. Rebekah served it with slices of soft potato. She'd told them that at home the fruit would be pineapple, which Ruth had never seen and couldn't imagine what it looked like.

Robbie surprised them as they were all eating by suddenly saying, 'I've got it! How about yer offer yer curry to Bett to sell?'

'Bett?' Rebekah was quiet for a moment. Ruth waited, not sure what to make of this new development.

'Yes, you could make a big pan of curry, and Bett could sell it from her stall.'

'But Robbie, she hates the smell of it when it wafts over from Bardri's shop. She calls it a stench.'

'That's because she's jealous of how popular it's getting.

'Some of her clients of a Friday dinner-time go there instead as African foods are getting very popular, especially when the weather's colder. I reckon if she could sell it herself, she'd sing a different tune about it.'

Ruth wasn't convinced. 'How would she keep it hot?'

'Rebekah has a pot. It can stand on an open fire and will keep anything hot for hours. We would have to get some dishes, but there's a market stall that sells them, some have little chips in them, but they'd do. We'd have to take them clean in the morning with the curry, and then bring them home at night. It'll be a lot of work, but it could be a solution.'

'You mean, yer really think Bett would go for it? I'm telling yer, she hates curry.'

'I doubt she's tasted it, Ruth. Look, why don't we take her some? We could put the proposition to her and ask her to taste it. She can't fail to like it. And a pot of this every couple of days ain't going to cost yer much. Rebekah has spices on her shelves to last a lifetime and they're the main ingredient. But to Bett, it could mean loads of profit and cover any risk she's taking.'

'I'll get some of me curry, Robbie. I have a small earthenware pot too, I made it with me own hands when I was a girl and did bring it with me on the ship.'

As Rebekah did this, she told them how the women used to make their own pots from clay that they shaped and baked.

Ruth never ceased to be amazed at all she heard of Rebekah's life and the skills she had, but then, Rebekah had told her there were no shops where her tribe lived, only merchants who would visit sometimes with cloths and silks and spices and for which the tribe would barter. Everything else they needed and what they bartered with, they made themselves out of the materials God had given them in abundance. 'Even the clay of the earth gave up to us the means of making our pots, ovens and pans.' She told them now.

It all fascinated Ruth and made her feel sad too, that Rebekah had been happy at home, but had dreamed of something more. What she'd found hadn't been anywhere near as good, but now she was stuck and could never afford to go home, where she longed to be.

While savouring the last spoonful of her delicious curry the thought came to Ruth, *If ever I achieve my dream of getting rich, I will take Rebekah home*. But then she smiled to herself as she wondered if she would have time to get rich, go to Canada and then to Africa too. She didn't know where either were, but it would help if they were next door to one another.

This thought made her giggle as she imagined jumping from one to the other holding Rebekah and Amy's hands.

'You're liking the idea, I can see.'

Ruth didn't tell Robbie what was really making her smile, she just nodded her head and told him, 'All right. It can't hurt to try. We'll take a curry to Bett, but I don't give much for our chances.'

'If you don't try, girl, you get nothing. Life is about doing, not putting obstacles in the way of doing. Rebekah has many lessons to teach you, honey child.'

Robbie stuck his tongue out at her as if in victory. She slapped his arm. 'All right, you win, but we'll see.'

Going to Bett's when she felt cross at her for what she was doing, wasn't something Ruth wanted to do, but she had to fight for the stall. Without that, her dreams were in tatters.

Chapter Seventeen

'Who the bleedin' hell is that knocking on me door? I ain't bloomin' well been home five minutes. If it ain't important, yer can bugger off!'

Ruth trembled at the sternness of Bett's voice calling out from the kitchen. She and Robbie stood on the step of Bett's open door. She looked at Robbie. 'Let's go.'

Robbie grinned. 'No, she'll be fine. She's just tired. She gets like this. It's a hard day for her from early morning and on her feet all the time.'

'Well, why don't her sons help her?'

'They give her anything she wants, but Bett's Bett. Everyone reckons she's got a fortune stacked away, but goodness knows what for.'

'Bett, it's us. Robbie and Ruth.'

When Bett came into view it was as if she'd stampeded through to them. Ruth cowered towards Robbie as visions of Matron came to her.

'Well, and what do you two want? I can guess. Come in while I go for a pee. I ain't been all day.'

When she disappeared out to the small part of the yard that was hers and that held a shared lav with the tenants upstairs, Robbie said, 'There, I told yer not to be scared.'

Bett strode back in within minutes. 'Now then, what yer looking like a terrified rabbit for?'

Bett looked at Ruth and put her arms out. 'Come here, luv.'

Ruth flooded with relief as she went into the soft squidgy cuddle.

'You're never to be afraid of me, Ruth, luv. I say it how it is, but I'd never hurt yer, or let anyone else either. Yer know that first hand, girl.'

Ruth felt her troubles leave her as Bett rocked her.

'Now, tell me, what's this all about, Robbie? And what's that yer've got in yer hands?'

Robbie explained.

'What? Me, sell that stinking stuff?!'

'There's full profit in it, Bett. Yer'll get a couple of pans a week for wavering the cut out of Rebekah's profits and whatever yer sell it for, you'll keep. Yer know how many of yer customers go to Bardri's? Well, his curry ain't a patch on this.'

'Oh, yer've tried his then?'

'No, the first I tried were Rebekah's, but I just know.'

'So, I'm to base a business deal on Robbie know-it-all's word, then?'

Robbie laughed. 'Just taste it. What can that hurt, eh?'

'Hmmm. But whether I do or I don't, and I ain't bleedin' keen I can tell yer, the fact is that you, Ruth, need to toughen up. I had no intention of making you and Rebekah pay straight off. Not until yer began to see a profit. I only thought to take the stall on a quarterly basis for yer, so that way you'd have paid the rent upfront, and if yer not doing any good by then, I'd have pulled out. But I'm taking a risk after that, and that's when I think I should have a cut to cover that. What you and Rebekah should have done is acted more business-like, Ruth. Yer should have come to see me to tell me that yer can't pay anything for the first few months, then I'll get double what I was asking for, till the backlog was paid. But Rebekah comes asking me for help and then gets upset 'cos I want something for it and you come offering curry.'

Robbie spoke up. 'That ain't fair, Bett. Ruth ain't yet fourteen, and yer thinking she should have the head of a businessman.'

'There's nothing fair in business, Robbie, and if Ruth is going into it, she needs to learn, and learn fast.'

Bett had let Ruth go and she stood with her fists stuck into her waist and her elbows stuck out. She posed a frightening figure in this mood.

But Robbie didn't flinch. 'Couldn't yer just try the curry? Surely that's what a businessman would do when offered such a deal?'

'Ha, yer don't bleedin' give up, do yer? Well, I'm glad. Ruth needs someone with a nose for it on her side, so with you and me she'll do all right. Put the bloody pot on the table, then. I ain't promising though. It's the smell I can't take.'

But when she lifted the lid, Bett's expression changed. 'Well, that ain't bad. Freshly cooked smells, nothing like that stuff that wafts over to me brazier.'

'No, and tastes like nothing yer imagine . . . Look, Bett, yer know that restaurants are opening and doing well selling curry. Why not you? Yer'll be the first to do it from an outside outlet.'

Bett took a small bit of the curry on her spoon and gingerly took it to her mouth. Ruth wanted to laugh out loud at her expression – it was as if she thought it might suddenly jump out of the dish and bite her.

'Mmm, yer right, Robbie, that tastes good.' She took another spoonful. 'Bleedin' hell, it gets better, what does Rebekah put in it? She could make a fortune.'

After another spoonful, she said, 'But how will it work? I can't plonk a ladle of this into a cutting of newspaper.'

Robbie explained as Bett put spoonful after spoonful into her mouth.

'Right, that sounds as though it would work . . . Now, I'll tell yer what I'll do. I'll take yer offer, but if I do well, then Rebekah and Ruth will have a cut of the profits. What your share will be Ruth, I've yet to work out. But I'll take roughly what I want first then share the rest. I can see this working, I really can.'

On the way home, Ruth and Robbie held hands and skipped with joy, Robbie going a lot further as always and twirling her about and dancing around her until she begged, 'Stop it, yer making me look daft, mate.'

'Oh, Ruth, do yer think it daft that I dance?'

'No, of course not. Yer a good dancer, but there's a time and a place. Through the streets in broad daylight ain't either.'

'But I don't care where I am, when I get the urge to dance, I dance.'

'Ha, in the workshop, even?'

Robbie became serious, 'No, not there. They make enough fun of me as it is.'

'You never said, mate, aren't yer happy there?'

'I'm all right, but it don't feel the right sort of thing for me. Ruth, would yer think me daft if I said that I dream of being on the stage?'

This didn't surprise Ruth and she said so, adding, 'But how do the likes of us ever get to do such a thing?'

'Well, I was thinking about it lately and I thought there

must be lessons yer can take. Them on the stage now in the music halls, they don't just go in off the streets. Anyway, I talked to Ted about it as I used to dance in the evenings sometimes when all the stall-holders had gone and entertain them sleeping on the street. I used to make them laugh, and none of them minded. You said once it wasn't sissy for a boy to dance, Ruth, well, they didn't seem to think so and used to ask me to lighten the evening for them when they had a long cold night to look forward to.'

'It isn't sissy, but what did Ted say?'

'He told me of a couple who take lessons in a church hall and that in their younger days they were known to train many famous dancers and actors. He knew them then and has heard about them since from some of his mates.'

'That sounds wonderful, mate. Yer should . . . well, at least find out how much it costs.'

'I know, it's a farthing a lesson.'

'Is that all? We could easily spare that and yer deserve it, Robbie, yer the only one bringing money in at the moment.'

'Would yer come with me, Ruth?'

There was nothing Ruth could think better to do than to go with him. To learn to dance properly sounded such a nice thing to do, and she had to admit to herself that since meeting Robbie and Rebekah and the times that they danced, she'd imagined herself on the stage. But there was so much going on at the moment.

'I'll think about it, but I'm going to be so busy from now on and I can't let Rebekah work all day on the stall with me and then go out in the evening leaving her to it. But you do it for sure, mate, Yer've got to.'

*

It was a couple of nights later when Robbie was in the back-yard working on finishing the stall he was making for them that he told her he'd found the hall and had booked in for a lesson.

'I told them about you, and they said, for the first lesson they'd only charge for one of us so they could assess us. The man said he so rarely got a youngster like me wanting to learn to dance that it was worth it to him if you gave me the confidence to do it, and yer do, Ruth. I feel like I can do anything when yer with me.'

Ruth felt herself blush. 'All right, as long as we see that Rebekah don't mind.'

'She was the one to encourage me, so I don't think she will . . . So, you'll come? You'll really come?'

Ruth latched onto his excitement. 'Yes, I will! I really, really will!'

'Oh, Ruth, I could dance right now.'

'Not with all this wood about, you silly sod.'

'You swore! Ruth Faith, yer swore! You wait till I tell the preacher on Sunday.'

Ruth skipped away from him, laughing as she went. She didn't think 'sod' was swearing, Bett said it all the time.

Sunday couldn't come quick enough for Ruth and when it did, she was up with the lark. Only one day till they went to market, and today she would give Hettie her bonnet, but before church, she needed to sew one last decoration onto a hat. This one was black, which Ruth hadn't really liked making, but when she'd tried it on herself, Rebekah had said she should keep it as it so suited her.

On the side she was to sew a small piece of black beading that Rebekah had made. She'd simply threaded the beads, all black and shiny like some of the coals for the fire were, and wound them into a flat, round circle. She said she thought it should be kept plain and elegant.

This done, Ruth turned to the project that seemed to be going on and on – the ruby red with the wide brim. At last, she felt pleased with it, and loved how she achieved turning one side of the brim up in a lovely curve with no dents in it. That hat, to Ruth, was elegance, and she wondered what Rebekah would think of it. Not that she was ready to share it yet. She wanted to keep going back to it, as it had to be perfect.

A noise in the yard caught her attention, but as her bedroom overlooked the street, Ruth had to go to the window on the landing to see what had caused it. She was surprised to see Robbie hard at work sawing away, as she knew he'd finished the stall and it was ready to be assembled. Bett was sorting something out to help them to transport it to the market.

Curious, she ran down the stairs into the yard.

Sawdust flew everywhere. Wafting it away, she could see that there were parts of what looked like a stool.

Robbie had beads of sweat dripping down his face when he looked up. He wiped his brow with his sleeve. 'It's for Rebekah. I've been thinking how it will be a long day for her to stand. But it ain't easy with not having the right tools. I've had to make the seat square as there's a proper cutter for making round ones, but boring the holes for the legs, which again have to be square as I couldn't get hold of spindles, is a lot harder when you've only got a saw and a chisel.'

'That's so kind, mate. I was worrying about that too.'

'Yer've not forgotten that it's after yer first day on the market that yer've to come to the dancing lesson with me, have yer?'

'I haven't but I wished it was another evening. I think Rebekah might need us, and it'll feel like abandoning her.'

'I told yer, she's fine with it.'

'Anyway, are yer coming to church, yer'd better get yerself hurrying if yer are.'

'I wouldn't miss it. I love the singing, and how they all clap and sway.'

'Oh, yer don't go to talk to God then?'

'Shurrup, yer daft thing.'

'It's not daft. At least, not if yer talk to Holy Mary.'

Robbie answered this with a wide grin. Not wanting to hear him make fun of the Holy Mary, Ruth left him to it.

As soon as they rounded the corner onto the street where the church was, Hettie screamed her name and came charging for her.

'Oh, Ruth, Ruth. I've longed for today.'

The way she said this sounded more like a relief the day was here rather than really longing to see Ruth.

'Are yer all right, mate? Where's Ebony and Horacio?'

Hettie hung her head.

'Hettie?'

'Ebony's hurt bad, Ruth.'

Rebekah gasped. 'What happened to me Ebony!'

'I'm sorry, Rebekah, I couldn't get away till today, but it happened on Friday . . . Cook . . . She hit Ebony with her rolling pin.'

'Oh God, Hettie!' Ruth's heart dropped. 'What did Ebony do to deserve that? How bad is she?'

Hettie looked down at the floor once more, 'Badly. She was unconscious. They sent her to the hospital.'

'And Cook? Is she still there?'

197

'No . . . I'm Cook now, Ruth – well, I'm on trial due to me age – but I can't stay now. I've to go straight back as I've lunch to see to and then dinner tonight. Only Abdi and Housekeeper got me a concession to come out to tell yer, Rebekah. He said to ask you, Ruth, to take Rebekah to the hospital and see Ebony, she's in the Bethnal Green Infirmary. The family made sure she went to the best, not to any work-house hospital.'

'Were you there, Hettie? Did yer give Cook what for?'

'I – I . . . it all happened so quick, mate. I couldn't do anything.'

'No one's blaming yer, Hettie, are they Ruth?' Robbie stepping in like this made Ruth realize that her questions seemed like an accusation. She hung her head, feeling worse as she listened to Hettie continue.

'Ta, Robbie. I do feel responsible, but I couldn't help her. Ebony just snapped. That Aggie said something, and Ebony just stood there and screamed at her to shut her mouth. Then Cook told Ebony to watch herself as she'd be out on her ear, and Ebony turned on her, telling her that she'd prefer to be on the streets than to work with animals. Cook just picked up her rolling pin and swung it. We all screamed, but it was too late, the blow struck, and Ebony went down. It was awful, Ruth . . . I can't get the picture out of me mind . . . the blood! Oh, Ruth.'

Hettie's body shook with sobs. Ruth gathered her to her. 'I'm sorry, luv, I was just shocked, I didn't mean that yer should have, or could have, done something. But poor Ebony.'

'Rebekah wants to go to her now, Ruth, please take me.'

'Yes, Rebekah, we will, luv.'

'I'll get one of them cabs to take us. We've got our church offerings – that should be enough.'

'Ta, Robbie, yes, I've got some money in me purse.' Rebekah's voice shook as she asked, 'Hettie, will me Abdi go to the hospital?'

Hettie looked from Rebekah to Ruth as if she needed help. 'No. He . . . he, he broke his heart in the yard with me, but he said he's afraid for his job. The bloke who is the under butler, is working against him. Abdi said that he keeps wrong-footing him and putting himself in a good light. That after all his years of service, Mr Peterson had a word with him in his office and asked if there was a reason that he was slipping in his standard of carrying out his duties. He was mortified and feels that he should stay there.'

Rebekah huffed. But Ruth partly understood, as she knew how difficult it would be for Abdi to get a job if he lost that one, and then how would he take care of his family?

Then another thought occurred. 'Hettie, what about Horacio? Poor little chap, how will he cope?'

'I haven't seen him since. Abdi said he was in the nursery and didn't want to come out as he was afraid that Cook would hurt him. Abdi is trying to help him. He told him that I was now Cook, but he said Horacio is frightened of all cooks. He has slept in Abdi's bed for the last two nights. But all the staff are against them, Ruth. I hear things, and it's horrible. They all hate a Black man lording it over them. But I'll change things as Cook.'

'I'm glad for yer, Hettie, though I know yer wouldn't have wanted to get the job like this, mate. But now yer have it, Ebony wouldn't want yer to lose it on her behalf, so tread carefully till yer see how it goes. Oh, the cab's here now, I'll come by the back gate later, luv, and let yer know how Ebony is so yer can tell Abdi.'

'Ta, Ruth. I'll see yer then, mate.'

'Oh, Hettie, I nearly forgot. Your bonnet, luv. Hope yer like it.'

Hettie beamed. 'I know I will, luv.' Then she put her arms out and hugged Ruth. Her whispered 'I'm sorry, Ruth' worried Ruth a little. Why did Hettie feel the need to say sorry, when they'd all acknowledged it wasn't her fault?

As they all stood around Ebony's bed, having been let in by a kindly nurse, who said she couldn't give them long as the ward sister was only on a tea break and would have her guts for garters if she came back and found visitors when it wasn't visiting time. 'But the poor soul hasn't had anyone come since Friday. When she wakes she asks for Horacio and Abdi, but we're not sure who they are.'

'They be her man and her son, but her man is a slave, and not free to come to bring her child.'

'A slave! I didn't know there were any slaves in England, missus.'

'No, not many do know, but it goes on, you believe me.'

'Well, I'm sorry, it shouldn't. Mind yer, I feel like one working here. If it weren't for being me calling . . . but as it is, I can't qualify as I ain't got the money. I can only work as an orderly.'

Ruth thought this strange, but didn't pursue it, she wanted to talk to Ebony.

'Ebony, luv, we're here. Me, Rebekah and Robbie. Wake up, luv.'

Ebony's eyes flickered open. Tears flowed down her cheeks. Her whispered 'Horacio?' was hardly discernible.

'No, we haven't brought Horacio, but Ebony, Rebekah's going to take care of you, honey child, you ain't never going to be treated like this again.'

Rebekah bent and kissed Ebony's cheek. 'You going to get well, girl. And then, you and Horacio, you going to come and live with me.'

Ruth felt a warmth go through her. This is how it should be. And she so wanted little Horacio with her, and Ebony too. She wouldn't let anything happen to them ever again.

'Abdi?'

Rebekah huffed. So, Ruth leaned forward. 'He's trying to save his job, Ebony, so that he can care for you and Horacio.'

'No. I want Abdi.'

Ruth was at a loss. But Rebekah spoke soothingly to Ebony, 'We'll work something out, honey child.'

'I want to come with you.'

'We'll get you out of here as soon as we can, but you're going to have to stay, girl, until the doctor say you're all well.'

'Get Horacio out of there, please.'

Ruth determined that she'd do just that. She didn't know how, but she would.

'We'll come back later when it's the proper visiting time, honey child, you're going to have to rest till then.'

'I'm going to the house, Ebony. I'll get a message to Abdi and see what he says about Horacio coming to us.'

Ebony smiled and nodded.

Ruth touched her hand. 'Get well, Ebony. Make sure yer get well, luv.'

As they walked outside, Robbie kicked a stone. 'Why ain't the cops doing anything? It ain't right.'

'It's one rule for Blacks and another for Whites, boy, you should know that. Now, Rebekah is going to take the cab back home. I'm very tired. But you go up to the house, and then come and let Rebekah know what Abdi says . . . I don't know where I'm going to put them all, but we'll figure something out.'

'Yer know, Ruth, it should be us that sorts something out, for ourselves,' Robbie told her. 'Rebekah's house is the rightful place for Ebony and her husband and child.'

'Abdi won't come, Robbie. He's lovely, but he likes the authority he has there – all have to look up to him and he won't get that anywhere else. Ebony can sleep with me, there's room for another bed if we shift the stock to the attic room, and Horacio is fine with you. He loved it up there last time.'

They walked in silence, and Ruth wondered if there would always be troubles for them to face. Sometimes she felt a lot older than her years and as if so many depended on her. Rebekah did. She did a lot and was the talent behind all Ruth did, but she couldn't do the work. That had to be Ruth. And Robbie, he did, though he'd never admit it, but would he go to the dancing lessons without her? She didn't think so. Hettie did in her way, though now she seemed settled for life if she made a good job of being cook at the house. And now it seemed Ebony and Horacio might.

So many times, she'd wished she had a mum. Right now, she yearned for one.

Chapter Eighteen

Hettie let them in the gate. 'Abdi knows yer coming and I've only to tell him yer here, luv. How's Ebony?'

They quickly told Hettie how they'd found Ebony to be, and then after a quick hug she disappeared back inside and Abdi came out looking as regal as ever but once the door was closed behind him the anguish any husband would feel showed on his face. 'How is my Ebony?'

Ruth told him, and also what Ebony wanted to happen now.

He leaned against the wall, held his lip with his forefinger and his thumb and shook his head.

'Please, Abdi, we'll take care of them both and no one will hurt them. Yer know that Horacio gets bullied – well, why should he?'

'Ebony should come back when she's well. She should do her husband's bidding. Things have changed. Cook has left so there is nothing for her to be afraid of.'

'But Aggie's still there and she used to shove Ebony if she met her on the stairs.'

'You know a lot for the short time you were with us, Ruth.'

'I do, I saw a lot and . . . Well, Ebony told me things at church on a Sunday.'

'Hmmm, that not good to talk about your master's house.'

Robbie, who hadn't spoken till now, exclaimed, 'Blimey . . . unbelievable,' in a voice that showed his disgust.

'What did you say, young man?'

'This is Robbie, me mate. He didn't mean anything.'

'I did. You're a prince, you shouldn't call anyone "master".'

To Ruth's relief, Abdi said, 'Perhaps you're right.'

'I didn't mean to be rude, but me mate, Reg, he says if a man loses his self-respect, even if he's reached rock bottom, then he ain't a man anymore. And he was a captain in the army.'

'Oh? Your reference, Ruth?'

'Yes, but he's a decent man. He's been through wars and things and now can't help but have a drink.'

'But he ain't lost his self-respect, Abdi.'

'No, I'm sure he hasn't, Robbie. Well, you've given me a lot to think about. When can you go to see my Ebony again?'

'We're going later, when it's proper visiting time.'

'Tell her that I agree. And tell her that I will change things.'

'You mean, she and Horacio can come to live with us?'

'Yes, Ruth.'

'Can we take Horacio with us now?'

'Oh . . . I – I, well, yes. I can tell my mas . . . Mr Peterson that I have made the decision.'

'Why, would he object, then?'

'Yes, Robbie.'

This worried Ruth. 'Can he stop Horacio from coming with us?'

'He wouldn't want any of us to go and may put obstacles in my way, but it will have happened by the time I tell him. I'll go now and fetch him. I have an hour off duty so I'll tell the housekeeper that I'm taking him to the park.'

Ruth didn't think this had ever happened before. 'What about his things?'

'I'll bring him some clothes down with me, and then have the rest sent over to you once I've told Mr Peterson. I'll see you at the park in a few minutes.'

Hettie popped out of the kitchen as they got to the gate. 'Ruth, luv.' She ran forward and grabbed Ruth in a big hug. 'Yer will come to see me, won't yer? Only I can't get out to church as that's the busiest time.'

'I'll come on a Sunday after church and see yer in this yard, is that all right?'

'Yes, mate. Housekeeper said that this time she's going to get help in the kitchen, so I'll arrange it that I can come to the park for a bit with yer while me assistant gets on with things here. But what is upsetting me is that I can't get to see Cook at the home.'

'She told us to call her Flo. We were going to go there after church, but it will have to be another time now. I don't know when, but we'll let her know how you're fixed, luv, and take messages to her for yer.'

'I could take a message to her after work one night and tell her how things are, if yer like.'

'Ta, Robbie. Wait a minute, though, Ruth . . . oh, Ruth. Cook, I mean, Flo, would be perfect for this job here with me. We could work it between us . . . Robbie, how soon could yer go and see her, mate?'

'Tuesday night.'

'Right, I won't be a minute.'

Hettie ran back inside.

Ruth wanted to call her back as concern at the situation hit her. 'Oh dear, Robbie, I don't know about this. If Flo's taken on, she'll have to work under Hettie, or, worse, might be given the main job and poor Hettie would have her dream taken from her!'

'Well, I think it's a great idea, mate. Flo ain't happy at the orphanage and she'd be really happy here with Hettie. I'm sure they'll work it out between them.'

With this logic, Ruth felt better and the idea began to appeal to her. 'You're right, I worried there for a mo, but yes, it could be the best thing ever. And the sooner the better. Look, if I take Horacio back, would yer go to the home now? We promised Flo some chocolate and she'll be looking forward to it.'

'All right. I can do that and let's hope I have a good message to take to her, eh?'

Hettie came out at the same time as Abdi and Horacio. For a few moments Horacio took all the attention as he ran at them and hugged them both. He didn't speak and Ruth could see he was near to tears.

'We're going to the park, son. Poppa wants to be with you before you leave, come along.'

'I'll be over in a minute, Horacio. Go and enjoy time with yer poppa.'

Abdi looked a bit put out and Ruth could have bitten her tongue as it had sounded as if she was taking over. But Hettie took her attention. 'Housekeeper says that Cook . . . I mean Flo, sounds just what they need. She said an older woman would feel right in the kitchen. That we'd both be joint cooks. Oh, Ruth, I can't believe it.'

Ruth felt herself grinning. Most of what was broken with Hettie telling her the awful news this morning seemed to be mending bit by bit, and with the added chance for Flo to have a better life.

'I'll go now, Hettie. I'm going to the home, so what am I to tell Flo?'

'Ta, Robbie, tell her she's to come to see the housekeeper here tomorrow afternoon. Tell her to come no matter what. That Housekeeper understands that she'll have to work her notice, but she needs to interview her, and she will need references.'

'Sounds like we might have to get Bett to tell her boys to give another warning to Matron 'cos she ain't going to like this.'

'Whatever it takes, Robbie, but please do all yer can to persuade Flo. Oh dear, it don't feel like I'm talking about me lovely Cook calling her that, she never ever told me her real name.'

Ruth didn't know what to say to this, she just hugged Hettie. 'It'll happen. Oh, Hettie, yer'll have yer mate back with yer and I'll feel so much better, luv, with me not being able to get to see yer often.'

'Well, if Cook comes, I can come to church, mate, and nothing need change.'

'Flo!' Ruth laughed. Suddenly it really did seem that all the problems that had reared up were being sorted as they left Hettie with a beaming smile on her face.

As they got to the gate she called out, 'Give me luv to Ebony. And, Ruth. I love yer, mate.'

In the park Horacio once more ran at her and clung to her waist. Still, he hadn't spoken much, and this wasn't like him at all.

'Where's Robbie, Ruth?'

Ruth told Abdi what was happening.

'Well, that's good and I'm pleased for Hettie. The kitchen needs two to work and it has always been in the plan but that woman, whose name I will never speak again, only had herself to blame for having to work with scant help as she upset anyone who was employed as assistant cook and caused them to walk out.'

Abdi reached into an inside pocket. 'Please give this note to my Ebony for me. And this one, give to Rebekah. Don't lose that one whatever you do as all my savings are inside it.'

Ruth took the envelopes. The one for Rebekah was bigger and very bulky.

'I have a plan, Ruth, which will enable me and my family to be together. I've had it for a long time and have saved almost every bit of my salary towards it. Ebony doesn't know of it, but I have outlined it in there for Rebekah. Only, there is an evil man working in the house. I am afraid he may steal it, as he is trying to steal my job.'

Ruth felt a weight lift off her shoulders; she smiled up at Abdi.

'Ruth, you have brought something different into our lives. Now I am looking forward to making changes in my family's situation.'

'There are a lot of folk like me. There's Bett, a friend of mine. She's helping Rebekah to get a market stall.'

'A what?'

'Hasn't Ebony told yer?'

'She said you were making hats and hoped to sell them . . . but Rebekah . . . a market trader? Is it possible?'

'It is.' Ruth had the feeling that living and working in the same house and hardly ever leaving it, had left Abdi with no idea what it was like in the world outside.

She told him all about Rebekah's plans. He couldn't understand why Ebony hadn't said, but Ruth had an idea why. Abdi had strong ideas of his and Ebony's standing in life. He accepted what he thought he had to. Ebony was probably waiting for it to be a reality before telling him as he would have laughed at the idea as being impossible.

Looking mystified, he called Horacio to him. 'Give Poppa a hug to last him till he sees you again, son, and be happy with Ruth and Momma when she comes to you from hospital.' He went down on his haunches. 'Poppa promises you, Horacio, that everything is going to change. Me, you and Momma will live together away from here, but Poppa has a lot to put into place before that can happen. Be a good boy until then.'

Horacio flung his arms around Abdi's neck and began to cry huge sobs that tore at Ruth. She gently took his arm. 'Come on, luv. I'm going to take you to see your momma and then yer can sleep in Robbie's bedroom and he'll take yer to play football.'

'Will he take me to the Hammers?'

Ruth smiled. The Hammers referred to West Ham Football Team, who Robbie adored, and he was always saying that one day he'd go to the ground to watch. She nodded her head. 'He promised he would, and Robbie always keeps his promises.'

Abdi gave her a huge grin. 'I think my son is going to see life at last, but take care of him, Ruth. Remember, he won't be seen in the same way as you are. There are those who would hurt him.'

'I'll take care of him, I promise, and if anyone hurts him, they'll have me to contend with, mate . . . Oh, I mean . . .'

'Ha, mate will do fine. It makes me feel that I belong, after feeling like an outsider all my life. Right, I'll have to go. See ya, mate.'

Ruth laughed out loud, and whether it was because she did or whether he really had seen the joke, Ruth didn't know, but Horacio laughed out loud with her.

When they got home, they found Rebekah lying on her bed fast asleep. For a moment, Ruth felt afraid as she gazed at her. Her cheekbones seemed to jut out and her eyes sat deep into their sockets. She didn't know how old Rebekah was but at this moment she looked very, very old and frail and for the first time Ruth noticed that she'd lost weight too.

She put her finger to her lips and whispered, 'Let's not wake her. Let's take your things up to my room, eh?'

'Will my momma and Aunty Rebekah die, Ruth?'

They were sat on the bed. Ruth had opened Horacio's little case and was pondering where she would put everything that was packed tightly inside it.

Spotting a rag doll with a lovely smiling face and knowing that Ebony had made it, she took it out and handed it to him. 'No. Your momma's going to get better and come to live here with you. And Rebekah is only resting. Cuddle your doll and you will feel the love your momma has stitched into it for yer.'

'Momma told me that. She said that every stitch had her love in it and when I'm not with her, I am to hold it and then I am holding her.'

'There you go, then. Nothing can happen to her while you are holding it, can it?'

Horacio smiled. The smile seemed to open him up as he became the lovely little question-a-second boy she knew.

'Where will I go to school? Will Poppa come to see me? Will I make friends in the street?' And on and on till Ruth felt weary of it.

'Look, young man, everything will happen when it happens. We'll find yer a school and I'm sure the boys in the street will love yer, and you heard your poppa. He is arranging something so that one day soon you will all be together.'

Throughout these questions and many more, Ruth gleaned the anxiety Horacio was feeling and understood it. How often she'd been plagued by uncertainty and fear.

'Look, as I'm all cramped in here, we'll take your case up to yours and Robbie's room and you can be the suitcase boy, living out of your case, eh?'

'A suitcase boy!' Horacio giggled and chanted the phrase, 'I'm a suitcase boy,' as he climbed the stairs two at a time.

By the time Robbie came in, Ruth had made a cup of tea and was about to wake Rebekah to see if she wanted to go to the hospital with them. Horacio sat quietly drawing with some charcoal that had been wrapped up in paper in his case.

Putting her finger to her lips she beckoned Robbie to go outside with her.

'So? What did Flo say?'

'She couldn't believe it, she was over the moon, but she did say it might be a few weeks before they'd release her and that getting to see the housekeeper might be very difficult for her.'

'Oh dear, I don't think she would be taken on without seeing the housekeeper. There must be a way! Did she say she'd try?'

'Yes, she said she'd have to pull some trick or other, but she didn't know what as she daren't tell Matron the real reason, or she'd never release her. But why are we outside here? Is Rebekah all right?'

'She's sleeping. I've made a cuppa, so we'll wake her now. Horacio may take a bit of settling in so tread careful with him, mate.'

211

By the time the tea was poured, Rebekah stirred. Horacio went up to her. 'I'm here, Aunty Rebekah. I'm going to live here with my momma.'

Rebekah rubbed her eyes and then peered at him before she gave him a lovely big smile. 'Then this is the best day that Rebekah did have, boy. Get up on me bed and let me have a cuddle.'

Horacio giggled as he did as she bid.

'Here yer go, Rebekah, tea. Now, be careful Horacio, don't make Rebekah spill it, mate.'

'I won't, I promise.' He spotted Robbie then and forgot his promise as he jumped off the bed. Rebekah raised her eyebrows as she juggled with the wobbly cup.

'Ha, he's going to be a handful, Rebekah, but a lovely one.'

'He is that, honey child.'

'How're yer feeling, luv?'

'Ole Rebekah's just tired with all that's happened. It knocked me off me legs to think of me lovely Ebony hurt.'

'I know, it was a shock. Here, I've got something from Abdi for yer, luv.'

'My, that's a thick envelope. Did Abdi write me a book?'

Ruth smiled. 'He said there's money inside and a note explaining everything.'

Rebekah frowned, then shoved it under her pillow. 'Rebekah's gonna save that for later.'

'What about visiting Ebony? Are yer up to it?'

'No. I'm better staying here. You give me Ebony me love and tell her ole Rebekah will be waiting for her, so hurry up and get well and come home.'

'I'll stay, Ruth. You take Horacio. I can get tea ready with instruction from Rebekah.'

'You, cook?!'

'Yes, men are chefs, and anyway, yer always saying it's all right for me to do what girls do.'

'I know, yer just surprised me, that's all, mate. Course it is.'

Robbie and Rebekah waved them off as, holding Horacio's hand, Ruth walked down the road. The street was deserted, which was usual on a Sunday afternoon. Most kept this day as a family day and rarely did you see children out playing so as not to disturb the peace of the neighbours.

As they reached the market square, Horacio spotted the horse-drawn cabs and jumped up and down with excitement. 'I've never been in a cab, Ruth. Are we really going to have a ride in one?'

'Yes, luv, we are. Come on.'

Seeing things through Horacio's eyes always gave Ruth such a different view of what had become familiar to her. He took such joy in passing parks, seeing a flock of pigeons taking to the air as the noise of the wheels of the cab disturbed them, a dog chasing a cat, and even the pictures the clouds in the sky made.

'Here yer are, luv. That'll be twopence halfpenny, and cheap at half the price. Let me help yer down.'

Ruth took the cab driver's hand as she alighted, but Horacio jumped into his arms. 'So, who's he then, mate, a son of one of them tea merchants? He's dressed in some fancy clothes. You'll be his nanny, no doubt?'

Not wanting to explain, Ruth just nodded, but she did wonder why he even speculated, though felt pleased he'd taken her as old enough to be a nanny.

Once they were inside the hospital the receptionist queried her bringing a child. 'Have yer permission from the ward sister, luv?'

'I didn't know I needed it. His mother's in here, she was attacked, and he really needs to see her. I've no one I can leave him with.'

'Well, on your head be it, mate.'

Luck was on Ruth's side when she stepped inside the ward as the same nursing orderly she'd seen earlier was on duty and seemed to have been left in charge of visitors.

She shook her head as Ruth approached. 'Kids ain't allowed, luv.'

'Please, mate, just for a minute. It'll help Ebony to see him and put her son's mind at rest.'

'Well, don't stay long. If Sister returns, then I'll be for it.'

Ebony was sat up against her pillows. She gave a little cry when she caught sight of Horacio.

'Momma!'

Once on the bed he asked, 'Why are your eyes sticking, Momma? And they're all red.' His lip quivered and his look was one of fear as he glanced at Ruth.

'Momma's all right, little one. Me eyes will soon look normal.'

Horacio snuggled into her. Ruth wasn't convinced he believed her.

Stroking his hair, Ebony asked of Ruth, 'Did you see Abdi, then?'

'I did, luv, he sent yer a note. He said not to worry about anything. Here it is, but I can't stay long, Ebony. How are yer?'

'I'm better, much better, girl. I still have a headache, but the doctors say no real damage has been done. I feel a bit shaky, but then Cook did nearly knock me brains out.'

'She's a bully and ought to have the cops after her.'

'That ain't going to happen, girl. Besides, a bit of me's

glad she did it – I couldn't stand it there no longer, nor did I want me Horacio to. Abdi did wrong in keeping us there. I ain't pleased with him.'

'Well, I think Abdi has plans to change things for yer, luv.'

'Poppa said it won't be long before we are all together again, Momma.'

Ebony smiled and hugged Horacio to her. 'That there's good news. And when Poppa says something, then it will happen. Be a good boy for Ruth and Aunty Rebekah, child.'

As they went to leave, Ebony caught hold of Ruth's hand. 'Ta for everything, Ruth.'

Ruth bent and kissed her cheek. 'It's me who is the one to be grateful. You and Rebekah have done so much for me. Now, just get well, Ebony, luv.'

Once outside, Ruth took a deep breath. Tomorrow was a big day – their first running the market stall. A few days ago, this would have been the most wonderful thought, but now, some of the shine had gone from her dream as she worried about those she loved. But there was hope for Ebony, Abdi and Horacio and she would take care of Rebekah. Robbie had his dancing classes to look forward to, so everything wasn't so bad.

With these things settled in her mind, Ruth took another deep breath. Despite everything she had to remember, it was her first step to a better future.

Chapter Nineteen

Ruth felt a mixture of excitement and nerves as she and Robbie set out just after four a.m. the next morning with the parts of their stall balanced on the four-wheeled handcart that Bett had borrowed for them.

The precarious pile threatened to come off more than once as they journeyed over cobbled stones.

When they arrived, a cheer went up as Reg and Ted stood waiting to give Robbie a hand. Mick the Irish had volunteered to go back with Ruth to help her to load the cart with her stock.

Ruth knew they would do all this for her out of the kindness of their hearts, but she planned on giving Reg enough to buy them all a jug of ale and a hot spud.

The final journey to collect Rebekah, Horacio and the huge pot of curry, Robbie would do before setting off to work.

Mick was adept with the cart and kept her entertained with his tales of his childhood in Ireland when he used to push a cart through the streets selling his father's produce. 'It is that me father had a farm in those days, but to be sure, the beer and the women were his downfall.'

Ruth felt sad that Mick had suffered a similar fate of having nothing due to his love of the drink, though she didn't know if he had a fancy for the women or not. How often she wished there was something she could do for all those on the streets. The one night she slept rough had told her how bad it was, and she hoped it would never happen to her again.

But all thoughts of this disappeared as the Bethnal community spirit that Ruth had experienced in the past came to the fore on their return and all the stall-holders chipped in to help.

In no time the structure was up, dressed and being admired.

As Ruth blew the steam from the tea Bett had given her, she told Bett, 'I never thought this day would come. Me first day of me dream.'

'Well, yer only have to work hard to achieve it now, luv. I can see yer now, boss of yer own store with departments for hats, frocks and accessories.'

The idea zinged through Ruth, giving her hope. She would make it happen, she would.

'Here they come mate, ha, Robbie looks knackered. Awe, look at the little one, is this the lad yer were telling us about?'

Horacio jumped down. His face changed from a huge beam to shyness as he looked around at the motley crew: Bett with her hair caught up in a scarf, wearing a long overall tied with string, Mick looking scruffier than usual with a flat cap pulled down on his head, Ted with his jacket tied with a piece of rope and string tying his trousers to his ankles, and Reg looking smart in his worn-out, fraying suit and neckerchief.

Seeing the fear in Horacio, Reg said, 'Now then, young man, I am the captain, and this is my army. Would you like to be one of me soldiers?'

Horacio nodded.

'Well, stand smart then, shoulders back and march with me.' Stamping his feet Reg turned towards the others. 'Fall in men, and you, Ted, play a marching tune. Let's get the morning drill under way.'

Staring out of his huge eyes, Horacio nodded and joined Reg.

'Now, same foot forward as the captain. Quick march!'

Ruth fell about laughing as everyone watching did.

'Never will yer see an army like that one, anywhere, Ruth.' Bett clapped her hands before turning to Rebekah. 'Close yer mouth, Rebekah, love, yer'll catch all the flies and me spuds'll go without. They taste better after a few flies land on them.'

This increased the laughter and Ruth was glad to see Horacio had a big smile on his face too.

'Well, I've got to go. I wish yer luck, Ruth. And you, Rebekah. Make a fortune,' Robbie told them.

As they waved Robbie off to work, the market women swarmed Ruth and Rebekah's stall, oohing and ahhing at what they had on display. Whether it was to help them or genuine interest, Ruth didn't know, but she sold two bonnets and took two orders for different colours to those she had in stock. And as if she was an expert hatter, she soon had them measured and wrote the details of what they wanted in her little book.

'No cold lugs for me this winter, Bett,' Ethel from the jewellery stall said as she adjusted the bonnet she'd bought. 'This is lovely, girl, even though yer gave first bleedin' choice to Bett. I tell yer, mate, I'd have had that one. Blue suits me.'

'Well, when yer the matriarch, yer'll be a bit luckier, won't yer, but I ain't being kicked off me seat yet, Ethel, mate, so yer can put that in yer bloomin' pipe and smoke it.'

Everyone laughed, including Ethel.

'Well, I'm more than pleased with mine.' Rosie, who had the ribbon stall, did a twirl.

'Ha, I'm surprised Ruth was able to make one big enough to fit your head, Rosie girl!'

Rosie spun round. 'Well, Ethel, it seems she did, and I think your Hector'll fancy me in it, he fancies every bleeder else.'

Ethel's face went purple, she went to go for Rosie, but Bett stepped in.

'Now, now, Rosie that weren't called for. No one's going to fancy anyone, in or out of a hat. Let's get on with the day's work, shall we?'

'Well, she always has something to say.'

'I fancy you, Bett, luv. I'll fill yer bag with me spuds for nothing if yer'd give me a kiss!'

'Bert Entwhistle, yer couldn't fill me knickers, let alone me bag with them spuds of yours.'

'I could have a good try, girl.'

The laughter that filled the air made Ruth's spirits soar, even Ruby was joining in and for once had a smile on her face – not that Ruth fully understood all the innuendos, but it somehow boosted her confidence and before she knew what she was doing, she joined in with those who'd begun to call out their wares and yelled, 'Lovely winter bonnets. Keep yer lug'oles warm in winter. All handmade.'

There was a second or two of pause, and then a cheer went up.

'My, girl, yer a natural.' Bett put her head back, 'Come and have a gander, lovely bonnets, scarves and mittens, all exclusive.'

Then, Rebekah, who'd been very quiet sitting on her new

stool, suddenly surprised them all by shouting, 'And we do take orders from yer all, if you can't see the colour you like.'

This pleased Ruth as she still held a niggly worry about Rebekah's health. She just hadn't been the same since she'd heard of what Cook did to Ebony.

Horacio played well on his own, between drifting to one or the other of the stalls and having a chat with the holders. Ruth knew he would be asking all sorts of questions, but none of them seemed to mind and this warmed her heart.

At one stage, she looked up to see him sitting on Rosie's knee helping her to wind ribbon into neat rolls. She didn't think any other child of his age could have done this task, but Horacio always surprised her.

Lunchtime brought a flurry of customers to all the stalls as the workers from the local factories poured into the square.

Ruth was soon surrounded by a group of laughing young women and was having a job to keep tabs on the bonnets as they passed them from hand to hand.

A voice cut across the rest, 'Did you really make all these, girl?'

'I did, and Rebekah here knitted the scarves and mittens.'

The woman looked over at Rebekah. 'Oh?'

The sound was one of disdain.

'Well, I'll take a bonnet, please. A brown one – that one with the butterfly on the side.'

Ruth felt like slapping her face with it. Sensing her feelings, Rebekah tugged at her skirt and smiled up at her. But Ruth's temper had risen. She snapped out, 'That one's a shilling!'

'Only a shilling? You're selling yourself too cheaply. I'll take it. And when I've had a chance to look at the workmanship, and if it is good, I may well be in touch with you. I own

Melinda's Milliner's shop. I may be able to give you some orders. Can you make different hats, or just these cloches?'

Ruth was dumbstruck.

'Yer should see her lovely brimmed ones, lady, only she didn't bring any today, as she's wanting to sell her stock and then will take orders for the posher ones.'

'Oh?' The woman looked round at Bett. 'That's all the better. Here's my card.' She went to hand a card to Bett, but Bett said, 'You give that to Ruth, it's her business, I only spoke up as she was a bit tongue-tied for a moment. It's her first day.'

Ruth took the card and thanked the woman.

'Good. Not saying I will take this further, but we will see.'

As she left the stall one of the girls said, 'Stuck up cow!'

Ruth nodded her head, but that didn't stop her feeling excited about what the woman might bring for the future.

'Rebekah am proud of you, honey child. One day, you will go far.'

'If I do, Rebekah, you will too.' She bent down and kissed Rebekah's cheek.

When the stall had calmed, the girls crowded around Bett.

'Curry, Bett? We ain't seen yer sell curry before.'

'You should try it, girl, it'll put hairs where I doubt yer've got them yet!'

All the girls giggled. But the one who'd asked said, 'I don't know. I ain't tasted it before.'

Bett served up a small plateful and a spoon. The girls dived in and loved it, which made Ruth feel so proud and filled with happiness as they learned who had made it and gave compliments to Rebekah.

A few minutes later, Ruby, who had gone back to her usual grumpy self after having a laugh with them earlier, came over to the stall. Her friendly tone surprised Ruth, 'Well, yer did well, girl. You landed on your feet when you found Rebekah. And I'm pleased for yer. I reckon yer'll bring more trade here as the word gets round. Now, what I want is gloves. Not now, but if yer could knit gloves, Rebekah, that'd suit me better. I need me fingers free to sort me fruit out and to weigh it and I think you'll find a trade for them amongst the other stall-holders, too.'

'Rebekah can knit gloves, Ruby, luv. I just did do mittens and muffs as they the quickest to get us stocked up. Let me see yer hands, girl.'

Ruby held up her puffy, ruddy-looking hands.

'Got it. I'll have some as'll fit like a glove by next week,' Rebekah cackled. Then something happened that stopped a few in their tracks. Ruby laughed out loud – a real belly laugh.

Bett did a double turn. If her stall wasn't so busy, Ruth knew Bett would have something to say, but no one commented as Ruby went back to her pitch.

All quietened in the afternoon, and Horacio, who'd busied himself helping everyone, showed signs of being weary.

His 'I'm hungry, Aunty' came out as a whine.

'Rebekah does have a sandwich here for yer, boy. There, eat that.'

'I've a few sacks here, luv, they'll make a bit of a seat for the boy.'

'Ta, Ruby, Rebekah am grateful.'

As Ruth settled Horacio, she told him, 'You've made me feel hungry now.'

Before Ruth and Rebekah had finished their own sand-wiches, Horacio was curled up in a ball, fast asleep.

'It'll be the fresh air that's knocked him out.'

'That and his busy day, Rebekah. It's a long day for him,

but we can't do anything about it till Ebony comes out of hospital and gets him into a school. He'll just have to come with us.'

It was gone five in the evening when they packed up. Mick the Irish helped them. 'I'll be leaving one side of the cart free for you to be sitting yerself on, Rebekah, and it is that I'll give yer a hand to be pushing the cart home, Ruth.'

With a lot of the hats sold and the boxes that had held them flattened once more, it was easy to make space for Rebekah to sit. Horacio was lively again and so skipped along beside them chattering ten to the dozen.

When they arrived home, Ruth didn't like the look of Rebekah and worried about how tired she was. 'You sit down, Rebekah. Robbie'll soon unload the cart for us when he gets in. Take yer shoes and socks off and I'll get a bowl of hot water for you to soak yer feet in, eh?'

'Ta, honey child.'

As Rebekah lay her head back, fear zinged through Ruth. Rebekah's face had sunk once more, giving her the look of someone very sick. The thought came to Ruth that maybe they wouldn't have her for long. Tears pricked her eyes as she stroked Rebekah's wiry hair. The time they'd been together was so short and yet, to Ruth, Rebekah was like the mother she'd never had, and she loved her with all her heart.

With the kettle and the stew they'd prepared the night before simmering on the hot plate, Ruth filled a bowl with warm water and took it through. Her heart almost stopped at what met her. Rebekah's head and top half of her body had flopped to one side. Horacio kneeled by her knee holding her hand with his head on her lap.

223

'Shush, Ruth, Aunty is sleeping again.'

Spilling water as she put the bowl down in haste, Ruth touched Rebekah's hand. 'Rebekah, luv, wake up!'

Rebekah didn't stir.

Frantic, Ruth ran out into the street. A couple of women she'd only said hello to stood chatting outside the house opposite.

'Can you come, please, I – I think Rebekah's . . .'

Before she could finish the sentence, one of them docked her fag, put the stub end in the pocket of her pinny and came dashing across the road. 'What's up, luv?'

'Rebekah . . . she . . . she's not well!'

'Bleedin' hell, I thought she was as strong as a horse that one, she's never been ill since I've known her. Come on, Joyce, we'd better take a look.'

'I've left me pan on, Gert, I'll be over in a minute, mate.'

'Well, young miss, let's get inside. I know yer name's Ruth and where yer come from, as Robbie told us. We all know Robbie; he's hung about these parts for a good while and is well-liked. It was a surprise when Rebekah took you and him in though . . . So, what's to do?'

Ruth didn't have to answer as Gert spotted Rebekah and went over to her. 'Now then, ole girl, you're not looking yerself.' Gert patted Rebekah's hand. 'Get me some cold water, Ruth, I think she's fainted.'

Horacio's eyes opened like saucers.

'I'd go outside if I were you, boy, there's some kids playing football, go and join in, eh?'

Horacio got as far as the door and looked out but didn't venture out, yet Ruth had no time to worry about him as she went into the kitchen.

Within seconds of Gert sprinkling water onto Rebekah's

224

face she opened her eyes. 'It's Gert, luv. How're yer feeling, eh?'

Rebekah just stared into Gert's face. "Ave a drink of this water, luv, yer mouth looks all dry.'

As Rebekah sipped the water, she gradually became more alert.

'Get her another one, Ruth. I think it's lack of water and in this heat that can make yer faint.'

The more she drank, the more alert Rebekah became. Ruth sighed with relief.

'So, looks like yer've got a bit of a venture going, then? We've seen the comings and goings, but Rebekah doesn't mix much so we let her keep herself to herself. She ain't ever given us any bother.'

Ruth told Gert what they'd been doing.

'Well, that's good, but for Rebekah to be out all day like that ain't good. Were yer in the shade?' Gert nodded her head at all Ruth told her. 'Right, mate. To my mind, yer've a nice set-up, but all that's too much for Rebekah at her age. I daresay she wants to help yer. She's a kind soul. Like I say, she don't mix a lot, but she's made stuff for most in the street.'

Rebekah had never said she'd been lonely, but Ruth wondered now if she had been and that's why she so willingly offered them a home. She'd heard the saying that you could be lonely in a crowd – thinking that this had happened to Rebekah caused a pain to stab at her heart.

'Look, I can see that's hurt yer and I'm sorry. I ain't lived here long, and I understand her grandfather bought this house, so her family have been here longer than most. But I reckon that not knowing her well is as much down to her as it is to us.'

Rebekah put her hand out and took hold of Gert's. Gert patted it. 'Yer all right now, luv. We'll all look out for yer. I'm sorry we ain't been good neighbours but some have the wrong idea about you people and others. Well, anyway, don't bother about them. We just didn't get to know yer. But we all thought kindly of yer and yer've been kindly to us and to these kids, taking them in and giving them a chance. From now on, yer one of us, mate.'

Rebekah smiled, her weakness clear to see.

'Do yer think I should get a doctor to look at her, Gert? I've got some money.'

'Yes, I would if yer can afford it. We all pay a penny insurance to Doctor Price, he's a good man. But do these people like our doctors, don't they do other things to heal themselves?'

Ruth couldn't understand why Gert kept talking about Rebekah as if she wasn't the same as them, but didn't want to get cross and upset her as she liked Gert. She was saved from answering as Rebekah spoke. 'I'm made of flesh and blood, Gert, same as you.'

'Don't fret now, I didn't mean any harm, luv. I'll see yer get a doctor. Young Ronnie across the road'll always run an errand for a farthing, I'll send him.'

Ruth followed Gert to the door. She was surprised to find Horacio gone. She looked up the street and saw him kick a ball to a big lad, who called out, 'He's a good little football player, Gert.'

Gert grinned, then turned back to Ruth. 'I'm sorry, Ruth, I was just ignorant, but things'll change, luv.' With this she shouted back to the boy, 'Come here, Ronnie.'

The boy gave Ruth a cheeky grin as he asked, 'What's up, Gert?'

'I want you to go for the doctor, mate. Tell him a lady

226

named Rebekah at number three ain't well and needs him to come as soon as possible. Tell him she can pay his fees.'

Not sure if Ronnie was going to say he would go, Ruth told him, 'I'll give yer a farthing for going, Ronnie.'

'All right, I'll go. What's yer name then?'

'Ruth. You won't be long, will yer?'

As he doffed his cap and turned to go, Ruth heard Robbie's familiar whistle. Ronnie called out to him as he ran by him. 'I'm getting the doc to your house, mate.'

Robbie started to run towards her, 'What's happened, Ruth?'

'Don't you be worrying about Ole Rebekah, the two of yer. I'm all right.'

This call from Rebekah lifted Ruth as she sounded so much stronger. In a low voice, Ruth told Robbie, 'She had a bad turn.'

Robbie kneeled next to Rebekah. 'Are yer sure yer all right, luv? We don't want anything to happen to yer.'

'I'm a bit better now, boy, but me heart, it's going like a steam engine and making Rebekah feel strange.'

'It'll be all right, Rebekah, don't worry. I bet Gert's arranged to fetch Doctor Price and I've heard that he's really good.'

He looked up at Ruth, the fear in his face matching her own. So much was going through her head, but the loudest was screaming at her that she didn't want to lose Rebekah. She lifted her eyes to heaven, and even though she hadn't prayed for a long time, she fervently asked Holy Mary to make Rebekah well.

When the doctor arrived, Ruth liked him very much. A gentleman with ginger hair and a ginger handlebar moustache, he had a ready smile. After she told him who they all were and that it was Rebekah who needed him, he went over to her. 'So, this is a house I haven't been to before. What seems to be the trouble, dear?'

'I'm thinking Ole Rebekah's heart's playing up, Doctor.'

'Well now, have you been overdoing it?'

Ruth knew a pang of guilt to attack her. She hadn't thought for one moment that the hard work they'd been doing was too much for Rebekah.

'No. Ole Rebekah is strong.'

'Maybe not as strong as you used to be, my dear.' He looked up at Robbie, 'Now young man, can we have some privacy? I need to examine Rebekah, but don't want to move her.'

Robbie blushed. 'Sorry. I'll go outside.'

'Shall I go too, Doctor?'

'No, Rebekah needs a familiar face to help her not to be anxious. You come and help her, Ruth, I need to get my stethoscope onto her chest.'

Ruth hadn't any idea how to unravel Rebekah's frock but she started with the part of the cloth Rebekah swirled around herself that tucked into the under layer, and with Rebekah's guidance, she gradually achieved getting the top half of her just covered by her underslip.

'That's fine. Now, this may be a little cold, Rebekah.'

After a few minutes, the doctor looked into Rebekah's face. His expression held concern. 'Well, my dear, I can detect an uneven rhythm. Now, that means you are going to have to take things easy. Very easy.'

'Will Rebekah get better, Doctor?'

This plea from Rebekah tugged at Ruth's heart.

'Yes, this can settle down, but you have to do as I say and take life easy. Let these young people do anything strenuous.'

He looked around. 'This room looks as though it's a hive of activity, a little factory almost, what have you been up to?'

Ruth told him about their work. 'It's my fault, Doctor, Rebekah's trying to give me a start in life. She's teaching me skills and we've worked very hard to get our market stall going. I make hats and Rebekah, gloves and scarves. It was our first day today.'

'Ahh, I see. Well, no market stall for you, Rebekah. You are on the verge of being very ill, but you can stop that progress by leading a very calm and gentle life. Will you do that?'

Rebekah nodded.

'Well, now, I am going to make a few visits to keep an eye on you, so would you all like to join my insurance scheme? You pay one penny a week for each of you and I treat you whenever you need me. Otherwise, my visits will land you with a bill at the end of the month.'

'Is it going to cost Rebekah a lot for this visit, Doctor?'

'Hmmm . . . It could, or . . . well, I'm intrigued about these hats you say you make. May I see them? Sometimes people pay me in goods, such as jars of jam they've made, or, in the case of one patient, lovely brown beer that she brews. I think my wife would love a new hat.'

Robbie brought a few boxes of hats in at a time. The doctor looked at them all. 'They're lovely and so well made, my dear. How old are you, Ruth?'

'I'm thirteen, Doctor.'

'You're very talented. May I take the green one instead of being paid? My wife has a green coat with a fur collar, and I think that one will match it.'

Before he left, the Doctor had signed them all up to his scheme. He hadn't realized they had a child and had charged half price for Horacio. He counted Ebony in and said he would go up to the hospital to see her.

'We so want her home, Doctor. Horacio is pining for her.'

'Well, I will see what I can do as I can visit her here at the same time as I visit Rebekah.'

As soon as he stepped outside, Horacio came in. 'Are you all right, Aunty?'

'I am, my boy. Sit at me knee again, eh?'

As Horacio kneeled down, both Ruth and Robbie went to Rebekah and sat on the arms of her chair. Ruth felt near to tears as she put an arm around Rebekah's shoulder. 'Oh, Rebekah, I'm sorry. I shouldn't have let you work like yer have.'

'Don't be sorry, honey child. Ole Rebekah had a very proud moment just then. The Doctor loved the work you done.'

'No more going to market, luv. I'll manage. There's always someone about to help me if I need it.'

'What about the cart? It's heavy for one to push, girl.'

'I can help on the way to the market in the morning. And we can get the bowl of curry onto it at the same time. Then, if you load it and leave it in the charge of Reg, I'll come by that way after work and bring it back.'

'Ta, Robbie. I can get home quickly like that.'

A voice interrupted them, 'It's only me!' Gert popped her head around the door. A tall, thin woman, Gert had dark hair rolled up into bun, and small dark eyes.

'Well, how did yer go on, luv? He's nice, ain't he? I saw him leave with one of your hats. Most of us find a bit of something for him. Well, those who can't pay the penny do.'

Ruth told her what the doctor had said.

'So, Rebekah, that's what you've to do, then. Hearts are funny things, and we can't live without them, that's for sure. If I can help in any way, yer've only got to ask.'

'We do need help, Gert. Just to watch over Rebekah in the daytime while we're both at work.'

'Consider it done, Robbie, luv. We cockneys stick together, and you're one of us now, as are Rebekah and Ruth. So, anything yer need, I'll be here for yer.'

The air had cooled by the time Ruth and Robbie sat on the step together. Neither had eaten much of the stew and while Ruth cleared everything away and followed Rebekah's instructions on making the curry for Bett, which was simmering and smelling delicious, Robbie had settled Horacio into bed. 'He went out like a light, poor little kid. He's had a lot to contend with.'

'That's good. Let's hope Ebony gets well soon and comes home. I won't worry so much about Rebekah then, and she can get Horacio into a school.'

The street was alive with folk gossiping and kids playing – who, unlike before, included Ruth and Robbie – and people called out that they were sorry to hear Rebekah was poorly and, if they needed anything, then their door was always open. Ruth began to feel that she belonged here in this street and she hoped she'd never have to leave it.

Chapter Twenty

When all had quietened down, Ruth and Robbie still sat out sipping the cocoa Ruth had made after helping Rebekah to bed.

The light was fading but it was still warm.

'Have yer thought any more about rearranging the dancing lessons, Ruth? I can call round tomorrow and tell them what happened to stop us coming.'

'I ain't, mate, I ain't had a minute to breathe. I'm scared of managing everything on me own and if I'll be able to keep up with having to make all the stock as well.' She told him about the lady who owned a milliner's shop.

'Well, if things change and yer can't manage the stall, maybe she'll give yer a job?'

'I don't know. I love having me own stall – well, mine and Rebekah's. It felt like me dream could really come true, but now, I don't know. It could all go.'

'There'll be a way. And don't forget Ebony coming. She might be a big help to yer. She'll make the curry for one thing. And be here to take care of Rebekah. '

'Yes, she'll be a godsend now.'

'And another solution could be that yer stand market on three days a week and work making your stock and filling your orders on the other days.'

'That would work! Bett only wants the curry twice a week, so it wouldn't be too much for Ebony. And Bett was saying that Thursday, Friday and Saturday are sometimes the only days that are worth doing.'

'Sorted, then. Now, about the dancing.'

Ruth sighed. 'OK, Robbie. Arrange it. But not until Ebony's here and well enough to leave.'

'That could be weeks. I'll ask Gert. I know she'd look after Rebekah and it's only for a couple of hours.'

'You never give up, I'll say that for yer. All right, if Gert don't mind keeping an eye on Rebekah, then I'll go with yer . . . You know, I think I'll make her a bonnet-type hat for her trouble.'

'That's a good idea. It's how it works around here. What yer can't pay for in money, yer pay for in kind.'

The next day was much slower and seemed to drag. Horacio decided that he would take the money and give out the change. By noon he'd earned a halfpenny in tips and was glowing. But as trade slowed to nothing, he became a little bored, until Ruth sent him to play in the park, but gave him strict instructions he must stay within her sight.

Just as he ran through the gate, Bett came over to the stall. 'So, luv, yer not going to be able to keep this up are yer? I'm sorry for yer and would help if I could.'

'Me and Robbie talked about this last night.' Ruth told her of Robbie's idea.

'That's all right by me. I can change the arrangement on the stall easily, so that will save yer money. And folk soon get to know what days yer here. Some of the others share their stall doing a couple of days each with their produce and their regulars always turn up to buy.'

'I think for now, it's the best idea for me to reduce the days as I said, rather than find someone to share, but would you do me a favour when I'm not here and keep an eye out for that woman coming, Bett? Her from Melinda's Milliner's?'

'I will, luv, but if I were you, I'd follow that up in a couple of days. Take that brimmed hat to show her, the one yer were telling me about.'

Ruth didn't know if she'd have the courage to, but she didn't say so.

'Anyway, I'll nip into the council later. Bert'll watch me stall and then I can make the arrangements for it to start next week, would that suit yer?'

'Yes, I can manage till then. I'm really hoping I'll have news on Ebony soon as the doctor who came to Rebekah said he'd go to the hospital to see her.'

'I hope so too, luv, or this little chap'll be worn out. He should be in school by rights.'

The news was good when Ruth arrived home. Rebekah looked a lot better and had sat knitting the gloves Ruby wanted.

'Rebekah does feel useful doing something, and it ain't no strain as it be relaxing and takes me mind off things.'

'Ha, she won't lose them in a hurry.' One of the gloves was complete up to the fingers and already had a thumb in it. It was multicoloured stripes and very bright.

'Rebekah thought to bring some colour into Ruby's life, and they'll match her fruit and vegetables.'

'They look as though they are going to be lovely. How yer knit with two pins is beyond me, but four!'

'Rebekah will teach you all me skills, honey child, as long as the good Lord gives me time.'

This hurt Ruth; she wanted Rebekah to have a lot of time – years of it, but before she could say, a knock on the door took their attention.

Doctor Price walked in. 'Sorry to call so late, but I wanted to catch you at home, Ruth. I've been to see Ebony and she is doing well. I have arranged for her to come home in the next couple of days.'

'Ole Rebekah is that pleased to hear that. Ta, Doctor.'

'I'm glad you're pleased. Now, I'll just take a quick look at you while I am here, my dear.'

To Ruth, it was as if the goodness of this man glowed from him as he smiled at Rebekah. And he gave her the feeling that in his hands, everything was going to be all right.

She put her hand out to Horacio. 'Come on, Horacio, let's me and you go into the kitchen and see what we can get for tea, eh?'

When she opened the door to the kitchen a surprise met her. On the side was a lovely pie with a golden crust. A note propped up against it said, *I baked this meat pie for you all, be lovely with some mash and gravy. Love, Gert x*

Ruth swallowed hard. The kindness of folk overwhelmed her.

'That looks nice. I like pie,' Horacio told her.

'Well, you can help me with the spuds to go with it, eh, mate? I'll stand yer on the stool and you can wash the spuds ready for me to peel. Roll yer sleeves up.'

'May I come in?'

Ruth had only just stood Horacio on the stool when the doctor opened the door to the kitchen. 'Well, my dear, it's good news. Rebekah is no worse. Her heart is weak, but she hasn't overdone it and put it into stress, so that's good. Mmm, something smells good.'

Ruth told him about the pie.

'You're in for a treat, I've had a few of Gert's pies. Now, do you think you could go up to the hospital and take some clothes for Ebony? They had to dump most of what she had on as it was covered in blood. The woman who did this should be prosecuted, but Ebony told me that she doesn't want that to happen.'

'I'll get some things to her, Doctor.'

'Good. You've a lot on your plate for a thirteen-year-old, young lady, but you seem more than capable. Rebekah was telling me you and Robbie came from the home?'

Ruth held her breath, worried as to what else Rebekah had said.

'If anything ever worries you . . . I mean, if things change for you, you will let me know, won't you?'

Ruth coloured.

'It's just that young ladies of your age go through a lot of stages. All normal development, but sometimes you need advice. My wife is a nurse and will see you if you need to see her. She oversees all the women's problems and is the local midwife at times.'

Ruth had the feeling that he knew what had happened, but then, if he did, wouldn't he do something about it? Maybe he also knew that it had been taken care of.

'Well, I'll say my goodbyes. I'll pop in as soon as I know Ebony's home.'

Ruth could feel her cheeks burning, and a feeling took her that what happened hadn't gone away and would always come back to haunt her. Her hand shook as she tried to peel the potato Horacio handed to her and for once she was glad of his questions.

*

When Robbie came home with the cart, despite being tired, he said at once that he'd go up to see Abdi about some clothes for Ebony. 'I'll take Horacio. You'd like that, mate, wouldn't yer?'

Horacio showed his pleasure by hugging Robbie.

'Rebekah does have the money for a cab, Robbie. Horacio will be too tired to walk, and you'll have things to carry.'

Ruth didn't know about this helping Horacio but could see Robbie was glad of it.

As they sat eating the delicious pie, Robbie told them how Abdi was going up to the hospital himself tonight. 'He said he'd been waiting to hear from us, but I explained how busy we were and about Rebekah.'

'Poppa said he will make everything how he promised very soon, Aunty Rebekah.'

'That's good, boy. Rebekah thinks you'll be very happy then.' She looked at Ruth and Robbie, 'I haven't told you that Abdi has told me his plans. I can't tell you them as he asked me to keep his confidence. He wants to be the one to tell Ebony, but Rebekah ain't sure how it will work out for him.'

Horacio looked worried.

Robbie had noticed this too and tried to make him feel better by saying, 'I'm sure he'll only do what's right, Rebekah. He strikes me as a careful man.'

'He is, Robbie, he done a lot of years at that house because of how careful he is, but it ain't the same out of them walls, he ain't never had the experiences that I have. He hasn't wanted them and that's what's kept him there when he should have left for Ebony's sake a long time ago.'

Ruth agreed, but didn't say so out loud. She found Abdi a difficult man to fathom. How could he not act when he knew what his wife and son were going through? Surely anything would have been better than that? But if him being out in the wide world was all that was worrying Rebekah, then that was a relief. The great news was that Ebony had left that place and she had hope for the future – they all did, if only they could keep Rebekah well.

Just as Bett had told her, her first day had been a fluke, and had generated her a lot of custom because of her stall being new and creating interest. Yesterday, Wednesday, had been hardly worth coming out for, and made her feel better about Robbie's idea. And yet today, the market was buzzing again. By lunchtime she'd sold two hats and taken orders for three more.

She did have a moment when she felt annoyed that they couldn't just choose from her stock – why did they all want different colours, or different decorations! But she was glad that her little order book now had six hats listed and it was only her third day.

The afternoon died for a while, but Bett told her it picked up again later when women fetched their kids out of school, and the part-timers in the factories finished their shifts.

As they were sipping what seemed to Ruth to be their umpteenth mug of tea and chatting, it occurred to Ruth that she could make better use of the time. 'Bett, I could do with getting off really. I've to pick up Ebony from hospital today, and it would be good if I could do that earlier rather than later.'

'Yes, and little Horacio's had enough. Look, we'll watch yer stall between us and Mick knows how to pack it up. But how do I take any orders for yer, luv?'

'Well, all I do is measure their head around the forehead to the back. Yer could give them the tape measure and ask them to do it. Are yer sure yer wouldn't mind?'

238

'Not at all, luv. We all help each other out as you've seen, and I don't do anything much now till tea-time.'

'If Ebony's all right sitting with Rebekah and watching over Horacio, I'll come back. Ta, Bett. It would really help me. I've got the prices all written down here, and they're easily identified.'

The horse-drawn cab they got to the hospital had an open top. Horacio loved it. He made Ruth giggle by waving to folk as well as noticing things she would have gone by without seeing, as she always did. She hoped that it wouldn't be long before Ebony or Abdi got him into school, though she wondered if he was too clever for a church school as she had never learned the things that he came out with during her schooldays.

As they helped Ebony out of the hospital and into the cab, Ruth worried that she really didn't seem strong enough to come home yet. Her face and eyes were still swollen, and she winced when Ruth helped to get her cardigan on. Why were some people so cruel?

Horacio sat close to Ebony all the way home. Ruth worried about him as he was so quiet. She wondered what was going on in his head. She knew the feeling of being so troubled that you couldn't speak.

Her mind went to Amy and Ellen. Where were they now? Did they still have moments like this, were they happy? She longed to know. Sighing, she turned her attention back to Ebony and saw her shiver.

'Are yer cold, luv? Here, I'll put me cardi over yer knees.'

'Ta, luv, I am cold, but excited and so happy to be going to Aunty Rebekah's.'

'She can't wait for you to arrive. Did Abdi tell yer she's not so well?'

'He did, and me heart's been aching for her. But I will take care of her and make her well.'

'And I will look after you, Momma.'

Ebony looked lovingly at her son as he said this. 'Good boy.'

Wanting to make them laugh, Ruth said, 'And I'll look after the bloomin' lot of yer!'

But Ebony didn't laugh, and Horacio didn't see anything funny. It seemed to Ruth that this wasn't the same Ebony she'd got to know, and that saddened her.

'We made some friends in the street, Ebony, and they will look out for you and Rebekah till you're stronger.'

Ebony flashed a look of fear towards Ruth.

'There's nothing to worry about, they love Rebekah and Horacio and will love you too. One's called Gert and the other's Joyce.'

'They're really nice, Momma. Gert makes lovely pies.'

Ebony didn't respond. It was as if she didn't trust anyone anymore. When she did speak, she said, 'I don't want no neighbours in. I can manage.'

'Oh, Ebony, I can't stop them. They've been so good to us over the last few days since Rebekah took ill. They don't interfere but have been popping in to make sure Rebekah's all right while I'm at the market and Robbie's at work. They make her a mug of tea, and a sandwich at dinner-time.'

Ebony nodded.

Ruth felt at a loss as to how to find the Ebony she knew.

'Momma, Poppa's going to make everything change. He said we will all be together soon like a proper family.'

At last, Ebony smiled. 'He is, son. Then no one can hurt Momma again as I'll have me man by me side protecting me, and me big son too.'

240

Horacio grinned at this. 'But I will have to go to school, Momma.'

'You will. Poppa is looking for a school nearby as soon as he can, my child.'

'I have my rag doll at Aunty Rebekah's and I cuddled it. Did you feel me cuddling you, Momma?'

Again, Ebony smiled. A tight smile as her swollen face didn't move a lot, but it did Ruth good to see it.

'I hope you've been good for Ruth and helped her, Horacio.'

'I have, I counted the money, and washed the spuds. I love Ruth, Momma.'

For the first time Ebony giggled. 'Me and you, both, son. We am lucky to have her in our lives.'

Ruth blushed, but felt relief as more and more of the old Ebony came to the fore.

Everything was going to be all right, she was sure. Ebony just needed to get well. And she hoped that whatever Abdi had planned would mean that all three of them were happy.

Chapter Twenty-One

A week later, Ebony was a lot better. Ruth had helped her find her old self, and the two of them had slipped back into their easy-going way with each other.

Ruth's workload had been easier too, as she hadn't been into market since Saturday and wasn't due in till tomorrow – Thursday.

Already her orders were almost completed, but she wasn't feeling stressed over them as she had told everyone they would be ready in a fortnight.

Horacio was to start at the church school on Monday. The preacher had signed him up after the service on Sunday and told Ebony that he could start the next day, but Ebony wanted more time with him and so the preacher had agreed to put him down for a week later but had warned that was all he could allow.

Rebekah seemed to be getting tired earlier and earlier and slept most of the afternoon. 'I fear for my Rebekah, Ruth.'

Ruth nodded as she shifted her bum to get comfortable. The stone step felt colder these days and a chilly wind used the street like a tunnel at times. She pulled her shawl around her, and then adjusted Ebony's.

'Ta, Ruth. I'm feeling the cold.'

'Do yer want to go inside?'

Before she could answer, Gert called over, 'Yer at the market tomorrow, ain't yer, Ruth? Do yer want me and Joyce to pop in, or do yer think you'll manage, Ebony?'

'I think I'll be all right, ta, Gert, but can I send Horacio for you if I need you?'

This exchange made Ruth feel settled as she was worried about going and leaving Ebony. It was good to see her not being afraid of the neighbours in such a short time too.

'Righto, luv. We'll come if yer need us.'

With this, Gert went inside.

'I'm glad yer all right with Gert, luv. As yer know, Robbie's rearranged our dancing for tonight, so will yer do the same then and send Horacio if yer need help while we're out?'

'I will. You go and enjoy yourselves. Me and Rebekah know how much you deserve to.'

'We will, and ta for helping Rebekah to make me a new skirt, I love it.'

'Rebekah, she taught me much about sewing on a machine while I did it. I'm going to make one for myself too.'

When Ruth came downstairs later wearing the skirt, she did a twirl. She felt silly in it really, but it had done both Rebekah and Ebony good to work together on it and they were so happy with it.

Made out of dark blue taffeta, it rustled as she walked along the pavement with Robbie.

'Yer don't think I looked overdressed do yer, Robbie?'

'No, yer look lovely.'

He guffawed as he said this, and Ruth hit out at him. 'What could I do? I had to wear it, but I feel foolish now.'

'No, I'm only teasing. You left yerself open to that, seeking reassurance. Yer look lovely, I promise.'

243

Changing the subject, she asked, 'Are this couple really called Romano and Juliana?'

'I don't know, sounds a bit exotic, but then they would need fancy stage names and I told yer, they did stage work once.'

When she met them, Ruth thought Romano and Juliana were more like characters that had stepped off the stage than real people.

Romano, a very thin man who looked ancient, with sleek black hair and a pencil thin moustache, wore a frilly shirt in bright pink that was more like a woman's blouse. And Juliana, just as sleek as Romano, with her jet-black hair pulled tightly into a bun that rested in the nape of her neck, wore a flowing frock in a matching colour. Their elaborate greeting intimidated Ruth, and she could see it had done Robbie too, as the couple sort of sing-sang together, 'Hello, darlings. Welcome, welcome.'

Then Romano, who seemed to be in a constant pose, said, 'Let me look at you both. Yes, the right figures for dancers. But you, young man, will need to wear tights.'

Robbie coloured.

'And you, young lady,' Juliana bent forward in an elegant way. 'You are dressed perfectly. Except, you both need dancing pumps. Or, if it is ballet you want to learn, then proper ballet shoes.'

Ruth found her voice first. 'We don't want to learn ballet, just dancing.'

'Ballet is the ultimate in dancing – it tells a story with your body. A whole play can be put on without a word spoken, only by the beauty of the movement of the body.'

Robbie helped her out. 'We just want to dance. We'll get some pumps, only . . . well, how much do they cost?'

'We know a stage shop that sells second-hand ones very cheaply. These will do you for a start. I will write the address down. But first we need to assess you. Juliana, put on some music. Let me see . . . Strauss, I think, something lively.' As he turned back to them, Romano's movement was like a dance in itself. He clapped his hands. 'Now, show me what the music does to you. Paint pictures and words with your bodies.'

They looked at each other, unsure what to do, but once the music filled the room it seemed to fill Ruth's soul too.

She closed her eyes and began to sway, and then to twirl and twist her body. Her cares and shyness left her. Opening her eyes, she saw that Robbie was mirroring her, his steps sweeping him around her. His hand caught hold of hers and he spun her around him. It was as if they were at one with the music.

As the music came to an end there was a silence. Robbie drew her to him. She grinned up at him, as the applause came.

'Bravo! Bravo!'

They both blushed.

'Come, come, sit down here with us.'

Beads of sweat stood on Ruth's forehead as she walked across to where Romano indicated she should sit.

'You are amazing – wonderful. You have a natural talent. You will go far in the show business world. Stage productions are crying out for dancers. What you did was like a ballet, you told a story. I could feel the hardships you've both been through, and your deep connection to one another. Then at times, I could feel your joy, as if the hardships are behind you and you want to tell the world . . . Well, you shall. I will coach you, and then we will seek an agent for you. Juliana and I will manage your interests. We will make you the talk of London!'

Ruth couldn't take all this in. *Famous? How?*

Robbie's face expressed his excitement. It seemed this was his dream, as his, 'Thank you,' came out in a gushing way and then he said, 'It's all I ever want to do.'

'Ahh, but there are more strings you can get to your bow. An all-round entertainer is much more sought after. Now, I want to hear you sing and then see you act!'

They both looked at him; Robbie looked as unsure as Ruth felt. Where was all this taking them?

'Here. These are the words to a popular song. Juliana, put the music on . . . I want you to listen to a short piece of "Put On Your Old Grey Bonnet", and then when we play it again, I want you to sing the words. Robbie takes the first two lines, then Ruth the next two, then the next two you sing together. Stand up and breathe in deeply to get yourselves ready.'

Ruth recognized the music but didn't know where she'd heard it as she hadn't had many opportunities in her life to listen to music. She read the words in time to the music, singing them in her head.

Now it was their turn, Robbie's clear tone rang out:
'*Put on your old grey bonnet with the blue ribbons on it,*
And we'll hitch old dobbin' to the shade.'
His confidence gave Ruth courage.
'*Through those fields of clover,*
'*We'll go down to Dover.*'
Then the chorus together:
'*We gonna go down to Dover on our golden wedding day.*
'*Grey bonnet, ribbons on it. Gonna go down to Dover on our golden wedding day.*'

They both giggled as it came to an end.

'Excellent, not only can you dance but you can hold a tune and put just the right amount of comedy into a lyric. Now to acting . . . Juliana, I'm very excited at this find. I think we have the protégés we have been looking for!'

Ruth had no idea what a protégé was, or how everything had progressed as it had. She'd come along to learn to dance and hadn't any ideas of becoming the talk of London, but she couldn't deny the excitement heating her insides and filling her with a sense of really wanting what Romano was offering.

'Robbie, I want you to make an imaginary pot of tea. Really make me know what you're doing without saying a word.'

Robbie didn't flinch at this but went over to where a small table stood and picked up something that wasn't there, but you soon knew was a kettle as he filled it with an imaginary ladle from an imaginary bucket. All his actions were exaggerated and some made her giggle as he tried to light the gas and then burned himself and dropped an imaginary something made of china, and it obviously broke into many pieces as he made a fuss about picking up the pieces. It was all so funny that she, Romano and Juliana were in fits of laughter by the time Robbie finally sat down, let out a huge sigh and then drank his imaginary tea with a loud smacking of his lips.

All three applauded.

'It's as I thought, you've got a great leaning towards comedy.' Romano rubbed his hands together. 'Whatever it is you do for a living, Robbie, give it up. I want you here every day. I have a part in mind that I want to prepare you to audition for.'

'You mean, the stage? In theatre? But—'

'No buts. This is a marvellous chance I am offering you.'

Robbie looked towards Ruth. She nodded her head. 'We'll manage, Robbie, say yes.'

'But it isn't just Robbie I want, my dear. You have equal talent . . . Show me. Not comedy this time, as I want you to act out a scene of someone kneeling at the bedside of her dying mother, begging her not to leave you.'

Ruth went forward. Already she could feel the emotion he wanted from her. She kneeled next to a chair and began her mime of someone imploring. In her head she was begging that one day she would find her mother, and that she would want her. The tears tumbled down her face.

When she looked up, all three were dabbing at their eyes.

'You're both amazing. I want you both to stop following other careers and come to me at once, I will make you stars. You're young yet, but that's when to begin.'

'I couldn't give up. I've a market stall and me friend who's taken us in to think about.'

'Taken you in? You don't have family?'

Ruth told him their situation.

He seemed undaunted. 'I can change your life, my dear.'

'It ain't for me, not yet. I want Robbie to take it though.'

Robbie pulled her to one side. 'We've got to do this, Ruth, it's a good chance for us.'

'What about Rebekah and Ebony? I need to earn money. You know Rebekah isn't well. I've got to carry on with the market, for her.'

'But Ebony's getting stronger. She and Abdi will take care of Rebekah. Please, Ruth, I don't want to do it without yer.'

'You must, Robbie. I can't give up. Rebekah's done everything for me and so has Bett with taking the stall. How can I turn around now and throw it in their faces after just such a short time!'

Even as she said these words and knew them to be true, Ruth's heart felt like a heavy weight in her chest. She'd been given a dream she'd never dreamed before, and yet, she hadn't known that such a thing could be for her, but just as suddenly, it had been snatched away. Still full of the emotions that had visited her while performing, her eyes readily filled with tears.

She could see that Robbie was torn. He must feel like he was taking a prize meant for them both. She squeezed his hand, 'Do it for me, Robbie. Please, mate.'

He nodded, 'If yer'll take me on me own, I'd like to join yer, Romano.'

'Consider it done. Give your notice in at work, but until you finish I want you here every evening. We have work to do, Robbie – hard, punishing work. Work that will make you wish you had never taken the chance offered, but work that you will look back on and be grateful for. And don't worry about paying, we will recoup what we invest in you a thousand times over.'

'Ta, Romano. Ta for giving me this chance.'

'Your talent gave you this chance, now you have to harness it and make it what it should be. And my dear Ruth, come along whenever you can. We will have to charge you our fee each time, but if we guide you and teach you there may come a day when you can change your mind.'

This cheered Ruth. 'Really? Oh, ta, ever so much. I'd love to. I think I could get here about twice a week.'

'There! Things aren't so bad after all. What is it you do at the market?'

Ruth told him about hers and Rebekah's venture.

'That sounds wonderful. Maybe in the future we can give you some business as the cast of ladies often wear bonnets and not all of the costume designers can actually make them. They nearly always get outside professionals to do that work. I will keep you in mind.'

'Ta, that'd be a big help and I'd love to be involved.'

'Good, and with you coming here for two sessions a week, we may have you ready to take a bit part in a production by next year. But you, Robbie, I want you ready much sooner than that. Much sooner. I have plans for you.'

On the way home, Robbie was full of it all. He went from saying how wonderful it all was, to worrying if he was putting too much onto Ruth's shoulders.

'For the first weeks that I lived with Rebekah, you were the breadwinner as Rebekah and me concentrated on getting everything ready for the stall. And yer made our stall for us and shelves for me room, and Rebekah's for our stock, so I think you have done yer bit and deserve this chance. Just think, Robbie, yer may get rich! Then yer can take care of us.'

'And I will, Ruth. I'll always look out for yer, I promise.'

As he often did, Robbie took her hand. He had a swagger to his step and Ruth was glad for him. She'd do anything for him. She'd work her fingers to the bone to keep him and to make it possible for him to follow his dream.

Rebekah looked a lot better when they arrived home. She was winding wool around the back of the chair. A delicious smell came from the kitchen and despite having had a bowl of stew earlier, it made Ruth feel hungry.

Ruth rushed over to Rebekah and kissed her. 'We've got some news, Rebekah.'

It lifted Ruth to see Rebekah as lively as always as she clapped her hands at their story. 'My, that be the best news Rebekah's heard today. And don't you be worrying, Robbie, we'll all manage. I think the stall is going to do well.'

'And Abdi is going to pay for me and Horacio's keep, so there will be money enough coming in for us all.'

'Ta, Rebekah, but are yer sure?'

'I am. Didn't I tell you, Robbie, that you have talent? Well, Rebekah is willing to back that talent, we all are, boy.'

Ruth knew Robbie to grin a lot, but she'd never seen him grin so widely as he did now as he looked round at them all, but then typically of him he came out with, 'I'll tell yer one thing, dancing makes yer hungry. What is that delicious smell?'

'Ebony did cook bunny chow. It be the most delicious thing you did taste, boy.'

'Bunny chow? Is it made with rabbit?'

'No, though it don't matter what meat you use, I used the lamb that Rebekah had in for the curry. I made plenty so you can take a pot to your friend. And I made bread. This dish we eat with bread, not rice. Ebony will serve you some.'

When it came out, it looked a lovely creamy colour and was piled into a scooped-out base of a bun loaf. Just to look at it made you enjoy it, but then, the taste. Ruth didn't think she had the words to describe it. Rebekah had said that they hadn't tasted a curry dish until they'd tasted Ebony's and she knew that to be true as she tucked in.

'Well?' Ebony looked eagerly from one to the other.

Robbie summed it up. 'The best ever.'

'And you think your friend's customers will like it?'

'They will love it, Ebony. It's . . . it's divine.' Ruth laughed at herself – she had no idea where that phrase came from, but then, maybe Romano and Juliana's way of talking had rubbed off on her.

'This just be a sample of what Ebony can cook.'

'Mmm. Is there more?'

They all laughed at Robbie as he held his empty plate forward and put on a little boy expression.

When Ebony had served him another helping, she asked, 'So, the English would buy this food?'

'We would. Yer'll see tomorrow. I'll tell yer when I come home how it went down.'

'That's important to me. Me and Abdi want to open a restaurant.'

'You do? But that's wonderful.'

'Abdi, he will serve the people, and I will cook the food.'

Ruth could easily imagine Abdi, looking all regal, serving the poshest of folk. Suddenly she felt excited for them. 'When? Where? Ooh, Ebony, it'll be bloomin' smashing!'

'Ha!' Ebony clapped her hands together.

Rebekah clucked her teeth and shook her head. The mood dropped.

'You don't think it a good idea, Aunty?'

'I don't know. I worry. Is it for us to own business? I mean, a market stall, maybe, but a restaurant?'

'There are others doing it, Rebekah. Up west there's a few African restaurants and one near to the market that does really well, and look at how the factory girls love yer curry.' Robbie took another mouthful. 'It can't fail with food like this.'

'Well then, Rebekah she worry for nothing?'

'Yes.' Ruth reached out and took her hand. 'I don't think they can fail.'

Rebekah smiled. 'Then I am pleased. Now, Rebekah has

252

another idea for the stall, Ruth. You need other items to attract all customers – Beads! Not just on them there hats, but necklaces, bracelets and pictures. While Ebony is here, she can help me, as she does have all the skills that I have in this field.'

'No, Rebekah, the doctor said—'

'Now don't yer be listening to no doctor – at least, not taking his words in the way he said them. He said Rebekah was to take it easy, not be a statue. I love making things, and I've been thinking that some of me beaded pictures might be very good sellers, so I'm planning on making a couple to see how they do.'

'And I can help. I won't have to be at me dancing lessons at the times you go to and come back from market, Ruth, so I can give yer a hand at both ends of the day once I start.'

Ruth began to feel better about it all. The extra help from Rebekah, Ebony and Robbie would make things a little easier for her, and on the days that she didn't stand market, she could concentrate on making the hats.

'Now, you gonna put on the music and show me and Ebony what you did at this lesson?'

The next hour was a lot of fun, and Ruth felt for the umpteenth time, how lucky she was to have landed with Rebekah and to have met Robbie. She tried not to think of her disappointment but couldn't deny how part of her so wanted to work towards being on the stage.

But then, she had two dreams now and being on the stage was an added one that she knew would have to be shelved for the time being, as she told herself she would concentrate on the dream that she was on her way to achieving, to own a milliner's and make her fortune.

Chapter Twenty-Two

Life over the next few weeks became a whirl of work, dancing and lovely times with all who Ruth looked upon as her family.

She and Ebony were back to their giggly selves, especially when lying in bed at night after a fun few minutes with Horacio, who wouldn't go up to his own bed until he'd had this time with them.

Ruth would tell Ebony stories of what had happened in the daytime on the market stall, or of Romano and Juliana's ways during the dancing classes and these would set them off.

Ebony was better than Ruth had ever known her as she was no longer afraid and bullied and had a wonderful future to look forward to.

The stall was busy. Orders piled up including a couple from Miss Melinda from Melinda's Milliner's.

In the hope of her turning up again, Ruth had taken the brimmed hat to market every day in a box that had to be very carefully handled. Miss Melinda had loved it and ordered one in a moss green and one in a chocolate brown.

Horacio had settled in at school and was a real chatterbox in the evening, telling them all he'd been doing. And Abdi had sent word that Mr Peterson was sorry to hear he planned to leave but was very interested in his plans and had a property in mind for the restaurant that he would lease to Abdi on terms that he could manage, which would increase as he became more successful.

Hettie, too, was happy in her job and even more so now as Flo had at last joined her in the kitchen. This meant she could now have a day off, and that was to happen this coming Sunday. Ruth could hardly wait for it to come around as she, Hettie and Robbie had planned to go up to the West End. A treat she couldn't even begin to dream how it would be.

When at last the day dawned, the late October weather was dogged by a cool breeze. Ruth welcomed it though as she had been dying to wear the lovely woollen, going-out skirt, one of two Ebony had made for her and just right for the warmth it gave, besides being the smartest skirt she'd ever owned. It was a light grey with little kick pleats at the hem. She'd laid out a silk blouse in a darker blue – a purchase from one of the market stalls – and a crocheted pale blue shawl that Rebekah had made for her, to wear with it.

Silk always kept you warm, but not taking any chances Ruth decided to wear her liberty bodice and long pantaloons underneath.

Once dressed, she donned the new dark blue bonnet she'd made for herself and she slipped her feet into soft, black leather boots. Doug the shoemaker had made these for her at a cut price. In return, she'd made a hat for his missus.

Doing a twirl, she caught her breath as the image in the mirror showed her a young woman, not a young girl. And that's just what she felt like with the responsibilities she had.

Pushing out her chest and lifting her chin, she told her image, 'A young businesswoman, in fact!'

Footsteps coming down from the attic bedroom were

accompanied by a giggle as a little voice said, 'And Horacio is a young boy!'

'You are, love. Momma's downstairs cooking breakfast; we're having eggs! Is lazy old Robbie up yet?'

'He's dressing, but he washed and dressed me first.'

'You look very smart. Ooh, we're going to see Hettie!' Horacio clapped his hands together.

As soon as they were in sight of the church, Hettie ran at Ruth. Their hug warmed Ruth's heart. 'Oh, Hettie, luv. How are yer? How's Flo?'

'She's fine and loving working in the kitchen with me, and I'm loving having her, mate. She was shy at first, but she . . . Oh, Ruth . . . I . . .' Hettie's body trembled. A huge sob came from her.

'Hettie? What's wrong, mate?'

'I ain't said anything but . . . Oh, Ruth, I can't go into church, I can't.'

Robbie joined them, 'What's wrong, Hettie, has someone hurt yer, luv?'

'I— I— Oh, Robbie, it's—'

'Hettie! I don't like to see you upset, girl. What's happened?' Ebony asked.

Rebekah didn't speak as she stood holding Horacio's hand, but her face held concern. Ruth didn't know what to do. She couldn't think what might have happened.

Ebony took charge. 'Robbie, you take Horacio inside. I think this is for women to talk of. We'll join you soon, son. Come on, Hettie, girl. I know that a worry shared is a worry halved. Let's sit on the wall, eh?'

When they were sat, and Hettie spoke, Ruth felt shock zing through her. Nothing prepared her for Hettie saying, 'I –

256

I ain't seen me monthly since . . . since before Belton . . .'
Another sob, and Hettie became inconsolable.

Ruth couldn't speak. Hettie had said that Belton was careful not to make them pregnant. *No, it can't happen to me, can it?* But then her panic subsided – she'd been on her monthly the week before.

As Ebony rocked the sobbing Hettie, Ruth felt for her hand. When she found it, Hettie clung on as if for dear life.

Feeling bad about her initial thoughts that had come through fear, Ruth told Hettie, 'We'll help yer, Hettie, luv, don't worry, you ain't on yer own.'

'They'll put me away . . . the workhouse . . . and take me baby.'

'Rebekah ain't going to let that happen, girl. You'll always have a home at mine.'

Ruth couldn't see where, but then remembered that Abdi would soon be taking Ebony and Horacio to live with him, and though her heart was heavy at the thought of not being with them every day, it would mean that Hettie could come to Rebekah's. She patted Hettie's back. 'It'll be all right, luv.'

'What will everyone think, Ruth? I'll be called a slut.'

'Rebekah does think the good Lord will sort all your problems out, Hettie girl. Let's get inside and you talk to Him. He does listen.'

'I can't. I – I'll wait here, yer can go in. I'll be all right.'

Ruth could see she wouldn't, her face was a flood of tears. 'I'll stay with Hettie, Rebekah. We'll walk a little way and then be back here for when yer come out.'

Rebekah went to protest, but Ruth so wanted to be alone with Hettie that it was a relief when Ebony said, 'I'm for thinking that's the best thing to do right now. Come on Rebekah, everyone has gone in.'

257

Ruth and Hettie walked a little way, holding hands but not talking. Hettie stopped crying, but every now and again her body shook with rebound sobs. Ruth felt at a loss as to what to say until they turned into the square and the haven of Bethnal Green Gardens lay ahead.

'Shall we go and sit in the park, luv?'

Hettie nodded.

The breeze rustling the trees gave a chill to the air as their branches swayed. Ruth pulled her shawl around her but still she shivered when they sat on a bench and she felt Hettie's body trembling too. 'Huddle up to me, luv, we'll keep each other warm, eh?'

As they snuggled in close, Ruth asked, 'How're yer feeling, Hettie, luv, are yer scared?'

'I am, Ruth, so scared, and sick, and . . . lonely . . . I know I ain't alone, but inside I've got this feeling of never being more so. That no matter what anyone does, or says, it's just me and me baby.'

'Will yer be able to love it, knowing . . .'

'I love it now, Ruth. I ain't thinking of that pig who put it inside me, only that it's my baby. Someone that belongs to me . . . is mine, me family.'

'Oh, Hettie. We ain't never had anyone like that.' Ruth looked down and swallowed hard as she wondered what it would be like to have a mum, sisters and brothers and to live with them.

As if reading her thoughts, Hettie said, 'I – I don't mean . . . Well, you're still like me family, Ruth. As I think of yer as a sister, but me baby will be me own flesh and blood.'

'I know what yer mean, mate. I think of you, Robbie and all of Rebekah's family as my family, but there's that something missing, that . . . Oh, I don't know.'

Ellen and Amy came to her mind and she had the sudden urge to say that she'd felt like that since they'd gone out of her life, but she thought this might be hurtful to Hettie, and in any case she couldn't understand it herself, or how to explain it.

How she longed to hear from them. It had been six weeks now since Amy sailed away and she doubted she'd reached Canada yet, and Ellen she knew was in London somewhere, but where did you start to look in such a huge city?

'It's like a hole inside yer, ain't it? But after I missed one and got so scared, I began to think of trying to make it come out of me. I thought of poking something up . . . you know . . . where he put his thing, but I was scared. And then after I missed two, I started to imagine what it would be like to hold me own baby and it became real and I didn't want it to never know its mum, that if I let anyone take it from me it would go through what me and you have been through and I couldn't bear that. I was still frightened and didn't know what to do but I did know I didn't want to lose it.'

'Rebekah'll have yer, luv. Once Ebony's settled with Abdi in their restaurant. We'll be together and I can help yer. I can teach yer how to make things for me stall and you can look after Rebekah and make the meals.' Warming to the idea, Ruth began to fill with hope. 'It'll be all right, and then when the baby comes, we'll help yer to look after it.'

Hettie smiled for the first time. 'Ta, Ruth. Yer the best friend I ever had.'

'And you me, mate. Shall we get back? And what about the West End? We don't have to go if you don't want to.'

'I do. It'll take me mind off things.'

As they began to walk back to the church, Hettie suddenly said, 'Oh, I forgot to tell yer, luv. Something happened last

259

week, I was introduced to the family. Housekeeper came to me and told me to put on a clean hat, pinny, collar and cuffs, and then to go to her office. I got the shock of me life when she took me to meet Mr and Mrs Peterson and their son Abraham. Anyway, Mrs Peterson asked Housekeeper about my previous experience. And when she was told where I'd come from, she raised her eyebrows and spoke to me for the first time. She asked how I had learned to cook so well as she wanted to compliment me on me food. I told her it just seemed to come natural and that in the while I'd been there as a maid, I'd watched Cook and learned a lot from her.'

Ruth knew what a big thing this was in such a household. 'Ooh, Hettie, luv, I bet yer feel so proud.'

Hettie nodded. 'But that's not all, because the strangest thing happened then. When we came out of Mrs Peterson's living room, Housekeeper told me to get back to the kitchen and she went up the stairs. She'd only just gone, and I was about to open the door leading down to the kitchen, when a voice said, "Excuse me." I turned and it was Abraham. He said, "I was wondering, do you know Ruth?"'

'What!'

'I know, me mouth dropped open, I couldn't answer him. Then he said, "I just wanted to know that she is all right. I heard she'd been taken, well, I've heard all sorts of stories".'

'He didn't?'

'Yes, I bet it was that Aggie. She gets to know all she can and she's the only one who goes upstairs where she's likely to see him. I can just see her smarming up to the family. I mean, they seem to me to know everything . . . Or the house-keeper, but she would see it as her duty to keep the mistress informed and he could have been there when she did.'

'What must he think?'

260

'Well, he can't think bad of yer wanting to know how yer are. Anyway, how come he knows of yer?'

'I met him on the stairs.' Ruth told how she'd tripped, and he'd helped her and asked her name.

'Blimey, mate, but why should he ask after yer?'

Something in Ruth knew why, and yet she couldn't understand it. She'd felt something when he'd looked at her. It was similar to what she felt now, as her legs seemed to have turned to jelly. 'What did yer tell him?'

'I was caught off guard and blurted out all you were doing and about yer market stall.'

Ruth didn't know what to make of this but had no time to ponder it as now they had reached the church and the parishioners were spilling out onto the street.

Robbie ran over to them. 'Phew, I'm glad that's over this week, it weren't half the fun without yer both, no one to have a secret giggle with and I've been worried sick about yer, Hettie.'

'I'm all right, Robbie.'

But suddenly, as she told Robbie what her problem was, she wasn't all right as her lip trembled. 'I – I just don't want this to be happening, it . . . well, it changes so much, and . . .' A tear plopped onto Hettie's cheek.

Ruth felt at a loss. Robbie kicked a stone – Ruth had learned he did this when unsure or angry. This time she knew it was anger as he said, 'I could kill that Belton, and I wished Bett's blokes had.'

'Hettie, luv, it will be all right, I promise. You can take up yer cooking later when yer baby has grown up, eh?'

'I – I know, Ruth. I know there's a way out for me. I just feel . . . dirty, soiled. I want to be as I was before Belton did that thing to me.'

They were all quiet. Ruth's heart wrenched for Hettie, but it did for herself too. She wanted the same. She wanted to be the pure girl that she used to be, and not to have the memory of that thing happening.

'If yer come to Rebekah's, I'll look out for yer, mate.'

'Ta, Robbie.'

'So, are we going up west, or not, Hettie? Are yer still up to it?'

'I am, ta, Robbie. I think it will make me feel better and forget about it for a while.'

After saying their goodbyes to Rebekah, Ebony and a tearful Horacio, who wanted to go with them, they set off for Bethnal Green Tube Station, not the happy crew Ruth had thought they'd be as she knew so many emotions to be churning her insides – fear for Hettie, nervousness about her first ride on a Tube train, an experience she couldn't even guess at, and overriding them all, her funny tickly stomach over hearing that Abraham had asked about her.

It was her nerves that won as they began to descend the steps. It looked to Ruth as if they were going into the bowels of the earth and this feeling worsened when they were on the platform and she looked along the long dark tunnel. Were they really going on a train into a hole that looked too small? She tried to concentrate on the adverts on the wall – Thomas Cook's Travel, an orange globe of the world with people standing around it in front of different countries; Pears soap with a beautiful lady looking down on them; and then one for Bovril which wrenched at her heart. It showed a mum looking confused, standing next to a table. Two kids were under the table tucking into a jar of Bovril. The caption said, 'Wherever did I put that Bovril?'

As she stared at it, the emotional feelings visited her once more. Oh, to have a proper family – a mum, sisters and brothers – your own flesh and blood, as Hettie had called her baby.

'Penny for them, yer look like a scared rabbit, Ruth.'

Ruth grinned at Robbie. 'I am a bit, luv. I can't imagine what it's like to be on a—'

Her words were taken by a noise that made her jump. The ground beneath her trembled. She flung herself at Robbie.

He held her close. 'Ruth, it's all right, mate, come on. It's safe as houses, you'll love it.'

Once she was settled and the train set off, Ruth began to relax as excitement gripped her. She loved looking at all the people as they crowded onto the train and to wonder where each was going and what their lives were like – all had an air of expectancy as they called out to one another.

It was when they got off that she saw him. He stepped out of a carriage marked 'First Class' and looked directly at her. 'Ruth!'

Ruth wanted to run and hide.

'Ruth . . . and, um . . . Cook. Hello.'

Struck dumb, Ruth nodded her head.

'Well it's nice to see you. I wondered . . .'

The noise of the train took his words. When it quietened, Abraham looked a little embarrassed. 'I'm sorry, I didn't mean . . . well, it's good to see you looking so well. Are you going anywhere in particular?'

At last, she found her voice. 'No, sir, we're just going to have a look around.' She bobbed as she spoke.

'Me too. I got bored. I tell you what, why don't you join me . . . you and your friends? I was just going to get a cab and have it drive me around the sights, I know them all, but never tire of them. I'm going to study history you see. Only, I'm taking a rest – a sabbatical before university.'

Ruth couldn't believe what he'd just asked her. She couldn't fathom him. Why should he be interested in her?

'Look, I'm intruding.' He looked from one to the other, and then addressed Robbie, 'I'm Abraham, I'm the son of the Petersons, the owners of the house where Cook works. I met Ruth when she worked for us.'

He held his hand out. Robbie took it. 'Robbie, sir.'

'No need to call me sir, I'm guessing that we're pretty much the same age. Look, would you mind if I joined you? Or rather, would you join me? To tell the truth I'm feeling a bit lonely.' He coloured then and looked sheepish. 'I'd be grateful if I could tag along.'

Robbie grinned. 'Be glad to have yer. Yer obviously know more about the sights than me, and these two are expecting the full tour – Buckingham Palace being at the top of their list.'

'Robbie!' This urgent whisper came from Hettie.

'Don't worry, Cook . . . may I call you Hettie?'

'Yes, sir.'

'Well, Hettie, I won't tell if you don't. It's only for a few hours and you'll be doing me a great service. I just wanted to escape for the day. Do something different. Have some fun.'

Suddenly, Ruth felt sorry for him. What he was doing was breaking the rules of his standing in society, whilst they were free to do what they wanted. Well, why shouldn't he? He was only young, like them. As she thought this, she saw him in a different light. Just a young person, like themselves.

'We'd be glad to go in your cab with yer, ta, Abraham.'

Abraham smiled that lovely smile she remembered. His deep blue eyes shone as he looked into hers. Once again, she wanted to reach up and brush back his hair from flopping over one eye. She clenched her fist to stop herself, but that didn't stop the feeling she had that Abraham was someone special to her life.

Chapter Twenty-Three

Outside Marble Arch Central a long line of horse-drawn and motor cabs waited for fares. Abraham hailed a landau. Ruth was captivated by the beautiful black horses wearing plumes in red and white. They looked magnificent. Part of her wanted to stroke their manes, but the biggest part of her was a little afraid and in awe of them as they snorted and shook their heads.

It was a relief when Abraham offered her his hand and helped her up into the landau. He did the same for Hettie before he and Robbie got in and sat opposite them.

What followed was a magical tour starting with Marble Arch, which Abe, as he insisted they call him, told them commemorated the Napoleonic wars. Some of his words were a bit long and Ruth didn't understand them, but she just loved listening to him saying them.

Hyde Park was next and she learned of Speakers' Corner.

His voice and the gentle pace of the horses lulled her into forgetting who it was she was with. 'Oh, just look at them swans, mate, ain't they a picture?'

'They are, Ruth.'

'And look at how the water sparkles in the sun, and the trees look like giants . . . it's all so beautiful. I ain't never seen anything like it.'

'Are you all from the children's home?'

This jolted Ruth to realizing who he was once more. Robbie answered, 'Yes, we are, and all glad to escape.'

'So, didn't they ever bring you out of the gates? I – I, well, I took a stroll up to look at it after I knew you had run away from there and had been taken back, Ruth. It looked an awful place. I was hoping to see you to tell you I would help you, but you never came out into the playground.'

Ruth looked down at the floor. 'I wasn't well.'

'She was beaten.'

Ruth gasped. 'Hettie!'

'Beaten? Oh my God! Are you all right now?'

'I am, ta.'

'Where do you live?'

'Me and Robbie both live with Ebony and her aunt.'

'Ebony? Do I know her?'

Ruth told him who Ebony was.

'Oh. There was a to-do in the kitchen I believe, and that is why the old Cook left. I like Abdi very much, I hope he and his wife are very successful in their new venture.'

They were all quiet for a while as the landau took them through the park gates and along a busy road, weaving in and out of motor cars.

Robbie was leaning forward with his elbows on his knees and clenching his hands. Ruth couldn't read his expression, but she got the feeling he was fighting a battle within himself.

But her attention was taken from her as suddenly the magnificent Buckingham Palace came into view and she gasped at the sight of it. She clutched Hettie's hand, realizing for the first time how quiet Hettie had been and bringing sharply into focus poor Hettie's dilemma. It must seem to her that they'd brushed over it as something they could manage, but in truth this was going to change Hettie's life. And now she was having to sit in a carriage with the son of the family she worked for, which broke all convention.

Suddenly, something she hadn't thought of before made her cringe inside – what if they met someone who knew the Peterson family! What could be the consequences for Hettie?

But these thoughts were dispelled as Abe got her attention again, 'Well, there it is, Ruth, in all its glory. Oh, look, the King's carriage!'

Their own landau came to a halt and the driver dismounted and stood to attention by his horses. Abe stood up. They all followed suit. Ruth gasped to see, not one, but two queens sitting in the carriage. She couldn't take her eyes off the beautiful Queen Alexandra and Queen Mary as the sun caught the shine of Queen Mary's golden-brown hair and Queen Alexandra's light-brown locks.

Suddenly, Queen Alexandra looked back at Ruth and it was as if there were only the two of them in the whole world as she smiled a beautiful smile. Ruth clapped her hands together, and this started a ripple of applause through the crowd that had now gathered. The King acknowledged this by waving to them all.

It was, to Ruth, the single most beautiful moment in her life.

She turned to look at Abe, her face stretched in a wondrous smile. He smiled back and Ruth thought he looked beautiful. He bent towards her. 'I arranged all that especially for you, madam.'

This set her giggling. It wasn't until Robbie and Hettie joined in with her that they came into her focus again, as for a moment it had been as if there was only her and Abe in the lovely world the experience had transported her to.

'Oh, Hettie, that was magical!'

Hettie grinned and seemed to relax for the first time. 'I can't believe what just happened, mate. I were in awe of being in a landau and all that we've seen, but never did I think to see the King and the two queens. Weren't they beautiful?'

'The most beautiful women I've ever seen in me life. They looked like they were made of porcelain.'

This from Robbie made Ruth look at him for the first time since they'd had to stop for the royal carriage. His expression was one of wonder as he said, 'It made me feel like dancing with joy.'

Abe looked at him in surprise. 'You dance?'

'Robbie's the best dancer in the world, he's going to be on the stage, ain't yer, mate?'

Robbie coloured. 'Not the best, Ruth. But I do love to dance and am training for the stage.'

This amazed Ruth. She'd regretted highlighting Robbie's passion, and hadn't expected him to admit to it, when he always said it was sissy, but Abe didn't flinch. 'Really? Well, I've never met a performer before. I love the theatre. My next place to take you is the Prince of Wales Theatre where I went to see a much-talked-about musical comedy, *The Prince of Pilsen*. My father uses an agency to buy all the tickets the family need. Which production are you in training for, Robbie?'

'Not any particular one yet, mate, but working towards auditioning.'

As the carriage continued on its journey Robbie told Abe about his dream and how it was materializing.

To Ruth, it was as if the two had been mates forever as they got into deep conversation, laughed together, and at times, Robbie listened intently to Abe telling him about shows he'd seen. But he took the wind out of their sails when he suddenly said, 'We'll go together to the Prince of Wales, all of us. I'll buy the tickets. Oh, please say yes, it would be such fun.'

Ruth couldn't speak. Today had been so strange, not a bit like the day they had planned. It was as if she was taking part in a fairy tale, and yet here was Abe, a young man far above their standing, asking them to be his guests for a night out at the theatre!

'It ain't for me, sir.'

'Hettie, you really don't have to keep calling me sir, not today. But why don't you want to come to the theatre? You will love it. The theatre transforms you into another being and takes you to a different world, everyone should experience that.'

'I ain't one for that sort of thing and I'd feel out of place. I do today, though I've enjoyed it, ta very much, Sir Abe.'

This made Ruth chuckle, but she did it quietly, she wouldn't want to hurt Hettie's feelings. She saw Abe turn away to hide his amusement and this endeared him to her even more.

She looked over at Robbie who hadn't said a word since Abe had surprised them all. Robbie looked dismayed like a child that might suddenly have a treat taken from him. Ruth knew she could speak for him – this was one time she wasn't going to stick by Hettie.

'Me and Robbie would love it, Abe, but are yer sure? What would we have to wear, as we ain't got that many going-out clothes.'

'That's wonderful! Oh, I'm so glad. And don't worry about clothes. What you have on now will be fine, you look lovely.'

270

Ruth blushed.

'And you look smart enough for any theatre, Robbie. I just know that one day I'm going to come and watch a show with you as the leading man. I wonder, would it be possible to come to one of your lessons? Just to watch? The theatre and actors just fascinate me. I'd really love to see behind the scenes.'

'You'd be very welcome, mate, and ta for the invite. Part of me dream is to go to a show at the theatre . . . Yer know, you ain't a bit like I thought toffs were. Yer more like a cockney; friendly and generous and having no side to yer.'

'Ta very much, mate.'

They all laughed at this, even Hettie, who, since Robbie had engaged with Abe seemed more relaxed.

They'd reached the Prince of Wales Theatre in all its splendour. Ruth felt her heart pounding as she gazed up at the magnificent building which seemed to be wrapped around the centre of two streets and almost resemble a huge ship, like the one Amy had left on. She didn't let her mind dwell on Amy as she wanted nothing to spoil this moment of staring at a real theatre. 'It's beautiful!'

'It is, Ruth. But you should see the inside! I can't wait for you to do me the honour of accompanying me to a show as then you will see it for yourself.'

Caught up in the moment, Ruth didn't stop herself from nodding her head. 'Yes, oh, yes, I can't wait, mate, I'd really love it.'

And suddenly, that's what Abe felt like, a mate, no different to them, just a lovely young man who Ruth loved to be with.

As if he'd read her thoughts Abe said, 'I can't thank you all enough for joining me. Since I left school, I've felt very lonely and at a loose end all the time. Usually, it's school

271

hols when I am at home and I have my brother, Andrew, at home too. But I've really enjoyed today. Would you let me buy you all lunch?'

Robbie looked over at Ruth. Ruth didn't know what to say, she did feel hungry but lunch sounded too posh for the likes of them.

'There're not many places open on a Sunday, but I know a couple.'

'Them places ain't for the likes of us, mate, how about we take yer to a cafe I know near to the docks. It's the only one that opens on a Sunday and serves the dockers, but yer'll never taste a better pie, mash and liquor in yer life. You'll love it. And it'll be my treat from me last week's wages. As from tomorrow, I dedicate meself to me dancing career.'

'I'd love that. I've heard about pie and mash, but never tasted it. Thanks, and I'll take your generous offer, Robbie.'

Abe put his hand out. Robbie took hold of it with both of his and shook it, his grin wide, his eyes not leaving Abe's face.

Ruth had a weird feeling as the two men looked at each other. Holding the gaze for longer than she thought necessary. She looked away. Confused feelings and thoughts juggled around in her head. Did friends look at each other like that? A small part of her felt a tinge of jealousy as the sensation of being excluded really hurt.

When, at Abe's instructions, the driver turned to take them back to the station, Ruth stared at the people they passed, wanting to look anywhere but at Abe and Robbie, who she could hear were in deep conversation again about each other's plans.

One couple – a man and girl – caught her eye. 'Ellen! Oh God, it's Ellen! Stop! Please stop the landau . . . ELLEN! ELLEN!'

As soon as the landau came to a halt Ruth was out and running towards Ellen, 'Oh, Ellen, Ellen!'

'Ru-u-th!'

They were in each other's arms laughing and crying with joy.

'Ellen! Stop this! Who is this young lady? Come back here . . . Oh my God! Ellen, come here at once!'

'Dad, it's Ruth. You know, Ruth. I told you about her.'

'I said, come here, do you hear me? Come here now! Go away whoever you are, we don't want you interfering with us. Get away!'

'But Dad . . .'

'Do as I say! I warned you and I'll carry out my threat if you disobey me on this.'

Ellen stiffened. She looked at Ruth. Her eyes held pain, 'I have to go. I love you, Ruth and miss you so much.'

'Oh, Ellen, I love you too, mate. Write to me at—'

'She will not! If you don't leave us alone, I will call the police!'

'There is no need for that, sir. I'm Abraham Peterson, this is my friend, Ruth. She is a perfectly respectable girl and would do no harm to Ellen. They are obviously very fond of each other. What reason can you have for this attitude?'

'A Jew! Don't try to tell me what to do, Jew boy. I know your family – step on anyone to further themselves. Well, neither I nor my daughter want anything to do with you, or your so-called friend. What do you pay her, eh? Ha! Knowing you Jews, not much, but then the likes of her and her kind aren't worth much . . . Ellen, we are leaving.'

Ruth stood as if turned to stone. Why should Ellen's father say such things about her? And how could he talk to Abe like that?

Ellen looked intently into Ruth's face. Tears filled her eyes then spilled over and glistened on her cheeks. She turned and walked towards her father.

As Ruth watched her retreat, she knew she just couldn't let her go without telling her where she lived. She'd sensed Ellen's unhappiness, and not just because they were having to be torn apart again, but there was a deep unhappiness in Ellen and yes, fear, too. 'Ellen! I live at number three, Little Collingwood Street!'

Ellen went to look over her shoulder, but her father pulled her roughly by the hand and jerked her back round.

'Oh, Ellen . . .' This anguished whisper from Ruth brought Abe closer to her side.

'Ruth, come on. Let me help you.'

Robbie appeared at the other side of her. His gentle hold on her arm helped her. 'Come on, mate.' But before she could move, Hettie's voice, brash and angry, hollered down the quiet posh street. 'Yer bleedin' monster you! Think yerself somebody, eh? Well, yer bleedin' nobody – a bleedin' child-snatcher!'

'Stop her, Robbie, please, mate. I'm so sorry, Abe. I – I wouldn't have caused this for the world . . . and I'm sorry that man spoke to yer like that . . . Hettie, please, don't!'

Robbie jumped back on the landau and held Hettie by the hands. 'Calm yerself, Hettie, yer making a scene, luv.'

'Well, I think Ellen didn't want to go with him, she looked scared, and how dare he talk to Sir Abe like that?'

Abe turned to Ruth, his eyes were smiling, 'Well, seeing that I have been elevated, allow your knight to help you to your carriage, dear lady.' His bow was deep. His free hand did little elaborate circles. Ruth giggled but the giggle turned to sobs. 'I – I'm so sorry.'

Robbie jumped off the landau and was by her side in seconds. His arm came around her shoulders. Never had she known a boy to be as caring as Robbie, though Abe was too as, though he didn't hold her, he took her hand. 'Let's get out of here, shall we?'

When she was seated, he said, 'Don't worry on my account, I have been called worse things than Jew. I am proud to be Jewish as it happens.'

'I didn't realize yer were, mate.'

'Yes, Robbie, our family is Jewish, we're not orthodox, though I did have a painful episode as something that should have been done when I was a baby didn't happen till I was a toddler.'

His laugh made them all laugh with him. Ruth hadn't a clue what he was talking about, but Robbie seemed to. She didn't miss the look that passed between them and wondered at the strong bond that was obviously growing between them, and how quickly it had formed.

Just as Abe signalled to the driver to leave, a voice called out, 'Abraham! Is that you?'

Abraham took a deep breath. On releasing it, he muttered, 'Oh, Lord. Now I'm for it.'

Ruth recognized Mr Peterson as he came nearer. His voice was low but his anger bristled from him.

'What on earth? Get down at once! Who are these people? How dare you get yourself involved in a public brawl? That was disgusting to hear and to witness, but to think it was my own son! I am appalled.'

'These are my friends, Father. They weren't to blame. The gentleman with the child was.'

'Friends! These! For God's sake, have you lost your senses? Get down at once!'

Abe was beetroot red. Ruth felt so sorry for him but didn't know how to help him. She sent a silent prayer to Holy Mary to keep Hettie from trying to, but then saw that Hettie was trying to hide her face and didn't have any intention of interfering.

'I should go, mate, if I was you. We'll be all right, we understand. Yer know where to find me.'

'Thanks, Robbie . . . Ruth . . . I'm sorry . . . I—'

'Do as I say. Now!'

'Yes, Father . . . but I must pay the landau, I hired him.'

Mr Peterson spoke to the driver. 'Take these . . . these people to where they need to go and charge the Peterson of Victoria Road account, driver. Thank you. Good day.'

With this he grabbed Abe roughly by the arm.

Hettie made the mistake of looking round at that moment.

Mr Peterson stopped in his tracks, frowned, then said, 'Don't I know you? My God! Our cook! Are you out of you mind, Abraham? I'm incensed with and ashamed of you.' Turning to look at Hettie, he said, 'And as for you, don't even bother to come back to work at my house. You are never to step foot inside my door again. Kindly tell me where I can forward your belongings to.'

Hettie burst into tears.

'Well!'

For the second time today, Ruth recited her address.

'That pigsty! Well, I happen to own most of that street, so you might find yourselves out on your ear!'

This touched a nerve with Ruth and the temper that hadn't risen in her for a long time came to the fore. 'Well, you don't own the house we live in, mate, so yer can't hurt us. And yer should be ashamed if yer own them hovels me mates live in. Besides, Hettie doesn't need yer poxy job, thank you very much, she has a home and another job to go to. So, stick that in yer pipe and smoke it!'

'Ruth! Don't . . . I'm sorry, Ruth, forgive me.'

'Yer've done nothing wrong, Abe. We'll always remember today. Ta for giving it to us . . . Driver, can yer take us to the station please.'

As the carriage drove away, Ruth heard Abe call out, 'Ruth!'

She turned and waved to him. It broke her heart to see his father wrench him away, but he managed a wave back. When he was out of sight, she saw Robbie was still looking back to where he'd stood. Somehow it was a pitiful sight as Robbie looked devastated.

They didn't speak till they got to the station, then as they sat on the platform, Hettie suddenly made a funny wailing noise.

Ruth turned, stunned by the sound, which was taken into the approaching train.

Shock held her as if turned to stone when Hettie stood, rushed forward and jumped.

Screams resounded around Ruth, but still, she couldn't move.

The train rumbled on and then came to a halt. Men in uniform shouting unfathomable instructions passed her by, blowing whistles and stampeding towards the train, but she could do nothing.

Beside her, Robbie uttered, 'God, no – no – no!'

All Ruth could do was stare. Dribble ran down her chin, snot ran from her nose, but she couldn't wipe it away, nor could she blink her eyes.

'Miss . . . miss . . . were she a friend of yours?'

Ruth lifted her eyes and looked into the kindly eyes of a station worker. She nodded her head.

277

'Here, wipe yer face, girl. Yer've had a shock . . . we all have.'

'Hettie?'

He shook his head. 'I'm sorry, love. She's gone. Why did she do it, do you know?'

Robbie answered, although his voice didn't sound like him. It was high and squeaky. 'She . . . she had a lot of problems . . . we were helping her, but . . . why? Why?'

'All right, son, I know these things are hard to understand. Sometimes it just takes one thing to tip someone over the edge and you say she had a lot of problems. Maybe she couldn't see a way out, even with your help. I'm sure you did all you could for her. I expect the police will want to interview you both, so will yer write yer names and addresses down for me. I've a little pocketbook and pencil. I'll just get it. Then you'd best get on yer way home. There'll be no trains for a while, and no use waiting as they'll not be much of yer friend to see. I'm very sorry.'

'Ta, mister. I'll give yer the details for both of us as we live in the same house.'

Robbie sounded more like himself now, but Ruth felt as though she'd left her body and couldn't get back into it. She looked towards the spot where Hettie had jumped. People crowded around it. Her mind echoed what Robbie had said. *Why, Hettie, why? Oh, Hettie, Hettie, I can't live without you.*

Chapter Twenty-Four

This question still pounded around Ruth's head the next day as she lay on her bed, where she'd been since it had happened.

Her eyes, puffy and swollen, would hardly open. Her mind was a turmoil of thoughts, her emotions a rollercoaster of hate, love and extreme sadness.

The hate was for such people as Belton and Gedberg, Ellen's father, and Mr Peterson. Her love was for all those she looked on as family and for Abe, and those lost to her – Amy, Ellen and Hettie. Her sadness was for these three too, and for herself – so deeply for herself at the injustice of it all.

'Ruth, luv, there's a copper here. We've got to talk to him.'

'I can't, Robbie . . . Oh, Robbie, why? We were going to help her . . . She seemed all right.'

'I don't know. But I do know she wasn't all right, mate, we just didn't see that. We thought it, and carried on as if everything was all right . . . We just didn't see . . .'

Ruth knew this to be the truth and felt the guilt of it.

'Come on, luv, we have to do this.'

'Does Flo know?'

'Yes. Look, I'll tell yer everything later. Let's get this over with, eh?'

Ruth sat up. 'Tell me now, Robbie. I want to know how Flo is.'

'She's broken. Like we all are but . . . she told me something that I know'll add to yer sadness as it has mine . . . Mr Peterson has sent Abe away.'

'What?'

'Yes. I think it was the shock that made Flo blurt it out, but at first when I told her about Hettie, she just stared at me and said, "Trouble comes to every corner when it comes, Robbie. There's been trouble at the house, shouting and carrying on and the mistress in tears. The master's sent the son away. They say he's going abroad until his university begins."

'Then she said, "And now you tell me this," and then, "It ain't happened. Robbie." Then she began to wail and cry. "Tell me it ain't happened. Tell me me lovely Hettie ain't dead."'

Robbie sat down. His head bowed. A tear plopped onto his knee.

'Oh, Robbie, I can't bear it. Everyone's going. I don't want them to.' This last came out on a wail. Robbie turned to Ruth. His arm came around her and he held her to him. She felt no comfort, just a feeling that Robbie was stopping her from falling.

'We have to do this, luv. Let's get it over with. We don't want him coming back when Horacio is home from school. Poor little chap is lost as it is as he doesn't understand how Hettie could so suddenly have gone to heaven.'

This helped Ruth to make her mind up to do as Robbie asked. She allowed him to help her to sit up. 'Hold on a mo, mate.'

He went to her washstand and came back with a wet flannel. 'It'll be cold, but best to wipe yer face, luv.'

The coolness felt good. It helped to steady her.

'Right, let's get it over with.'

Downstairs, Ruth stared into the face that was etched onto her mind – the policeman who'd captured her and called her names, had handed her over to Belton like a lamb going to slaughter, to the man responsible for her nightmares and for killing lovely Hettie. The man who had slaughtered her girlhood.

She curtly answered all his queries. No one could miss the hate clipping her every word, because at this moment, she hated this man with all her guts.

'I know you from somewhere, don't I, Ruth?'

Ruth nodded.

'Oh, I remember – the runaway. So, from what we know of Hettie Randall, she was at the same home as you. And I'm assuming that as you were with her yesterday that you'd remained friends. Can yer think of any reason why she should jump in front of a train and kill herself?'

Something burst inside Ruth. She gritted her teeth and snarled at him, 'People like you are to blame – you more than anyone, 'cos you wouldn't believe what yer were told. Yer believed yer filthy mate over those he was hurting. Belton killed Hettie, just as sure as if he pushed her off the platform. His filthy raping of her night after night, leaving her pregnant! And the swine bleedin' well got away with it, because the matron helped him and Gedberg to cover up what they were doing, and bleeders like you wouldn't believe us when we told yer. Well, he can't hurt any more girls, we saw to that, and I wished we'd had him killed . . .' Her voice rose, spittle sprayed from her mouth. 'He should be dead, not Hettie and her baby. And you should be too because you didn't stop it. I hate yer, do yer hear me. I hate you and all yer stand for!'

281

The policeman stepped back, his face a picture of astonishment. A voice had pleaded throughout her tirade, 'Ruth, no, honey child . . . Ruth!' And Robbie was saying over and over, 'No, don't, Ruth.'

She reeled round to face him, 'Don't? Don't? I tried to tell that . . . that pig, what Belton was doing, and he called me names. He forced me to go back to the home to be raped . . . Raped . . . Oh God!'

Ruth's knees gave way, her voice went into a hollow, rasping sob. Her fists beat the ground. 'Hettie . . . I want Hettie!'

Robbie kneeled beside her. 'Ruth, luv . . . Ruth.' His arms held her tightly to his body. But he couldn't save her, she was drowning, drowning in the horror of all that had happened to her and to Amy and Ellen, and all the girls at the home, and those who disappeared in the night, never to be seen again, and Hettie. Lovely Hettie.

Faces bounced at her, clawed at her, girls, then Belton, then Matron. She had to scream them away, she had to . . .

'Ruth, no. Oh, Ruth, stop it, please, please . . .'

'Honey child, Rebekah is here. Lift her, Robbie, lift her into me arms.'

'I can't, Rebekah. She's a dead weight.'

'Ebony will help you. You get that arm, Robbie, and Ebony this, when Ebony says lift, we lift together. Right, lift!'

Ruth felt her body rising, then she was sitting and the familiar smell and feel of her beloved Rebekah enveloped her in love and a calmness descended on her.

'Well, after that show, I am arresting you, Ruth Faith, on two counts of causing grievous bodily harm. Two counts of slander intending to blacken Mr Belton's and Mr Gedberg's good names. And for false accusations and insulting a police officer while he attempts to carry out his duty.'

282

'No, no, not me Ruth. Please don't.'

'Look, if you think I'm going to listen to a Black woman, you've another think coming.'

'Please, sir, Ruth doesn't know what she is saying.'

'I do, Robbie. And . . . yer know . . . I'm speaking the truth.'

'You heard her. Now, out of me way.'

Ruth looked into the hateful face and spat as hard as she could. The policeman wiped her spittle off with the back of his hand. 'Now, I can add assaulting a police officer to our charges.'

His look was evil as he grabbed her hand and went to snap a handcuff on it. 'You'll be lucky to see daylight this side of next Christmas, young lady.'

Sheer terror gripped Ruth as memories of the dark room at the home they'd called 'the cell' came to her. She pulled her hand free and, lifting her leg, she kicked out with all her mite. The policeman sank to the floor.

Ruth pulled herself from Rebekah's grasp and headed for the door.

Just as she got there, she looked back. Robbie looked as though he would climb over the stricken policeman but tripped and fell across him.

Ruth ran like the wind down the street to cries from Gert for her to stop and asking what was going on.

But Ruth couldn't stop, she ran and ran, not knowing which way to go. But then Bett came to mind, and she made for hers, knowing she always left a key under the mat.

Once inside Bett's house, Ruth flung herself on Bett's sofa and sobbed her heart out as despair washed over her. *What have I done? Holy Mary, help me. Please, help me.*

*

'What the bleedin' hell? Ruth! Ruth girl, wake up!'

Ruth opened her eyes to see Bett staring down at her.

'Aw. Luv, is this over yer friend, eh? I feel sorry for yer, mate, but yer best place is to be with Rebekah and Robbie, luv.'

Ruth's head shook from one side to the other. 'No. I – I can't, Bett . . . Help me, Bett, help me.'

'Now then, girl, what's all this about? Are you in some sort of trouble?'

'The . . . police . . . Oh, Bett, I'm going to prison!'

'Prison? Good God, what have yer done, girl?'

Through her sobs, Ruth told Bett what had happened. 'Don't let them lock me away, Bett, please don't.'

'You're going to prison over me dead body, mate. What did that copper call himself, can yer remember?'

Ruth racked her brain for his name. Suddenly it came to her. 'Veners. PC Veners.'

'Ha! Worry no more, luv, he's one as is in the pay of me man. I'll soon sort him. He's a bad un. Anyone can pay him off. Yer say he took that Belton's word over yours? Well, it would be my bet Belton were paying him too. He'd turn a blind eye to anything for a bob. Stay here, and don't go outside. I won't be long, I've to get word to me man.'

Putting her head back, Ruth felt the weight lift off her shoulders. She took a deep breath. With it came the memory of how Rebekah had looked and how she'd struggled and gasped for breath. She sat bolt upright and once again prayed, *Don't let this make me Rebekah ill, Holy Mary. Please don't.*

The door opening made her jump round. Robbie came through. 'Oh, Ruth, Ruth!'

Ruth ran to him and into his arms. Her sobs shook through her.

'Rebekah, I've hurt Rebekah.'

'Rebekah's all right. She was glad yer got away. The cop left after he recovered. Ebony's with her and I came looking for you. I met Bett hurrying down the street and she told me you were here. She said she's sorting everything. You're going to be all right, Ruth. But, mate, that were a daft thing yer did. Yer scared the life out of me.'

'I'm sorry, Robbie. I just go out of meself at times and can't stop me actions.'

'I know. I've seen yer before. Sit down, luv. Bett told me to put the kettle on and make yer a cuppa with lots of sugar in it, so I'd better do that.'

Robbie was stopped in his tracks by a loud banging on the door. When it opened, the policeman stood there. 'So, you just added "resisting arrest" to your charges. Ha, you're never going to see the light of day again, girl, let alone next Christmas!'

His nasty face screwed into a sickly smile as he strode towards her. 'And don't even try your tricks again as there are more officers on the way to assist me.'

With this, he grabbed Ruth and clamped handcuffs on her before she could collect herself to get over the shock of him appearing.

'Bett's sorting this out, sir.'

The policeman turned towards Robbie, his look changed to one of fear. 'Bett? Bett Stabler?'

'Yes, this is her flat.'

He looked around him. 'Bloody hell, of course it is!' His shocked tones made him sound like a trapped animal as his head darted from Ruth to the open door. When he turned back to Ruth, his teeth gritted. 'You little bleeder! I had no idea you were a friend of Bett's. You made me so angry, I wasn't thinking. You were seen coming here . . .' Again, he looked around him as if expecting Bett to jump out at him any minute.

'I'm sorry for what I did, sir, I was scared, and yer just won't believe a word I say when it's all the truth.'

'Yer mean . . . Belton did them things?'

Robbie answered. 'He did, he . . . well, he interfered with almost every girl in the orphanage. He made their lives hell . . . and, poor Hettie, he did it to her more than most. He made her pregnant, and then she lost her job and, well, I think she just couldn't face everything. Belton ruined her life, and you stick up for him.'

The policeman stared at Robbie. Ruth could see the truth dawning on him, and then his look said, 'What have I done?' as he sank down beside her on the sofa. Dropping his head, he shook it from side to side. 'I – I'm sorry. I . . . He's an upstanding man in the community . . . a churchman . . . a godly one . . . I – I just don't know what to say.'

'Can yer take the cuffs off Ruth, sir. She'd been through such a lot and she's still in shock over Hettie.'

Veners undid the cuffs, his trembling hands fumbling, but at last they clicked open.

'Did Bett arrange for what happened to Belton and Gedberg?'

Ruth looked at Robbie.

'Don't answer that, I think I know the answer. I never thought I'd say this, but maybe it was the best way. Neither will hurt anyone again, though it's too late for your friend and I'm sorry about that.'

Ruth still felt like kicking him again. Fear of the same happening to him had made him listen to her at last, but if she hadn't had the threat of Bett's man to hold over him, he'd have dragged her to prison, when the one he should be doing that to went scot free.

Suddenly, she wanted that. She wanted justice for Hettie, for herself and for Ellen and Amy. 'It ain't the best way. He's still free, ain't he? He may be crippled, but he still lives his life. Everyone should know what he's done. Yer should be at his door arresting him and then going for Gedberg and Matron. Kids disappeared, they were fetched at night by Belton and never seen again.'

'Are you saying you think some kids have been murdered?'

Now she heard the word, Ruth could only nod.

Veners got out his little black book. Ruth had seen this before and knew he'd written things in it about her. The sound of him tearing pages filled her with relief. 'That's the end of this matter, but I will be questioning Belton, Gedberg and Matron. If anything comes of that, you will be required to stand witness to what you've told me . . . and, Ruth, I'm very sorry about what I've put you through and your mate too, poor girl. I just couldn't believe what you were saying about Belton.'

Bett's booming voice made them all jump. 'Get out of me house, you scumbag!'

'Now, now, none of that, Bett. You may have might behind yer, but I've got the law and I know me rights.'

'Rights! Yer protect them as grease yer palms, well, Ruth's part of the family that does, and you lay a finger on her and you'll live to regret it – that's if yer do live!'

'I'm in no one's pay, Bett, and if that son of yours has told yer different, then he's lying. But I know what he's capable of and I was scared, but grateful too, as the fear made me listen to the truth from these two young ones. So, you've nothing to worry over, I've scrapped me accusations against Ruth. Mind, I will give Ruth a warning. Her behaviour towards a man of the law was very wrong.'

With the wind taken out of her sails, Bett let out a massive sigh. 'Well, that's good. And no, me son ain't said that about yer, I just assumed as he seems to have every bleeder else in his pocket and with you taking the word of that Belton, I thought yer were in his pay too.' She turned to Robbie. 'Come outside a mo, luv, I need yer to run an errand and undo what I just did.'

With Robbie gone, Bett sat down. 'I'll tell yer, Ruth girl, from the moment yer slept rough on the market and I found yer, I ain't had a minute's peace.'

'I – I'm sorry, Bett.'

'No, no, it ain't your doing, luv, and I'd do anything for yer. But the stuff that's happened to yer breaks me heart and I've only one way of dealing with it, other than to give yer me love, which I do, mate. Yer like the daughter I never had.'

Ruth rose and went to Bett. Sitting on the arm of her chair she put her arm around her shoulders and leaned her head on Bett's. 'I love you, Bett. You're like a mum to me. I wished I hadn't caused you all this trouble.'

'I know, me little luv. Get yourself off home, poor Rebekah must be out of her mind.'

With Bett mentioning Rebekah, the way PC Veners had spoken to her came back into Ruth's mind. Her anger rose once more. 'Some don't give Rebekah the respect she should have, Bett.'

Veners coughed.

'I'm sorry, I didn't mean what I said. Rebekah seems to be a good woman. Belton told me she'd taken you and your mate in. Look, if he could he would tell yer, I stuck up for them when he told me. But I'll call round and apologize,

288

and I'll keep an eye out for her from now on. I know she does some lovely work, sewing and knitting, I can maybe put some business her way.'

'And she taught me how to make hats as well. I stand market now.'

'Do yer now? Well, that's interesting. I ain't seen yer, but I'll look out for yer and tell Mrs Veners about yer stall.'

'Ta, though Rebekah don't do so much now as she's frail, but her niece Ebony does, so the business would be welcome.'

'Look, why don't I take you back there now, eh? I can drop in and say I'm sorry to Rebekah then.'

Ruth gave a goodbye hug to Bett then went to sit in the police car. She hadn't thought how it might look until the car began to move, and then giggled to herself as she thought, *Folk are usually taken away in one of these, not brought back.*

When they arrived at Rebekah's door, Gert was straight out of her house. 'Ruth girl, you're back. I've worried meself to death.'

'She's all right, missus. A misunderstanding, but I've brought her home safe.'

'Well, that's good. I've checked on Ebony and Rebekah and they're all right. I went in to them when yer ran off and after this copper left.'

'Ta, Gert. I'll tell yer about it all sometime, but . . . I – I lost me friend.' A huge sob came from Ruth, though she hadn't meant to cry.

'I know, me darlin', and I'm sorry. You get in now and put Rebekah's mind at rest, I can hear all about it another day.'

Once through the door, Ruth went straight into Rebekah's open arms.

'Ruth, Ruth girl, Rebekah did worry about you.'

'You've no need to worry anymore, Rebekah. I know the truth of everything now. And, well, I want to apologize.'

PC Veners had taken off his helmet and stood twirling it in his hands. 'I shouldn't have spoken to yer how I did. I don't why I did as I don't have thoughts of you being below me through the colour yer are.'

'That's all right. Rebekah am used to it. But it's very good of you to apologize. That means a lot to Rebekah.'

'Well, from now on, I will be looking out for you. If I hear anyone calling yer names or see them not treating yer right, I'll sort them out.'

'Rebekah am grateful, but I don't get many that do. Most are kindly, if a bit wary of me. I didn't make any friends in the street till Ruth came, now me doorstep's never empty for long, and that makes Rebekah not feel lonely anymore.'

'That's good to hear. Well, I'll go now, but I will be back in a couple of weeks to get a full statement from you, Ruth. I just think you need a little time as there'll be arrangements to make and a lot for you to go through.'

Ruth couldn't match this man to the one who had caught her all those months ago and who had terrified her earlier today.

When he'd gone she could hold back her tears no longer. Her legs gave way. Rebekah sat down next to her and stroked her hair while Ebony sat on the other side.

'You cry, Ruth, cry a river of tears, as that's what the soul needs at such a sad time. I will cry with you as me heart is breaking for Hettie.'

To Ruth it was more than her soul that was crying, it was her heart and her head and even her fingers and toes – the whole of her wept for Hettie and for Ellen, who she was sure wasn't happy, and for Amy all those miles away. Would she ever see any of them again?

Chapter Twenty-Five

1913

Three years to the day after Hettie had died, Ruth stood with Robbie next to her grave.

'I cannot believe all that happened to us three years ago, Robbie.'

'I know. Your birthday was a moment when I thought back. Sixteen! Yer were a snotty-nosed kid when I met yer.'

Ruth laughed, but then became thoughtful again. 'Yer know, we were blessed in many ways when yer think what could have happened to us. But I fear things are changing, mate, and I'm not sure what I shall do.'

But before Robbie could answer, Rebekah called over, 'Rebekah is getting cold, Ruth, the flesh on me old bones don't keep me warm no more.'

Ruth looked back to the bench where she'd parked Rebekah's bath chair. Rebekah gave her a lovely smile, but this didn't dispel the fear in Ruth that the woman she loved like a mother was fading fast.

As they went back towards her, Robbie said, 'I'll have to go anyway, mate. I've rehearsals in a couple of hours and I haven't eaten.'

'Neither have we. Let's go and get a hot spud from Bett, eh? It may be our last chance as she's retiring yer know.'

'Take Rebekah home first, Ruth, love. I need to lay on me bed. Gert will sit with me and I don't want anything to eat.'

Ruth sighed, 'All right, luv. Here, let me tuck yer in, your blanket's dragging on the ground.'

As always it was with a heavy heart that Ruth left Hettie there in the graveyard. Nothing had ever come of the investigation into Belton and the others, but now, she hardly thought about it. She'd had to get on with her life. And that had meant working harder than ever at her successful stall and especially keeping the stock levels up and fulfilling the orders she was given. All this had been single-handed for the last eighteen months as Ebony and Abdi had been running their restaurant in Stepney and doing a roaring trade in all of that time.

And now, Bett was retiring, and Ruby had done so already.

Other stall-holders had changed too, but all were still like a huge family who looked out for one another.

Sadly, there was no longer the usual gang of homeless either, as Mick the Irish had been knocked down whilst drunk and had died instantly, leaving a gap in their hearts. And Reg had a well-to-do fancy woman and was always gadding off. Ruth knew it wouldn't be long before he went off into the sunset with his lady love.

She was happy for Reg, though the more she learned about his heroism in the Boer War, the more she wished he had a better life.

So, now there was only Ted most days. Lovely Ted, who still played his flute for pennies, but who was still a big help to her. He always carried her stock from behind the cafe where she now had a storeroom and packed it away again at night.

They were nearly home when Robbie broke into her thoughts, 'How about yer come to see the show this weekend, Ruth?'

'I'd love to, mate, but—'

'You go, honey child, Rebekah will be all right once you've got me into bed. You know I never disturb till morning.'

'We'll see.'

With Rebekah settled and Gert happy to look in on her, Ruth and Robbie walked to the market together, chatting about everything and nothing. They didn't see each other often now – a couple of times a week, when Robbie only did a matinee, and he would come round for his tea – as now, he shared a flat with a few other showbusiness people and rarely stayed at home.

They were sitting in the park juggling their hot spuds when Robbie asked her again.

'I don't know, Robbie. I'm really worried about Rebekah. Doctor Price warned me that it's only a matter of time, and I worry that it will happen while I'm out.'

'You need a break. I'm worried about Rebekah too, but I'm just as worried about you, Ruth. It's relentless for yer, mate.'

'I know, but I'm coping, honest. Tell me about the show. I love you to transport me there with yer tales.'

'Well, it's a daft tale called *Miss Hook of Holland*. The gist of it is that there's this really rich man – Mr Hook, a liqueur maker. Well, his daughter, Sally, invented this liqueur called Cream of the Sky and Mr Hook loses the recipe. Papp, who loves Sally, buys the recipe from the man who found it as he wants to use it to win the favour of Sally. There's a whole host of choruses of market folk, soldiers, cheese merchants, villagers, and assistants at the liqueur distillery. I am in most scenes at one time or another. I even sing a solo as one of the soldiers. And we dance and generally fill in the scene changes. I love it, Ruth. It's me biggest part to date, and the best bit is that I am the understudy for Papp!'

'Oh, that's wond— Oh my God! Abraham!'

'What?' Robbie swivelled around then stood as in the one movement, his graceful body lifted effortlessly from the bench. 'Abe! Oh, Abe.'

Before Ruth could react, Robbie put his spud on the bench and ran to Abe. Ruth could only watch as nineteen-year-old Robbie, and the now twenty-one-year-old Abe, hugged each other. Both tall, dark and lovely-looking men, they looked beautiful to Ruth – like two people in love.

Shocked at this thought, she stood and stared . . . They couldn't be, could they?

A pain gripped her heart as the love she had for Abe – had dreamed of for all this time – was crushed under the helplessness she felt against the strong feelings she was witnessing.

She looked away, unable to process how it could be that two men loved each other, and trying to dispel the loneliness the realization had given her.

'Ruth!'

Her name on his lips quickened her heart but when she looked back expecting Abe to be coming towards her, he still stood with his arm around Robbie in a way that said to Ruth that he never wanted to let go.

They came back to the bench together. 'How are you, Ruth? It's good to see you. I've thought so much about you – about you both.' He smiled at Robbie.

Ruth had never seen Robbie looking so happy. His grin truly did seem to reach from ear to ear, as she'd read happened in books.

But as she looked up into Abe's eyes, Robbie faded, and she felt there was only her and Abe in the world. 'I – I'm all right ta, mate.'

Mate? Why had she called him that as if he was no more

294

than someone she hadn't seen for five minutes, when every night she'd lain awake dreaming of him and longing for the day he came back into their lives.

'Ha, I've missed being called that while abroad. But well, I have been called it very recently. I sought Cook out, wanting to know if she knew where you were and what had happened to Hettie. I wanted to know how you were. I expected her to tell me that Hettie was with you. I was so shocked when she told me that I burst into tears. Cook called me "mate" as she comforted me – such a nice lady. I'm so sorry. I feel responsible. Was it my actions? Did she do it because she lost her job? Only Cook said there were underlying reasons.'

Ruth threw the remains of her spud away and sat down. Abe sat beside her and Robbie followed suit, sitting next to Abe. Out the corner of her eye, Ruth saw Robbie throw the remains of his spud away too.

As she watched the birds dive after it, she heard herself say, 'Hettie was pregnant.'

'What? How . . . ? Who . . . ? I mean . . .'

Without thinking, Ruth blurted out, 'At the orphanage, she was raped . . . We all were.'

Abe's head swivelled round. 'Robbie?'

Robbie nodded. As he did, a tear plopped onto his cheek and Ruth had a moment of knowing the suffering Robbie had been through and yet, he was always strong for her.

Abe slowly looked back at Ruth. 'Not you . . . No . . . Oh my God!' His arms came around them both and he pulled them to him.

They sat like that for a moment, till Ruth reached for Robbie's hand. She wanted to thank him, to tell him she loved him as if he was her brother as that was what he was

295

to her. A big brother who'd always looked out for her and been there for her.

'I don't know what to say. I've thought so much about you both over the past three years, but never dreamed you had suffered like that. Or that poor Hettie . . . I could have helped. I could have given her money . . . Well, anything . . . I'd have done anything.'

'Nothing would have made any difference, Abe. We tried. Rebekah offered her and her baby a home. And all of us offered her help and love. Flo – the cook you spoke to – was like a mother to her. But Hettie was hurt inside. Like a wound that festered, and she felt worthless no matter how much we all loved her . . . I didn't know this at the time. Everything seemed simple back then – as if everything could be fixed one way or another. But it can't. No one can fix how yer feel inside, only yerself. I've learned that the hard way.'

'Are you fixed? I mean, have you come to terms with what happened?'

'Mostly.'

'And you, Robbie? Oh, Robbie.'

There it was again, that special thing between Abe and Robbie. Could it be possible for two men to love each other?

Her mind wouldn't give her an understanding of this. She'd never heard of such a thing; did it happen?

'I'm all right most of the time, mate.'

'I don't want this thing to have happened to you, to either of you. I hope the man that did it rots in hell.'

'He ain't dead yet, but he ain't got much of a life.'

This shocked Ruth. Was Belton still alive? Before she could react, Abe asked, 'You still know of him, then?'

Robbie stood and did what he always had done when in

a bit of a situation – he kicked a stone. Shoving his hands in his pockets, he shrugged. 'I have seen him. I mean, not the bloke who interfered with the girls – a different one.' He looked at Ruth. Ruth gaped back.

'You are in touch with Gedberg?'

'I'm sorry, Ruth, I never told you because I knew it would upset you, but I sought him out. I had to. I had to confront him. I wanted . . . Oh, I don't know . . . An apology . . . To see him grovel and laugh at him as his life had become difficult, and to rub it in that we had that done to him, but it didn't turn out like that. I found a broken man living in squalor. His family had left him, he had no job, no money, he couldn't even take himself to the toilet and sat in his own mess. He stank, was starving, and near to death, and well, he told me that Belton was still alive but not good. He can't walk and needs constant care.'

Ruth still couldn't react. She sensed Abe's shock.

Robbie sat again and hung his head in his hands. This time, Abe didn't touch him, but stared into space. Ruth wondered what he thought of them – what was Robbie thinking to do such a thing as to seek out the man who . . . she couldn't even think the word.

'I – I helped him. I cleaned him and his house up. I got food for him . . . I did that for months. And, well, I forgave him and that made me feel better. He died a happy man not long after that.'

When Robbie looked up, Ruth saw the anguish in his eyes. And yes, the loneliness. Because she knew what loneliness you could carry even though surrounded by people who loved you. It was about the things you couldn't share. Well, Robbie was sharing now.

She rose and went to him, going down on her haunches

297

next to him. 'Robbie, mate. Yer did right. It was how yer were driven. You were true to yerself. But I could never deal with it that way. I couldn't seek out Belton. I don't ever want to see him again as long as I live.'

'It helps to forgive, Ruth, it really does. And it especially helps me now that you know and yer ain't condemning me. It was something the preacher said about forgiveness that prompted me.'

'I know, mate, I've thought about it, but know I can't do it. If I forgave for me, I've no right to forgive for Hettie, Ellen, Amy . . . and there was a girl called Doris, who always tried to act as if it wasn't happening and used to tell us to snuggle down in bed afterwards as if it hadn't. I never knew if she could really do that . . . and well, all the others it happened to. I can't forgive for me and I can't forgive for them. So, I just want to forget. I have done that, till today.'

'I really don't know what to say to you both. I knew there would be pain in meeting up again because of Hettie, but I never dreamed anything like this. But I do understand. A lot goes on in boarding school . . . Anyway, I don't want to talk about that. Can we salvage anything from this poor meet-up? I've longed to see you both again.'

Robbie blew his nose and wiped his eyes. 'Sorry, mate, you didn't deserve this. I don't know what possessed me. Part of it was talking about Hettie and part of it was just seeing you. It made me feel like me again and as if I could unburden.'

Abe put his arm around Robbie. 'You can always do that with me, Robbie. I'm here now.'

And with this, Ruth knew for sure that Abe loved Robbie. Not just as a friend, but he was in love with him, and her world suddenly became lonelier.

'Well, it has to be short this time as I have to go to rehearsals.'

'Rehearsals! Has your career moved on?'

They got into a deep conversation about Robbie and how he'd progressed and how he lived mostly with some artistic types in South London.

Ruth had gone back to her seat. She watched the birds still fighting over the last remnants of hers and Robbie's lunch and tried to come to terms with her newfound knowledge. She loved both Robbie and Abe, so if they truly loved one another, she must stand by them, as surely, they would be ridiculed?

It was this thought that gave her remembrance, of how Gedberg was referred to as 'queer' because he preferred to do things with the boys. Is this what being queer meant? Did Robbie and Abe prefer that? Were they queer?

Somehow, she couldn't think of them in that way. If they loved each other, she knew it would be a pure thing. A beautiful thing, not something sordid. But, oh, she wished she understood.

Interrupting them, she told them that she had to go to get back to Rebekah.

Abe stood. 'I'll walk with you, Ruth.'

'Oh, I thought you'd want to go with Robbie.'

This sounded like a petulant child when she hadn't meant it to.

'No. I'm going to the show tonight and then we're going to supper after. I want to catch up with all your news and tell you mine, Ruth.'

Robbie gave a little laugh, 'Oh dear, I've gone on a bit, mate. I ain't given yer a chance to tell me where you've been or what's been happening in your life.'

'I know, but I think you needed to talk, Robbie. About anything and everything except what you initially told me. I will bend your ear, as they say, tonight. Ha, you won't be able to shut me up. And I expect you to take me to this special place you've been telling me of.'

A smile that was like a coded message went between them and Ruth thought, how little she knew of Robbie and his new life. She'd never heard of a special place he knew of, nor had he ever invited her to it.

'Well, I'll see yer later, then. And Ruth, I'm sorry.' Robbie held his arms out, his head on one side, his look appealing to her. She went to him. When his arms enclosed her, he whispered, 'I'll always love yer and be here for yer, Ruth.'

A flash of intuition came to her. Robbie was trying to tell her that though his feelings were different to hers about everything, she and him were forever. She decided to lighten the moment. 'Yer better had. You're me big bruvver and I rely on yer.'

He pulled away and looked into her face. 'That's what I've always wanted to be and'll always be, no matter what yer find out about me.'

'There's nothing I don't know about yer, Robbie, mate. And none of it makes any difference – well, no, that's not right. It makes me love yer more, because yer going to need it. I'll always be here for you too, Robbie. Nothing can change that.'

He looked quizzically at her. 'You know?'

He didn't have to say what he thought she knew. Ruth could see he was still looking for reassurance. She nodded. 'I know, mate. And I love yer more for it. Now get off to rehearsals or you'll be late and that won't do.'

Robbie kissed her cheek. 'Ta, Ruth. I thought I would always have to keep the real me secret from you. And I never wanted to have secrets between us.'

She kissed him back, landing her peck on his lips. 'I'll see yer soon. And I will try to get to the show on Saturday night, luv.'

Abe didn't speak for a while as they strolled out of the gates of the park.

A sudden breeze broke the ice between them as he helped her to wrap her shawl around her shoulders from where it had been slung low on her arms. 'Watching your acceptance of Robbie really moved me, Ruth. How did you become so wise? How did you ever know about such things as the love men can have for each other? And women too, for that matter?'

'Women, I sort of knew, but . . . I – I, well, the penny dropped watching you both.'

'Oh? It was that obvious?'

'Yes.' Ruth couldn't believe how comfortable she felt talking to Abe like this. The companionship she felt was almost like having Hettie back with her.

'I try to fight the feelings. Giving in can lead to a lot of trouble. Men are in prison right now, because of their love for another man.'

'No! Oh, Abe, that won't happen, will it?'

'If it becomes known, yes, it could. I don't want it to, and that's why I chose to study far away from here. But I worry about Robbie. The special place he talked of is a place of acceptance. It's a seedy club – not because it provides a space where men like Robbie can be themselves, but it also provides drugs, and not all men that frequent it are men in love, or looking for love. There are those who exploit them – perverts. Don't get me wrong, I fully understand why Robbie goes there, but I don't really want to. I'll go to his show and then try to persuade him to just have supper with me and leave it at that.'

Ruth knew that what Abe was saying was a warning – a kind of plea to her to stop Robbie going there, but how could she? She rarely saw him.

'Where he goes is the sort of place that the police raid every now and again and that results in a lot of men getting prison sentences. Oh, it doesn't happen often, and when it hasn't for a while the men get complacent and begin to feel too safe. They may come out onto the streets still holding hands or with their arms around each other and then the local community begin to complain, and the harassment starts all over again.'

'How do you know all of this, Abe, have you been there?'

'No, but I have a friend who has and is now in prison. He has a terrible time and there doesn't seem to be any hope of getting him out. His father has disowned him. He really is wretched.'

'Oh, Abe, promise you'll stop Robbie from going. I couldn't bear that to happen to him.'

'I will. Anyway, I wanted to hear all that's been happening to you. How your business is thriving. How the lady that you live with is, and how Abdi and his wife are . . . and . . . Oh God!'

Ruth looked around to see what had caused this reaction. But then Abe fished out his handkerchief and held it over his nose and for the first time in a long time the stench of the street where she lived registered with Ruth. The place she'd always seen as a haven – a home – suddenly became the stinking hovel it was with blocked drains smelling of urine. It was a regular sight to see one of the housewives empty the chamber pot out of the window.

As her colour rose in embarrassment, so did her repulsion. How could she have just lived with it?

She looked at Abe, saw his eyes watering and him gagging. 'I'm sorry, Abe. Yer can go and leave me here, I understand, mate.'

'No . . . I – I'm sorry. I just didn't expect it. You . . . you live here?'

The way this was said rattled Ruth. 'Yes, I do. We weren't all born with privileges yer know. This is me home. This is where I found love and acceptance, and if yer don't like it yer can leave, it won't bother me!'

'Ruth!'

'Don't Ruth me! I know it don't smell that good, well, at least I'm aware of that now that you've made a show of it, but it's the only home I have.'

Abe hung his head. 'I'm sorry, Ruth. I was insensitive. I didn't want to hurt you. I would never do that.'

He caught hold of her hand. 'I have feelings for you, Ruth. I have from the moment I set eyes on you . . . Oh, I don't know, I'm so confused.'

Ruth felt her own confusion flood her. It had started in the park, then she'd felt an understanding and a love that could surmount her own feelings, and now, here she was longing for Abe to take her in his arms and to love her and no one else – not Robbie, not anyone. But she knew that couldn't happen as she watched the emotions Abe was suffering darken his face.

'I'll see yer sometime, Abe. I've to go.'

He didn't stop her. Ruth didn't know if she wanted him to or not but knew a great relief when she closed the door of her home and leaned on it. As she did, she looked over at Rebekah and knew her love for this lovely woman could fill her. It compensated for all her other hurt feelings and gave her the strength to cope with them.

Chapter Twenty-Six

When Saturday evening came and Ruth alighted from the cab outside the Prince of Wales Theatre, she looked around her, afraid that she would look out of place. But no, she could hold her head up high as her dark green velvet costume, with its fitted jacket and straight ankle-length skirt, fitted in well with what the other ladies waiting to go into the theatre were wearing.

For a moment, she stood in awe looking up at the building – not remembering its grandeur from that fateful day three years ago, only the feelings that had visited her later.

And now, here she was to watch Robbie on stage. To her he'd made it – achieved his dream – but he spoke as if he still had a long way to go and wouldn't rest until it was his name up in lights instead of Harry Grattan and Isobel Jay's – the stars of *Miss Hook of Holland*.

The excitement of what might have been tickled her tummy – how she would have liked to have kept up her dancing and gone on to do what Robbie was doing. But, to see his happiness was worth the sacrifices she and Rebekah had had to make to get him this far. Now he was able to look after himself most of the time but did come home if he was out of work and going hungry.

The thought of the other evening made her shudder. Thank goodness nothing had happened – well, nothing as far as Robbie getting arrested. If anything else had taken place, she didn't want to know, but she had lived in dread all day Thursday wondering if she would hear that Robbie and Abe were in prison.

She had given a lot of thought to Abe and come to an understanding of how difficult it had been for him to hide his feelings when he'd turned into Little Collingwood Street. He wasn't used to squalor.

She pulled herself up. She must stop thinking of her home as being in squalor . . . But then, everything had changed since Abe had turned up in the park – where from, or where he'd been all this time, they never got around to asking him, and she hadn't thought much about it as to her, it was as if he'd never left.

She'd cried buckets that night when she'd finally got into bed after having had a difficult few hours with Rebekah feeling so poorly. Tears of lost love – not that she had ever been given Abe's love, but she'd always hoped – and tears of fear for Robbie. This last had given her nightmares of seeing him in a cell. Only the cell kept turning into the room in the cellars of the orphanage and Robbie's jailor into Matron.

'Well, are we going in?'

Ruth jumped around to look straight into Abe's eyes. Thrown off balance, he had to catch her as she almost fell. He held her close for a moment. 'Am I forgiven, or shall I let you fall and step over you?'

His giggle was as she remembered it from all that time ago when she first met him.

'Not forgiven, but I understand now the repulsion you

felt. But, mate, friends are friends no matter what their circumstances.'

'I know. And I always want you as a friend, more, but . . . Anyway, I have our tickets, I bought two, just in case you came.'

'Really? Oh, Abe, ta, mate. I was nervous at going in and trying to buy one. I have no idea how much they are, or what to ask for.'

He just smiled at this. 'Come on then, we can get seated and then chat till the curtain comes up. I would say, we could have a drink before going into the auditorium, but you are too young.'

Ruth blushed at this. She didn't feel too young. She felt older than Abe and full of the knowledge of the world – well most of what she shouldn't know yet anyway.

And at this moment as she took Abe's arm, she felt even older than her years as he steered her through the lobby.

Once in the auditorium, Ruth gasped. 'It's so beautiful.' To Ruth, it looked like a sea of red and gold, so brightly lit it dazzled her. Red seats, curtains and frontage to the balcony seating, outlined in gold.

Abe smiled down at her as he took her almost to the front. It all felt so strange and, yes, wonderful. It was if the atmosphere of the place was seeping into her. She wanted to run up onto the stage and fling her arms wide and sing and dance and hear the audience cheer her.

'Ruth? Are you all right? You look as if you've been transported.'

'Oh, I have been. This is what I really want to do – entertain, be on the stage.'

'Really? I never knew. But then, I feel as though I know you like my own skin, and yet, don't know you at all.'

307

This seemed a funny thing to say as they had met on only four occasions in their lives, and yet Ruth understood what he meant as when with him she too felt as if she'd known him all her life and, as he had said of her, didn't know much about him.

When they took their seats, they chatted about everything. Ruth learned that Abe had been sent to Germany to live with an uncle there who was a doctor. To her surprise, he now wanted to study medicine after gaining his history degree and had secured a place at a medical college in Edinburgh.

'You really meant it when you said you were going away again, then?'

'I did, and I hope to be able to . . . well, sort my feelings out.'

Ruth didn't want to discuss this further, she tried to change the subject, but Abe didn't let her. 'Nothing happened the other night, Ruth. Me and Robbie had a good talk and agreed we had a deep attraction to each other, but that we were both confused, and decided that for now, we would remain friends. But I was able to persuade him not to frequent that place as it was the one that I had heard of. He promised, though said he would find it difficult as when there, he felt he could be himself. And that means a lot to anyone.'

'I'm glad. But now, he can be himself with me as I know and it ain't changed the way I feel about him. I don't understand and didn't know there was such thing as . . . well, anyway, it might help him to know I don't think badly of him for it.'

Suddenly, and to Ruth's relief, the air filled with the sound of music. The theatre darkened, and the curtain rose.

Forgetting all of her newfound discoveries that threatened to change her world, she immersed herself so deeply into the atmosphere that it became her up there on the stage, playing the part of Sally, singing and dancing. And then it happened – Robbie appeared. Ruth wanted to clap and clap his every step, his every sway of his body and his upright depiction of a soldier. To Ruth he was wonderful and the star of the show.

When the curtain fell on the first act, she stood with everyone else and called out, 'Bravo', making Abe giggle.

But as she sat down beside him, she knew his giggle was excited and pride-filled.

'How long before the second half starts, mate? I can't wait. It all feels like magic to me, and Robbie stands out. Wasn't he wonderful? He should be the leading man, not dancing and singing in the chorus.'

'It's magic for me too. And I agree, he has a magnetism on the stage. I don't think it will be long before that is noticed.'

'Do yer really think so? Just imagine, his name up in lights outside the theatre. It'd be a dream come true.'

As she turned to look at Abe, she found him looking at her intently.

'It's funny, Ruth, but I loved every minute of the show when I saw it for the first time the other evening and yet, tonight, it seems even better watching it through your eyes . . . You look lovely, Ruth. You are very beautiful.'

Ruth held his gaze but didn't speak.

'I connected with you from the moment you slipped on our stairs, Ruth. Do you have any feelings for me?'

She wanted to shout, 'Yes, yes, I love you,' but all had changed. Not her feelings, but how she now saw him. 'I'll always be your friend, though it ain't easy as yer showed yer repulsion of me home and that hurt, and well, I'm not of your standing.'

'I'm ashamed of my reaction, Ruth. I don't know how to

make that right. I've been cosseted all my life. I've only ever known the finer things of life. But I can learn. And you have to think, would you be comfortable in my world? If I took you to a posh restaurant, would you not find it strange and react against it?'

She knew he was right and it did help to think of it that way. She smiled a cheeky grin. 'I could learn.'

His smile held his relief. 'And I would love to teach you. May I visit you at home tomorrow?'

'I go to church tomorrow, but I come out at lunchtime. Robbie sometimes comes too, so yer can come and meet me outside if yer like and come home with me for a mug of tea.'

'I'd like that. Thank you, Ruth. We can start again, eh?'

He reached for her hand. She didn't resist as the feel of his touch zinged through her, but she did try to caution herself as this Abe wasn't the Abe she'd always imagined him to be. He was two people – the one she loved and the one who could love another man.

When the final curtain fell, Ruth once more stood to applaud. Never had she seen anything so wonderful.

'Let's go backstage and see Robbie as he can be a long time coming out. I'd like to take you both to supper.'

'Not to one of your posh places. I ain't ready yet.'

'No, it's a popular supper bar not far from here. I promise you won't feel uncomfortable, and they serve pie and mash along with other foods. A bit heavy for me though. I usually have the cheese board and a glass of port.'

There it was in a nutshell to Ruth. His world and hers meeting and he chose his. She supposed it was natural as she'd go for the pie and mash any day, but was it a difference they could ever make meet in the middle? She didn't think so.

310

Backstage was a hustle and bustle of folk in costumes rushing around all punctuating their every sentence with 'darling'. It was as if they were captured in an exciting world that was different to any Ruth had experienced and yet knew she wanted to be a part of.

Even Robbie had a different air about him as he came to them. 'Wasn't it wonderful? Oh, darling, Ruth, I'm so excited you're here. Come and let me show you around.'

Ruth giggled. 'What's with the "darling", mate?'

His laugh was her Robbie. 'Sorry, luv. It rubs off on yer. Oh, Ruth, it's a wonderful world to be part of. Everyone loves each other and yet can be really bitchy about each other – I can't explain, but I love it.'

'I can see that. I've never seen yer so relaxed and happy. And you stood out on that stage, Robbie. Me and Abe were saying, yer should have been the star of the show.'

'Ta, luv.'

Robbie smiled down at her. It was a funny smile from his lipstick lips and a face caked with pan stick make-up, but she knew it held something different to how he'd been with her since he'd entered this stage world. He was his old self and she welcomed that.

'How's Rebekah? Did yer leave her on her own?'

'No. Gert came in to sit with her.'

'Ahh, lovely Gert. We'll have to treat her one of these days. But I am worried about Rebekah.'

'I know, I am too. I'm hoping that Abdi, Ebony and Horacio can spend some time with her tomorrow, that always lifts her.'

'I'll be there tomorrow, mate, I promise. I'm not going out late tonight – or ever again, by order of Abe.'

The two men laughed, and Ruth saw a difference in their

311

relationship. The intensity they'd shown was gone and they seemed more at ease with one another. Maybe Abe had found out that he wasn't the same as Robbie? She sighed. It was all so confusing to her.

'Well, I'm glad to hear it. Abe told me about your special place and it frightened me, but yer know, Robbie, yer can always be yerself with me, mate.'

Robbie blushed. He didn't say anything but put his arm around her and went to draw her to him. Ruth resisted. 'Hey, I don't want your make-up all over me best costume, mate. Wait until you've cleaned up, then yer can give me a cuddle.'

Their laughter at this, and the banter that set up about him liking to wear make-up and dress up, seemed to Ruth to set the new way they would be with each other – more or less back to their old selves, but with a deeper knowledge and understanding and, yes, she thought, finally leaving their childhood days behind and being grown up with each other.

The supper bar was busy. Chatter and laughter gave it an atmosphere that Ruth loved as theatre-goers on a high from the place the show had taken them to, and actors winding down from the magical place they had been to, swilled down wine, sherry and beer with their food and became rowdier by the minute. And all addressed each other as if they were lovers, all were called 'darling'.

She'd hardly had this thought when a fussily dressed gentleman came up to them. 'Darling, Robbie, you must introduce me to your friends. Especially this beautiful man.'

Ruth found that she didn't even blush at this, that it seemed natural now, and she was glad as Robbie shot her a look. She grinned at him to tell him not to worry.

Introductions done, Jeromy, as she'd learned his name was, paid attention to her. 'You, darling, are so beautiful, you have a Spanish look – a regal beauty. Oh, if only you could sing and dance, you would be my next leading lady!'

'She can. She has the voice of an angel and dances like a fairy princess.'

'Really? Why haven't I met her before? Darling, have you been keeping her to yourself?' He turned back to Ruth. 'Darling, you must audition for my pantomime. Oh dear, the very thought makes me shiver with anxiety. Here it is late October and I haven't yet been inspired by anyone to be my leading lady.'

'Have yer chosen yer leading man yet, Jeromy?'

'Robbie, darling, I need my leading lady, then I will know. She will determine who I choose. You are still in the running, darling, and if I could get this divine lady, you would be it, as you two go together like two peas in a pod. I could feel the connection and love between you as I watched you and that is what I want to capture for my Cinderella and her prince. Darling – work on it.'

With this he was gone, moving away like the swish of a curtain, his tone above all of the others as he said, 'Darling, how lovely to see you, you are looking so beautiful,' to another lady sat just behind them.

A shocked Ruth, caught up in the moment, could only giggle a girlish giggle as she looked at Robbie in disbelief and asked herself, did that just happen? Did he mean it? And felt an excitement bubble up inside her.

'Well, what do yer think, Ruth?'

'Did he really mean it? Me? A starring role? I can't take it in, Robbie.'

'Can you really sing and dance, Ruth?'

313

'She can, Abe, she is amazing to listen to and watch . . . and well, she gave it all up so that I could follow me dream. She was only thirteen at the time but determined to do that for me. I can never repay her.'

'Well, yer me big bruvver, Robbie. I'd do anything for yer, you know that. Besides, yer saved me when I ran away. You gave me yer friendship and support, and I had me hat business, so it seemed the best way then.'

'I agree with Robbie. You are amazing, Ruth, and the more I learn about you, the more amazing you become. You were thirteen and you had your own hat business – a milliner at that age! That's astounding. I was still learning to tie my own shoelaces then.'

Abe laughed his lovely laugh.

'But seriously, your achievements are fantastic. Would you really consider auditioning for the part you were just offered?'

'I don't know, Abe. Me heart wants me to but me head is saying that I have too many responsibilities and I can't just give them up.'

'You can, Ruth and yer should, mate. I ain't just saying that because it would give me a chance to make a break-through, but because I know you've always wanted to do it. Yer heart was in it as much as mine was.'

'Oh, I don't know. I'll think about it.' But though she said this, she knew that she'd love to grab this opportunity with both hands.

Excusing herself and going to the ladies' closet, Ruth sat a moment on the lav trying to contain an excitement she dared not give into. She had to think of Rebekah, of the stall, and . . . oh so many things. And she knew as she rose that her answer couldn't be anything other than 'no'.

Shock held her in the doorway for a moment as Abe and Robbie came into view. They were looking into each other's eyes and once again, she saw the love they had for one another. Sighing, she went towards them.

'Well, I'll have to go now, mate. I'll get a cab to the station and see yer both tomorrow, eh?'

Both stood up. And both coloured a little. She didn't want them to feel embarrassed, 'It's all right, I'll be fine, you two carry on and have a great night together.'

'But, Ruth, you ain't made up yer mind.'

'I have, Robbie. I can't do it. It's just not possible. See yer tomorrow, mate.'

Grabbing her shawl, Ruth turned and hurried to the door. Just before she opened it an attack of nerves hit her at the prospect of going home alone. She looked back. Neither of them looked as though they'd given her a second thought. They were engrossed in one another.

Hurt and a little angry, she sighed as a pain sliced through her heart, for at this moment, it felt as though she had lost them both. She didn't want that – couldn't live without them. It was then that the thought came to her, that the only way to keep them both was to let them be free to love each other. With her blessing and her love.

Chapter Twenty-Seven

Outside, Ruth looked this way and that, but there wasn't a cab in sight. Unsure whether to start to walk and hope that one would come along, or to go back inside, she hesitated, but then froze as a familiar voice shocked her and filled her with fear.

'Gone up in the world, ain't yer?'

Swivelling around, she peered into the darkness. Two feet, as if not attached to anything appeared in the dim streetlight from around the corner of the building. Ruth's heart thumped against her chest. She could only stare as more of the person came into view and she realized that whoever it was was in a wheelchair. She held her breath.

'Got yer, you rotten bleeder! Yer had me crippled for life. Oh yes, I know it was you. The bloke who did this to me named yer.'

'Belton!'

'Yes, it's me. I've been watching yer every last movement since I found out where yer were.'

Ruth stared in disbelief.

'Well now's me chance. I've waited and waited for it to happen. Ha, I'm yer worst nightmare. And I'm gonna haunt yer for the rest of yer life. Yer mine now.'

At last, finding her legs, Ruth turned, but then a woman's voice spoke. 'Yer can run, but we know where yer live.'

There was something in the tone that Ruth recognized.

'Ha, I can see that you remember Gwen? Snotty-nosed kid? Well, she ain't that now, she's me saviour and me favourite.'

Sick with fear and disgust, Ruth looked back towards the supper bar door, praying that either Abe or Robbie would come out looking to see if she'd got off safely, but they didn't. Instead, she was chilled by the sound of Gwen's laugh mocking her.

'I look after him in all ways now, Ruth, but he can't forget you. He needs to have his revenge on yer, so you're coming with us.'

'No! Don't touch me, Gwen. I'll scream the place down if yer do. I'm warning yer.'

'Ha, we don't care.'

A shrill whistle disorientated Ruth for a moment, then a pain sliced her legs as Gwen viciously drove the wheelchair at her, causing her to tumble on top of Belton.

Bile rose to her throat as his hand came around her mouth preventing her from calling out. Kicking as hard as she could, she caught his shins. His hand released her as he cried out in pain. With all her might, Ruth screamed and screamed.

Belton pushed her off him sending her crashing to the ground.

'Where's the bleedin' van, Gwen?'

'I don't know, he said I only had to whistle.'

'Well, bleedin' whistle again, girl!'

But before Gwen could do this, the door of the bar opened and Belton shouted, 'Run, Gwen, for bleedin' hell's sake, run!'

As they took off, Ruth couldn't move. She couldn't even feel the relief she should.

'Oh, my dear, what happened? Who were they? Are you hurt?'

Ruth looked up into a kindly woman's face. 'I'm all right, I – I . . . Please, will yer get me friends for me? They're inside.'

'The two men you were sat with, dear? Yes, of course I will.' She turned to the man with her. 'Bertram, help the girl up while I fetch her friends.'

Robbie and Abe came rushing out of the bar. 'Ruth, Ruth! Oh my God! What happened?'

Ruth looked from one to the other of their frightened, concerned faces. She felt so let down by them. How could they have let her walk into the night? But then, she knew why; they'd been so engrossed in one another they hadn't given a thought to her safety. At this moment, she felt like hitting them but her legs, still feeling like jelly, would only let her flop into Robbie's open arms.

'Oh, Ruth. The lady said you'd been attacked, mate.'

The lady told them, 'Yes, I came out just in time. I saw a man in a wheelchair being pushed by a young woman – he was shouting, "Run, Gwen".'

'Here is my card, my wife and I would be willing to testify to what we saw and heard. I am a retired lawyer, and we abhor this kind of threat to a young woman's life, or any crime.'

Abe took the card from the gentleman who had helped her. 'Thank you very much. We'll look after her now.'

As Abe said goodbye to the couple, Robbie asked, 'Why did they do it? Were they after stealing yer purse, Ruth?'

She could only answer with one word. 'Belton.'

'God! Who? Belton? How? Where?'

'H-he was going to take me. He had a van!'

She felt Abe's hand stroke her back. 'I'm sorry, so sorry,

Ruth. I should have come with you. What were we thinking, Robbie? I'm disgusted with myself for letting Ruth step outside on her own at this time of night.'

Robbie held her closer. 'Oh, Ruth, Ruth, I don't know what to say. It's unforgiveable what we've done.'

When a tear plopped onto her forehead, Ruth put her hand up and touched Robbie's face. 'It's all right, mate, I'm all right. Just get me home to Rebekah.'

'We will, luv, if yer sure you're all right?'

'I – I don't know if I'll ever be right again, I . . . I thought he'd gone, Robbie. You won't leave me, will yer? Will yer stay the night? Don't leave me.'

Though Robbie assured her he would stay with her, she didn't miss how he lifted his head and looked at Abe. With the look, she knew that she'd lost more than her feeling of being safe and thinking that Belton could never hurt her again – she'd lost Abe. He belonged to Robbie.

A cab pulled up the moment Abe put his arm up. Both got in with her.

'Give the driver Ruth's home address, Robbie. Neither of you are going on a train, now.'

As she sat between them with their arms around her, Ruth felt no comfort as the fear she'd known as a kid and just now, wrapped her in a cloak of misery.

'We'll have to go to the police tomorrow, Ruth. This has to be reported. That, well, I can't express what he is, but he has to be brought to justice.'

Ruth nodded. She knew Abe was right. No more of Bett's solutions. Belton deserved to go to prison.

Finding a little strength, she told them about Gwen being with him and him calling Gwen his favourite now. 'They were going to hurt me, Robbie. Belton said he wanted his revenge as he knew I was involved in him being beaten up. I'm scared, Robbie.'

'Don't be, I'll always look out for yer. I know I let yer down back there, but I'll never do that again, Ruth.'

Ruth found his hand. 'It's all right, mate, I know. And I know that you two have a lot to talk about. Yer couldn't have known that would happen.'

They both fell silent. Ruth reached for Abe's hand. These were her friends, and they were in a turmoil over their feelings – forbidden feelings that she had no understanding of or even knew existed until a short time ago. 'Everything'll work out. I'll always stand by yer both.'

How she knew this was what they needed, Ruth couldn't fathom, but something told her that by letting them know it was all right, they might be able to find peace.

When they opened the door to their home, Gert's greeting made everything seem normal again.

'Robbie! Well, it's good to see yer, mate. Yer the hero of the street, with you being a star of the stage. Rebekah's talked about yer all night, until she dropped off. She's sleeping like a baby now.'

'Ta, Gert.' Robbie managed a little forced giggle, 'But I haven't made it yet. A long way to go.'

'Well, yer our star, and we're all proud of yer. And of you, Ruth. The pair of you are the darlin's of the street. Anyway, I'll say goodnight now and see yer in the morning.'

Ruth caught hold of Gert's hands. 'Ta, Gert, for looking after Rebekah for me.'

'Yer welcome, girl. I was glad to give you the break you deserve. Now, did yer have a good time, eh? That's all that matters.'

320

Taking a deep breath, Ruth made herself smile. 'I did, luv. Ta. It was magical.' She leaned forward and kissed Gert's cheek.

Gert patted her shoulder, 'Yer a good un. I'll get off now. Night both.'

As she passed Robbie, he took her hand and kissed her cheek too. Gert beamed. 'Ha, I'll not wash that spot now, mate. It's been kissed by a future star!'

They all giggled at this and Ruth began to feel better – safer even.

They'd said goodbye to Abe in the cab, not wanting to ask him in at this late hour and with knowing Gert was here and Rebekah asleep in her bed in the corner of the room. Besides, she felt nervous enough about his visit tomorrow as she remembered his reaction when he'd only just turned into the street, but then, they were what they were, and he had to accept that.

Though it wasn't that warm out at the late hour of midnight, Ruth and Robbie sat on the step drinking cocoa together like they had so many times in the past.

'About tonight, Ruth, I really am sorry, mate. I shouldn't have even considered letting yer go off on yer own. I, well, I was distracted.'

'I know. I was surprised you did, but when I looked back and saw the two of yer, I understood. Robbie, the situation needs resolving, mate. It's . . . well, things are a bit funny between the three of us.'

'I know. Ha, who'd have thought we'd both fall in love with the same bloke, eh?'

Ruth couldn't help laughing. It was the most ridiculous situation and yet, one that hurt. But then, that was a hurt that she could talk to no one about. Nor ask for help. No

321

one would understand. She had a job understanding it all herself. But she did know that somehow it was down to her to help things get better. 'Abe's very confused. But I don't think you are, Robbie, luv. You seem to have accepted being . . . well, I don't know what yer call it. I mean, I know what folk say but that don't fit you, Robbie. I don't like the word, it sounds horrid.'

'Queer, you mean?'

Ruth nodded, feeling embarrassed to be even talking like this, but knowing things had to be said. 'I can't think of calling you that word, mate.'

'No, we don't like it. Oh, Ruth, why do I feel like I do? I don't want to. Was it Gedberg that did it to me?'

'I don't know, luv. I wish I understood.'

'I always thought I would marry you one day.'

'Did yer? Ha, yer daft thing, yer like me bruvver.'

'I know. I think I was clutching at anything rather than admit what was really inside me.'

Poor Robbie sounded full of anguish, and she felt at a loss as to how to help him. She only knew that they had to talk about Abe. 'So, you're in love with Abe, but how does he feel about you?'

'Like yer say, confused. He talks about a love triangle. I don't know what he means, but he says the three of us are in one and he thinks the only solution is if he goes out of both of our lives.'

Ruth didn't want this but could see the sense in it. 'He might be right. It may unmuddle things for a bit. But I can't bear for yer to be unhappy, Robbie, mate. Will yer be all right?'

'I will. But what about you? You love him, don't yer?'

'I don't know. I think I'm too young to be in love properly. I do sort of have dreams about him, but I don't think he is really confused. I think he really loves you but just doesn't want to. I mean, he wants to be normal. No, I don't mean that . . . Oh dear, luv, I can't express it right.'

'I know. I don't feel normal either . . . and yet, I do. I know this is the way I'm meant to be. And when I'm with like-minded men, it all feels very normal and right.'

'Yer won't go to that place again though, will yer, Robbie?'

'I don't know, luv. I'll try not to. I know the dangers. I knew them before Abe told me, but the feeling I get when I'm there – the acceptance, the normality of men like me and no pretence, it's so . . . well, liberating.'

Ruth put her head on Robbie's shoulder, 'But I couldn't bear yer to be arrested. Yer can be all of them things with me.'

'Huh, yer a good un, but yer can never really understand. Anyway yer the best mate in all the world, so I'm lucky to have yer.'

He kissed the top of her head.

They sat in silence for a while until Ruth yawned.

'Time for bed, methinks. Come on, mate. We'd better go up. Good job I keep some of me clothes here, as I can hardly go to church in this!'

Ruth laughed. He did look a bit overdressed in his light brown suit with a sheen on it that made it seem different colours in different lights. But very handsome. 'Your grey trousers and navy blazer are in the wardrobe, luv, and I washed and ironed yer white shirt, so you'll do. And yer nightshirt's always on yer pillow, just in case.'

'Ta, Ruth, I miss living here, yer know, and being with you both, but it just ain't practical, the hours I keep.'

'I know, luv, and we miss you like mad.'

His arm came around her. He smiled down at her. 'Come on, let's go to bed, eh?'

Inside, while Robbie put the mugs in the sink, Ruth went over to Rebekah and found her gently snoring. She didn't stir when Ruth bent down and kissed her cheek. Nor when Robbie came over and did the same.

'She'll be happy to see yer here in the morning, mate.'

'I know. We were lucky to find her, Ruth. She means the world to me.'

'She's like our mum, ain't she?'

'She is. The only one we've known, and we couldn't do better.'

'Right, up to bed now. I'm whacked.'

'Me too, but can I lay on yer bed with yer for a while, eh? I still have the need to talk a bit.'

'Oh, Robbie . . . All right then, come on.'

They lay in the dimness the street gaslight provided through the window, when Robbie brought the conversation around to her being on the stage, asking her to at least give it some thought. 'I know Jeromy, he meant what he said. His casting is often done by the look of people. He always says as long as they look right and have a modicum of talent, they'll do for him. He can develop talent, but he can't change a face to be just what fits his vision.'

Ruth sighed. 'I can only say what I did before, Robbie. I want to, but . . . Well, you know the rest. It just isn't possible. I've Rebekah to care for and I'd have to give up so much for a career that ain't steady.'

'You've an old head on yer shoulders, and it ain't right that you have, Ruth. Yer shouldn't have these responsibilities, yer should be living the life of a sixteen-year-old, not a thirty-year-old. Yer haven't lived or followed yer dreams. I feel guilty about that.'

'Please don't, Robbie. I have lived me dream in a way – I

324

dreamed of being a milliner from the moment Rebekah taught me to make hats.' Ruth yawned. Her bones felt tired now. It had been a long day and though they hadn't talked about it, the horror of earlier hadn't left her. She still had to face going to the police station – and what if they didn't find him and Belton tried to take her again? A shudder trembled through her.

But Robbie didn't notice, nor did he give up.

'I think we should talk to Abdi and Ebony. They have gone off and are making a fortune for themselves while they leave you to care for their aunt.'

'Robbie! Don't even think like that, mate. Rebekah is as we just said, a mum to me. I'm caring for me mum and I'd have it no other way. Now go to bed before I fall out with yer.'

Robbie rolled off the bed. 'I'm sorry, luv. I just think . . .'

'Well, don't think. I can't and that's that.'

Robbie bent over her. 'Yer shivering. Ruth, are yer all right? Oh God, did I do wrong? I tried to talk about anything other than what had happened as I thought that would help yer, luv.'

'It did for a while. But I'm scared, Robbie.'

'I'm going to sleep with yer, mate, I can't leave yer. The street light'll go out soon and then you'll be in the dark. I know the nightmares of the dark. I'll just nip up and get me nightshirt on.'

Though Ruth didn't think it right that he should sleep in her bed, she welcomed it and was glad when he slipped between the sheets and held her in a lovely brotherly cuddle.

'You're special, Ruth, but yer don't know it, and that's what I love about yer.' He kissed her hair. 'Goodnight, luv. Yer safe now.'

His voice became sleepy, 'But yer know, mate. I'm going to hound yer till yer give in about the stage.'

She snuggled into him, feeling safe in the special way that Robbie had always made her feel, as if he would protect her. She wished they could stay like this forever. Tomorrow he would be gone again and it might be weeks before she saw him.

Chapter Twenty-Eight

The service lifted Ruth as she joined in the singing and the clapping and saw the joy in Rebekah's face and how well she looked. It also strengthened her resolve not to give in to her desire to take the offer to join Robbie on the stage, even though her own joy when singing made her long to do so.

Outside, Abe was waiting. He was so gracious to Rebekah, kissing her hand and making her go all coy and giggly.

But Ruth didn't have time to greet him, as Horacio, tall for his eight years and reaching Ruth's shoulder, grabbed her and hugged her as if he was still a five-year-old.

She hugged him back.

'I can come to Aunty Rebekah's house, Ruth.'

'Oh, that's lovely, mate. I was happy before, but now I could jump over the moon.'

Horacio laughed, but soon became serious. 'Why is the master's son here, Ruth?'

'There is no master now, Horacio.'

'Well, Poppa said to Momma that he saw the master's son waiting outside, and then when we came out, there he is!'

Ruth knew that Abdi was a little late for the service and had slipped in after it had begun, but she hadn't realized that Abe had been there that long. 'I expect your poppa finds it difficult to stop referring to Abe's dad as the master, but you don't have to. Anyway, Abe is coming back to our house with us. He's coming on a visit.'

'Does that mean we won't have curry? I never knew us to have curry at his house.'

'It doesn't, I started the curry off early this morning – a lamb curry, with rice and bread.'

'But it will mean that Robbie won't play football with me. Look, he's too busy talking to even say hello to me.'

Ruth looked over. Abdi had joined Abe and Robbie and was talking intently to Abe. Robbie looked angry. He stared at Abdi. Ruth prayed he wouldn't say anything about looking after Rebekah. That wasn't what she wanted, and nor would Rebekah.

Ebony coming over to her took her attention away from the men. 'I heard that man tried to grab you again, Ruth girl. I am sorry. Are you all right?'

'I am, ta. But I'm scared. I keep thinking he may be hiding somewhere as he said he watches me. Anyway, me and Robbie are going to the police now with Abe. Do yer think yer could stay with Rebekah and Horacio until we get back home, Ebony?'

'I can, girl, and be glad to. So, you ain't got no hug for me, then?

'Oh, Ebony, of course, I'm sorry. I need a hug, luv.'

When they came out of the hug, Ruth heard Robbie saying, 'Well, good, because it ain't right. She shouldn't have to take the full burden of it all.'

Her heart stopped.

'You all right, girl?'

Ruth shook her head. 'I think Robbie is saying something to Abdi that I don't want him to. It ain't what I want. He has no right.'

'What is it, Ruth?'

'Oh, Ebony. If I tell you, you won't think it's anything to do with me, will yer?'

Ruth looked around to where Rebekah was. Happy she wouldn't hear as Horacio was telling her something and she was listening intently, she told Ebony what Robbie thought should happen. Ebony took the wind out of her sails with her answer.

'Well, girl, I'll tell you something now, and I want you to know that this ain't me thinking or saying this, but, well, Abdi, he been talking about this very same thing. He needs more money, and he says he cannot wait till Rebekah dies, he needs his inheritance now. He says he's gonna take Rebekah into our flat and sell her house.'

'What? Oh no. No, Ebony, he wouldn't, would he?'

'Abdi is one determined man. I told him to think of you, but he says Rebekah did right by you, but now she can't and he doesn't owe you anything. He can be a selfish man, Ruth. He is a good man, but when he wants something, or thinks it's right, he sticks to his guns. Look how long he kept me at that house, knowing I was being beaten and his son bullied. He tells me that he had one aim, and that was to save for our future, and that I had my part to play. I'm going to take a long time to forgive him, but I'm only a wife and have to do what my man says.'

Ruth stared at Ebony. 'He can't . . . I mean, it would kill Rebekah. She—'

The expression on Ebony's face stopped Ruth in her tracks.

'Why do you think that, girl? I take loving care of Rebekah.'

'Oh no, I didn't mean . . . I just meant, taking her out of her home.'

'This is a shock to you, I know that, but think about it.

You will be welcome to come and see Rebekah and me and Horacio anytime you want, girl. And you can follow that career on the stage that awaits you. My Abdi says that all the hat-making stuff will be yours, and he will help you to find a place to live, so you can still make your hats. That skill will never leave you, girl.'

Ruth felt her body begin to shake. The shock of this on top of what she endured the night before was too much for her. She looked over towards Robbie. He was smiling now. She realized Abdi had told him his plan and she could tell it suited him. Well, it didn't suit her. They were taking the only home she knew away from her.

Her head swivelled to look over towards Rebekah. Unaware of what was happening, dear Rebekah was still being amused by Horacio. Ruth knew this would greatly upset her but felt powerless to stop it happening.

'Are you all right, Ruth?'

A feeling of being lost gripped Ruth, leaving her unable to answer Abe. She didn't even know how it was he was so suddenly by her side.

'Ruth?'

She looked up at him.

'Did you hear what was being said? Oh, Ruth, I'm sorry. I don't know what to say. I think it harsh and ruthless but I don't know what to do to stop it.'

Ruth looked to where Ebony had stood. But she'd moved away and was sitting on the wall next to Rebekah. Was she telling Rebekah . . . ? *Oh, Holy Mary, don't let this happen, please. I beg you.*

'Ruth, are you all right, do you want to sit down?'

'Can he do this, Abe? Can he really sell Rebekah's house from under her feet?'

'He'll have to have her consent, but with that, yes. Would she give it to him?'

'I – I don't know . . . Oh, Abe, she's so frail. This could kill her.'

'Look, I don't know her, but life couldn't have been easy for her. And if it hasn't then she has more strength than you realize. It's you I'm worried about. How you will live and where. I wouldn't want you living where Robbie does.'

'You know where he lives?'

'Yes . . . Well, I mean . . . Look, I've seen it and the people he lives with. They're arty types and up to all sorts that isn't normal to me. They're Bohemian, anything goes types of people. I'm not saying they're not nice, they are . . . Oh dear, I'm digging a hole for myself here. But I'm worried about you, Ruth.'

Ruth had no answer.

She excused herself and went over to Rebekah. Horacio's hand came into hers. She loved how he was still so affectionate towards her, even though most lads of his age would reject any show of fuss.

'Ruth, is there a man after you?'

His face looked full of concern and fear. She couldn't deny it as he'd heard what Ebony had said. 'Don't worry about it. There are bad people in the world, but our policemen soon deal with them. I'll see you later, luv. I'm going to the police station now to report it, then the bad man will be locked away and not be able to hurt anyone ever again. How are yer getting on at school, mate? Still loving it?'

'I do, but I am still learning things I already know and that gets boring. But Poppa is going to get me into a school where he has to pay the fees. Mr Peterson is going to recommend me so I will get in, only Poppa is waiting to get some more money.'

'Oh? That's . . . that's wonderful, and all you deserve. You have a good father, Horacio.' The penny had dropped. If only Ebony had said this was the reason Abdi wanted the money, then such a different light would have been put on everything. For Ruth knew she would sacrifice anything for Horacio – as long as Rebekah was happy about it all too.

'He's worried though. Poppa says that to get the money, he may have to cause unhappiness, so I told him not to do it.'

'No, he must do it, and he won't cause unhappiness. Look, we'll talk later, eh? I've just got something I have to do.'

Going over to Abdi and Robbie, who'd once again been joined by Abe, Ruth tapped him on the shoulder. 'Abdi, can I have a word, please.'

Abe caught hold of Robbie. 'We'll wait over by the wall, Ruth, only we should get going soon as the police station doesn't open to the public all day today.'

'No, don't go. I know you both know all about what I want to talk about.'

'Ruth, I'm sorry, I—'

'Don't be, Abdi. I was very upset when Ebony told me, but she missed out the reason why. I want yer to know that I'm behind you. Your reason for wanting the money is very important to Horacio's future and that to me is worth the sacrifice, but what about Rebekah? Yer won't do it if she'll be unhappy about it, will yer?'

'Rebekah is family. It would make her unhappy not to. And, thank you, Ruth. I won't leave you destitute. What I have been told I can get for the house will be more than enough to make a gift to you, which will be enough to set yourself up in a flat.'

'And I'll share with yer, Ruth, mate, so yer won't struggle to pay the rent. It's the answer! It's what we wanted.'

'It's what you wanted, Robbie, not me. I still don't want it, but Horacio is the important one, and I'm thinking of him. I need to talk to Rebekah though. When will yer tell her, Abdi?'

'Today. I won't tell her, I'll ask her, and if she doesn't want to, that'll be that.'

'How much does it cost to send Horacio to school? I have some savings and would help yer out if Rebekah is too upset to agree, Abdi.'

'That's kind of you, but it is a lot of money to continue for his schooldays and on to university. Mr Peterson is going to make a donation to the school and that entitles him to choose a child to be schooled for half the yearly fees, meaning I have to find twenty five pound a year, besides his uniforms and books and his board.'

'He will sleep there?'

'Only during the week.'

'Oh!' Ruth didn't like this idea. 'What if he's bullied? Yer know yerself that it's possible.'

'The school would not stand for that.'

Ruth knew it was no use her arguing. She just said she hoped it didn't happen and that Abdi was able to find the money. 'But don't be short, 'cos even though I haven't a lot, if I can buy the odd few books or something, I'd do it willingly.'

'You have a good heart, Ruth. I did worry about you but knew I couldn't hold myself responsible for you, except to make sure you had enough to sort yourself out.'

'No, don't worry about that. I'll be all right. I have to go now. Ta for taking Rebekah back for me.'

They all waved her, Abe and Robbie off. Ruth stood a moment and watched them turn Rebekah's bath chair around. Was there a plea in Rebekah's look? Did she know? Was she wanting someone to stop it happening? Ruth felt a tug on her heart.

'Are yer all right, mate?'

Ruth sighed. 'Oh, I don't know. I do know that Horacio deserves the best start that he can have but at the expense of Rebekah's happiness?'

'She will be happy, luv. I wouldn't even think about it and would fight it, if I thought any different, but she'll be with her family. Ebony adores her, Horacio worships her, and Abdi, well, I know he doesn't show his emotions, but I am sure he won't let Rebekah suffer any unhappiness. Besides, we'll know. We can visit whenever we want to. We get Sundays off in the theatre.'

'Really? Well, yer've been busy at something, Robbie, so how come you'll now be able to visit regularly?'

'I know yer mad at me, when you use that tone. What have I done?'

'Oh, I don't know. I'm not cross, I'm just upset about the whole thing.'

Robbie put his arm out. 'Come on, mate. It'll work out.'

At the police station they were met with an almost mocking response as the duty officer looked Ruth up and down. 'These things happen to young women who go out alone after dark. What did yer expect, eh?'

His attitude changed when Abe stepped forward. 'I beg your pardon. It is your job to prevent them happening, sir, and to make our women safe on the streets. I want to speak to your superior. He may know my father, Mr Peterson, the property developer? My father sits on many committees and I believe the governing body of the local police force is one of them.'

'I'm very sorry, sir, I didn't realize that you were with this young woman. Of course we take genuine complaints seriously, but more often than not we find that the woman in these circumstances is to blame.'

'That isn't for you to judge. There is background to this story. You need to take a proper statement from Miss Faith and find this man and stop him before he does her some real harm.'

'Yes, sir, of course, sir.' Licking the tip of his pencil and flicking open his notebook, the constable asked, 'Now, you say his name is Belton? Now, wait a minute, I remember a case a while ago involving a Mr Belton . . . Yes. The man was beaten up by someone who had the interests of the kids at the home at heart, as I remember, and besides not being able to get any substantial evidence of his wrong-doing it was considered he was no longer a danger. But yer saying that he tried to kidnap yer? That you're one of the girls involved? And that he threatened to have revenge on you?'

'Yes. And he means it. He said he'd been following me.'

'Well, these are serious allegations. Did you men see anything?'

Both shook their head.

'But there was a lady who did. She gave me her card. She and her husband helped Ruth. To our shame we were inside the bar and allowed Ruth to make her way home on her own. This lady's husband is an ex-lawyer – he said they would both stand as witnesses if the man was brought to trial.'

The policeman looked directly at Ruth. 'You do know that if this goes to court a lot more than this attack will come out and be made public? I mean, the church run that home, don't they? And I believe it was all dealt with in the way it was to save face for them and their home once it was sure that none of that kind of thing was still going on. You must remember that the church is a powerful body.'

'Do you want to go ahead, Ruth?'

'I want to know that Belton is where he can't hurt me again. I can't live me life in fear of him, Abe.'

'In that case, we will take on the church, or any other body to get justice, sir.'

'Very well. Let me take a few details and then one of our detectives will call on you to bring you in to get a full statement. Only there isn't anyone on duty today.'

Back home, Ruth could sense the atmosphere. Everyone was polite and welcomed Abe, but Rebekah was visibly upset.

'Robbie, Abe, take Horacio to the park, eh? It'll take me about half an hour to get the meal ready.'

With them not making any fuss about this and Horacio pleased to escape, Ruth soon had just the three of them left. She dreaded speaking to Rebekah about the plans but knew she must. 'Are yer all right, Rebekah, luv?'

'They take Rebekah away from you, Ruth.'

Ruth hurried to her side. She was sitting in her favourite armchair. Ruth sat on the arm and gently eased Rebekah's frail body closer to her own.

'Rebekah understands, Ruth, and must do this for Horacio, but I want to be with you.'

'And I want to be with you, Rebekah, luv. But like you, I knew it was what we must do for Horacio's future. But if yer want to live with me, yer can. I'll find a place like Bett's on the ground floor, eh?'

Rebekah patted her hand. 'Ta, luv, Rebekah would like that.'

'Aunt, you should be with us. We should be taking care of you. Ruth can come to see you whenever she wants to. Ruth, what about your stage career?'

Shocked that Abdi knew of this, Ruth told him, 'It isn't important to me, Abdi.'

Rebekah looked shocked. 'What you talking of, Abdi?'

'Ruth has a chance to join Robbie on the stage, Aunt. She's turning it down because of her responsibilities to you.'

'I'm not! I haven't given it a lot of thought. Robbie has made his mind up that I should follow this chance, but I only heard of there even being one last night. It isn't as important to me as it is to Robbie. He had no right mentioning it to yer, Abdi.'

'Rebekah is hearing you, Ruth, but I know this is some-thing you should do. I'll go with Abdi, honey child, but my heart will miss you.'

'Rebekah, I – I . . . Oh, Rebekah, I don't know what to say. I can't lie to yer. I do harbour a dream of the stage, but I have me business. And you set me on the path to that. I ain't throwing it away.'

'You can go back to that at any time, Ruth girl. Chances to go on the stage don't come that often. Give it a go and see what comes of it, eh?'

'But will you be happy, luv?'

'Rebekah will be happy with Ebony and Abdi, but I was worried about you, honey child. This though, could be the making of you, and if that happens, then that will make Rebekah even happier.'

'Oh, luv, ta. Ta, ever so much. I will come to see you every day, I promise.'

Rebekah tapped her hand and Ruth knew she was too full up to speak. She felt the same and wanted to say that she would rather live with her than go on the stage, but she knew in her heart that it was better for Rebekah to be with Ebony and Abdi and as she'd said, she couldn't lie to Rebekah.

The rest of the day was lovely. Abe fitted in so well and Rebekah loved him. Abdi talked to him a lot about the house, his father, and Abe's future. It was lovely to see Abe so relaxed in her home. More than once he looked at her.

Ruth couldn't deny the quickening of her heart when he did, but nor could she quieten the feeling that he really did love Robbie, and she must find a way of bowing out.

Chapter Twenty-Nine

The pace of how quickly everything happened had left Ruth in a whirl at first, but here it was, November, and she was in full swing of rehearsals and loving it.

'Darling, you are almost perfect!'

Jeromy took her hand. She loved him, he was so very lovable, full of compliments and praise, kind and fair and really patient with everyone, especially her, knowing she hadn't had the benefit of formal training.

Robbie was in his element, and an amazing teacher and talent.

'You're both going to be a hit. I just know it, my darlings.' He clapped his hands. 'Right. Go through the scene when the hour strikes twelve and you have to run. I need more drama in this moment. You, Robbie, must be showing your feelings through your look and your dance around Cinderella, and you, Ruth, need to show your distress.'

'This time, mate, eh?' Robbie whispered to her.

Ruth nodded, letting her mind think about how it would be if this dream suddenly ended. Immersing herself in this distressing thought, she drifted into the music. Before she knew it Jeromy was clapping enthusiastically. 'We're ready! That was perfect, hold that feeling and use it every time, and you will both knock the socks off the audience. Remember, with no recognized leading couple I am taking a chance, so opening night is all important – we need those reviews, darling. Now, off you go, rest day tomorrow.'

Outside, Robbie hugged her. 'Oh, Ruth, only two weeks to go and we will be the stars of the show!'

'I know, luv. Brrr, it's freezing. Let's hurry home. I'm exhausted.'

They'd been so lucky to find their need for a flat coincided with the one above Bett's becoming empty. Bett had secured it for them and revelled in looking out for them.

So far, they had managed to pay their rent from their earnings, which they supplemented by working some evenings in the theatre, seeing people to their seats, and helping to run the box office.

Ruth had found, too, that she'd been able to earn money in the costume dept. Her hat-making and sewing skills had come in very useful for the current productions as well as for the upcoming pantomime she was going to star in. She loved making the decorations for the elaborate wigs all the lady cast members had to wear for the ballroom scene.

'I know, it's draining, but yer amazing, mate. I'd have never got me chance without yer.'

'Don't be daft, Robbie, of course yer would.'

'Oh, I don't know. Anyway, I'll get the tin bath filled for yer when we get in, and you can relax in front of the fire while I make tea, eh?'

'Mmm, sounds lovely, luv. Ooh, yer a good un. Will yer come to see Rebekah with me tomorrow?'

'I will, but I won't stay, I'm meeting friends.'

She didn't question him. Gazing out of the window of the train, her thoughts were of fear for him, and for herself.

For Robbie, it was knowing that on the odd evening when he didn't come in till the early hours that he was going to the club, but she knew she had to let him lead his own life.

For herself, she feared that once again, nothing had come of the police's promise to arrest Belton. This incensed her and left her scared to be alone at any time, day or night.

Opening the door to their flat, the lovely smell of cooking met them, as did a warmth from the roaring fire. Bett came out of the kitchen carrying a wooden spoon. 'There you are. Yer late tonight, I've had a job to keep the stew and dumplings from sticking to the bottom of the pan. Ooh, shut the door, mate, it's bleedin' freezing.'

'Hello, Bett, luv. That smells good.'

'Well, it comes along with good news. Sit down, both of yer.'

The serious tone Bett used had Ruth curious. Neither of them sat down but stared at Bett.

'Right. Veners called round, which I ain't happy about, I don't like the Ole Bill on me doorstep. Anyway, they've arrested that Gwen yer told me about.'

'Gwen? Not Belton?'

'No, Robbie. Gwen's on a charge of murder – she did Belton in.'

Ruth's mouth dropped open. They were both looking at her. After a moment she managed to ask, 'Belton, dead?'

'He is, luv, and good riddance. It seems he couldn't stop talking about you. Veners said Gwen got jealous and clocked him across his head with a rolling pin. He died instantly, apparently. Good bleedin' riddance! I thought yer'd be pleased, girl.'

'I – I, well, I am, but shocked as well.'

'Will Ruth be called to testify? I mean, won't the court want to know why Gwen was jealous of her?'

'If she gets to court. Veners said she'd poisoned herself and left a note as to why. She ain't dead, she's in hospital, but still under arrest.'

'God, I hope she dies, Ruth, that will save this spoiling everything. Jeromy won't like bad publicity being in the papers.'

'Robbie!'

Robbie hung his head. 'Oh, Ruth, Ruth I – I . . .' His head shook from side to side. 'I'm sorry. What's happened to me? I've got so caught up in me ambitions I ain't thinking right. Come here, luv. I didn't mean it. And I can see this has been a shock to yer.'

Ruth didn't feel like being hugged. 'You've changed, Robbie. No hug will make everything better. And life ain't all about you and yer mates, and the stage. You just wished someone dead – a girl who's been through the same as us. And yer seem to forget that there's people who love you and deserve a part of you. Rebekah, for instance. She shouldn't come second to yer mates. And me. But everything that happens is how it affects you and yer stage career.'

Robbie put his arms down and stared at her.

'Now, you two, yer ain't gonna bleedin' fall out are yer?'

'No, Bett. I'm going to apologize again to Ruth, and I know I've done wrong, so I'm going to change.'

'Good, because Ruth ain't wrong, I've noticed it, and if I have, Rebekah must have, and she don't deserve to be second best to anything in yer life.'

'I know. I don't know where I'd be without her, or you, Bett, or you, Ruth. I'm sorry, really, I am. I'll not wish Gwen to die, even though she did wrong to you, Ruth. And I'll come with yer tomorrow and spend the day with yer. Look, I know, we'll take Rebekah out, shall we? She'd like that as

342

she don't get out much. And what about you, Bett? Will you come too?'

Robbie was like a little boy who didn't know how to make amends. Still cross at him, Ruth didn't answer, but Bett did. 'I would, Robbie. I'd love to. Where yer thinking of, eh?'

'Hmmm, not sure . . . Wait a minute. What about the zoo in Regent's Park, mate? Rebekah would love seeing the animals from her native land.'

Ruth sighed. 'Oh, Robbie. That's more like you, thinking of others, and all right, I'll forgive yer, but think on in future. And as for yer idea, as lovely as it is, we could never get Rebekah onto the trains. Getting her on one would be hard enough, but we'd have to take at least two to get there.'

'We'll have a cab! I'll pay. Now I've been promised a trip like this, I ain't bleedin' losing out, girl. Robbie, nip to you-know-who and tell him to get a message to me man. Tell him I want a cab here tomorrow at ten o'clock and it's to be at me disposal all day.'

Ruth suddenly felt the excitement that she could see was in Bett, and yet, she hadn't really taken in the shocking news of what Gwen had done.

The relief she should feel didn't come to her, instead all she could think of was what would happen to Gwen. Would she live? If she did, would she face being hung? What had she been put through to get to this stage? Her heart went out to Gwen and she wanted to go to her, to comfort her, but she couldn't do that.

As Robbie went to leave, Bett called after him. 'And here, take this bob and bring me a jug of ale back with yer, I feel like celebrating.'

Robbie grinned. It was a grin that Ruth loved and brought with it a feeling that all would be all right from now on.

As the door closed on him, Bett turned to her. 'Right, girl, I've filled the bath for yer in yer room and lit a fire in there so yer'll be nice and warm. You go and get a soak while I see to getting the table ready. The stew's fine simmering, I was only kidding when I said it was overdone.'

'Ta, Bett. Oh, Bett, what would we do without yer?'

'Yer'll never know, luv. Because I ain't bleedin' going anywhere. Now, go on with yer.'

Ruth got into the hot water and lay back, her mind a turmoil of thoughts. Memories had been evoked that she didn't want to revisit and that stopped her rejoicing at the realization of how she was safe now and truly free at last.

She should feel happy, but all she could feel was her heart heavy with sadness at the destruction Belton had caused – Hettie, lovely Hettie, unable to live and face a future with a child, and the job she'd loved taken from her, and all the other kids who'd suffered. Amy, lovely Amy. Images of her crying in the dark came to her, and she hoped with all her heart that she was happy now. But oh, how she longed to hear from her and from Ellen. Was Ellen happy? Something told her that she wasn't as her dad had been a nasty piece of work.

These memories and longings brought tears streaming down her face. Exhausted, she allowed them to flow. Let her heart empty of the sorrow of them all.

When at last she was drained of emotion, she felt better. More able to face the future and to take it in, though she wished with all her heart she could change so many things, she knew that life would be better for her now and she would grasp it with all her might. Throw her heart into it and try to realize her dream.

*

344

The wind was keen the next day, but that didn't deter them as they got ready for the day out.

Bett hollering up the stairs only added to the excitement that Ruth felt.

'I hope Rebekah's in agreement with this, as I ain't not going now. Come on the pair of yer, the cab'll be here any minute. Me man never lets me down.'

Why Bett always referred to her son as being 'her man' was something Ruth and Robbie had often giggled over. They both knew the identity of the gangster and wondered if it made her feel better about it all if she distanced it from her family.

'Nearly ready, Bett, just waiting for Ruth. Yer know what women are like.'

'I should do, I am one, in case yer hadn't noticed, yer cheeky bleeder.'

Ruth heard Robbie laugh at this, but she didn't join in the banter. Instead she grabbed her coat from the hook on the back of her door, and her warm cloche she'd laid out ready on the bed, but then hesitated as she went to put it on. It all seemed so long ago since she'd made it for herself. Her very first hat. In some ways she missed the hat trade. She'd loved the feeling of creating a new design and the orders from Melinda's Milliner's had begun to increase just before she finished, giving her scope for more and more elaborate hats.

Thinking about this as she pinned her cloche into place, the thought occurred that maybe she shouldn't have stopped taking orders from the shop. There were only two a month at most ordered, and she could manage that.

She looked at the shelf that held all her hat moulds and piles of felt alongside a box that contained her tools and the idea grew, giving her the urge to go to see Melinda and discuss with her the possibility of carrying on.

As she skipped down the stairs, her step was light with anticipation and excitement, for more reasons than the outing – she knew she could really make her two careers work side by side and that would mean she always had something to fall back on.

'You look happy, Ruth, I was worried about yer this morning, you didn't look like yer'd slept much, mate.'

'I didn't, Robbie, but I've had an idea. Yer know how folk at the theatre are always warning of lean times when work dries up? Well, I've had an idea.' They stood and chatted about it for a moment before joining Bett.

'It won't be too much for yer, will it, luv?'

'No, there's hours when I sit up there alone with nothing to do. I could fill that time by doing something I really enjoy. I don't know why I haven't thought about it before.'

'I do. You've not been yerself since Belton attacked yer. His death has sort of released yer, really.'

'It has, Robbie. I feel free at last! And yes, that might be the reason. So, yer think it a good idea, then?'

'I do. Yer right, we do need something else, there's a few lean times in the theatre world. I might take up something meself, but I don't know what.'

'Carpentry. You were really good at that and you help out with making the sets sometimes. Well, yer could make bits of furniture – small tables and the like.'

'Oh, I don't know. I'll think about it, But I'll help you out all yer need, luv. And, Ruth, I promise yer, I'll change, or rather, go back to being meself. I've had a lot on me plate.'

'I know, luv. Come on, I feel like a kid again. I can't wait to see Rebekah.'

346

'Be great if Horacio's there too, but it being a schoolday it's not likely.'

'We'll take him another time. We'll have our hands full with Rebekah and Bett!'

They giggled at this as they went through the connecting door to Bett's flat – a door that they'd never known was there as it had had a Welsh dresser in front of it before they moved in. This now stood next to the fireplace.

The door not only gave them freedom to come and go, but Bett liked the idea of having access to the backyard. She said she would sit out there when it was nice weather and have a line for her washing. Ruth loved it as having the two dwellings was like living with Bett, and yet having their own place – a great combination as she loved Bett.

It was as they waited on the step that the postman came along. 'One for upstairs, Bett!'

'That's these two then, which one is it for?'

The postman read out: 'Ruth Faith and Robbie, is that three people?'

'No, me name's Ruth Faith.'

'And what's yours, young man?'

Robbie had recently adopted the name of Grant. Jeromy had given it to him, saying it had a strong ring to it.

'It's Robbie Grant, and I'm an actor and dancer, so is Ruth, so look out for our names on the Prince of Wales Theatre around Christmas time – we're going to be stars for two weeks in the pantomime!'

The postman took off his cap and scratched his head. 'Well! That's a turn up. Pleased to meet yer both. Here yer go, and yes, I'll look out for yer.'

Robbie gave one of his ear-to-ear smiles that always filled Ruth with joy. She forgave him his boastfulness as it had

347

been a good moment and had given her a thrill to hear it said out loud . . . *Yes, I am truly going to be a star!* For the first time it sank in with Ruth.

Robbie was already ripping open the envelope when the cab pulled up. No ordinary cab, but a huge shiny green one with a bench seat open to the elements, with just a glass screen in front of the steering wheel and a back that looked like a pram hood and could be folded down to make the carriage open air.

'Hello there, missus. Cab for Bett! And I was told you'd want to put a bath chair in, so no problem, mate, two of yer can sit up here with me, and one in the back to look after the lady we have to pick up. I've plenty of blankets, so yer'll all be warm enough.'

As Ruth gazed at the car in wonderment that she was going to ride in such a vehicle, she had mixed feelings – one that she'd freeze sitting up front but knew she couldn't ask Bett to, and the other of deep excitement.

'You sit in the back, Bett, we'll get up on the front seat.'

'Ta, Ruth, luv. I feel me bones chilling already. Let me get me bonnet yer made me, I didn't think I'd need it, but me lug'oles feel like icicles.'

Ruth smiled. She didn't think it was for this reason as Bett had tied her usual headscarf around her head and knotted it above her forehead, but the car had made her feel she wanted to look more dressed up. When she came back out, she looked lovely in the blue bonnet with the darker blue butterfly on one side of it.

As the car spluttered into life more than one curtain twitched and eyes peered out to watch them go.

Ruth wasn't sure about the sensation at first as the wheels jolted over the cobbles and the car belched fumes from its

348

side exhaust, but she could see Robbie was in his element, asking questions about something called pistons.

Nudging him, she could wait no longer. 'Robbie, the letter!' She didn't have to ask who it was from; she knew it would be Abe writing to them.

Robbie passed the letter to her. Her heart gave an involuntary flip as she looked at the beautiful writing and read:

Hello, you two.
I hope this letter finds you both well.
I was excited to read that you are starring in the pantomime. I will be home for Christmas and will catch a performance. Then I want to take the leading lady and leading man to supper afterwards. I cannot wait.
All is going well here. Well, sort of. I miss London and you both, and the studying I have to do sometimes wears me down.
Love to you both, Abe x

'Well, that was short and sweet. Do yer think he's all right?'

'Who knows with Abe? He's a complicated fellow, Ruth. He doesn't know who he is, but let's hope he finds himself if nothing else.'

'I miss him, though, Robbie. It'll be good to see him.'

'I do, but well, somehow it's easier when he ain't around. Anyway, let's enjoy our day, eh? Can't wait to see Rebekah's face, but I'm nervous that she won't want to come and'll just want us to sit with her all day. I really want to go to the zoo now and I know Bett does.'

'Me too. I can't begin to imagine what it's like.' Though she said this, Ruth did feel a little apprehensive, as she thought of the huge animals they would see and hoped they were truly, safely caged.

When they reached Rebekah's, they found her really perky. She hugged Ruth as if she would never let her go and repeated over and over, 'My honey child, my honey child.'

Ruth felt the tears prickle her eyes and wished for the millionth time that things hadn't worked out as they had.

When she released her, Rebekah looked up into her face. 'Rebekah is proud of you, honey child. Leading lady, from not having been on the stage before. That's some achievement.'

'All down to the way I look, Rebekah, not talent as such. I fit the bill.'

'Well, that's good because it gave Robbie the chance to shine too. Come here, boy, let me cuddle you. Ooh, it's good to see you, I was afraid you wouldn't come – not that Rebekah would mind. I know you must live your life now and hope I gave you the confidence to do that.'

'You did, Rebekah, how are yer, luv?'

'Rebekah is well and happy. Thanks, Robbie.' She looked past Robbie. 'And am pleased to see you too, Bett.' She put her arms out to Bett and the two women hugged.

'Well, luv, we've come to take yer out. We're taking yer back to yer own country, in a way – we're going to the zoo, luv.'

'The zoo? Rebekah am going to the zoo?'

'Yer are, luv.'

While Bett and Rebekah were having this conversation, Ruth was hugging Ebony.

'I am pleased to see you all. How are you, Ruth? I'm excited about yer new career.'

'It's good to see you too, Ebony. Has Rebekah been behaving?'

'She's no trouble.'

'Why don't yer come to the zoo with us, there's room in the car.'

'No, ta. I've to get down to the restaurant. It works well with just having to go downstairs. Whenever I get a moment, I can come up to see Rebekah is all right. And I always find that she's fine. She's started her knitting and her pictures again, and do you know what happened? I did go and put one of her pictures up on the wall of the restaurant and it sold!'

'But that's wonderful!' Ruth's heart swelled. To hear this was as if Rebekah had come alive again and was no longer deteriorating. She even looked a lot better.

Though this thought pleased Ruth, it also gave her a pang of guilt. Maybe she'd cossetted Rebekah too much? Treated her like a sick old lady, instead of someone who was still useful?

'What's that mug for, Ruth? Yer look like yer lost an ha'penny and found a farthing.'

'Nothing, Bett, sorry. Just me thoughts.'

'Well, no bleedin' thought that puts you in the doldrums is allowed today, girl. Come on, we're going to the zoo!'

Ruth smiled. Bett was like a kid being given a treat. But then, thinking about it, since she'd retired, Bett's life had been very different, and maybe a little humdrum. 'We should have more treats like this, Bett, to keep us all going.'

'I wish I could come, but it's not possible,' Ebony said. 'I'll get Rebekah's coat and blankets. Oh, and a pillow. I'm going to make you cosy in your chair.'

'Ta, Ebony, love. Oooh, I can't wait.'

The joy on Rebekah's face pleased Ruth so much she did a little twirl, then bowed and said, 'Cinderella will go to the ball!'

Rebekah laughed her cackly laugh and to Ruth, everything was wonderful in her world.

*

It took them a good fifteen minutes to get the excited Rebekah wrapped up warm, down in the lift, and into the car, but at last they were on the way. Ruth felt like a kid again as they rolled along, but more than once had to put her hanky over her nose as the fumes from cars mingled with dollops of horse manure. At other times she held on for dear life as they weaved in and out of the slower, horse-drawn vehicles.

The noise was deafening as horns were beeped, and cars and busses driven by noisy smelly engines rumbled over uneven roads, but still she felt like a princess in her carriage.

By the time they turned into Regent's Park the sun had broken through and lit the golden leaves with its rays as the last of the autumn oranges and reds clung on before winter killed them off.

To Ruth it was beautiful. She took a deep breath and felt the happiness of now fill her. She was already having a wonderful time and that was made even more so as she was with dear Rebekah.

Chapter Thirty

Once inside the zoo Ruth felt she'd been transported to a different world and could see this was so for Rebekah too, as memories of the animals she'd known in their native habitats flooded her.

These memories sometimes made her tearful and sometimes made her radiate with happiness, as she did when she told of seeing a herd of elephants at a waterhole. 'Them love the water, girl. Look at the baby, ahh, it's loving its bath. Mama elephant will fill her trunk and squirt the water out like a cannon. Look, she do it now.' Rebekah clapped her hands.

At the giraffe enclosure, Rebekah's tears were of sadness. 'Them shouldn't be caged like this, girl. Them do run like the wind across the plains. They run all day and feed off the tops of the trees where the leaves be tender and sweet. This am cruel.'

But at the monkeys and chimps, she laughed at their antics. 'These I am happier for, because they're safe and have lots of space.'

It was all a wondrous sight to Ruth, she loved all the animals even though some were a bit scary. And she could tell Robbie was in his element. But the best bit was when Rebekah clapped her hands again and said, 'I've had happy memories today, Ruth, girl. Some of the animals we've seen lived close to my village. Sometimes we saw them, but never as close as this. It has all made me think of home.' Then she reached for Bett's hand and looked up at her. 'You am a good friend, Bett. Ta for today.'

While they sat having a cup of tea, Rebekah never once took her hand out of Ruth's. And every few moments she looked up at her and gave her a lovely smile.

'You're tired now, luv, shall we head home?'

'Yes, Rebekah is tired, but very happy. I feel as though I have been home, but one thing Rebekah would ask, could we go by the old street? I want to say hello to Gert . . . and, well, just see it one more time.'

Ruth's heart dropped at this, she couldn't answer, but Bett did in her usual way. 'Of course yer can, yer can do any bleedin' thing yer like, luv.'

All Little Collingwood Street came out as the car pulled up, and when they saw who it was some of them cheered. Gert was among them and came running towards the car. 'Rebekah! Oh, it's good to see yer, mate.'

The two women kissed, before Gert turned to Ruth. 'My Ruth, yer've blossomed, girl. Yer beautiful.' With this she hugged her and kissed her cheek.

'I've so much news, Gert, but I'll have to come another time to tell yer everything, luv. We've to get Rebekah home, only she wanted to come to see you.'

Gert lowered her voice. 'She don't look well, mate. It's a good idea to get her home, and quick, if I was you.'

This alarmed Ruth. But one glance at Rebekah told her the truth of this. She caught Robbie's eye. He nodded. His look told he'd seen the same, as did Bett's.

'Well, Rebekah, luv. Say goodbye now, eh?'

'Rebekah just wants to gaze at her old house, Ruth. See how nice it looks with them there net curtains.'

'The people who live there are lovely, Rebekah. They are looking after the house with love.'

'That am good, Gert . . . Oh, Gert, I miss yer.'

'And we miss you, luv.'

Gert swallowed loudly and wiped away her tears. Putting on a smile she told Rebekah, 'Come and see me again, luv, only next time, leave enough time to have a cuppa with me, eh.'

Rebekah nodded.

It was with a heavy heart that Ruth said goodbye to Rebekah. Almost asleep, Rebekah smiled a weak smile and whispered, 'That be one of the best days in me life since leaving Africa. Rebekah will go home again soon.'

Ruth clung on to her, until Bett tapped her on the shoulder and gave her a look as much to say, that was all now. Ruth understood.

Robbie's goodbye was a gentle kiss on her hair. 'Ta for everything, Rebekah, luv.'

With this, Ruth wanted to give Rebekah her proper place. 'Mum. Ta for everything, Mum.'

Robbie nodded. 'Yes, ta for everything, Mum.'

Rebekah's face lit up. 'Goodbye, my children. Grow in yer lives and be happy, that will make Rebekah happy.'

As she hugged Ebony, Ruth could feel her body trembling. 'Will yer be all right, Ebony?'

'I will. I'll make Rebekah comfortable and by that time Abdi will be home. He goes to the bank with the lunchtime takings.'

355

Once in the car, Ruth broke down. They sat in the back with Bett, and both held her. None of them denied her tears and when she looked up, they too were crying.

'W-we won't see her again, will we, Robbie?'

On a sob, Robbie said, 'No, I don't think so, but if this is her last, we can be proud to have given her a day that brought so many memories of her homeland to her.'

Ruth nodded. She couldn't speak. She didn't want Rebekah to go. To her, she'd found the mum she'd always wanted. *Holy Mary, don't take Rebekah from me yet . . . Please don't.*

They were sitting drinking their cocoa when they heard a loud knocking on Bett's door downstairs. Ruth froze. Robbie stared at her, his look telling her of his fear.

They listened to the adjoining door click open and then Bett's voice coming up the stairs to them. 'Ruth, Robbie! Come on down, me darlin's, there's not good news. Abdi's here.'

'No . . . No, Robbie, I don't want to hear. Don't let it be . . . Please don't.'

Robbie took her hand and led her downstairs. Abdi sat at the table, his head in his hands.

It was Bett who spoke. 'She's gone, me darlin's. I'm sorry.'

'Oh no, Bett. No . . . No!'

Abdi lifted his head. 'I haven't ever seen her happier. Thank you for what you did today. In her mind's eye, she saw her homeland once more.' He dabbed his eyes. 'She lay down to have a sleep when you left and when I came in, I looked in on her and she was gone. She had a lovely smile on her face. Thank you. That was your doing.'

This gave little comfort to Ruth's broken heart as she sat on Bett's sofa and sobbed out the pain that consumed her.

*

Standing by the graveside after a service of joyous celebration of Rebekah's life but that hadn't touched the empty space in her heart, Ruth looked around at the mourners, so different to what she was used to. All wore bright colours – yellows, reds and blues. Their voices had raised the roof of the church as they'd sung all Rebekah's favourite hymns and clapped and danced in the aisle as they did so.

The preacher had told of the hope that death brought eternal rest with the Father and assured them that he knew no better soul than Rebekah's and that she was surely sitting on the right hand of God.

Ruth looked up and away from the grave as they lowered Rebekah's coffin into it. The sky looked full of snow – Rebekah hated snow. She loved the sunshine and everything light and bright in the world. She would love the scene around her resting place.

Did I do wrong, to leave you when you were so near the end? Couldn't Horacio have waited to go to school?

As if in answer, a small hand came into hers. She looked down into Horacio's face, saw the tears swimming in his eyes and she knew, this little boy was the future Rebekah hoped for for her people, and the sacrifice they made was worth it.

Hugging Horacio to her, she couldn't speak words of comfort. There were none for either of them, they just needed to show the love they had for one another in their shared grief. 'Do you think Aunty Rebekah is happy, Ruth? Is she happier than she was with us?'

Ruth didn't know what to say, she had no words to fit what Horacio needed to know, but she did feel that Rebekah was happy. 'I think she is. Look, I can only think of the time the priest said that if we live a good life by God's rules, then when we die, we will know eternal peace and happiness. He said, we will give up all our earthly feelings and only know joy. So, I think that though we feel sadness because she isn't here anymore, we should be glad that Rebekah has found that peace. She so deserves it.'

'So, she don't feel sad and lonely, like we do?'

'No, she can no longer feel those things . . . Look, don't tell anyone I said this, but I love the Holy Mary.'

'The mother of God?'

'Yes.'

'But why can't I tell anyone? I love her too. She's pretty and kind and God loves her.'

'Just because . . . well, some congregations think it wrong to worship her like I do. I pray to her all the time, and now I think of her with her arm around Rebekah, as one mum to another, and loving her for her good work.'

'Aunty wasn't a mum though.'

'She was. She lost her child when still in Africa, but she went on to be the greatest mum yer could ever know. She took two homeless kids in and cared for them like a mum and gave them the start they'd never have had – that makes her the greatest mum.'

Horacio didn't speak for a moment, but when he did, he smiled for the first time. 'I like to think of two mums cuddling. I will pray to the Holy Mary too.'

Ruth found that she was comforted now. If Horacio hadn't grown so big, she would pick him up and swing him around like she used to, but instead she squeezed him tighter and smiled back at him.

Holding his hand, she walked back to the church with him, following Abdi and Ebony. Though Abdi didn't attend church as often as they did, when he was present, it was like a god was amongst his people as he was treated with such reverence. Even the preacher took second place to him. Ruth wondered for the umpteenth time what all their lives would have been like in their native country, and at how cruel it was to ship them away to a cold and distant land to be slaves to others.

Thinking of this, she imagined heaven to be a warm and sunny place full of the joy that Rebekah spoke of her people having, and that Ruth had witnessed so many times, and some peace began to settle in her, for she'd want that for Rebekah. She'd want her to feel that she was back home.

Ruth and Robbie threw themselves into rehearsals, earning elaborate praise from Jeromy and the admiration of all the cast. And now, it was opening night and Ruth felt sick.

The curtain was up, and the audience had given an uplifting applause of encouragement. Once the dancers finished, Ruth was to go on with her mop and bucket followed by the ugly sisters who would take delight in taunting her.

Standing waiting in the wings was nerve-wracking, but once her cue came, she took a deep breath. 'This is for you, my dear mum, Rebekah.'

Seeming to glide onto the stage, her nerves left her as she became Cinderella.

By the end of the performance when the audience stood and applauded for so long that they had to take three curtain calls, Ruth knew this was what she was meant to do with her life.

Coming off stage she ran straight into Abe, holding the biggest bunch of flowers she'd ever seen. 'You were amazing, both of you. I'm so proud.'

The three of them hugged.

'Ruth, Ruth!'

Coming out of the hug to the biggest smile of the night,

she giggled as she took Horacio into her arms. 'You weren't Ruth on the stage, but you are now.'

'Well, mate, that's the best compliment anyone can give me, for you to only have seen me as Cinders as we call her, I must have done me job.'

He took her hand. 'It's Christmas tomorrow!'

'Ha, I know. I'm surprised yer managed to sit through the performance with yer excitement, luv.'

'It was easy, as the show was just magical, I loved it.'

Abdi put his arm around her shoulder. 'You were magnificent, both of you. I couldn't believe it was you.'

'Ta, Abdi. That means a lot . . . Ebony! Oh, Ebony, did you enjoy it?'

Ebony hugged her. 'It was wonderful, girl, you are beautiful.'

'Ta, luv. Well, I'd better go and change, I'm covering you all in face powder and this costume's very hot to wear.'

'Not before yer hug me, me darling. I want powder on me too, yer know, mate.'

'Bett! Oh, Bett, it was wonderful, did yer like it?'

As Bett swamped her into her big body that always enveloped her in love, she said, 'I did, I loved it, mate, and so did me boy. He brought me here in a flipping landau. He said if it were good enough for the royals it were good enough for me – I were bleedin' freezing, mate.'

Ruth laughed out loud. 'Oh, Bett, I do love you.'

'And I love you, girl, yer like the daughter I never had.'

'And I'm lucky. I started out with no mum and ended up with two of the very best.'

Bett held her from her for a moment. Her eyes had filled with tears. She didn't speak but drew her back into the circle of her arms. After a moment she released her. 'I've to go now, luv, enjoy the rest of yer evening. I'm going back to me son's to have Christmas with him. You have a lovely time. Happy Christmas, me darlin'.'

'Happy Christmas to you too, Mum.'

Bett went off shining with happiness and Ruth's heart warmed even more. Sighing, she stopped the thought coming to her that she wished she could hug Rebekah and cheerfully told Ebony, 'Me and Robbie will join yer at the cafe, eh?' She turned to see Robbie and Abe in what was more than a hug. Her heart did a little disappointed flip. 'Come on Robbie, mate, we've to get changed.' Then she laughed as Abe turned around and his face had lipstick all over it. 'Oh dear, my colour and Robbie's. We've smothered yer, mate.'

Robbie grinned his lovely grin. 'Abe's coming to me dressing room to clean up . . . And Ruth, oh, Ruth, mate, you were magic. Come here, I ain't had a moment to congratulate yer.'

As she went into Robbie's arms, she could feel his extreme happiness and knew it was down to being with Abe once more. 'Robbie, mate.' Her voice was a whisper just for him. 'I'm all right with yer loving Abe and him loving you. Be happy, luv.'

'Oh, Ruth, I do love him, he's me world, but it's up to him in the end.'

'I know, mate, just be ready when he finally realizes that you are the one. I love yer, Robbie, mate. You were magnificent tonight. Ta, luv, it was an honour to be on stage with yer.'

'No, you were the one who made it . . . And we have made it, Ruth. After this performance, if we get the reviews, when we come back after Christmas we'll play to packed houses and be in big demand.'

Excitement at this zinged through Ruth. At this moment, she could think of nothing she wanted more in the whole world. She looked up and knew that Rebekah was smiling down on her and this warmed her heart, more than any promising future could and it helped her to come to terms with having truly lost Abe to Robbie.

Supper was a chatty affair with everyone talking at once, but as they sat in church for midnight mass the feeling Ruth had surpassed everything as they joined in the wonderful celebrations.

At the stroke of midnight, Horacio had the honour of carrying the baby to lay in the crib, but just before that, the preacher turned to face them all. 'I have a request. We have our two stars with us, and I would very much like them to come and sing to us – "Away in a Manger"? – as Horacio carries out his duty.'

The congregation all cheered. Robbie took her hand and together they walked to the alter amidst many pats on the back and happy comments.

When they stood together, Robbie squeezed her hand. Looking up at him, she thanked God for him, for him being – to her, her big brother, always there to catch her, always there for her to lean on. They'd been through so much together, and separately, that their bond was strong and everlasting.

She joined her voice to his as they watched Horacio with pride and love.

The song conjured up memories of those lost forever and those no longer near, but the Christmas story was about hope. Soon it would be a new year, and new years always brought more hope, didn't they? Ruth prayed that this next one would be the one when she finally heard from Ellen and Amy. This time she prayed to baby Jesus to make it so.

Chapter Thirty-One

1914

'Ruth, we got the part, mate! A full summer season of music hall!'

'Oh, Robbie. That's amazing.' Ruth put the last stitch in the brim of the hat she was making for Melinda's – the shop had kept her going over the first three lean months of the new year.

A new musical had followed in April, but had only run for one month, leaving them both out of work for all of May. But luckily, Melinda had ordered a range of summer hats. For the last four weeks, Ruth had worked long hours to complete the assignment and was so near doing so. Then she could look forward to collecting the money for them. It was good to know she would be able to contribute to keeping them both going and to pay back what she'd had to borrow from Bett.

'When do rehearsals begin? I've a few more hats to make, so could do with a week at least, luv.'

She didn't tell him that she had news of her own; his was exciting news and she needed that right now.

'Not till the first week in June, so I'll have a chance to finish that window seat that I'm making for Abe's mother.

We'll be in clover then, and with no money worries can really concentrate on rehearsing for long hours.'

'Maybe you'll get more work, though. I mean, we can't turn anything down.'

'If I do, it'll have to wait. We did say we would only work at our other skills when we were resting between stage jobs. Anyway, I ain't much for doing more at the house, it's been funny working there, knowing this was where Abe grew up. I've wished a hundred times that he was still there.'

'Have yer heard from him again, luv? It seems ages since his last letter.'

'Yes. I forgot to tell yer. Or rather, I didn't have much to say about it. His letter was full of concerns for what was happening in Europe and his fears about the future, very little news about himself – except to say, well, he said if there was a war, he would join up to fight.'

Ruth's heart did a flip. Although she and Robbie didn't talk about what was happening and how there was still unrest following the end of the Balkan War, Bett did, and the newspaper stands were full of pacts we'd made with this country and that, and how Germany didn't like what we were doing. 'Will there be war, Robbie?'

'I don't know. I don't see why there should be. Don't start worrying about it, mate.'

Ruth couldn't leave it there. 'What would you do if there was, Robbie?'

'Well, I'm not a fighting man, or soldier material, but I would go if needed. I'd have to. If our country and people are threatened, then men have to fight.' He laughed then. 'I could hardly dance them to death, could I?'

This tickled Ruth and she felt better for the laughter they

364

shared, but in her mind, she prayed to the Holy Mary not to let it happen.

'So, how have yer got on today? Do yer think you'll finish the hats in time?'

The time was on her to tell her news. 'I will, but today brought a bit of a shock. I had a visit from Veners.'

'Oh?'

'Gwen was found hung in her cell in Holloway Prison.'

'What?!'

Though Ruth had wanted to cry for poor Gwen, she hadn't, but somehow this horror-filled exclamation of Robbie's triggered her.

'Hey, mate. Don't upset yerself.'

'I can't help thinking what that beast put her through and wishing I'd gone to visit her to see if I could help her.'

Robbie was quiet for a moment. He held her hand as she sobbed little, helpless sobs.

'It never leaves us, does it, Ruth?'

'No. I still have nightmares.'

'I know, I hear yer call out a couple of times in the night and I've gone to yer bedside wanting to wake yer. Once, I sat on the side of yer bed and cried me heart out. You were calling for Hettie, Ellen and Amy.'

'Oh, Robbie.'

'I know. But all we can do is to keep on going. We've a lot to look forward to, so let's not look back, eh?'

Ruth dried her eyes. 'At least Gwen's at peace. What it must have been like in the prison I can't think.'

'And she faced having to go to the gallows . . . and, luv, I don't want yer to take this the wrong way, but she's saved herself and you a lot of agony.'

'I know. I was dreading being summoned to be a witness.'

'There, yer see. Look, it's a lovely evening. Why don't we go for a walk, eh? We could take a couple of plates, knives and forks and get pie and mash and take it to the park. We ain't done anything like that in a long time.'

Ruth smiled. 'I'd love that, mate. I've been cooped up all day – all month, it seems, apart from going to church on a Sunday.'

Even as she said this, she knew she didn't get the same joyous feeling from going to church now, so that hadn't been a real break for her. It seemed those who gave her the joy were missing – even Horacio, who was now at boarding school during most of the term. A sigh escaped her. Life kept rolling along. In a couple of months, she'd be seventeen! She could hardly believe it.

As they sat talking and balancing their delicious meal on their laps they attracted more than one glance.

'Ha, folk ain't seen anything like us, picnicking in the park. No dainty sandwiches for us, girl!'

This set the tone for a few giggles and Ruth began to enjoy herself. Robbie was in top form cracking jokes. 'Look at them all – Mr I-Know-It-All over there with Mrs Butter-Wouldn't-Melt on his arm. Miss Got-It-All, riding her horse side-saddle, and . . . Ted! Hey, Ted, how are yer, mate?'

There was no time to ask for explanations as Robbie jumped up, leaving his pie and mash on the bench and ran to Ted, shaking his hand and patting his shoulder. 'Good to see yer, mate, I ain't seen yer in an age. How are yer?'

Ted beamed. He looked so well. Ruth wasn't far behind Robbie and went into a hug.

'You haven't been in the market square for ages, Ted, what have yer been up to, mate?'

'I got a job, and I'm living with a mate. I'm in a band

and we play in theatres. Not the big ones, but the less known ones. We've been playing The Ambassadors, but the show came to an end, so we're looking for more work. Nothing like you two. Blimey, mate, the Prince of Wales! It don't get much better than that.'

'That's wonderful, Ted.' Ruth squeezed him.

'Come and sit down. Have yer eaten? I've some of me pie left yer can have, Ted.'

'Ta, Robbie. No, I ain't eaten yet.'

'Yer can have me mash as well, Ted, well, half of it and me and Robbie can share the rest of me pie,' Ruth told him.

'I've missed you two, yer know, but yer ain't changed and that's good.'

'We might be able to help yer a bit, Ted. We're doing music hall next. Not sure of the set-up yet, if they've auditioned a band or not. Tell me more about your band.'

They learned that the band had seven members and played classical as well as popular music. 'Here, I can show yer a cutting.' Ted fished in the pocket of his very nice jacket – gone was the khaki one tied with string. And his hair – a light golden colour – was cut neatly when it had always looked wild. His moustache was neatly trimmed too, and met his tiny beard. He looked like the musician he was as they both knew how wonderfully he could play his flute.

It was as if another member of Ruth's family had returned. When he'd finished talking about his band and Robbie had said he would talk to the producer of the show, she asked him if he knew how Reg was.

'He's champion. I'm meeting him later for a beer. Why don't yer come along? We're always talking about yer both.'

'I'm up for that. It'll be great to be together again. What about you, Ruth?'

Ruth nodded. She could think of nothing better, though she wasn't sure about having a beer.

With their food finished, they all linked in and walked to the Albert Arms. As soon as they walked in Reg spotted them. He stood and held out his arms to them both.

For Ruth, it was a wonderful moment and took her back to when she first met the three of them. She didn't let herself dwell on why their paths crossed but enjoyed the moment of the reunion.

Reg, it turned out, now had an office. He'd married his fancy woman. 'I made an honest woman of her, and I've never been happier. Now, I write for the local paper, and still write letters for those who can't. I even take up their cases of complaint or injustice and highlight them in my article.'

Ruth was in awe of him. He looked every inch the captain and she was proud to be in his, Ted's and Robbie's company.

Suddenly a huge woman sat on the piano stool next to them and for a moment Ruth feared that it would collapse, but no, she lifted the lid and began to play. The bar filled with the sound of singing, 'Down At The Old Bull And Bush'.

It didn't matter that they were in the Albert Arms, the song fitted any London pub as far as they were concerned.

Ruth sang as loudly as the rest of them, and laughed as Robbie, always the performer, stood on a chair and led the singing.

Someone shouted, 'You should be on the stage, mate.'

Reg shouted back, 'He is, this is Robbie Grant, star of *Cinderella* at the Prince of Wales, and this is his leading lady, Ruth Faith, Cinderella.'

A round of applause started as well as calls for them to do a song from the pantomime.

After they'd only sung a line or two of a song especially composed for their performance at the Prince of Wales, and which no one could know, the woman pianist was playing along with them. Ruth loved it and was in her element.

As the applause rang out, Robbie whispered, 'This is what music hall will be like, mate. We'll have an audience who will join in and sing along and shout out remarks. You'll love it.'

'I know I will, Robbie. This has been one of the best evenings. Made the more so because I shouldn't really be in here at my age.'

'To me, you've always been grown up, luv. No one's questioned yer. But we can go now, if yer like. I don't want any more beer, it's gone to me head.'

'Ha, I can see that. Come on, let's say our goodbyes. Now we've found Ted and Reg again, we won't lose touch. I'll tell them they'll be welcome at ours anytime.'

Though Ted had to go as he had rehearsals with his band, Reg walked a little way with them.

The talk turned to war again, but this time with Reg speaking so knowledgeably, Ruth couldn't dismiss it.

As the men talked, she thought about family, as meeting up with Ted had brought back to her how much certain people in your life could be called that.

She had a family – a wonderful one with a real mixture of characters, but she loved them all. Some were gone forever, others missing with their presence, but they were tucked safely into her heart. Lovely Hettie. Mum Rebekah, and Ellen and Amy. How she longed to hear from them both, but knew she stood little chance now with the change in her address – though Gert knew the new people and had promised to ask them to pass on any letters that arrived for her.

She wouldn't give up hope. No. She would never give up hope.

This resolve was sorely tested just a few weeks later when war was declared. And more so in December as she stood on Victoria Station waving goodbye to Robbie and Abe.

Through her tears she saw the officer and the soldier, both in different carriages, both waving a handkerchief through the carriage window and she wondered if she would ever see either of them again.

But she wouldn't leave them to fight this fight alone. The Red Cross had accepted her and come Monday she would sign up for her training. She was ready and hoped she was sent out to France too.

As she turned away, Bett stood waiting for her. 'Come on, girl. Chin up.'

Ruth smiled through her tears as she was enveloped in the place that meant love and protection to her – Bett's arms.

Acknowledgements

My heartfelt thanks to those unsung heroes of the pandemic who worked hard at home to keep the wheels of the publishing industry turning so that the nation could be entertained during lockdown: my wonderful editor, Wayne Brookes, always there for me; my agent, Judith Murdoch, who stands firmly in my corner and who, along with Wayne, encourages me and smooths the paths I tread in my writing career; Samantha Fletcher and her team of editors; Victoria Hughes-Williams whose edits make my words sing off the page; and Philippa McEwan, my publicity manager, and all her team, who do an amazing job. And to all at Pan Macmillan who play a part in getting mine and so many books, beautifully presented, onto the shelves and never wavered in doing so during the difficult circumstances that have prevailed. I am grateful to you all and send you all much love.

My thanks, too, to my beloved son, James Wood, who always lightens my load by helping me with the revisions of my manuscripts and by combing the final proofs for errors that may have slipped through.

And to all my beloved family, especially my husband Roy, whose support and love sustain me while I write and, together with our beloved children, grandchildren and great-grandchildren, cheers me on, helping me to climb my mountain. I love you all with all my heart x

Letter to Readers

Hello again, dear reader.

I hope you loved this, the first in a brand-new trilogy. The second book will be Ellen's story, and the third Amy's. Ellen's book is already well along the process that every book goes through before you hold it and read it. A process that takes many months after we authors submit our manuscripts.

Firstly, there is the read-through to determine the work is good enough and holds all the elements that Pan Macmillan judge as essential for the target market it is aimed at, as they care passionately about the millions of readers they serve.

Once the story passes muster, then the editing begins – a procedure many authors dread and yet accept as a necessary step in bringing their work to pristine condition and to make their words sing off the page.

There are three edits:

The structural edit. This validates the research and makes sure the story isn't over-written with lots of unnecessary detail that may slow the pace. Often, when cuts are suggested, the author angsts over making it as they may love that scene, but we come to realize how other detail comes strongly to life, which had been overshadowed.

Then comes the copy-edit. Oh dear, this is when we see our manuscript in the state that we often saw our schoolwork, with red lines striking out misspelled words, or misused words, and punctuation corrected, as well as repetition highlighted and rewrites needed to fix all the errors – hard work, but once again, we see a difference. The work is still ours, but now it has come to life in a way that lets the heart of it shine.

Next, the final proofread, when we see our work laid out how it will look in the book. This is when we must root out all errors that have slipped the net – our final chance to do so – and then a crisp, clean read will be presented to our reader.

Why, might you ask, does an author have so many errors in their work when they first present it?

This is because an author will write from their heart, spilling the words onto the page in a frenzy of excitement as their story unfolds and new characters are created, brought to life and loved – or hated, but real people to them. They don't labour over every word as that would stop the flow of creation. Of course, once the first draft is completed, we will read our story through and polish the manuscript as best we can. But our best isn't enough as errors we don't see glare out to a fresh pair of trained eyes.

Other work carried out behind the scenes, during the long process of bringing the final book to you, includes designing a cover, writing a blurb that will attract readers to want to know more, the printing process, and the all-important publicity work.

And all overseen and brought together by a commissioning editor – the main person, along with an agent, in an author's working life. These are the people who guide an author's path, take care of them, encourage them, and make or drive all the important decisions that will determine if another of our books reaches the shelves. Much loved figures who we depend upon.

And so, I hope this has helped you to understand what a book goes through before it reaches you and may give you an idea of how much a review from you means to the whole team. To an author, it is like hugging them for their work, and for the team behind the author, who have all carried on through the pandemic working under difficult circumstances, it is a verification of all the pride and effort they have put into the book too.

We all thank you for taking the time to do this for us as we so value your feedback.

Thank you for reading my letter. Your support means the world to me.

Please continue to take care of yourselves and others. And keep on keeping in touch with me. I love to interact with you and can be reached by email via my website:

www.authormarywood.com

You can also interact with me on Facebook, where I run many competitions to win personally signed books:

www.facebook.com/marywoodauthor

And if you are a tweeter, I'm here on Twitter: @Authormary

Much love to all,

Mary Wood

If you enjoyed

The Orphanage Girls

then you'll love

The Jam Factory Girls

**Whatever life throws at them,
they will face it together**

Life for Elsie is difficult as she struggles to cope with her alcoholic mother. Caring for her siblings and working long hours at Swift's Jam Factory in London's Bermondsey is exhausting. Thankfully her lifelong friendship with Dot helps to smooth over life's rough edges.

When Elsie and Dot meet Millie Hawkesfield, the boss's daughter, they are nervous to be in her presence. Over time, they are surprised to feel so drawn to her, but should two cockney girls be socializing in such circles?

When disaster strikes, it binds the women in ways they could never have imagined. And long-held secrets are revealed that will change all their lives . . .

The Jam Factory Girls series continues with
Secrets of the Jam Factory Girls and *The Jam Factory Girls
Fight Back*, all available to read now.

The Forgotten Daughter

Book one in
The Girls Who Went to War series

From a tender age, Flora felt unloved and unwanted by her parents, but she finds safety in the arms of caring Nanny Pru. But when Pru is cast out of the family home, under a shadow of secrets and with a baby boy of her own on the way, it shatters little Flora.

Over the years, however, Flora and Pru meet in secret – unbeknown to Flora's parents. Pru becomes the mother she never had, and Flora grows into a fine young woman. When she signs up as a volunteer with St John Ambulance, she begins to shape her life. But the drum of war beats loudly and her world is turned upside down when she receives a letter asking her to join the Red Cross in Belgium.

With the fate of the country in the balance, it is a time for bravery. Flora's determined to be the strong woman she was destined to be. But with horror, loss and heartache on her horizon, there's a lot for young Flora to learn . . .

The Girls Who Went to War series continues with *The Abandoned Daughter*, *The Wronged Daughter* and *The Brave Daughters*, all available to read now.